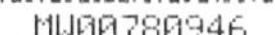

KICKER'S JOURNEY

LOIS CLOAREC HART

Martin, Kathy, Laura, and Carol
With profound love and gratitude for this journey we've taken together.

ACKNOWLEDGEMENTS

Kicker's Journey began as a short story I wrote for my wife in late 2002. It was posted online as *Kicker's Heart* and grew over six years to the novel it is today. It would never have reached fruition without the input of many people.

I am grateful for the steadfast help and support of Kathy GramsGibbs, Debra, Glenda, Verda Foster, and my mother, who generously offered their insight and editorial critiques.

Thanks also to the wonderful women of Ylva Publishing for taking me on and putting out this second edition of *Kicker's Journey.*

Lastly and most profoundly, my unending gratitude to my beloved wife and primary editor, Day Petersen. *Je t'aime,* little sweetie.

HISTORICAL NOTE

For the most part, I stayed true to the history of western Canada in 1899-1900; however, there were two significant anomalies in *Kicker's Journey*.

At the time, the new century was considered to start in 1901. I changed that apprehension for narrative purposes.

Additionally, mining in the Crowsnest Pass did not truly begin until 1903. I advanced that context by three years. For an accurate and entertaining history of the Crowsnest Pass, I highly recommend the Frank Slide Interpretative Centre in the Municipality of Crowsnest Pass, Alberta, Canada. The stories Pudge relates to Seamus and Kicker from the Pass come directly from newspapers of the era, showcased at the centre. (http://www.history.alberta.ca/frankslide)

PROLOGUE

On an unseasonably hot spring day, fourteen-year-old Kicker Stuart stopped in front of her destination. Her ragged, ill-fitting clothes were caked with dust, and her feet burned within shabby boots from the remorseless pounding of the last two hours. She wiped one grimy sleeve over dry, cracked lips and blinked away drops of sweat. *Should ha' brung water wi' me. Twas foolish not to.*

Kicker's discomfort quickly melted into awe as she stared at the stately stone pillars that flanked the entrance to the Grindleshire Academy for Young Ladies. She had never seen such an imposing entrance, nor felt more keenly the lowly circumstances of her birth. *Bless'd Jesus. I'll fit here wors'n a mare in a chicken coop.*

Kicker swallowed hard and peered in concentration at the bronze tablet on one pillar. She could make out the numbers as 1868, but could not read aught else on the sign that marked the founding of the Academy.

"Huh, twas here ten years b'fore I were e'en born, an' I ain't ne'er bin by this way b'fore." She allowed herself a moment to muse on the boundaries of her life to date. Kicker had walked only five miles from her home village, carrying a small sack with all her worldly possessions slung over her back, yet the world she was about to enter was as alien to her as a London drawing room.

I hope you ain't sent me into the lion's den, Adam. Kicker mentally directed the admonition at her older brother, who was responsible for her presence at this gate. She squared her shoulders and passed into the grounds of the finishing school for daughters of families who did not have the status or influence to secure more elite placements.

Kicker trudged up the long driveway and gaped at the massive stone building with ostentatious turrets on all corners. *I ne'er seen nothin' so gran'.*

The Academy's position on a rise dominated two hundred acres of lush green lawns, manicured gardens, cultivated fields, and thickly wooded land alongside a turbulent river. The institution was comprised of academic facilities, student dormitories, teacher and household staff quarters, as well as the Grindleshire family's private suite. The four wings of the main structure enclosed a cobble-stoned courtyard.

Behind the edifice, several small cottages for senior employees flanked the vast vegetable gardens that supplied the school's kitchen. Kicker's destination lay to the west side of the Academy—the stable, paddocks, storage, and maintenance buildings.

It was Saturday and students wandered the lawns and lingered in the lush gardens. Some of the girls were around her age, yet Kicker felt their differences keenly. Though an oddity even in her village, at least there her common clothes and scruffy hair did not mark her so blatantly an outsider.

Kicker nodded politely at two girls who crossed the driveway, sweeping their elegant dresses far from her path, only to be stung by the disdainful looks she received in return. Their giggles trailed after her as Kicker hastily detoured off the long driveway toward the stable.

Kicker relaxed as she headed away from the scornful students and toward the familiar environment. *Leastways I won' ha' to muck about wi' their sort. I hope Adam's right about this, though. Gonna be a long, thirsty walk home if he ain't.*

Her tempered optimism lasted until the moment she came face to face with the stable master, who viewed her approach with a scowl.

Kicker snatched the cap off her short, dark brown hair. "Would you be Ol' Thomas, Sir?"

"Aye. You're Henry Stuart's girl—Adam's sister?"

"Aye, Sir. I am."

Old Thomas looked her up and down.

Kicker tried to project strength, but there was only so much she could do about her short stature and wiry body.

The stable master spat, an eloquent comment on his newest employee.

Kicker refused to wither; this was nothing new. Since the age of seven, when her parents reluctantly acknowledged she was useless at traditional female chores, she'd had to prove herself in the male domain.

Her father had finally yielded to her pleas and allowed Kicker to join her brothers in his smithy. As the years passed, Kicker had learned the ins and outs of the farrier's trade. Now she was starting anew, but Kicker was confident her skills and industry would win Old Thomas over.

"Don' be thinkin' I'll go easy on you jus' cuz you're a girl, got that?"

"Aye, Sir. I kin do a full day's work, no less'n my brothers."

Old Thomas' scowl became less pronounced. "So says your da and Adam. They're good men, honest men." He turned away, but not before Kicker heard his final word on the matter. "I'll gi' ye a chance, but you set one foot wrong and I'll toss you out on your arse. Don' be thinkin' I won't, girl."

Kicker grinned as she followed the stable master into the barn.

Old Thomas pointed to a door at the end of the aisle. "You kin throw your gear in there, then we got work to do."

She hastened past the stalls and didn't slow to examine the horses as she normally would have. Even the exhilarating discovery that she was to have a room entirely to herself did not delay her hurried return to the stable master.

"You kin b'gin by muckin' out the place." As Kicker started off, Old Thomas called after her, "How'd you come by such an odd name, anyway?"

Kicker flashed him a smile as she grabbed the pitchfork and set to work. "Twas Adam, Sir. The firs' time he seen me, he called me a helluva kicker. Ma said she'd a'ready come up with thirteen names, an' Kicker would have to do fer me. Said she was too tired to think up 'nother one."

Old Thomas chuckled, then shot her a stern look. "Don' be callin' me Sir, girl. I ain't one of 'em up t' the 'cademy. I work fer my daily bread."

"Aye." Kicker fell into a comfortably familiar rhythm with the fork. *As do I.*

CHAPTER 1

FALL LEAVES CRACKLED UNDERFOOT AS Kicker trotted out of the gate mounted proudly on Grindleshire stable's latest acquisition. She brushed her hand over a stone pillar as she passed, and was able to reach higher than she ever had before.

Kicker rubbed the neck of the tall grey gelding. "Made this ride dozens of time o'er the last year, Banner, but I ain't ne'er gone home in such style."

Just outside the gate, Kicker had to pull Banner hard to one side to avoid a buggy loaded with students returning from a day in the city. She saw glances of irritation and disdain shot in her direction, but Kicker had become immune to those over the months. *Faces change, but the arrogance don'. Ain't gonna ruin my day, tis sure.*

On the way to the Stuart home, Kicker enjoyed the looks her mount received. She knew she was riding a special horse. By the expression on her brother's face as he waited at the fence line for her, he knew the same.

Adam pushed his hat back on his forehead and whistled appreciatively. "Damn, Kicker, that's one fine lookin' animal. Tell me you din't steal 'im."

Kicker cantered up to her brother, a wide grin on her face and her chest puffed up with pride. "Ain't he somethin'? The Academy jus' got him. His name's Banner, an' Ol' Thomas said I could borrow him fer my half day." She came to a stop in front of Adam and slid off Banner's back. "He stan's near eighteen han's."

Adam winked at her. "So how'd you get up on him, little sister? Jump off a stump?"

Kicker stuck her tongue out at her brother. "You're jus' jealous, cuz all you got to ride is that ol' nag." She jerked her thumb at the family mare grazing placidly in the nearby paddock.

Adam shrugged. "Maybe, but it ain't like you own this one anyway."

Kicker stroked Banner's neck. "No, but someday I'll own one e'en finer."

"Hah, by then there won'be anythin'but those newfangled motor cars about. That's what I'm gonna have one day."

Kicker frowned at Adam. Favourite brother and surrogate parent or not, such blasphemy regarding her beloved horses would not be tolerated. But before she could protest, Adam hooked her around the neck in a hug. Kicker punched him lightly in the ribs, and their customary greeting ritual was complete.

"Kin you get away fer a bit, Adam?"

"Could be, if we was to go fishin' and bring Ma somethin' back."

Kicker turned Banner out to graze with the mare. The siblings grabbed fishing poles from the woodshed and headed down to the creek and their favourite hole.

Kicker caught two, and Adam one, by the time their conversation picked up again.

"Looks like you grew some, Kicker."

"You jus' saw me las' month. 'Sides, bin well o'er a year since I lef' for Grindleshire. Wasn't gonna stay that scrawny fore'er."

Adam cast a glance his sister's way. "It's been that long, has it? I 'spect you think you're all growed up now." He pointed down the bank about twenty feet to a thick copse of trees and bushes that overhung the river. "'Member the day I foun' you there."

"Tis where you always foun' me."

"Aye, but I'm talkin' 'bout the day you ran from Ma."

"Wasn't runnin' from Ma; I was runnin' from Preacher Dodd's sons." Kicker shook her head in disgust at the memory. Though it had led to her current enviable living arrangement, at the time it seemed like the end of the world.

Adam chuckled softly. "If Ma'd had her way, you'd ha' bin married right 'longside June an' Edna las' summer."

Kicker shuddered at the memory of that horrible day.

Mary Stuart, had taken note of her seventh daughter, and realized that Kicker more closely resembled her brothers than her sisters. She wore her brothers' hand-me-downs, disdaining, from the moment she could talk, the dresses that her older sisters wore. The patched trousers were more appropriate for the work Kicker did for her father, so Mary rarely protested.

However, the new cleric in town had three sons of marriageable age. Kicker was only fourteen, but Mary had been given in marriage when she was fifteen and decided that her unconventional daughter was old enough to wed. Along with her three unmarried older sisters, Kicker was to be included in the display of available females when the cleric dutifully came to call.

To that end, Mary ordered all the girls into their best clothes and spent a whole morning washing and dressing hair. When it came to Kicker, however, Mary met full scale rebellion. The girl flatly refused to don one of her sisters' dresses for the occasion. When her mother grabbed her arm and tried to force her up the stairs to get into a frock, Kicker broke free and tore out of the house.

Adam had been sent to find her, and without hesitation headed straight for her usual hiding place. He'd found her down by the creek, nestled amongst the bushes that overhung the slow moving water. When he'd squirmed in next to Kicker, folding his six-foot frame into the small space with difficulty, she'd scowled at him.

"Don' e'en ask. I don' care what Ma wants, I ain't puttin' on a dress fer anyone, let alone Preacher Dodd's pig-ass sons."

"I know, Kicker, and I ain't here to ask you to go back. I jus' thought you might wanna talk, is all."

Kicker's expression had softened and became more puzzled than fierce. "Why'd she do it? I tol' her over and over that I ain't e'er gettin' married. Why don' she b'lieve me?"

Adam had wrapped his arm around Kicker's thin shoulders and given her a warm hug. "Because she don' really know you, is why. You gotta understan'. Ma truly does think that the bes' she can do for all of us is see us married off and startin' families of our own."

"Damned if I'm e'er goin' to marry. No way I'm birthin' e'ry year 'til I drop dead."

"Ain't jus' not wantin' babies, eh?"

She'd stared uncomfortably at her stained, too-large boots and then glanced up shyly. "Not really. I jus' don' get it, Adam; what the fuss is about, I mean. E'en when I was in school, I thought the girls were actin' so silly, fawnin' over the boys. Hell, I could beat any of them gits in wrasslin' or knife toss. They weren't no big deal."

"You'll understan' someday, little sister. Someone will come along an' steal your heart clean away, cuz you know, there's a little bit more to life than wrasslin' and knife throwin', sweetie."

"Course I know that—there's horses, too."

To this day, Kicker did not understand why Adam had laughed so hard he almost fell into the creek. However, since he had delivered on his subsequent promise to make things better, she did not care that she had been the butt of his merriment.

As always when it came to his favourite sibling, Adam went one step further than convincing their mother that Kicker was a poor candidate for matrimony. Within weeks, he procured for his sister the position as stable hand at Grindleshire's.

In the sixteen months since, Kicker had been content. She had her own small room—a luxury she'd never before experienced—work that she enjoyed, and the congenial company of a boss she respected, and who had come to respect her. She would never grow wealthy on the wages she earned, but she had enough and she was content.

Adam's voice recalled Kicker's attention to her present. "Looks to me like you've put on a poun' or two. They mus' be feedin' you right o'er there."

"Aye, Cook likes me fine. I bring her fish as a reg'lar thing. She's real partial to fresh trout, an' she'll fix it up special for us after t'others eat. Always saves me the bigges' piece of pie, too."

Adam smiled affectionately at her. "I'm glad. You foun' a home."

"Aye, I did, thanks to you."

They fished in silence for a while.

"Adam?"

"Aye."

"Ol' Thomas said somethin' t'other day."

"Aye?"

"He said the las' stable han' were in a scandal, an' tis why I got his job."

"Tis true."

There was distinct unease in Adam's voice and Kicker glanced up. She was surprised to see her brother shift uncomfortably. It piqued her curiosity further.

"So, what was't?"

"What?"

Kicker frowned. It wasn't like Adam to avoid a subject. "What was the scandal? What did the las' stable hand do twas so bad?"

Adam sighed deeply, and for a moment Kicker did not think he would answer.

"He...um...well, he d'spoiled a couple of the students. When twas foun' they was in a family way, he disappeared. After that, din't take a lot of convincin' to get Ol' Thomas to hire you, e'en if you was a girl."

"Huh." Kicker absorbed the new information. "Makes sense. He won' e'er have to worry 'bout nothin' like that with me."

There was a strangled sound from Adam, but when Kicker glanced at him, he shook his head. "No, I guess he won'." With an audible sigh, her brother changed the subject. "I got somethin' to tell you."

"Aye?"

"Aye. Me and Annie, we're gettin' married nex' month."

Kicker nodded slowly. She'd been expecting it. Adam had courted Annie Doyle for almost a year. Still, it would be hard losing him to another.

"Don' mean you're losin' me, jus' means you're gonna gain 'nother sister."

Like nine ain't enough? Kicker sternly set aside her jealousy. "Annie's nice. I'm glad fer you, Adam. You'll be a good husban'."

"An' some day, you'll be aunt to our chil'ren."

"Aye. Tis so." But as always, when Kicker considered the traditional ways of marriage, her stomach got queasy. *Might be a'right for Adam, but it ain't ne'er gonna be for me.*

"Mornin', Kicker."

"Mornin', Cook. The wood bin was low, so I filled it." It was getting cooler in the mornings as fall approached, and Kicker knew that bigger fires helped relieve the ache in Cook's aging bones.

The rotund sovereign of Grindleshire's kitchen beamed at Kicker. "You're a good 'un, girl. I kin always depen' on you. Wisht my lazy girls would take a lesson. I just ain't able to keep after them like I used ta, back when you firs' came to us."

Kicker winked at Cook and crammed the remainder of her breakfast into her mouth. "If I kin get away t'night, I'll bring you some fresh fish, too."

Cook's eyes sparkled with anticipation. The two of them would dine well this evening, though they generally did, fresh fish or not.

Kicker left the kitchen whistling as she headed for the stables. She had worked at Grindleshire's for more than six years. Over time, she'd slowly assumed the heaviest of Old Thomas' workload, though it had been almost two years before she was allowed to shoe the horses independently. It was now generally accepted around the school that when

Old Thomas retired, Kicker would take his place as stable master.

Under warm, sunny skies, Kicker could not think of one thing wrong with her world. *Life is good, eh?* Reaching the stables, she laughed aloud from sheer pleasure and drew an indulgent smile from Old Thomas.

Hours later, Kicker had just finished shoeing the elderly bay that the Grindleshires favoured for their excursions to the finer homes in the county when Old Thomas beckoned her aside.

"Need you to pick up the new teacher comin' in on the afternoon train."

Kicker nodded. She was often sent to make pick-ups at the station as another new school year approached, and she had expected this particular assignment. Kitchen scuttlebutt had indicated someone new was coming in to replace a teacher who resigned her post to get married.

Old Thomas frowned as he regarded her. "An' try to clean up a bit before you go. We don' want the woman thinkin' we're a bunch of clods just b'cause we're outta spittin' distance of civilization."

Unused to giving any thought to her appearance, Kicker glanced down at her dusty clothes. *Huh. You'd think I was goin' to pick up the Queen, herself.* With a shrug, Kicker stepped up to the trough to rinse off the evidence of her duties. She barely got her hands wet before Old Thomas growled at her.

"Go use some soap, and put on a clean shirt."

Instantly resentful of the unknown woman who was responsible for her having to bathe when it was not even Saturday night, Kicker stomped into the stable, muttering under her breath.

"Twould be a damned shame to offend Miss High 'n Mighty now, eh?" Kicker ignored the sleepy eyed chestnut that nuzzled her as she strode past the mare's stall. "God forbid she breathe in a little sweat an' horse shit."

Kicker paused to kick her boots against the post outside her door and was forced to admit that there was more than a little manure clinging to them. She sighed, entered her room and stripped off her footwear and clothes. She gave her boots a cursory brushing out the window, and then poured water from the chipped pitcher into the tin basin. Kicker seized the sliver of soap and made hasty work of her ablutions. She shivered as she dried herself on the threadbare towel and dragged a brush through short, riotous curls.

The small, cracked mirror, a discard from one of the students, reflected a young woman who was only several inches taller than the girl who had fled her mother's ill-advised designs. Small breasted, and deeply tanned from long hours in the sun, visitors to the Academy often mistook Kicker for a youth. She never bothered to correct anyone's assumptions. Still as wiry as she had ever been, Kicker's sinewy arms and leanly muscled back bespoke the manual labour that filled her days.

Kicker turned away with her customary disregard for the mirror's image and sought out her Sunday shirt and trousers. Mr. Grindleshire's rules insisted that everyone, from the lowliest stable hand to the Headmistress, attend Sunday services in the school chapel. She had learned early to keep one of her three changes of clothing in respectable condition.

Kicker dressed quickly and headed outside to find that Old Thomas had already harnessed the chestnut to the school's carriage. The bold maroon lettering on the side identified the small buggy as Grindleshire Academy's.

As Kicker sprang lightly to the seat and took up the reins, Old Thomas laid a hand on the buggy's edge. "Train'll be in at three if tis on time. The teacher's name is Miss Madelyn Bristow, and she'll likely have a trunk or two. Take 'er straight up to the school to see Mrs. Sheridan, and then put 'er things in 'er room. Got all that?"

He did not offer written instructions, as Kicker's literacy skills were severely lacking and Old Thomas' were non-existent, but they traded nods of perfect understanding.

"Aye. See you in a couple hours."

Kicker enjoyed the drive into town along the quiet country lanes. It was part of the comforting rhythms of her life. A familiar sight now to those she passed on the road and in the fields, many greeted her cheerfully. She quickly forgot her bathing inspired pique in the pleasure of the summer afternoon, as her earlier sense of wellbeing returned.

Kicker arrived at the station and was informed that the train was running late, so she settled back to wait, musing idly on the new teacher. In her experience, Grindleshire attracted two types of teachers. Some were hidebound spinsters who had taught so long that they could do it with their eyes and minds shut; others were young women barely out of school themselves, who would stay in the profession only until the first proposal of marriage came their way.

When the train pulled in, Kicker eyed the descending passengers and looked for a woman who had *teacher* stamped all over her. She readily disregarded the matrons returning from London, and the young mothers shepherding their noisy broods. Much to Kicker's surprise, when Miss Madelyn Bristow stepped down onto the platform, she did not fit either Grindleshire stereotype.

The woman looked to be in her mid to late twenties, neatly dressed in a pale blue shirtwaist and ankle-length, navy blue skirt, which was gathered at her slim waist with a thin black belt. Beneath a wide-brimmed hat, copper coloured hair was pulled back in a twist, and bright, inquisitive green eyes assessed her surroundings. Before Kicker could approach, the woman spotted her and walked quickly toward the carriage.

Kicker jumped down from the seat to greet the new teacher, noting that the other woman had three or four inches on her in height.

"Miss Bristow?"

"Yes. You're from the Academy."

It was not so much a question as a statement of fact, but Kicker nodded.

"Aye, Miss. D'you have a trunk, Miss?"

The teacher gestured over her shoulder where Kicker could see a porter hauling a large chest toward the carriage. She hastened to help him, and between them, they swung the trunk up on the back of the carriage. After tying it down,

Kicker rushed to assist the teacher into the buggy. She was surprised when Miss Bristow insisted on riding up front with her rather than in the more comfortable passenger seat behind.

As Kicker guided the horse away from the station and onto the road that led out of town, she stole a sideways glance at her passenger. This was no shy, awkward neophyte, nor a rigid, humourless old maid. At a loss as to how to categorize the new teacher, Kicker maintained her silence while Miss Bristow took in her surroundings with evident interest. She was startled when the other woman finally addressed her.

"You have the advantage of me, my dear. What is your name?"

"Kicker Stuart, Miss."

She could feel the teacher's stare boring into her, and felt herself colour under the intense scrutiny, but Kicker kept her eyes firmly on the road.

"Kicker, is it?"

"Aye, Miss."

"That is very...unusual."

The words were not critical, only curious. Rather than taking refuge in her usual reticence, Kicker felt compelled to explain. "M'brother Adam named me, Miss. Guess Ma thought it fit me good. Ne'er called me anythin' else since the day I were born."

"I see. So, Miss Kicker Stuart, tell me about the Grindleshire Academy for Young Ladies."

It did not exactly feel like an order, but Miss Bristow's expectant gaze and firm voice made it apparent she was confident of a full and informative answer.

Bet she don' have no discipline problems in her classroom. With a small grin at the thought, Kicker gave a half shrug. "Not too sure what to tell you, Miss. I don' stray too far from the stables mos' days. I kin tell you that Missus Sheridan, the Headmistress, is a fair hand so long as you don' cross her. She's really the boss, e'en though Mister Grindleshire owns the place. You gotta duck when Missus Sheridan and Missus Grindleshire get to arguin' cuz they kin shake the tiles off'n the roof and you don' wanna get betwixt them. I kin tell you that Cook ain't got no patience if you're late fer meals, and she won' be savin' you anythin' either. An' I kin tell you that Pastor Hubble preaches the boringest sermons in the county, but you're gonna hafta pretend to listen cuz the teachers all sit up front and Missus Sheridan will see you if you doze off."

Kicker thrilled to the sound of Miss Bristow's laughter. Then, embarrassed by her reaction, she jerked her cap lower over her eyes and stared straight ahead.

"Well, I shall certainly do my best not to fall asleep then, Miss Stuart."

"Tis Kicker, Miss. Ever'one calls me that." Kicker blushed at correcting a lady, but was reassured by Miss Bristow's friendly smile.

"Thank you for the invaluable briefing, Kicker. I shall remember to be on time for dinner, submit to Mrs. Sheridan's dictates, stay out of the line of fire between the two eminent grande dames, and pay strict attention to Pastor Hubble."

Kicker wondered if the teacher was mocking her, but before the suspicion could fester, Miss Bristow went on.

"So what do you do for entertainment?"

Kicker hesitated. *She mus' mean what t'other teachers do for fun. She surely don' mean what a stable hand does.*

"Cook said twas a poetry readin' las' weekend, an' I know some teachers wen' on a picnic two weeks ago. Oh, and the Grindleshires arrange a trip to London come spring for all the teachers that wan' ta go. Young Mister Grindleshire helps with that, since he lives in the city." Kicker shrugged. "Tis about all I know, but Missus Sheridan kin prob'ly tell you more."

Miss Bristow was quiet for a moment. "And what about you, Kicker? What do you like to do when your work is done?"

Kicker glanced sharply sideways, but the other woman's expression was calmly inquisitive. She decided that, for whatever reason, Miss Bristow's interest was genuine.

"I go fishin' quite a bit. Cook likes it when I bring her fresh trout. An' sometimes on my half-days, Ol' Thomas lets me take Banner home to see my family."

"Banner?"

Kicker warmed to the subject of her favourite horse. "Aye, Miss. Banner, he's the smartest one in the stables. Times are you look in his eyes an' you jus' know he's fixin' to put one over on you. So you gotta keep a tight rein, but boy, kin he run. Get up on his back, give him his head, and you feel like you're ridin' the wind. If he ain't bin out all day, I take 'im out for a run in the evenin'."

"You like to ride, then?"

Kicker was surprised at the wistful tone in Miss Bristow's voice. "Aye, Miss. I do."

"I always wanted to ride, but I grew up in London and have worked there since I started teaching, so I never really had the chance. I've ridden a little in the parks, of course, but it's not precisely the same thing."

"What d'you like to do then, Miss? Fer fun, I mean."

"Well, I practice those time honoured feminine arts of needlepoint and watercolour, though not terribly well." Miss Bristow chuckled, but Kicker did not think it was a happy sound. "I also read extensively, and write very bad poetry. In fact one of the courses I'll be teaching is Eighteenth Century Poetry. Add in Seventeenth Century Literature and Advanced Principles of Deportment, and I shall no doubt enjoy a full life at the Grindleshire Academy for Young Ladies."

The teacher fell silent, and Kicker pondered the edge of bitterness in the woman's voice. Unsure what to say, she concentrated on the road, even though the docile chestnut could have plodded the whole way with blinders on.

"Is staff allowed to take the horses out on pleasure rides?"

"Aye, Miss, but not many of 'em do."

"Your horse...Banner, was it? Do you think I might ride him now and again?"

Kicker blinked and absorbed the undertone of nervous anticipation in the woman's voice. "Well, he ain't mine, Miss;

he b'longs to the Academy. But if I might say, if you ain't done much ridin', you might wanna start with ol' Cherry here. She's as gentle as they come." The chestnut bobbed her head as if aware she was the subject of conversation. "She won' run off with you like Banner prob'ly would."

Miss Bristow laid a hand on Kicker's forearm and almost caused her to drop the reins in surprise. "But I wish to ride the way you described, free and unfettered, as if I had harnessed the wind."

"I know, Miss, and you kin do that one day, but please start with Cherry here firs'. I don' wanna see you break your neck or somethin'."

"Please, will you teach me? Teach me how to ride, teach me to taste the freedom that you so enjoy?"

"A'right, Miss, so long's you b'gin with Cherry and work up to Banner."

"Agreed. I put myself entirely in your hands."

Though the thought of teaching Miss Bristow enthused Kicker, and she enjoyed the teacher's eagerness, she seriously doubted that Miss Bristow would follow through. Their conversation about horses and riding would simply be something to store away as a pleasant memory.

When Miss Bristow showed up at the stable the evening after she arrived, Kicker blinked in amazement. *Well, damn me.* She hastened to saddle Cherry. "Sorry I were not ready, Miss. Won' happ'n agin."

"You didn't think I'd make an appearance, did you, Miss Stuart?"

There was distinct amusement in Miss Bristow's voice, and Kicker blushed. "My mistake, Miss. I promise, it really won' happ'n agin."

"Please don't apologize. The fault is mine if I misled you into thinking I was merely offering a lighthearted suggestion. I promise you that I intend to take your lessons seriously. I hope that if I apply myself, I may be able to keep up with you soon."

Startled, Kicker met Miss Bristow's penetrating gaze. "Keep up, Miss?"

"Of course. You will ride with me, won't you? How could you instruct me if you're not nearby to offer corrections on my technique?"

While preparing Cherry, Kicker had hazily visualized imparting some instructions before Miss Bristow rode out on her own. It did not occur to her that she would keep the beautiful teacher company. But as she went to saddle Banner, an unbidden, unexpected, and oddly exciting thought put a broad smile on her face.

I got an' excuse t' look at her whene'er I like.

Much to the surprise of Grindleshire's small community, the unusual friendship between the teacher and the stable hand flourished. Though the first month of school was busy for everyone at the Academy, the onset of colder weather meant a lightening of Kicker's duties, and more time for her to indulge her new passion for teaching the teacher. They rode at every opportunity, often for hours at a time.

Alone at night in her small room, Kicker mentally replayed their lessons over and over. Her mind lingered on the laughter they shared, warm smiles Miss Bristow bestowed on her earnest instructor, and Kicker's favourite reminiscence—any casual touch between the two. Most precious of all was the memory of the day Miss Bristow rode Banner for the first time.

On a blustery November afternoon, Kicker quietly handed the teacher Banner's reins and took Cherry's reins for herself. She knew that the pure delight in Miss Bristow's eyes would be added to her store of midnight memories. They kept their ride short, but Kicker was shivering by the time they turned back. She tried to conceal her discomfort from her companion.

When they came in sight of the Academy, Miss Bristow winningly entreated Kicker. "May I gallop Banner? Oh, do say yes. I am ready—honestly, I am."

Kicker was finding it more and more difficult to refuse Miss Bristow the slightest request, but in this instance, she was relieved that she did not have to. The teacher had become an accomplished rider under Kicker's tutelage, and she knew Miss Bristow could handle the big grey.

"Aye, go 'head. I'll meet you back at the stable." Kicker smiled as Miss Bristow and Banner raced away. She knew there was no use in attempting to keep up. Cherry would be highly indignant even to be asked for more than a sedate canter.

Kicker laughed aloud when she saw Miss Bristow reach the stable, only to wheel and race back toward her.

"Oh, my heavens, Kicker! It's like flying. No wonder you love Banner so."

Miss Bristow's eyes glowed with excitement, and her face was attractively flushed with the cold and the wind. Kicker's breath caught, and she could not prevent the violent shiver that overcame her.

Instantly, Miss Bristow reached over and touched Kicker's hand. "You're freezing. Why didn't you tell me how cold you were? Come. We shall return immediately."

Miss Bristow slowed Banner to keep pace with Cherry as they rode back together. Kicker had never felt such a strange and exhilarating combination of heat and cold. *I mus' be comin' down with somethin'.*

Confused, Kicker kept silent as Miss Bristow waxed enthusiastic about the joys of riding Banner. When they reached the stable, Kicker dismounted quickly so she could take Banner's reins as usual.

Miss Bristow jumped lightly to the ground, then spun and wrapped her shocked companion in an enthusiastic hug. "I can never thank you enough." She released Kicker, only to laugh aloud and seize her in an even longer hug. "My dear, you have no idea how much our rides have come to mean to me. They are the highlight of my days, and it is all thanks to you. I can never repay you for your kindness, patience, and consideration."

If Kicker had been able to speak, she would have told Miss Bristow it was entirely her pleasure, but she could not force even the smallest sound from her throat. Fortunately, Miss Bristow did not seem to require an answer. She gave Kicker a cheerful wave and departed for the staff quarters. Kicker stood stock still and watched Miss Bristow walk away.

"You look like you bin pole-axed, girl."

Kicker glanced over her shoulder at Old Thomas, who stood grinning behind her. "Don' be daft, ol' man. She's jus' grateful fer the ridin' lessons."

"Uh huh. Well, put Banner and Cherry in the barn. Tis a storm blowin' up."

Several days later Kicker returned to her room after her work was done and found a thick, quilted coat on her bed. There was a note with it, but she was unable to make out the meaning of the graceful script. Still, she had no doubt the gift and note were from Miss Bristow, and she fingered both reverently.

Thrilled by the teacher's consideration, Kicker could hardly wait until she saw Miss Bristow again. They had made arrangements to meet that day to ride. A soon as she heard the bell toll the end of the school day, Kicker swiftly saddled Banner and Cherry.

When Miss Bristow did not appear, Kicker waited until dark for her student, passing up dinner for fear of missing the teacher's arrival. Finally she accepted that Miss Bristow was not coming and unsaddled the horses.

Kicker knew that Cook would find her favourite something to eat if she went up to the kitchen, but her stomach churned and her appetite was absent. Profoundly dismayed by Miss Bristow's cavalier treatment, she lay on her hard, narrow bed, thinking.

Maybe that's it, then. Maybe the coat meant g'bye. Maybe now that she knows how to ride, she'll have naught to do with me. Maybe she'll jus' ride with her frien's now. Ain't like I'm but a dirty stable han' anyway.

The thought of being so easily dismissed roiled Kicker's gut. Tears burned her eyes, but she angrily brushed them away. *So be it, then. I don' need her takin' time from my days. I got things to do. Tis better this way. Should ha' tol' her myself not to come anymore.*

A soft tap on her door interrupted Kicker's anguished thoughts.

"Aye?"

The door opened and Miss Bristow poked her head into the room. "Hello, Kicker. If you don't mind the interruption, I thought I'd see how the coat fit."

Kicker swung her legs off the bed and sat up, but averted her face. "It fits fine, but I kin not take it."

Miss Bristow stepped into the room and closed the door behind her. "Why is that? Don't you like it? I just felt so badly about keeping you out in the cold the other day."

"Don' need charity."

There was a long moment of silence. "It wasn't charity. It was a gift from one friend to another, in gratitude, and the hope that it would keep you warm this winter."

Kicker refused to look at Miss Bristow, but she heard sadness in the teacher's voice. *Frien', eh? Some frien'.*

"Kicker? Kicker, please look at me."

Kicker studied the floor as if she had never seen it before.

With a sigh, Miss Bristow knelt in front of her. Kicker wanted to throw off the hands that came to rest on her knees, but all she could do was stare at them.

"Please, Kicker. It is apparent that you are deeply angry with me, but I have no idea why. I never meant to offend you with my gift; it came from my heart. I do apologize if it seemed any other way."

Gentle fingers tilted Kicker's face up. Miss Bristow's concerned face swam in front of Kicker's tear filled eyes.

"Oh, Kicker, what is it? What have I done to upset you so? Please tell me. I cannot make things better between us if you refuse to speak, and I do so want to restore our friendship."

Kicker blurted angrily, "Frien'ship? What kinda frien' jus' don' show up when she says she will?"

"But, I told you in my note that I would be unable to make our rendezvous today and wished to reschedule for tomorrow. Didn't you see my message? I set it right on top of the coat. I was sure you wouldn't miss it."

Kicker knew the moment Miss Bristow spied the square of paper sticking out from under her pillow. She blushed furiously. *Bless'd Jesus. Bad 'nuff I couldn't read it. Now she'll know I kep' it close anyway. She'll think...*

Before Kicker could decide what Miss Bristow would think, the teacher extracted the note and stared at it. Unable to bear what might be reflected on Miss Bristow's face, Kicker tried to look away.

Gentle hands stopped her, cupping her face. Eyes bright with emotion met hers. "I'm a fool. I never thought—I'm so, so sorry." Soft fingers brushed away Kicker's tears of shame. "You couldn't read my note, could you?"

Kicker shook her head wordlessly.

Miss Bristow rose and sat down on the bed. She took one of Kicker's hands and patted it comfortingly. "The fault is entirely mine. I hope you will forgive me for being so obtuse."

"I'm not stupid; I jus' ne'er liked school."

"Heavens, I never once thought you witless. However, you also never had the advantage of my being your teacher." Miss Bristow slid an arm around Kicker's shoulders and hugged her. "I shall teach you, my dear. After all, it is only fair. You have given me a gift of immeasurable value. Allow me to return the favour and initiate you into the beautiful universe of words. Please?"

Kicker blanched. She had loathed the dark, musty, village schoolhouse dominated by a teacher who wielded his thick, leather strap with an unstinting hand. Kicker escaped at every opportunity, despite the punishment she knew would await her unwilling return. Finally her father had stepped in and gruffly ordered that Kicker be allowed to spend her days helping him, rather than be subjected to fruitless attempts to expand her rudimentary education.

Without giving Kicker a chance to object, Miss Bristow continued. "I promise, I'll make the whole process painless. You'll see. Not to be immodest, but I'm almost as good a teacher as you are."

Miss Bristow smiled, and this time Kicker met her gaze. She was acutely aware of their bodies touching and the teacher's arm around her shoulders.

It was unthinkable to do anything but agree to as much time as possible in this woman's presence.

Kicker nodded her agreement.

"Cook, may I thank you again for allowing Kicker and me the use of your kitchen? It's been such a boon during these cold months, and I do believe I far prefer teaching here to my classroom."

Kicker hid a grin. She knew that Cook had succumbed as readily to Miss Bristow's charms as she had, and would have granted her the run of the whole kitchen if the teacher had asked. As it was, this warm corner, tucked away from the whirl of activity in the rest of the kitchen, had become Kicker's favourite spot in the Academy. Here, the winter months had seen her literacy skills expand by leaps and bounds under Miss Bristow's attentive tutelage.

I ne'er thought learnin' would be so... pleasant.

Cook set cups of tea in front of the teacher and her faithful student. "Guess wi' the weather turnin' nice agin, ye'll be back out in the gardens soon, eh?"

"Thank you, Cook. Yes, it was so lovely today that I almost suggested we take our lessons and go riding." Miss Bristow looked at Kicker over the rim of the steaming cup. "You've a half-day tomorrow, don't you? How would it be if I pack our books and we take Banner and Cherry out for a ride?"

"I could sen' ye wi' a picnic, if ye wan'."

"Why, thank you, Cook. That would be lovely. Kicker, what do you say?"

Kicker had planned to ride Banner over to see Adam and his family, as she had not seen them in two months, but she did not hesitate. "Aye, twould be nice." *I'll go see Adam nex' week.*

The following afternoon, Kicker waited at the stables with Cook's bountiful picnic basket and a blanket both tied to Cherry's saddle. Miss Bristow was prompt, and graciously insisted that Kicker ride Banner. Without discussion, they headed directly for a clearing by the river that had become their favourite spot to stop a while and talk.

By the time they reached the clearing, Kicker found she was unaccountably nervous. She was not unprepared for her lessons. In the five months since Miss Bristow began tutoring her, Kicker had often fallen asleep after a hard day's work with a book on her chest or her slate close at hand. But after she released the horses to graze, Kicker saw her hands shake as she spread the blanket on the grass.

When she took her seat next to Miss Bristow, she thrust her hands under her thighs to conceal their trembling. There was nothing she could do about her shortened breath, except to hope that her teacher did not notice.

Miss Bristow extracted the book they had been working on, and opened it to a page she had already marked. "So, where did we leave off yesterday?"

"You were talkin' about poetry."

"That's right, I was. Lord Byron, to be precise. Let me read you a passage, and then we'll discuss it." Miss Bristow's eyes barely glanced at the page as she began to recite.

Her rapt audience almost missed the meaning of the verse because of the way the teacher's soft, husky voice caressed the evocative words.

And on that cheek, and o'er that brow,
So soft, so calm, yet eloquent,
The smiles that win, the tints that glow
But tell of days in goodness spent,
A mind at peace with all below,
A heart whose love is innocent!

Kicker felt that she could drown in the eyes fixed so intently on her own. *Bless'd Jesus. What am I doin'?* She fought a wave of excitement and panic so intense that she feared she might swoon at the teacher's feet.

When Miss Bristow paused and looked inquiringly at Kicker, it was all she could do to speak. Clearing her throat once, then again, she asked, "Could you read it one more time, please?"

With an enigmatic smile, Miss Bristow read the passage again. The last line echoed in Kicker's mind, and the rest of the afternoon's lessons were lost in one overwhelming question. *Did she pick this one special for me? Is she tryin' to tell me—*

At which point Kicker rejected the question as nonsense, and tried to focus on the lessons, and later, the picnic. When the afternoon ended, Kicker was as exhausted as if she had worked a fifteen hour day. For the first time, it was more a relief than a disappointment to return to the stable.

Thankfully Cook had packed an expansive lunch for the two, so Kicker skipped dinner and retired to her room. She had a lot to think about.

A week later on her half-day, Kicker rode over to visit her brother and his growing family. Adam took her for a walk in the fields behind his small cottage. They hadn't gone far before he began to gently chide her.

"So, little sister, why is't you've not been to see any of us in more'n two months? I know how close you've gotten to your Academy frien's o'er the years, but you got blood family cares 'bout you too. You're getting' more and more nieces and nephews all'a time, an' you don' e'en know half of 'em."

Kicker looked up indignantly to see a half-grin on his bearded face, and she elbowed him. "Not true. It ain' bin that long."

"Has too. Young Jeremiah was just gone four when you las' came by."

Kicker thought about that as she automatically quickened her step to keep up with her brother's long stride. *Tis bin that long?* Ruefully she had to admit that it had. Kicker spent her half-days with Miss Bristow, if the teacher requested her presence. Lately it seemed that the dedicated teacher was eager to get all the time possible with Kicker to devote to lessons. It was purely guilt that had led Kicker to excuse herself today. She knew it had been too long since she had seen her family.

"I guess I kinda los' track of time. Sometimes, I can barely believe so many years have passed since I lef' here. Seems like twere jus' yesterday, but here's both of us long grown and gone from Da's hearth."

Kicker was unwilling to confess, even to Adam, that in these halcyon days nothing held more importance than spending every possible moment with her lovely teacher. "I'll try to do better, honest."

Adam stopped and turned to face her but Kicker refused to meet his eyes and toed the dirt. "'Fess up. What's goin' on?" When Kicker remained silent, a surprised, then delighted look came over Adam's face. "Kicker! Did you meet someone? Has someone finally stolen your heart?"

"No. Of course not." Kicker was dismayed at the thought of having her feelings for Miss Bristow hauled into the harsh light of day. This was Adam, who had loved and protected her for as long as she could remember, but even so, she couldn't share this with him.

Adam regarded her quietly, then turned to resume their walk. After a long silence, he spoke softly, his voice troubled. "Tis a'right, you know. I mean if there was some... someone. Jus'...be really careful, a'right? Tis prob'ly not somethin' you should talk about anyway. Not e'eryone would understan', you know?"

Kicker nodded mutely, and was deeply grateful when he changed the subject. For the rest of their walk, they discussed their youngest brother Brian's flight from the family home to join his two eldest brothers in the army. Later that day, when Kicker rode Banner back to the Academy, she finally allowed herself to contemplate what Adam said. *Would he be shocked if I tol' him how I feel for Miss Bristow?* Kicker shook her head in confusion. *What do I feel?*

She did not know how to define their relationship. What Kicker did know was that the class gulf between teacher and stable hand was sharply defined and never to be crossed. Their unlikely friendship was tolerated only because Miss

Bristow was regarded as something of a harmless eccentric. She was a talented and popular teacher, but one with an unusual fascination for riding that Kicker facilitated on demand.

Kicker did not dare to aspire to more than what they already had. She never sought Miss Bristow out between their scheduled lessons, though it was not unusual for the teacher to stroll down to the stables at unexpected times. Kicker would often look up from grooming Banner or one of her other charges, to find Miss Bristow watching her from just inside the stable door. Sometimes they would speak, and sometimes Miss Bristow would simply give her an inscrutable smile and go on her way.

Kicker knew the teacher was fond of her. Many times Miss Bristow had urged Kicker to call her by her Christian name when they were alone. But fearful of forgetting her place in front of others, Kicker had not allowed herself to do so, though she often rolled the lovely name over in her mind in the solitude of her bed.

Madelyn. Madelyn Elizabeth. Madelyn Elizabeth Bristow.

One day, Kicker had been too busy to go to the kitchen for lunch. Though she'd known Cook would bend the kitchen rules for her, she hadn't wanted to put her friend in a difficult position. So instead, Kicker had done something she'd tried to work her nerve up to do for weeks. Nervously, she'd made her way toward the academic wing. She'd known Miss Bristow conducted afternoon class on seventeenth century literature at this time, and which classroom her teacher would be using.

Kicker had become such an integral part of the school support system over the years that no one questioned her presence anywhere on the grounds. Still, she could not help feeling profoundly guilty about what she was about to do. And if she were stopped for any reason, Kicker had been certain her face would clearly broadcast her feelings. Much to her chagrin, it always did.

Kicker had reached a grove of trees and glanced around. There had been no one in the immediate area, so she'd quickly shinnied up an ancient oak tree. She'd settled herself on a branch and looked around. It was as she had hoped—a perfect place for her purposes. No one would be able to detect her presence, but she could see directly into Miss Bristow's second floor classroom. Though she had been too far away to hear anything, she could watch Miss Bristow's animated lecture.

At one point, Miss Bristow had laughed heartily at something a student said, and Kicker felt her heart fill with emotion. *She's...beautiful. No, more than jus' beautiful... she's b'witchin' like...enchantin' e'en...* She'd shaken her head in frustration. Words were so inadequate.

For weeks afterwards, Kicker had often taken her lunch break at that hour, until Cook chastised her for missing so many meals. Nervously, Kicker had recalled Adam's warning, knowing she should be more careful. She'd made more frequent appearances in the kitchen from then on, but had been helpless against the powerful pull of the oak tree and Miss Bristow's class.

Early May arrived, and with it Mr. Grindleshire's only son, Merrick, came to make arrangements for the staff's annual weekend in the city. The evening that Mr. Grindleshire the younger arrived, Miss Bristow was at the stable, inspecting the latest batch of kittens the stable cat had birthed.

"Ain't they adorable?" Much to her delight, Kicker found that though there were eight kittens, she and Miss Bristow often ended up stroking the same one. Their fingers could not avoid the occasional accidental touch.

"They are indeed. Do you think—"

Whatever Miss Bristow had been about to say was lost in the commotion of a rider approaching fast and hard. Kicker jumped up from the hay and rushed to the stable door. She frowned as she saw who was galloping up the long, curving entrance road.

Kicker did not approve of Merrick Grindleshire, though she would never be so brash as to say so. The man rode horses hard, with little regard for their welfare. Kicker was only grateful that he never again requisitioned Banner after he'd been tossed by the big grey gelding a couple of years earlier. It had taken Old Thomas' intervention with the senior Mr. Grindleshire to prevent Banner from being put down as incorrigible. Kicker never forgave the arrogant young man.

Cook reported that Merrick was overheard bragging about his intention to acquire a motor car. Kicker uttered a small prayer that he would do so soon, and spare the magnificent animals unlucky enough to fall into his hands.

Kicker brushed off the straw and walked quickly to the main house, well aware that Merrick would never deign to bring his mount down to the stable. He was more likely to simply abandon it where he dismounted, and it would be on Kicker's head if the horse ended up amidst the flower gardens.

Miss Bristow fell into step beside her. "Who is our visitor?"

Kicker frowned as she noticed the curiosity with which the teacher regarded the new arrival. "That's Mister Grindleshire's son, Miss. I expect he's come about the teachers' trip to the city. Since he lives there mos' of the time, his da makes him help with the staff weekend. Says tis good for the teachers' morals or some such."

A soft chuckle greeted her words. "I think it may well be their morale that is to be raised. Hopefully their morals are already in high order."

Kicker scowled. She had worked hard to improve, but she knew her rough ways still needed a lot of refining. Worse, Miss Bristow seemed more interested in the stranger than in her injured feelings.

Merrick appeared to be reciprocally interested. After greeting his father, who had come out to meet him, the newcomer turned to wait for the approaching women, his eyes fixed on Miss Bristow.

Without a word, Kicker parted from the teacher and made her way to Merrick's horse, which was still snorting hard from the exertion of their arrival. She ran her hands over the sweating flanks and listened to the conversation between the three.

The older man's voice boomed cheerfully. "Ah, there you are, Miss Bristow. I want you to meet my son, just down from London for a visit. Miss Madelyn Bristow, this is my youngest child, Merrick. Merrick, Miss Bristow joined us last summer, and has established herself as an excellent teacher, as well as a very promising poet in her own right."

"Enchanted, my dear Miss Bristow. It is truly a pleasure to meet you."

Kicker clenched her teeth at the smooth, ingratiating voice.

"The pleasure is mine, Mr. Grindleshire. Are you down for long?"

"Well, I had not planned to be, but perhaps I may find reason to extend my visit. And please, call me Merrick."

Kicker winced as she pictured the man's unctuous smile. She glanced under the horse's neck and saw Merrick still holding her teacher's hand. As she watched, he drew Miss Bristow's arm through his and guided her up the stairs.

Merrick's buttery tones floated back to Kicker. "So tell me, Madelyn, if I may call you that, do you ever give readings of your poetry? I have quite a passion for verse myself. At one time, I fancied myself another Browning."

Miss Bristow's response was inaudible as the trio entered the front door. Kicker stood numbly and felt as if Banner had just kicked her in the stomach. Her beloved teacher had not even bade her goodnight.

Glowering, Kicker gathered the horse's reins and led him to the stable. Her mind reeled at how casually she had been disregarded. Her heart was filled with a sense of betrayal, though her mind argued that she had no right to feel so.

Leading the horse first to the water trough, Kicker monitored his intake closely as she considered the man she could not help regarding as competition. *I s'pose some might think him han'some enough. His hair is a'ready thin, though, an' I don' trust his eyes. They're...shifty.*

"From the cut of his vest, he's bin eatin' a bit too well these days, too." Kicker emphatically pulled the horse away from the trough and scowled as she led him into the barn.

"Did you say somepin', Kicker?" Old Thomas asked as he passed her by. She shook her head and began to unsaddle the tired animal.

"I see the lad is down from the city." Old Thomas grinned and jerked his thumb up at the mansion. "That means the fillies will be tumblin' all over themselves to catch 'is eye. Wisht he'd just pick one of 'em and settle down so we don' have to go through this foolishness ever' time the princeling comes back to the school. Whene'er his royal highness visits, they're all atwitter up there, busy settin' their caps to snare him."

Along with the downstairs staff, Kicker had hung avidly on Cook's tales of the younger Mr. Grindleshire's legendary dalliances each time he visited. It had meant nothing more to her than a moment's entertainment...until now.

Kicker curried the horse with vigorous strokes and let her mind stray to the unthinkable. *Will she fall under his spell, questionable though it be? Surely not. Miss Bristow's far too smart to be taken in. Tis not like she's some callow girl to fall for a han'some face and good manners...is she?* Kicker stopped with a horrified look on her face. *What if she does fall for him? Will she marry an' leave for the city?*

Kicker had no experience with affairs of the heart, and her fears plagued her long after she bade Old Thomas goodnight. He headed for his cottage and his wife, and she took a seat on the top rail of the paddock fence.

By the dim light of a scant moon, Kicker's gaze flickered across the row of lights on the top floor of the school. She counted off until she reached Miss Bristow's window, illuminated brightly by the gaslight within. Being very familiar with her habits, Kicker knew that normally the light would be dimmed by now. She did not know if she should be troubled by that break in routine, or pleased that Miss Bristow was safely in the solitude of her room.

But what if she's not in her room? What if she jus' lef' a light on, knowin' she'd be back later than usual an' in the dark?

Kicker tortured herself for over an hour, then heaved a sigh of relief when Miss Bristow's window finally went dark. Sliding off the rail, she became aware that she had been perched in the uncomfortable spot far too long. She grimaced and tried to coax some feeling back into her numb flesh as she headed for bed herself. But even in her sanctuary, Kicker's thoughts did not allow her any peace.

Over and over Kicker pondered the improvements she had made in herself these past months. She'd studied intensely; her literacy skills were hard won, but solid. She had taken to bathing on a frequent basis so as not to offend Miss Bristow's ladylike senses. She washed her clothes more often and spoke more carefully, even when not around the teacher.

Kicker coaxed choice bits from Cook to take with them on their excursions. And she taught Miss Bristow horsemanship with as much dedication as she herself was taught grammar, spelling, and composition.

Cook and Old Thomas had noticed the changes, with the former bestowing approval for the betterment while the latter teased her about the reasons for her drive toward self-improvement. Yet it did not seem to make any difference to the only person that mattered, at least as far as Kicker could see.

She treats me kin'ly, jus' like she has since we met. Miss Bristow offered encouragement and praise in lavish measure, but Kicker had watched her do the same with her other students.

Sometimes Kicker could almost convince herself that Miss Bristow regarded her as more than just another student, perhaps even as a friend, but then the harsh reality of their respective positions set in, and Kicker chastised herself for being so foolish.

Wracked with unspoken longings and unfulfilled dreams, Kicker spent a sleepless night. She rose at dawn to begin her duties with a heavy heart and sullen demeanour. Even Old Thomas could not elicit a smile when he brought her some of his wife's breakfast cakes wrapped in brown paper.

When Miss Bristow came down to the stables the next evening, Kicker silently saddled Banner for her and stepped aside.

Miss Bristow regarded her with puzzlement. "Won't you join me?"

"Got too much to do. Can't be wastin' time goin' willy-nilly across the fields."

Kicker was too lost in her misery to notice the distress her gruff words caused, as Miss Bristow slowly left the paddock alone.

To her complete lack of surprise, Merrick arrived at the stable moments after Miss Bristow departed, and ordered his horse to be saddled at once. Kicker barely had time to tighten the cinch before he swung up and galloped off in the direction Miss Bristow had taken. Bitter, she glared after him. *Should ha' lef' the cinch loose.*

When the two of them rode back together, Kicker stubbornly kept her back turned while she worked on a bit that had separated from an old bridle.

"Girl!"

The peremptory demand was impossible to ignore, and Kicker slowly turned to face the couple.

"Her name is Kicker."

Kicker assumed the cool displeasure in Miss Bristow's voice was directed at her earlier abruptness. She refused to meet the eyes which regarded her sadly.

"Mmm? Oh, whatever. Kicker, then, come take our horses." Merrick swung down, and turned his attention to his companion. He flattered Miss Bristow with his brightest smile and offered his hand. "You ride very well, my dear, though I'm surprised that you shun the customary sidesaddle. I've never seen a lady ride thus. I would think it would be difficult to find the appropriate dress."

Miss Bristow accepted the proffered hand and dismounted gracefully. Kicker took the reins of both horses and led them away. Her ears strained to hear the couple's conversation even as she castigated herself for caring.

"I find I can control my mount better astride, and I simply modified some of my clothing to accommodate my preferred style."

"Well, you certainly maintain excellent control of that beast." A note of petulance crept into Merrick's voice. "Really though, do you think you should chance riding that grey? I happen to know that he can be very headstrong and highly unpredictable. Perhaps you should select a different mount for our next ride."

Kicker focused on the man's assertion of them riding together again and failed to detect the chilly tones of Miss Bristow's voice as they moved away.

"I assure you, Mr. Grindleshire, Banner is a delight to ride, and has always been utterly well mannered for me."

"Merrick, please, my dear Madelyn. And of course I do not for one moment doubt your skill, but..."

The voices faded across the lawn, and with a sigh Kicker began to groom the horses. With each stroke of the curry comb, she tried to console herself. *Twill be back to the city b'fore long. Countryside's too quiet for the likes of the grand Mister Grindleshire, that's sure and certain.*

The next four weeks were the longest of Kicker's life. The teachers' excursion to the city came and went, and still the younger Mr. Grindleshire lingered. Talk in the kitchen revolved around how smitten the Headmaster's son was by the beautiful Miss Bristow. Betting was fierce among the household staff as to the length of time it would be until the Academy hosted a splendid wedding. Based on the lustful looks bestowed on Miss Bristow by her ardent swain, odds ran heavily that a marriage would take place before summer's end.

In the days following the conclusion of the school year, Kicker and Old Thomas were kept busy ferrying students and their baggage into town to catch the trains that dispersed them to their families. With little time for reflection, Kicker was nonetheless keenly aware that staff would be leaving next. A few of the older, single teachers stayed on through the summer, as did some of the household staff. Most left, however, to return at the end of summer before the new school year began.

Kicker had not had a private conversation with Miss Bristow since Merrick's arrival. She had no idea what her plans were, though she could guess from the kitchen gossip.

One evening, sick at heart, Kicker took advantage of a lull in the constant travel between the Academy and the town to take Banner out for a ride.

She rode hard, urging the big horse to a gallop. As Kicker strove for an elusive peace, she gave Banner his head and let the wind whip the tears from her eyes. When finally the horse slowed to a canter, then to a walk, she wasn't surprised to see he'd brought her down to the river. It was their spot—hers and Miss Bristow's, but she could not remember the last time they'd visited it.

"Aye, you know, don'cha, old boy." Kicker slid off Banner's back and patted his damp neck affectionately. He nuzzled her as she knotted the reins loosely over his withers. The gelding ambled off to graze while Kicker walked to the edge of the bank.

Kicker stared at the river and reflected on the past year. She wondered wearily if she would be able to stand working at the Academy once Miss Bristow became Mrs. Merrick Grindleshire. It would be agony to see her beloved teacher on the man's arm, his possessive, victorious smirk clear evidence that she now completely and irrevocably belonged to him.

"Like there was e'er any chance..."

Kicker lacked the words to define her inchoate longings. The most she had ever allowed herself was the fantasy of years of cherished friendship with Miss Bristow. Perhaps one day she might allow herself to call the other woman by her Christian name when they were alone. She did not dare dream of taking any further liberties. But even without substance, unformed desires haunted Kicker, denied her rest, and deprived her days of the harmony that had characterized them these past seven years.

Lost in her thoughts and hypnotized by the turbulent water, Kicker failed to notice the sound of an approaching horse or Banner's welcoming whinny. When she finally sensed another horse nearing the river, Kicker spun around, only to gape at the sight of Miss Bristow on Cherry's back. She automatically glanced past her, looking for the woman's inevitable companion, but there was no sign of Merrick Grindleshire.

Kicker pulled her wits together and hurried to her side, taking Cherry's reins as Miss Bristow slid to the ground.

"Is e'erythin' a'right, Miss? Am I needed back at the Academy?"

Miss Bristow looked at her angrily. "At the Academy? No...not at the Academy."

Uneasy at the teacher's unusual demeanour, Kicker stepped out of the way and allowed Cherry to amble to Banner's side and the teacher to stride to the riverbank.

Miss Bristow said nothing as she stared into the waters.

In nervous uncertainty, Kicker stood quietly to the side. She fumbled for something to say, saddened at the unease that had replaced their once warm, effortless rapport. Finally, she could stand the silence no longer. "Are you a'right, Miss?"

Miss Bristow's shoulders tightened and her head snapped up.

Kicker took an involuntary step backwards.

"All right? Yes, I suppose you could say I was fine. Probably better than fine, really. After all, it's not every day that a woman is proposed to by a wealthy young man from a fine family, is it?" Madelyn's voice was tight and controlled.

Kicker froze. So Merrick had finally done it. Madelyn would be his, and all the amorphous dreams that had haunted her nights through this glorious spring would be as dust in the stable yard.

CHAPTER 2

Kicker's throat closed with grief. She started to back away before a thought halted her retreat. *If Merrick proposed t'night, what is Miss Bristow doin' out here? Shouldn't she be celebratin' with her betrothed's family and fellow teachers?*

Confused, Kicker shook her head as Miss Bristow turned to stare at her.

"What? You don't believe that Merrick Grindleshire would propose to me, my young friend? You don't believe that I would be a fine catch for such a gentleman?"

The words were light but it seemed to a baffled Kicker as if the teacher mocked herself. "Uh, no, Miss. I think you're a real catch, and anyone would be lucky to have you."

Never taking her eyes from Kicker's face, Miss Bristow advanced on the flustered woman. "Anyone? Really? Then you would approve if someone, say...the Prince of Wales, for instance, was to propose a union?"

The Prince? But I thought...well, din't Mister Grindleshire jus' propose? Aloud, Kicker mumbled her agreement, disconcerted by the intent glitter in Miss Bristow's eyes.

"So if you believe that I'm good enough to marry a prince, then it follows that I should be good enough for almost anyone—is that what you're saying?"

Miss Bristow was close enough that Kicker could feel the warmth of her body and smell the familiar scent of her lavender toilet water.

Kicker nodded, not trusting her voice.

Miss Bristow's expression suddenly gentled and she reached out to caress Kicker's face. She drew her fingers lightly over a tanned cheekbone and down a strong jaw to linger on lips that parted unconsciously. Her voice softened. "And if I'm good enough for those illustrious gentlemen, why then am I not good enough for you?"

"For me?" Kicker was amazed that she was able to produce even that squeak. "But, Miss, I'm not... I mean I'm not e'en fit'n..."

Miss Bristow sighed deeply and took Kicker's head firmly in both hands. "Yes, you are, dearest. You most surely are. God help me, I know the risks far too well. But I can no longer deny what I feel ... and what I have prayed night after night that you feel as well." Miss Bristow lowered her head and gave Kicker her first kiss, soft, sweet, but insistent.

Shocked, Kicker stood passively for a long moment, but as her lips absorbed the feel of the warm, demanding mouth that covered her own, her entire body began to respond. With growing urgency, Kicker strained against her, engulfed by a rushing torrent of sensations and emotions. Convinced that she was seconds from bursting into flame, Kicker was grateful when Miss Bristow broke their kiss with a joyful laugh.

"I knew you would be a quick learner. You were always my best student."

"Miss Bristow—"

"No. You cannot kiss me like that and still call me 'Miss Bristow', dearest." Her voice was mirthful, but firm.

"Madelyn..." Kicker rolled the sound on her tongue. "Madelyn, what about...him?"

"Let him find his own lady, dearest. I found mine many months ago, though she is a stubborn sort and refused to see what lay before her very eyes." Madelyn's voice was teasing, and part of Kicker simply wanted to let the unpleasantness go and return to kissing, but she had to know for certain, had to hear the words.

"You turned him down, Miss...Madelyn?"

Madelyn's fingers stroked Kicker's shoulders and elicited a sigh as they traced a path down the strong back. When those mischievous hands tugged her shirt from her trousers and slipped underneath, Kicker's eyes closed in delight.

Only a tiny vestige of her stubborn nature kept Kicker from surrendering without another word, but she forced herself to speak. "Mister Grindleshire? What about him?"

Madelyn's hands stilled and she rested her cheek against Kicker's hair. "I suppose I do owe you the whole story."

Madelyn eased her hands from under the thin shirt, took Kicker's hand and led her to the bank of the river. She tugged Kicker down to sit beside her as they dangled their feet above the water's edge.

"I suppose the long and the short of it is that Merrick asked me to marry him tonight, and I declined the honour he obviously felt he had bestowed upon me." Madelyn turned her head to look at Kicker. "I turned him down for several reasons, but the main one is that I'm in love with another."

"Another?" For an instant, Kicker wondered if there was a man back in the city that she did not know about. *Did I misunderstan'?*

Madelyn chuckled at the confusion on Kicker's face. "You, my sweet girl. I've been in love with you for ever so long."

"But, you spent all your time with him. I thought sure you was goin' to marry him." Even as Kicker protested, part of her mind told her to simply shut up and accept Madelyn's declaration at face value. "You e'en went to the city with him."

Madelyn shot Kicker a dry look. "And his parents, and twenty-two other women. Initially I tried to bow out, but all the Grindleshires put pressure on me. Finally I decided it would actually be a good opportunity to take care of some matters with my family's barrister." She squeezed Kicker's hand. "Besides, by then you were avoiding me. I couldn't even get you to come for a ride with me."

Kicker hung her head and focused intently on the small eddy at the edge of the water. "He was always hangin' 'round, and I din't want to get in the way."

"Do you think so little of me that you would believe for even a moment that I could possibly be interested in such a pompous, tedious, simpering ass?"

Stung, Kicker shot back, "He's rich, an' han'some, and all t'other teachers were after him. Wasn't hard to see he was smitten with you. Figured all he had to do was crook his finger an' you'd agree to marry him."

"Marry him? Never. I have no desire to become some man's chattel—to lose control over my body and mind and property; to be dictated to like some feeble minded child for the rest of my life; to never again taste the freedom that you have shown me. That I should take his name, bend to his will, and go to his bed...would you wish that for me?"

"No. But t'others seem to want it right enough. They was always fallin' all over him, like he was kin to the Queen."

"And I'm sure that one of them will make Merrick a fine wife, but it isn't going to be me." Exasperation was clear in her tone, but then Madelyn's voice softened. "I far prefer a most handsome lass who has thick, dark curls that my fingers long to get lost in; big, black eyes that look out on the world with such innocence, intelligence, and curiosity; and a mind and heart that have drawn my own from the first moment we met." Madelyn took Kicker's hands tightly in her own. "I know all your objections before you even voice them, dearest. It's not as if we can march up to Pastor Hubble's door and demand that he marry us. Nor can we spend a night together without causing a scandal at the Academy. Society would not approve of us even being friends, were it not for our unique situation here. In truth, dearest, by my words and actions this night, I'm trusting you beyond what I've ever trusted another soul. Women like us—women in love with each other—are so terribly vulnerable. Should one word of what has passed between us reach other ears, we stand to lose everything—reputation, position, potentially even our freedom."

Kicker nodded soberly. She had never dared to dream of more than friendship, but now that Madelyn had opened the gates to far greater aspirations, the impossibility of it all began to sink in. "Tis hopeless, is it not?"

She expected to be told that they would have to content themselves with stolen moments, and was startled by Madelyn's next words.

"Perhaps not, dearest. There may be a way, but it will not be easy." For the first time Kicker saw uncertainty on her face, but it cleared and Madelyn continued in a resolute voice. "I saw early on that Merrick had set his mind on marrying me, though I tried to dissuade him. From what I swiftly learned of him, I knew he would not take rejection gracefully."

Kicker thought of how Merrick had tried to have Banner put down for throwing him, and nodded.

Madelyn released Kicker's hands, rose to her feet and paced back and forth in the grass. Kicker was reminded of all the times she had watched Madelyn in front of her classroom—instructing, questioning, and debating.

"The fact of the matter is, when I turned him down tonight, I as much as ended my tenure here at Grindleshire's. They won't have me back after I refused the honour of marrying their precious son and heir."

Startled, Kicker blinked at Madelyn. She had not considered that aspect, but as soon as Madelyn put it into words, she knew it for the truth. The Grindleshires—mother, father, and five older sisters—had spoiled and doted on the only male scion since his birth. They would not tolerate the continued presence of any woman who so greatly insulted him.

Springing to her feet, Kicker stepped into Madelyn's path, and slipped her arms around Madelyn's waist. "Then what is our plan?"

Madelyn stared at her, a newborn smile growing. "Oh, I've chosen well, dearest. I could not ask for a truer companion, nor stouter heart in what is to be done."

Kicker appreciated the words, but she appreciated the kiss that punctuated them even more. This time they took their time, exploring each other avidly until they sank down to the grass, bodies entwined. When at long last they stilled, bodies nestled and touches lingering, they found that the long summer's evening had begun to darken.

"We mus' get back soon." Kicker did not really wish to move an inch. "They might start to worry."

"I know, dearest." Madelyn's languid voice sharpened urgently. "We don't have much time. Merrick will no doubt have informed his parents by now. I'm sure I shall be summoned to Mr. Grindleshire's office to be dismissed on the morrow."

Reluctantly Kicker drew just far enough out of her companion's embrace to rise up on her elbow so she could gaze down on the Madelyn's face. Fighting the urge to steal another kiss, she repeated her earlier question. "What is our plan?"

"While living in London, I was involved with a group working towards women's suffrage." Madelyn flashed Kicker a wry grin. "Actually, that's why I was asked to leave my last post. The Headmistress feared I might corrupt the impressionable young minds in my care."

"You're a Suffragette?" Kicker was surprised. She had heard of the movement, but it meant little to her.

"Well, an inactive member of late, but I've kept in touch with several old friends who were also involved in the movement. I believe one of them may hold the key to our freedom." Excited, Madelyn sat up. "Dearest, have you ever given any thought to leaving England, to sailing to a new country and making a life there?"

Leave England? Leave Adam and my family and Grindleshire's? Kicker shook her head. She had assumed that she would always live and work within a few miles of the place she had been born. "I've barely the money to take the train to the city. I don' know what it costs to take ship, but—"

Madelyn leaned forward and rested her hands on Kicker's thighs. "I have enough for both of us, plus a stake to get us started in the West, where my friend and her husband have settled. Kicker, that's what I did when I went to London. I settled my affairs and booked us passage to Canada. The ship is to sail a few weeks from now."

"Canada?" Kicker was dumbfounded. Without warning, she was being asked to uproot her whole life. As much as she had yearned after Madelyn, she was not entirely clear on what future was even possible with her. *I ne'er e'en heard of two women lovin' an' makin' a life t'gether.*

For the first time Kicker hesitated, and doubt crept in. A small voice reminded her that even if Madelyn had to leave the Academy, she did not. Kicker could go on working in the stables for the rest of her life, if she chose to do so. *I got frien's here. Cook treats me like her own daughter. I kin see Adam reg'lar. Tis work I like too, an' Ol' Thomas thinks I half walk on water. I kin ride Banner pretty much any time I choose...*

As always, Madelyn read Kicker easily. "I know the magnitude of what I ask, dearest, but think of the possibilities. We're in the last months of the nineteenth century. The twentieth century will be one of untold wonders, and we could welcome it in a young land, a growing land, one that is part of the Empire, too. It won't be easy, but the opportunities are endless for those with the courage and determination to seize them. If we find we don't take to life in Canada, we can always try America or even Australia. We can do whatever we want, Kicker. Just you and I, together."

"Why d'you think twill be any easier for us to be t'gether, even there?"

"Because we can reinvent ourselves, dearest. We can pose as sisters, and no one will question our living together. There is a desperate need for teachers, according to my friend, and your skill with horses and the forge will always be in high demand."

Kicker mulled over Madelyn's words. "No one will believe we're sisters. We don' look alike, an' we sure don' talk alike. What happens when some man sets his eye on you again? We'll have to keep movin' all the time."

"Cousins, then, and we will keep working on your speech. You've already made wonderful progress, dearest. As for men courting me, I shall wear a ring and say my husband is a soldier on foreign duty. He has sent me on ahead and intends to join me once his tour is done. After a suitable period, I'll receive word of his passing and enter a period of mourning. Like our good Queen, I will always honour his memory, and refuse to ever countenance offers of marriage."

Kicker stared at her in amazement. "You've got it all worked out, have you not?"

"Merrick made no effort to conceal his intentions almost from the start, dearest. I had to think quickly."

"An' you say you booked us both passage? You were that certain of me?" Kicker was not sure if she should feel taken for granted.

At that, Madelyn's gaze dropped. "No, I wasn't certain at all. I only hoped and prayed that you felt the same as I did. If you feel...if you do not...well, I can probably sell your ticket to someone else who is looking to book passage, but I am going, dearest."

"I don' know, Madelyn. I don' know what to tell you. I do love you, but to leave all I have ever known...tis a harsh thing you ask of me."

"I know, and I wouldn't ask it of you so abruptly had we more time, but the hours grow short." Madelyn sighed deeply. "I'll try to delay my leaving one day, to give you more time to decide. If you still haven't reached a decision, I'll give you my address in London before I leave. If you decide to take a chance on me...on us, come to me by the twenty-second, or it will be too late."

Madelyn stood, and Kicker followed. The ride back to the Academy was quiet, both women lost in deep thought. Neither spoke until they reached the stables and dismounted.

"Whatever you decide, please know that it will not change my love for you." Before Kicker could reach for her, Madelyn turned away and returned to the Academy and her living quarters.

Numb, Kicker cared for the horses, ignoring Banner's injured look at the cursory brushing she administered before leaving them fed and stabled for the night. She flopped on her bed and tried to quiet her mind as she considered her decision. Wild and conflicting emotions finally drove her from her stifling room to the old oak tree that had so often sheltered her.

Kicker climbed to her usual post, stared up at the stars and wrestled with her decision. *Tis all so sudden. Can she truly love me? If I gi' it all for her, my home, my family, my work, my country e'en, will I e'er regret it? Twill be no turnin' back from this choice. I know that well.*

But just when doubts threatened to overwhelm her, Kicker closed her eyes and let the memory of Madelyn's kisses inflame her body. *To touch her—to be touched so, could I live wi'out that e'er again? Bless'd Jesus. What she does t'me ... ne'er did I think to feel this way about anyone.*

Impulsively, Kicker pushed herself up off the branch, driven by an overwhelming need to hurry to Madelyn's side. Then another thought occurred to her and she sank back down against the tree's trunk. *What if I'm naught but a brief fancy? In all ways she is so far 'bove me. Tis passin' strange such a lady would settle on one such as me. An' havin' done so, havin' claimed me heart and body, will she then grow bored wi' me? Abandon me when another more comely, more learn'd, more ... e'rything catches her eye? Will she forsake me in a strange land?*

An unexpected tear fell from Kicker's eye as she contemplated that dire possibility, and a resurgence of uncertainty quelled her desire.

Finally, exhausted by hours of fierce internal debate, Kicker admonished herself aloud, "Grow up, you feckless whelp. Will you hang on to your family's coatstrings, muckin' out stables for the rest of your life whilst the woman you love sails alone to a new land? Or will you take the life she offers when you know bloody well tis what you want?"

As simply as that, Kicker made up her mind. She would miss Adam terribly, as well as the rest of her family, Old Thomas and Cook, but she would learn to live with their loss. But if Madelyn left without her...that Kicker did not think she could ever learn to live with.

Cheered, Kicker scrambled out of her haven, determined to tell Madelyn that instant. She was undaunted by the fact that she had only been to the Madelyn's room once, the day she brought her from the train station the previous year and deposited the new teacher's trunk in her quarters. Kicker had counted the windows of the teachers' dormitory by night often enough to be certain she knew her way.

Kicker entered by the same side door she had watched Madelyn disappear within only hours before. It occurred to her that it would be very hard to explain her presence should any of the staff wake up and confront her. So once inside the dark, quiet building, she climbed the stairs to the top floor with deliberate stealth. When she reached the top, she listened carefully before she ventured into the hallway.

The doors were all labelled with their resident's name, but it was far too dark for Kicker to read. She counted off until she reached the room she was certain belonged to Madelyn.

For a long moment Kicker stood silently and stared at the door, aware she was about to cross her own Rubicon. Then the thought of the woman asleep beyond that door drove everything else out of her mind. She drew a deep breath and tapped softly, hopeful that Madelyn was a light sleeper.

When no one answered, Kicker began to worry that she had the wrong door and she stepped back to count again. Just as she did, the door eased open, and Madelyn stood before her. Though dressed in a white nightgown, she had none of the look of a sleeper roused. Without a word, Madelyn reached out and drew Kicker into the room.

Once the door closed behind her, Kicker began to speak, only to feel Madelyn's finger over her lips.

"Hush one moment, dearest. Let me light a lamp first."

Kicker heeded the whispered words and held her tongue, though she longed to blurt out her news.

As the lamp flared, then steadied, Madelyn turned to look at her companion's face. Instantly a smile broke over her face. "You've decided."

"Aye."

"You'll come with me?"

"Now and always," Kicker vowed. She stepped into the arms that opened to her. She buried her face against Madelyn's neck and felt the promise of the slender arms that held her tightly.

"Wither thou goest... Oh, sweet woman, I swear to you, you'll never regret this."

Kicker pulled back and looked at Madelyn with twinkling eyes. "Well, I couldn't let you go by yourself. Who knows what kin' of trouble you'd get into without me about? They might not take kindly to Byron-quotin' Suffragettes over there." She sobered. "All I ask is that we go into town early enough that I might talk to Adam b'fore we leave. I cannot leave him without a word."

"Whatever you need to do, we'll make time for, dearest." Madelyn grimaced. "When I returned this evening, there was a note under my door requiring my presence in the Headmaster's office immediately after breakfast." She gestured at the trunk sitting open at the foot of her bed. "I've already packed up most of my belongings."

Kicker was aware that the morning's confrontation would not be an easy one. "Are you sad then, to be leavin' here?"

Madelyn cocked her head and smiled at Kicker. "Why would I be, when I'm taking the best part of Grindleshire Academy with me?" She shrugged a little. "Not that I'm at all thrilled to be terminated on Merrick's account, mind you."

Kicker allowed herself to indulge in a few seconds of revenge fantasies against the callow man who had ended their idyll. Then she was distracted as Madelyn tugged her over to the bed and drew Kicker down beside her.

Flustered, Kicker protested, "I think tis better I get back to the stables now. Twould be trouble if anyone caught me in here."

"Shhh," Madelyn soothed. "I won't rush you into anything you're not ready for, dearest, but rest here with me for a little while. When I went to bed this night, I didn't know if I would ever get a chance to hold you again, and I could not rest for the fear of it. Just hold me a little while until I sleep, please?"

Helpless to resist, and lacking any real desire to do so, Kicker quickly unlaced her boots and set them aside. Madelyn drew closer to the wall to make room on the narrow bed, but when Kicker lay down, she found the lack of space well to her liking.

Resting their heads on the pillow, their faces were only inches apart. By an unspoken alchemy, the women surged together until limbs entangled and lips pressed in wild demands.

Kicker had no sexual experience at all and little inkling what she should do next. Her body shook with nervous excitement.

With obvious effort Madelyn broke their kiss and pulled her hands from beneath Kicker's shirt. Breathing heavily, she dropped her head on Kicker's shoulders. "I'm sorry, dearest. I really didn't mean to rush you. I promise I'll behave." Madelyn smiled at her. "At least for now."

Madelyn deposited one last, lingering kiss on eager lips, rolled over and snuggled back into Kicker's body. Holding her companion securely, Kicker felt the moment when Madelyn finally drifted off, but no sleep came for her. Her body hummed with excitement. Although she was grateful that Madelyn was allowing her to set the pace of their physical explorations, Kicker was eager for the next opportunity to continue what they had begun that night.

When first light began to illuminate the clouds, Kicker slipped soundlessly out of bed. She left Madelyn with a soft kiss as she carried her boots out of the room.

Kicker encountered no one and hurriedly made her way out of the Academy proper and back to the stable just as dawn broke. With a quick splash of cold water to waken herself, she began her morning routine.

Kicker decided that she would keep things as normal as possible until she got word from Madelyn that it was time to leave. After feeding all the horses, she indulged in a long, careful grooming of her favourite. "I'll miss you somethin' fierce, Banner. Twill ne'er be 'nother like you for me. But min' you b'have yourself for Ol' Thomas. Don' be runnin' off on him or anythin'. I'm dependin' on you."

Kicker's heart lurched when she finally set the curry comb down. She wrapped her arms around the grey and hugged him as she whispered into his neck, "I'll ne'er forget you." Kicker brushed tears from her eyes, and resolutely began the walk to the kitchen for her last breakfast under Cook's affectionately bossy eye.

Sitting at the table with most of the household staff, Kicker wasn't a bit surprised to hear that talk was already of Miss Bristow refusing Merrick's proposal.

The general consensus was that the teacher must be mad, until Cook pronounced her opinion. "I b'lieve Miz Bristow knows bett'r'n any o' you lot the cut of young Mister Grindleshire's jib. I'm thinkin' she made a wise choice, an' I don' wanna hear no more 'bout it."

That was enough to stifle any further gossip.

Kicker watched as the housekeeper ordered everyone to their duties. With only the kitchen staff left, she made a point to thank Cook effusively for breakfast.

For a moment Kicker thought she had given herself away, as Cook eyed her shrewdly, but the large woman just laughed.

"Twas nothin' more than ye've eaten since ye first sat your scrawny self at my table. Now be off with ye. An' don' ye be hidin' in the hay catchin' forty winks, either. Ye look like a blessed raccoon this mornin', lass."

Kicker grinned and headed for the back door. Before she reached it, she could have sworn she heard a gruff, "Ye're welcome, lass." By the time she got back to the stable, Old Thomas had already harnessed the matched chocolate-coloured mares, Daisy and Brownie, to the large carriage.

"More runs t'make t'day." Old Thomas raised an eyebrow as he got a good look at his stable hand. "Good Lord, girl, did ya sleep at all las' night?"

Kicker shook her head ruefully. "Not much." To deflect any further questions, she asked, "So when's the firs' run?" She hoped that Old Thomas would take it so that she could be present when Madelyn came to relay the results of her summoning.

"Got four teachers goin' out on the mornin' train." The stable master adjusted another buckle. "Word is twill be at leas' one on the late train, too." Old Thomas looked at Kicker expectantly. "Did ya 'ear about your frien', Miz Bristow?"

"Aye. Twas all the talk in the kitchen. They said she turned Mister Grindleshire down las' night."

"An' you can bet she'll be on the late train out. Himself won' be allowin' her to stay after that." Old Thomas finished his task and came over to lean on the rail beside Kicker. They watched the spring foals gambol around the paddock as their dams grazed peacefully. "Guess you'll be wantin' to take 'er into town, then?"

Kicker nodded. There was a long silence between them, a comfortable, familiar interlude between two naturally reticent people.

"You know Norman, the gardener's boy?"

"Aye, I do."

"Seems to me he could be a lot of help around here. He's old enough, and has a fair hand with the horses."

There was an even longer silence, but neither moved to break it until finally Old Thomas gave a deep sigh. "Tha's the way of it then, is't?"

"Aye."

Old Thomas nodded, his face showing little emotion. "Thought it might be." He pushed himself back and began to walk away. "'S'pose Norman will do, then. Won' have your touch, though."

Kicker felt an overwhelming sadness that the decent old man, who had given her a chance most would not, would be burdened by her departure. For the rest of the morning, she moved about her chores in a haze of mingled excitement, exhaustion, and sorrow for the pleasant life that was swiftly slipping away.

Old Thomas had taken the morning run into town when Madelyn showed up at the stable. Her normal grace was absent and her shoulders were rigid as she approached the forge where Kicker worked. Kicker stopped hammering, and set the tongs aside as she waited.

Without preliminaries, Madelyn snapped, "Well, as expected, I've been summarily dismissed and ordered to be out of here by evening." She drew in a deep breath and visibly struggled to calm herself.

"Tis sorry, I am. You did not deserve that."

"Well, it could've been worse, though I would've happily dispensed with being called everything from Jezebel to a temptress... Mrs. Grindleshire's contribution, by the way. I suppose I should be grateful that Mr. Grindleshire found gumption enough to defy his wife and give me references. Perhaps there is still some decency in the man that harridan has not eradicated."

Kicker longed to take Madelyn in her arms and soothe the pain of the injustice. But, conscious of the broad light of day and her own dirty, sweat streaked body, she restrained herself.

"I've been instructed to be aboard the four o'clock train. The Grindleshires are taking Merrick to board the noon train and don't wish to run any risk of encountering me." Madelyn's eyes snapped angrily. "Apparently I've become something of an Untouchable."

"Not to me."

At those soft words, the women's eyes met and memories of what had begun the previous night flared between them.

"I'm counting on that, dearest."

The quiet intensity of Madelyn's voice made Kicker shiver. She nodded, barely able to speak over the thunder of her heart. "As am I."

"Walk me back?"

Kicker shook her head in regret. "Bes' not, but I'll pick up your trunk at mid-afternoon, and we'll go into town then."

Plans made, the two separated. When Old Thomas returned from town, Kicker told him of the next departure. "I can have Norman go with us an' bring the carriage back."

"No. I'll drive the carriage. Thought you might wanna ride Banner one las' time."

Kicker was deeply touched by Old Thomas' consideration. "Aye, tis a good idea. Thank you."

Old Thomas nodded gruffly.

Kicker could've sworn there was a suspicious wetness in his eyes, but he quickly walked away.

Hours later, cleaned up and packed, Kicker looked around the small room that had been her home for seven years. One corner floorboard was still askew where she had pried open her hiding place and removed the frayed leather sack that held her savings. It wasn't much—a little more than eleven pounds, accumulated over years of frugal living—but Kicker would not cross the ocean penniless. She had not had time for much introspection, but she knew that, at least, was important to her.

Kicker paused for a quick farewell with each of her equine charges, then left the stable and found Madelyn and Old Thomas waiting in the carriage. Banner whinnied as she walked out into the sunlight. Unable to speak, Kicker simply tossed her bag into the carriage and mounted the gelding. As they passed through the Academy's stone gates, she twisted for one last look at the lovely estate where she had found such contentment in her work and friendships.

Once on the road Madelyn suggested that Kicker ride ahead to see Adam and promised that they would meet at the station. Instantly, Kicker allowed Banner his head, and they flew down the road. When they reached the village, she slowed the horse and turned him down the road that led to her family home. Kicker knew at this hour Adam would be at their father's smithy.

Her brothers and father looked up in surprise when Kicker cantered into the yard and slid off. "Can I talk to Adam, Da?"

Their father frowned. "Don' be long. He's work t'do."

She nodded and Adam fell into step as they walked away from the forge, Banner trailing behind them. Without preliminaries, Kicker blurted her news. "I'm goin' away."

Adam blinked. "You are? Where? When?"

"T'day. To Canada."

"What! What d'ya mean to Canada? You can't just up and sail across the ocean all by yourself."

"Why not? People do it e'ery day."

"Not my little sister. What in God's name put this daft notion in your head?"

"Tis not daft, Adam. An' I'm not goin' alone. I'm goin' with someone special to make a new life. We cannot do that here, so we have to try someplace new."

Adam's shoulders sagged and Kicker saw reluctant acceptance enter his eyes. "So I was right. There is someone then." A worried expression crossed his face. "You're not in trouble, are you?"

"No. Well, at leas', not really, but we do have to leave t' be t'gether."

They had automatically headed for the creekside that had hosted so many of their talks over the years. Adam was quiet for a long time before he asked pensively, "Is she worth it?"

Kicker nodded, not at all surprised that he knew. "You can meet her if you wan' to come to the station with me."

Adam considered that, chewing on his scraggly moustache as he was wont to do in times of great stress. "Are you telling Da?"

"No, nor Ma. I thought you could tell 'em once I'm off."

That got a wry grin. "Coward."

Kicker shrugged, not denying the charge.

"Well then, tis up to me to meet her and make sure she knows to take care of my little sister."

They reached the creek, and watched as Banner waded in to get a drink. When the horse had his fill, they turned back towards the house, their conversation now deliberately avoiding what was to come. Kicker left Adam to make whatever excuse he could come up with while she went into the house.

Kicker found her mother in the kitchen, two small grandchildren hanging off her apron while she yelled at another for spilling flour.

"Ma?"

Mary turned in surprise. "Kicker? What're ye doin' 'ere mid-week?"

Kicker found her throat unexpectedly tight. "Had to run an erran' so I thought I'd drop by. How're you doin', Ma?"

Her mother waved her hand around the chaotic kitchen. "Same's always. Things ne'er change, ye know that." Mary snatched at a pitcher that one of the children was dangerously close to knocking over. Kicker watched the familiar scene as her mother took her wooden spoon to the offender, who ran squalling from the room.

"Sometimes they do, Ma. Sometimes they do." With those whispered words, Kicker hugged her startled mother and dashed out of the room, trying desperately to forestall her tears.

By the time she reached the forge, Kicker was under tenuous control. Adam had saddled his horse and was waiting for her. Mounting Banner, she called out to her father, "Be well, Da."

He barely looked up. "Godspeed, Kicker. See ye soon."

The tears threatened to overflow again as she turned Banner out of the yard. With Adam cantering beside her, Kicker twisted in the saddle for one last look as she tried to imprint home on her memory.

"You'll carry it...and us, in your heart, little sister." There was a suspicious break in Adam's soft voice.

"Aye, I will." At that moment, Kicker could not have said more to save her life.

When they arrived at the station, Madelyn and Old Thomas had just pulled in. The stable master volunteered to go get their tickets. Madelyn handed him the money and Kicker made introductions.

"Madelyn, this is my brother, Adam. Adam, this is Miss Madelyn Bristow."

Adam eyed the teacher intently and she returned his gaze steadily. Finally he gave a quick nod. "You'll be good to her? Take care of her a'ways?"

"I will."

It was as solemn a promise as any heard in a church, and appeared to satisfy Adam. He offered his hand and Madelyn took it willingly. They shook firmly and sealed the vow.

"When are you two off, then?"

"We sail on the *SS Assiniboine*, a steamer with the Dominion Line. We leave Liverpool on the twenty-fourth and should dock in Montreal eight to ten days later, depending on weather during the crossing. From there we'll take a train across Canada to Manitoba. I've friends that are homesteading outside of Winnipeg, and we'll stay with them until we get our feet under us."

Adam nodded gravely. "Make sure she don' ferget us."

"She won't," Madelyn replied with equal solemnity. "I'll ensure that she writes at least once a month."

Kicker rolled her eyes, feeling like an errant schoolgirl.

Old Thomas was returning from the wicket when Adam drew her aside and bestowed his blessing. "She seems like a good 'un, but you r'member you kin always come home if you want. No shame in admittin' when you made a mistake."

Adam looked half hopeful as he admonished her, and Kicker smiled at him.

"P'rhaps you and Anne could join us. Lots of room to raise a growin' family out there. You could have lan' of your own and a bunch of men workin' for you, 'stead of slavin' for Da for the nex' twen'y years."

Kicker was surprised to see an interested gleam in his eyes, but Adam just pulled her into his arms and issued a fierce order. "You write an' let us know where you are, soon's you get there."

Kicker buried her face in Adam's stained tunic and breathed deeply of the sweat and forge smoke she had associated with him for as long as she could remember. Tears ran freely and she made no effort to stop them as she hugged her brother with all her strength. Kicker's muttered words were almost inaudible against his chest.

"Love you."

"Love you right back, little sister. You better take care of yourself, or I'm going to kick your arse all the way to—"

"Canada?" Kicker pulled back as a grin broke through the tears.

Adam cuffed her lightly and released her. "An' don' think I won'." He kissed her on the forehead and turned away. Without a backwards glance, he mounted his horse and trotted down the dusty street towards home.

Kicker stared after him until he rounded the corner and disappeared from her view. Madelyn and Old Thomas, engaged in quiet conversation, politely faced away from the teary leave-taking.

Kicker mopped her face on her sleeve and walked over to them.

Banner was tied to the back of the carriage, and Madelyn's trunk, as well as Kicker's small bag, sat on the platform.

Old Thomas handed Kicker a thin leather purse."Your final wages, lass. Thought ya might have need of 'em."

Kicker hoped her eyes conveyed all she felt. "Thank you...for everythin'."

Old Thomas shrugged. With a nod that took in both of the women, he said hoarsely, "Best o' luck, ta both of ye." Pulling himself laboriously up into the carriage, he tipped his cap and gave a sly grin. "Nex' time I'm hirin' me one o' them eunuchs."

With a deep guffaw Old Thomas departed the station. The two women gaped after him in shock, then broke into laughter, too.

CHAPTER 3

What have I done? The thought reverberated through her mind as Madelyn watched the quiet figure opposite her on the padded train seat. Kicker had said little since leaving the station and the only life she had ever known. Instead she watched the pastoral countryside as they rolled steadily toward an uncertain future.

The speed with which events unfolded had left Madelyn little time to truly contemplate the measure of what she asked of Kicker. As she had so often done in her life, Madelyn acted on instinct and booked both of them passage to Canada before she even declared her feelings.

It had seemed so right. The instant Madelyn felt Kicker respond to her first kiss, everything fell into place as never before. And when she lit the lamp and saw the look on her midnight visitor's face, Madelyn was flooded with a joy so powerful that she could scarcely stand. Even up to the moment when she watched Kicker and Adam say goodbye, Madelyn was convinced of the rightness of her actions. Then they boarded the train.

Kicker was slightly ahead of Madelyn. When she began to mount the steps to the car, the conductor moved to block her, glowering at her presumption for entering the first class carriage. Madelyn quickly laid a hand on her companion's back and fixed the man with a haughty stare. She knew he instantly received the message, as he stepped back and touched his cap politely, though his scowl remained in place.

It happened so fast that Madelyn didn't know if Kicker even noticed the exchange, but the implications were not lost on her. Kicker was a fish out of water in her world, and Madelyn knew she was going to have to battle constantly to ensure her acceptance.

She was not sure she was up to the task.

Madelyn had been self-sufficient for so long that she had forgotten—if she had ever known—what it was to be responsible for another's feelings and welfare. Now she ached at the thought that someone's automatic imposition of social conventions might hurt Kicker.

I've taken her from a life where her oddities were appreciated. Dear God, let our new life offer her the same kind of acceptance.

Madelyn clung to the hope that Canada would offer a haven from the class-ridden society into which she and Kicker had been born. Despite her reservations, Madelyn allowed herself to dream of a place where the two women could truly make a home together, until she was wrenched from her thoughts by a quiet voice.

"What troubles you, Madelyn?"

Though her first name still sounded foreign on Kicker's tongue, Madelyn reveled in the sound of it. She shook her head, intending to brush aside her companion's concerns. But Kicker fixed her with eyes that had peered effortlessly into her soul from the first moment they met. *She is an adult. She's freely chosen to walk this difficult path with me. I owe her the respect of being forthright.*

"The conductor..." Madelyn said, and hesitated, unsure of how to explain her concern.

"Aye, he'd'a sent me to the back of the train did you not make it clear I b'longed with you."

"I should've known naught would get by you, dearest." Madelyn shook her head in chagrin.

"Why does't concern you so?" Kicker's voice was genuinely curious.

Madelyn wondered for a moment how her partner saw herself—if Kicker recognized how different she was from other women.

Madelyn looked around and noted gratefully that there were only a handful of people in their car. Their nearest neighbour was a portly gentleman who snored softly three seats away. Unwilling to take a chance, however, she leaned forward and spoke softly. "We must be careful, dearest. We must tread lightly until we slip away. Once we are established in our own home in Canada, we'll be able to relax somewhat...to be more ourselves."

Kicker shrugged. "Tis not my way to cause a commotion or get in trouble."

"I know, dearest, but sometimes—many times, I'm afraid—trouble seeks out those innocently going about their business." Madelyn drew in a deep breath. She did not want to disparage Kicker in any way, but she knew that they had to deal with the potential difficulties that would arise from Kicker's unorthodox dress and manner. "People often react badly to...unconventional ways."

Kicker nodded soberly and tweaked the worn fabric of her trousers between finger and thumb. "An' not many women wear these."

"Very few," Madelyn agreed, desperately hoping Kicker would not take offence. She loved every aspect of the unique woman with whom she had fallen so in love. In a perfect world, everyone would see Kicker as she did, but it was not a perfect world. Madelyn was determined that Kicker not lose the essence of what made her who she was, societal norms or not. However, she also knew that if Kicker was not willing to make some compromises, it would make both of their lives much more difficult, and potentially even dangerous.

"I don' own a dress, wouldna wear one if I did." Kicker stubbornly banged the heel of her boot against the floor for emphasis. "Cannot do my work like that."

"I know, dearest, but our journey might be smoother if you let me furnish you with one or two dresses once we reach the city." Madelyn held up a soothing hand as a rebellious look clouded Kicker's face. "Not for everyday use, but just for when you need to fit in." She winced at her own words, but did not retract them.

Kicker was clearly unhappy with the idea and Madelyn kept silent, letting her mull it over.

"I could pass as a boy. Happened all the time at the Academy."

Madelyn nodded. "I thought of that too, but then we wouldn't be able to share lodgings in London, or on the ship." Dropping her voice even lower, Madelyn delivered the coup de grace with a sensuous smile. "And I do so want us to share a room."

It was not difficult to see how her words affected Kicker. Madelyn let her eyes linger on the front of Kicker's thin muslin shirt and felt an answering response that made her ache.

Flushed, Kicker nodded and tucked trembling hands under her thighs. "Only when tis necess'ry, though."

"Agreed." Madelyn decided it might be prudent to outline how they would define "necessary." "It would be best to wear such garb when we stay at my parents' house, and when we board and disembark from our ship."

Kicker groaned softly, but did not protest. Changing an obviously unpleasant subject, she asked, "What are our plans?"

Relieved that they had cleared the first major hurdle with scarcely a stumble, Madelyn leaned back and relaxed. "When we reach London, our first stop is going to be at a shop run by a friend of mine. We'll be able to get suitable clothing for you there. Then we'll stay with my parents for the next ten days or so, making preparations for the trip. We'll need to decide what we should take with us and what can be left behind, for it may be a long time before we are back again, if ever."

The "if ever" hung in the air between them, and Madelyn did not miss the way Kicker flinched.

"I also wish to take you to the Canada High Commission later this week. They put on exhibitions and receptions for prospective immigrants. I thought you would enjoy seeing something of the land to which we are moving."

She breathed a small sigh of relief at Kicker's nod. Madelyn knew that the reality of Kicker's parting with Adam had not completely sunk in. However, she was determined to keep Kicker focused on the adventure that lay ahead, rather than on what she had left behind.

"How're you gonna explain me to your ma and da?"

There was a challenging note in Kicker's voice, and Madelyn grimaced inwardly.

"I've already discussed with them my plans to emigrate. I'll simply say that your father, who works at the Academy, asked that you be allowed to accompany me as you travel to meet your husband in Canada."

Kicker looked impressed by her inventiveness, and Madelyn felt a pang of guilt at her ability to prevaricate. It was a useful skill, one that had served her well as she lived her unconventional life, but it was not something of which she was proud.

"They don' min' you goin' all that way alone?"

"I think they will be glad that I've someone with me." Madelyn knew she had ducked the essence of the question.

Not surprisingly, Kicker did not allow the dodge. "But what do they think of you leavin' England? Tis not many women would do so without a husband by their side."

"When I informed them, I said I was going because I'd heard that the ratio of men to women in the Northwest Territories was three to one. My father said he didn't know why I hadn't accepted a proposal from a proper Englishman, but that if I wanted a cowboy, so be it. He thinks it well past time that I give up teaching and settle down. He told me rather sternly that he would expect a letter from me within the year saying that I'd found a suitable spouse."

There was an audible snort from Kicker. "And your ma? Does she approve of your plans?"

Madelyn could not help a rueful smile as she thought of her mother's incredulous look upon hearing her announcement. "Perhaps we should just say that, while Mother has her reservations, she's kept her own counsel."

"Huh." Kicker changed the topic. "Tell me about this frien' we're to stay with in Canada."

"Adelaide and I have known each other since we were children though she is somewhat older than me. She was the one who originally got me involved with the Suffragette movement. She has very pronounced opinions on women's emancipation, and she challenged many of my ingrained ideas. I owe her a great deal, and I'm very much looking forward to seeing her again."

Startled to see a troubled look cross Kicker's face, Madelyn stopped and leaned forward. "What is it, dearest? What's the matter?"

Kicker fidgeted. "Was she... I mean, were you and her... How close are you?"

Amused, Madelyn patted Kicker's knee. "Close, but not in the way that you mean. Adelaide is very happily married, and has been for a good decade and longer." She leaned back again, oddly flattered at the unexpected indication of jealousy. But when Kicker refused to meet her eyes and stared out the window with a faraway gaze, Madelyn became concerned.

"Kicker." Her companion ignored her, but Madelyn persisted. "Kicker, please look at me."

Reluctantly, dark eyes swiveled to meet hers. Madelyn held Kicker's gaze intently. She needed her companion to hear her next words with her heart. "Dearest, I will not deny that there have been others with whom I was involved over the years, but they were transitory affairs. They meant little to me then, for I was young and none acquired my heart, only my body. They mean nothing at all to me now. You, my love, you mean everything to me. If you believe nothing else, please believe that."

It seemed like forever before Kicker ducked her head in acknowledgement and gave her a sweet half-smile. "I do. Tis jus' I cannot believe you wan' to spen' your life with me, when you could have anyone you wanted."

The whispered words were almost lost in the rhythmic sound of the wheels clacking over rails, but Madelyn heard them loud and clear. She ached at the insecurity in Kicker's voice. Madelyn longed to reassure Kicker not only of the depth and resiliency of her love, but that their path would be smooth and unimpeded. She was a realist, though, and knew better than to make false promises.

Madelyn slid into the seat next to Kicker, took her hand, and cupped it as if it were the most delicate crystal. "I wish I could promise you endless days of happiness and boundless nights of pleasure. What I can promise you are these things: my undying love, my absolute devotion, and my commitment to never break my word to Adam. I will cherish you the rest of my days. I may not be able to make that vow in a church, but I make it with unequivocal sincerity."

The tanned hand curled around the pale fingers which cradled it, and squeezed firmly. They sat for a long moment in silent communion until the conductor entered the car at the far end of the aisle.

Their fingers loosened and drew apart as Kicker whispered, "About those boundless nights of pleasure..."

Madelyn stifled a shocked laugh and slid across to her own seat. She stared into eyes that sparkled back at her unrepentantly. She shivered and counted the hours until they would be safely behind closed doors, when she could begin to educate Kicker as to exactly what pleasures awaited them.

When they stepped off the train onto a crowded platform and Kicker set foot for the first time in London, she turned to Madelyn, eyes wide with awe. "I always heard, but I ne'er seen the like of it."

Madelyn smiled. She had been attuned to Kicker's amazement as they left the countryside behind and began moving through larger and larger towns, culminating in their arrival in London. She had worried that Kicker would be put off by the dirty, often blighted areas that they traversed. However, it seemed as though Kicker was far too curious about everything to draw any negative comparisons with the tranquility of her home village.

"I would like to show you some of the city before we leave, but for now let's concentrate on finding transportation to depart from this madhouse."

Before Madelyn could raise her hand to signal a waiting hansom cab, Kicker seized her forearm in excitement. "D'you think we might get to see the Queen, then?"

"I rather doubt it, dearest." Madelyn gently unlocked the powerful fingers from around her arm. "She's quite elderly now and rarely makes public appearances." Kicker frowned in disappointment. "But we'll go and see the Queen's Guard, shall we? I think you'll enjoy the spectacle; it is quite the occasion."

Suddenly Kicker slammed her boot down on the top of Madelyn's trunk and glared. Two grimy urchins had sidled up next to the chest and Kicker's bag of belongings while the women talked, their attention distracted.

One of the boys bolted, but the more brazen of the two sneered as he backed away. "'Ere, mister, don' be lookin' so queerly. We ain't done nuffin." Then the boy paused with a puzzled look on his face as he stared at Kicker. When she jerked her foot down from the chest, he decided not to hang around and took off running.

Madelyn shook her head and signaled the cabbie, who moved up to take the trunk as the two women climbed into the carriage.

"Mrs. Harrington's at 12 Wesley Lane, please, driver."

Though it was dusk, the streets surrounding the station were still tumultuous with people, carriages, and horses. Madelyn watched Kicker crane her neck to take in every detail of their surroundings. She was struck by how truly innocent her companion was.

When Madelyn glanced out the window, all she saw was the dirty, overcrowded, often crime ridden streets she was all too ready to leave behind forever. But Kicker's wonder reminded Madelyn of a long ago time when she, too, had thought the city magical.

Shortly they passed into quieter, more prosperous streets, where neat, attractive shops lined wide cobblestoned lanes. The cabbie pulled to a halt in front of a small, yellow sandstone house with a boldly lettered sign that read: *Mrs. Harrington's Fine Clothing for Ladies.*

While Kicker and the cabbie hauled the trunk up the short flight of stairs, Madelyn rang the bell that hung prominently to the right of the door. It took two more vigorous pulls of the chain before the door opened.

"I'm sorry, we're clo... Well, as I live and breathe, if it isn't Maddie Bristow!" The short, plump, white haired woman who stood in the doorway beamed and clasped her arms around the visitor.

Madelyn laughed with pleasure at seeing her old friend and returned the hug enthusiastically. When the woman began to explode with questions, Madelyn held up a restraining hand. "All in good time, Lil. First, before I send the cabbie on his way, I need to know if you've room for a couple of weary travelers." Madelyn indicated Kicker who stood quietly two stairs below Madelyn, bag over one shoulder.

The cabbie, with hands thrust in his jacket, awaited his fare.

"Of course, Maddie. You know I've always got room for you and any friend of yours. Pay the poor man and get in here."

Madelyn did so, and reached to take one end of the trunk.

Kicker shook her head and lifted it easily by herself as she followed Madelyn across the threshold.

Lil led the two through the front shop area, where several mannequins displayed the latest London fashions. Madelyn smiled as they passed the large rear room and fitting area, which featured a huge cutting table, two sewing machines, and reams of material stacked in every available space. When she'd lived in London, Madelyn had spent many pleasant hours in that room helping Lil and her business partner, Vivian, do finishing needlework on ladies' garments. When they reached the end of the hall, they came to a flight of stairs which led to the living quarters.

"Please, dearest, let me help," Madelyn pleaded as they came to the bottom of the stairs. "You'll hurt yourself."

Kicker shook her head and determinedly held on to the trunk. "Tis naught. A few of your fancies ain't be weighin' nothin'."

Madelyn caught the shrewd look Lil cast her way, but the older woman held her tongue as she led them up the flight of steps and along the narrow upstairs hall to a small room that overlooked the street.

"Here you be. Maddie, you know where everything is, so I'll let you get settled in while I go see what I can find in the kitchen. I imagine you're hungry."

As Kicker set the trunk at the foot of the bed, Madelyn took her old friend's hands. "I'm so very grateful, Lil. We'll be out of your way shortly, but I knew I could depend on you for succour."

Lil gave her another quick hug. "Always, girl, you know that." She pulled back and glanced to where Kicker peered out the window. "I believe you have more than a few things to tell me."

Madelyn nodded, and in an equally soft voice, though she knew that it would not escape her lover's notice, she promised, "Later."

The older woman closed the door gently behind her and Madelyn turned to see Kicker regarding her gravely.

"She din't ask my name."

"No. I'm sorry. I'll introduce you when we go downstairs."

"I'm thinkin' tis not the firs' time you've brought a frien' here."

Madelyn flushed, but there was no accusation in the calm voice or censure in the dark eyes. She chose her words carefully. "There have been times that I've found it expedient to spend a night here rather than at my own home, and yes, Lil has always been a very discreet hostess."

Madelyn crossed the room to stand in front of Kicker. "Dearest, I told you that my past is not unblemished. I thought it would be easiest to delay our arrival at my parents' home until we expanded on your wardrobe somewhat. But if it makes you uncomfortable to be here, we can go there tonight."

Kicker shook her head and reached for Madelyn.

Madelyn nestled into the wiry body and greedily absorbed the comfort freely offered.

"Tis no matter that you're not chaste, love." The soft words burred over Madelyn's shoulder. "I've no right to be down on what went before, and I don' mean to be." Kicker chuckled. "B'sides, seems to me one of us should know what we're doin', right?"

Madelyn sighed as she felt soft lips nibble at her neck. She wished fervently that they could skip supper and not leave the room until the morning. Though Madelyn had done just that with previous conquests, she refused to treat Kicker so cavalierly. She wanted to introduce Kicker to her old friend, and make it clear that this was no flight of fancy—that she had finally found the one who completed her. "As much as I would like to continue this... Oh!"

Kicker's hand cupped Madelyn's breast and her thumb gently rubbed a hardening nipple.

Madelyn swallowed hard against her body's response, laid her hand over the adventurous fingers and stilled their movement. "Dearest, if you don't stop, we'll never make it out of this room."

Kicker's slow, mischievous smile indicated that was exactly what she had in mind, but she obediently withdrew her hand and backed away.

Madelyn almost reached to draw her back, but she managed to restrain the impulse. "We should go down."

"Aye."

But neither woman moved, as they stood and stared at each other, their bodies shivering in erotic anticipation. In the end, it was only the realization that they stood in front of an open window that allowed Madelyn to break the profoundly sensual connection which pulsed between them.

"Please..." It was a whispered plea, and much to her amazement, Kicker responded by striding past her to the door. Wordlessly, she held it open as Madelyn forced herself to walk by without touching.

As Madelyn descended the stairs, she was acutely aware of Kicker close behind her. It had been over two years since she last visited Lil with a woman in tow, but she couldn't attribute the stark intensity of what she felt to the extended period of abstinence. The weakness in her legs, the uncontrollable trembling of her hands, and the powerful desire that kept her nerves thrumming unbearably were all due to Kicker.

It was obvious from Lil's amused smile when they entered the kitchen that their state did not go unnoticed, but blessedly the older woman did not tease them. She merely indicated that they should take a seat at the table, which was laid with an assortment of cold dishes.

Once settled, Madelyn looked pointedly at her old friend. "Lil, I would like you to meet someone very dear to me. This is Kicker Stuart. Kicker, Mrs. Harrington is one of my oldest and dearest friends, and you may trust her as you would me."

Lil smiled at Madelyn's statement, then at Kicker who regarded her with interest. "It's very nice to meet you, Kicker. You are most welcome in my home."

"Thank you, Missus."

"Ah, but if we are to be friends, Kicker, you must call me Lil."

"Lil, then. If you don' min', can I ask how you know Madelyn?"

Lil gestured for the two of them to start their supper, and settled back. "Many, many years ago I was Maddie's nanny. Outside of the midwife that brought her into this world, I was the first one to hold her. I diapered her, wiped her nose, and bandaged more than one scrape along the way."

"Of the visible and not so visible sort," Madelyn added, regarding Lil affectionately.

Lil's eyes were suspiciously bright as she continued. "And when the last of the Bristow children outgrew me, Mrs. Bristow very kindly set me up in my own shop. I've been here ever since."

"I'll never truly outgrow you, Lil. Many's the time I don't know what I would've done without you."

"Ah well, there are still some things that you can tell your old nanny that are best not told your mother," Lil acknowledged with a smile. "But no getting maudlin now,

Maddie girl. I suspect you've a purpose here tonight, and you might as well be telling me."

Madelyn turned serious and leaned forward. "I'm leaving England. Kicker and I are going to Canada to make a new life together."

Lil's eyes widened in shock. "Canada? But, so far, Maddie? Must you go so far away from...all that you've ever known?"

Madelyn sighed and looked across the table at Kicker. Their eyes held for a timeless moment. "I love Kicker. I need to leave here so we can find a place where we may fit in."

Troubled, Lil shook her head slowly. "Are you sure that place is in Canada? Do you not think you can find such a place here?"

"Under my father's omnipresent eye? You know I cannot—not in London, and probably nowhere in England or even on the Continent. But even Timothy Bristow's reach does not cross the ocean. It's a vast land we're going to, Lil. We can vanish there."

"Will I never again hear from you?"

Lil's voice was soft and sorrowful. Madelyn took the woman's hand and absently noted the profusion of wrinkles and dark spots that denoted the passage of time. She stroked it gently as she tried to impart reassurance. "You shall, I promise. I swear I'll write all the time. I'll tell you everything, and you will live the adventure along with us."

"But I'll never again open my door and see your wayward self standing there ready to share a story and a laugh. Never again to hear the cock crow because we've spent the whole night talking without the knowing of it." Tears began to seep over the woman's lined, and suddenly aged, face.

Madelyn bowed her head and simply kissed the hand she held as her own tears ran freely. All three women were silent as Lil absorbed the news, already grieving for the child she'd loved as her own, and the woman who had become a dear friend.

Finally Lil pulled her hand out of Madelyn's grasp and yanked a large white handkerchief out of her apron pocket. Wiping her eyes and blowing her nose, she sat up determinedly. "Well then, what can I do to help smooth your journey?"

It was Madelyn's turn to wipe away her tears, and in a shaky voice she laid out their plan. "And I thought that it would be easier all around if Kicker had some more conventional clothing—perhaps two day dresses and one for evenings?"

Lil looked at Kicker closely and gestured for her to stand. Kicker bolted a bite of cold beef and obediently stood, allowing the seamstress' professional eye to size up her body.

When Lil was satisfied, she motioned Kicker back to her seat. "There are a few things in the donation box that might fit her, and I can whip up a bit of finery in a day. I'll take her measurements tonight and get to work on the clothing first thing in the morning. I have just the rose coloured bit that will go well with her dark hair. There may even be a proper pair of shoes in the box, if they'll fit her. For certain she can't be wearing those old boots with my creations."

Lil hustled off to her sewing room as Madelyn chuckled at Kicker's look of consternation. "Calm yourself, dearest. It will be painless, I promise. Now finish up, so Lil can measure you."

Kicker looked doubtful, but dutifully finished her tea without protest. "What did she mean 'donation box'?"

"Quite often when ladies have her make them new dresses, they'll donate their older, unwanted things. Lil collects them and takes them to the Women's Benevolence Union. The people there help women down on their luck. They provide shelter, clothing, and often education to enable them to escape their fates. They also regularly send her a couple of girls as apprentices, and she trains them until they're ready to go out on their own. Quite a number of young women literally owe their existence to Lil's kindness."

Kicker nodded at the explanation and looked up warily as Lil bustled back into the room. She stood silently and endured the seamstress' fussing while Lil took measurements and noted down figures until she was satisfied. Kicker looked pleadingly at Madelyn and the teacher smiled.

"Go ahead, dearest. You'll find the water closet down the hall on the right, and I'll be up in a few minutes."

Kicker practically ran out of the room, and Lil shook her head. "Quite the skittish young colt, isn't she?" Pulling up a chair, she fixed a firm gaze on her former charge. "Right then, we've a few minutes to ourselves, so spill it."

Madelyn did not make any pretence that she didn't know what her friend meant. "I love her, like I've never in my life loved anyone else. You know as well as I do that things are exceedingly difficult for people such as us. My father has never forgotten or forgiven me for what happened in '91. I need to get Kicker far enough away that we at least stand a chance of living our lives peacefully together."

Lil scowled. "That Charity was tribulation right from the start. I never did understand what you were thinking, girl."

Madelyn blushed and shook her head. "I wasn't thinking; I was only feeling." Her tone became fierce. "Charity may have been tribulation to some, but she didn't deserve what my father did to her. I'm not taking any chance of Kicker suffering his wrath if he were to discover the truth about us."

"Are you sure you want to go over to your parents' place then, little one?" The very fact that Lil used the old endearment indicated the depth of her concern. "You know you're welcome to stay here as long as you need to."

"God, what will I do without you?" Madelyn gazed at her affectionately. "I wish I could take you up on that, but there are things I need from the house. I'd like to see you again before we leave, but I also want to spend some time with Mother before we go and see my uncle, siblings, nieces and nephews."

"Mmm, well, I can understand that. And I know your mother will be pleased to have you home."

Neither woman mentioned Madelyn's father, but his shadow pervaded their thoughts.

"You might want to talk to your mother about taking some of Roderick's clothes with you. I suspect that girl of yours will kick off her dresses as soon as she can, and Roddy was about Kicker's size when he passed on. I know your mother has never given his things away, but if you can come up with a good reason, I expect she might be ready to part with them at last."

Madelyn sighed at the mention of her brother who died in the worldwide influenza epidemic of '89. He was only fifteen, and the baby of the seven siblings. Their grief-stricken mother had withdrawn completely from her family, and at sixteen, Madelyn found herself virtually an orphan.

It was only in the most recent years that Elizabeth Bristow managed to regain the strength and force of will that was once so characteristic. Sadly, in the interim she and Madelyn had grown apart, despite their love for each other.

Madelyn's three sisters and two brothers had all married and produced children, which enabled Elizabeth to reconnect with them as a doting grandmother. But her youngest daughter's single-minded preference for teaching over marriage was a constant source of bewilderment for the Bristow matriarch.

"Please be careful in your father's house, Maddie. You can paint a pigeon like a peacock, but it's still a pigeon. You can dress Kicker up proper, but can you hide what's in her eyes when she looks at you? If your father gets the slightest inkling about the two of you..." Lil shuddered.

Madelyn considered Lil's caution for long moments. She could not deny that she was nervous about their stay, however short, under her father's roof, but she felt she had to take the risk if they were to sail with everything they needed.

Finally Madelyn met the worried eyes that regarded her steadily. "Perhaps we'll take you up on your invitation to stay a few more days while I coach Kicker as to what to expect. I do have a story ready to explain her presence, but you're right—she lacks the experience you and I have at concealing what must be kept secret."

Madelyn knew by the relief on Lil's face that she had made the right decision, but again she felt the uneasiness of responsibility. With the notable exception of Charity, Madelyn had kept the two parts of her life strictly separate, and for years it worked well. She briefly considered leaving Kicker at Lil's while she visited her parents, but she quickly rejected that. Madelyn did not want Kicker to feel abandoned or neglected. She would have to rely on her lover's intuition and innate intelligence to keep them both safe while in the lion's den.

"It will work out," Madelyn muttered, mostly to herself. "It has to."

Warm hands covered hers comfortingly, and the two women sat quietly in shared awareness of the difficult road that lay ahead.

With a deep sigh, Lil drew her hands away. "Your girl will wonder what's become of you; I expect she's waiting up." Lil eyed Madelyn shrewdly. "My apprentices will be here early in the morning, so be careful. They're good girls for the most part, but I don't wish to give them cause to chatter any more than they already do."

With a little grin, Lil stood and gave an ostentatious yawn. "As for me, I believe I will retire early. You know I sleep like a log the moment I lay my old head down. Good night, Maddie. I'll see you in the morning."

Madelyn could have sworn that her friend winked as she turned to leave, and she could not help the blush that warmed her face. Lil had never made any pointed references to Madelyn's occasional overnight guest through the years. Nor had Madelyn ever commented on why Lil and Mrs. Vivian Johnston, her late business partner and lifelong friend, had shared the same bedroom since Lil left the Bristow's employ after Roderick died. The longstanding current of understanding between them made such things superfluous.

Now, however, her friend's subtle insinuation set the butterflies dancing in her belly again, and Madelyn stood on unsteady legs to tidy up the kitchen. She took the lamp with her as she made her way down the darkened but familiar hallway. She stopped briefly to make her ablutions, then paused at the foot of the stairs and stared beyond the soft glow of the lamp.

Kicker was waiting for her...in their bed.

As never before, Madelyn was stunned by the depth of the commitment that Kicker had made, and the realization shook her, slowing her steps. She had never been with an innocent, and she feared that she would frighten or hurt Kicker.

Then comprehension of Kicker's courage and willingness to face the unknown flooded over Madelyn, and she chastised herself for her doubts.

Madelyn lifted her skirts and took one step and then another; her speed became quicker with each one. By the time she reached the landing, she was almost running. With a deep breath, Madelyn forced herself to slow her pace as she hurried down the hall to the small end room.

When Madelyn slipped quietly into the room, she was momentarily taken aback to see Kicker in a chair by the window, barefoot but still clothed as she watched the street below. Before she could wonder if her lover had changed her mind, Kicker stood, drew the curtains, and turned to greet Madelyn with a dazzling smile.

There was no hint of nervousness in the soft voice, and Kicker's eyes sparkled with anticipation. "I bin waitin' for you."

Madelyn gave a muted sigh of relief, set the lamp on a side table and advanced to meet Kicker. For a long moment they simply held each other and let their bodies say what words expressed so inadequately.

Finally, aware that this night it would be up to her to lead, Madelyn laid her fingers on the top button of Kicker's shirt. Not wanting to presume, she asked, "May I?"

In answer, Kicker moved her own hands to the long row of tiny pearl buttons that fastened the back of Madelyn's dress and began to work them open. Smiling, Madelyn made short work of the coarse shirt, and ran her hands lightly over Kicker's belly to the trouser buttons.

"'Tisn't fair, you know," Kicker murmured, only halfway through her task. "You'll have me naked before I kin get these bless'd fastenings undone."

Madelyn only laughed as she undid the last button and watched the trousers slip down over her lover's narrow hips. Kicker wore no underwear, and Madelyn could not resist trailing her fingers lightly through the dark triangle revealed to her avid gaze.

Kicker flinched. "Bless'd Jesus, woman. If you don' want me to rip these right off, you'll stay your wanderin' fingers."

Delighted by the effect she had on her lover, Madelyn nonetheless pulled her hands away and rested them virtuously on Kicker's lean waist as she waited.

When fumbling fingers undid the last of the buttons, Madelyn stepped back to allow Kicker to draw the dress down over her shoulders. She almost laughed aloud at the look of dismay on Kicker's face as she faced the laced sateen corset underneath.

Only slightly daunted, Kicker tugged on the top lace and began loosening the stays. "I hope you're not expectin' me to wear one of these contraptions. Tis worse than ol' Cherry's rig."

Madelyn could not help a chuckle at the comparison, but when Kicker finally worked her way down to the lace edged chemise and long drawers, she stopped laughing. And when Kicker knelt to unbutton the stylish French kid boots, Madelyn heard her heartbeat thunder in her ears. As Kicker unclipped garters and rolled stockings down her legs, the sensuality of the moment became almost unbearable.

Kicker scarcely had time to rise to her feet before Madelyn frantically pushed off the unbuttoned shirt and pressed against her. All thoughts of taking it slow and not rushing her inexperienced lover fled in the overwhelmingly erotic sensation of flesh against flesh.

In her sensual haze, Madelyn heard a small growl from deep in Kicker's throat and knew that she felt the same need. Later she was never sure how they made it to the bed, or who started what, or where one body began and the other left off. But Madelyn never forgot the primal ecstasy of their first touch, of initiating her lover to unfamiliar joys, or of being the first to coax the unrestrained sounds of rapture from Kicker's lips.

At length Madelyn rested her sweat soaked form on Kicker's exhausted body, and listened with enchantment to her soft, deliriously indecipherable sounds of pleasure. She knew that no matter what awaited them, she would cherish the memory of this night and pray for a thousand more.

CHAPTER 4

PEACEFUL EYES SURVEYED THE UNFAMILIAR room which was barely illuminated by the dim, predawn light. Despite the long day and late night with their succession of dramatic events, her body had awakened early, as it was long accustomed to do. This morning, however, rather than rising, Kicker lay still, her mind turning over yesterday's milestones.

What a day of incredible firsts it had been: her first train ride; her first visit to London; and the most exhilarating first of all—making love with the woman whose soft, measured breath she could feel on her hair.

Kicker fought the desire to turn over and wake Madelyn to begin anew the delightful explorations of the previous night. She knew that by the time they'd finally allowed sleep to overcome them, Madelyn was bone weary. She had barely settled her head on Kicker's shoulder before she was asleep. Kicker had fended off sleep a little while longer as she reveled in the feel of the naked body tucked against her own. She had been overcome with tenderness for the woman who had opened a whole new world to her.

In the end, it was simple need that drove Kicker from the warmth of their shared bed. She dropped to her knees and peered beneath the bed. She frowned at the absence of a chamber pot. As silently as she could, she slipped on her trousers and shirt and winced as she buttoned the rough fabric into place over tender flesh. Madelyn had been an enthusiastic teacher.

Kicker took one last look at her sleeping lover and quietly left the room, treading lightly down the hallway until she came to the stairs. As she descended, she heard the sound of someone in the kitchen and surmised that their hostess, too, was an early riser. After making use of the water closet, Kicker hesitated. She wanted to return to Madelyn, yet wondered if it would be impolite not to bid Lil a good morning.

An amused voice from the kitchen solved her dilemma. "You might as well join me for a cup of tea. Maddie won't wake until midday, if I know her."

Kicker followed the voice to the well-lit kitchen and shyly edged around the door. She found the elderly woman somewhat intimidating, despite her friendly demeanour. But she wanted to get off on the right foot with Mrs. Harrington, who so obviously meant the world to Madelyn.

"Sit down, girl. I don't bite. How about a nice cuppa to warm you up?" Lil, still dressed in her nightgown and an ancient yellowed night cap, beamed at Kicker as she took a seat. Without waiting for an answer, she poured a second cup. "If you're hungry, I think I can find a little something to tide you over until her highness arises. What say you?"

The cheerful, prosaic kindness reminded Kicker of Cook, and a surge of homesickness washed over her. But before she could be overwhelmed with sorrow that she would never again be fussed over by that brusque, good-hearted woman in the huge kitchen of Grindleshire Academy, a steaming cup was pushed into her hands. Kicker glanced up and saw shrewd, old eyes assessing her.

"Missing home, are you?"

"No, no... I jus'..." Kicker trailed off, not wanting Lil to think she wasn't completely happy with her decision to accompany Madelyn.

Lil sank back into her chair and pushed the worn Bible and her wire rimmed glasses to the side as she cradled her own cup of tea. "It's not disloyal to miss those you've left behind, my dear. You do your Maddie no disservice by honouring the memory of family and old friends. She doesn't expect or require that of you."

Kicker wasn't completely sure what Madelyn would expect and require of her in the days to come. That made her uneasy so she changed the subject. "How'd you know twas me comin' down?"

"Because I've been listening to Maddie's steps since she took her first one, and she was never as quiet as that. If it weren't for the squeak on the third step, I'd not have known someone else stirred in the house."

Kicker sipped the delicious brew and let her mind linger over an image of a youthful Madelyn, skipping down the stairs of her family home.

"What was she like as a wee 'un?"

"Maddie? Oh, she was a handful, that's for certain. I've been nanny to a score of children, and never did one test me as sorely as that child."

"She were bad, then?"

"No, not bad, just willful. She came into the world with her mother's looks, her father's brains, and a healthy dose of stubborn streak from the both of them. Lordy, didn't father and daughter butt heads over the years. If it weren't for Mrs. Bristow, I swear young Maddie would've been tossed out on her ear more than one time." Lil smiled sadly. "She learned fast, though. Learned how to stay out of her father's way, and learned how to get her own, by whatever means necessary."

Kicker frowned, not at all sure she liked this portrayal of her lover.

"No, lass, don't fret. All I mean is that Maddie had to learn early on to take care of herself. I did what I could, but I left the Bristow household shortly after young Roderick's passing and she was mostly on her own."

"But is her da not a rich man? Did he jus' abandon her?"

"Not in the sense you mean, no. She always had lovely clothes and a fine roof over her head. She had the best schooling allowed, considering she wasn't being groomed to one day stand in her father's shoes. Twas a battle when she decided to teach, but she won through by sheer willfulness. I think even Mr. Timothy grudgingly admired her spirit, sore though it tried him over the years."

"But you said she was mos'ly on her own."

Lil sighed. "Maddie has three older sisters and two older brothers, and she had one younger brother who passed on some years ago. The oldest five all obediently fell in line with their father's plans. The boys work in his company, and the girls all made approved marriages at an early age. Mr. Timothy didn't expect his sixth child to carve her own path, and that's what she's done almost since she was born. When he got tired of fighting with the child, he washed his hands of her for the most part. Her mother's a good and caring woman with a bit of the same independent streak as Maddie, but I've never seen her cross her husband. Plus, she doted mostly on her last baby, Roderick. I'm not saying Maddie was neglected or unloved, but she spent far more of her time with me than with her family. I don't think her parents even had much of a sense of who she was until..."

"'Til? 'Til what?"

Lil shifted uneasily and cast a glance at the ceiling. She was silent for a long moment, then nodded. "You do need to know if you're to protect yourself, and her."

"Protect?" Kicker leaned forward anxiously. "Is Madelyn in danger?"

"She could be. You both could be if you're not very careful." Lil laid a wrinkled hand on the old Bible. "Listen well. You are about to enter the lion's den, and you must beware, child. While in Mr. Timothy's house, you must strive to give no clue as to what lies between you and Maddie, else he will destroy you, and in doing so, her too. Do you understand?"

Confused, Kicker shook her head. It was not that she didn't know they had to keep their love a secret, but it seemed to her that the elderly nanny was being melodramatic.

Perhaps sensing the younger woman's scepticism, Lil's expression grew resolute. "Listen and remember, Kicker. About ten years ago, Maddie got...involved with a woman named Charity Hiller. She was the daughter of one of Mr. Timothy's junior partners, and as such, was welcomed freely to their house. She was somewhat older than Maddie, but the two hit it off right from the start and became inseparable friends.

"Now, understand that I wasn't there during this time, so I'm only going on what I've gleaned from Maddie and my old friend Sylvia, who's been housekeeper to the Bristows for nigh onto forty years. Apparently Maddie and Charity got careless as time went on, and the servants began to gossip about exactly how close the two were. Someone—I'm thinking the bloody butler, who always did put on airs like he was one of the family itself—went to Mr. Timothy with the tales. Furious, the Master stormed into Maddie's room, only to see the proof of what he'd been told right before his eyes.

"The way Maddie tells it, they were only kissing, but from what Sylvia told me, the Master's outraged roars could've raised the dead. The next thing Sylvia knew, Charity was literally hurled down the front stairs."

"Bless'd Jesus!"

"She didn't break any bones, but mayhap it'd have been better if she had, for perhaps then Mr. Timothy's anger would've been slaked. As it was, he did far worse to her than mere physical harm."

Lil paused to sip her tea as Kicker stared at her in shock.

"Mr. Timothy first ensured that all societal doors were closed to Charity. No man would consider courting her, and no well-born woman would dare entertain her company. I don't exactly know how, but I do know that he then wreaked his vengeance on Charity's entire family. Though he kept his own daughter's name out of it, he broke Mr. Hiller—implicated him in a financial scandal, fired him, befouled his reputation, and eventually drove the poor man to Australia to escape the calumnies that were being heaped on his head. As the family's fortunes ebbed and they became pariahs here in London, they turned their wrath on Charity. Her family would not allow her to accompany them when they finally fled."

"What b'fell her then?"

Lil stared morosely at the dregs of tea as if seeking an answer there before she slowly shook her head. "There were rumours, my dear, but no one knows for sure. She just disappeared."

"But Madelyn... What did she do while her da ruined her...friend?"

"Naught she could do, Kicker. She was locked in her room for many weeks before her father came to her. She told me it was the first time she was out and out afraid of him. He chose to take the position that Charity had taken advantage of his daughter's innocence and that Maddie really hadn't understood what was going on, but for a year after that, he never allowed her to leave the house without a minder. He really only loosened the reins after she became employed as a teacher at a fine school."

"She ne'er saw Charity agin?"

"Not that I know of." Lil reached across the table and laid her hand on Kicker's. "Do you understand what would happen if Mr. Timothy were to find out about you and Maddie? The first time he could dismiss and rationalize, but he's a hard man and would not do so twice. If you do not hide what you feel for her, if you do not guard your every word and every glance in that house, I fear for what will become of the both of you."

Deeply shaken, Kicker nodded. "I swear I'll not give her da any cause for suspicion. I'll wear the damn'ble dresses an' speak only when spoken to. I'll e'en bend my knee to the basti'd if need be...anythin' to keep Madelyn safe."

Lil saw the effect her words had and gentled her tone. "I did not mean to scare you, child; twere only a warning. Chances are Mr. Timothy won't even notice you. Stay below stairs as much as you can, and you'll be fine until you leave."

Kicker thought longingly of the little room upstairs that had been such a haven for the new lovers the previous night. She wished they could stay there until their ship departed. However, she could not deny Madelyn the chance for a last farewell with her family. She was acutely aware that once they sailed, the likelihood of ever seeing England's shores again was slim.

"Oh, listen to me rambling on like an old fool. Go back to your lady, now, and let her remind you why this is all worth it."

Kicker stood and faced Lil, her shoulders drawn back and a look of determination on her face. "I thank you for the warnin', Missus. I won' forget what you tol' me."

She turned abruptly, left the kitchen and missed the sadness in the old eyes that watched her departure.

"God keep you, child. God keep both of you."

So great was the need to see Madelyn that Kicker was running by the time she reached their bedroom. When she entered the room, she had to bite off an exclamation of relief at seeing Madelyn in the same peaceful position that she'd left her.

She shook her head at her foolishness, quickly shed her clothes and slid under the covers. Kicker curled around Madelyn's warm body and closed her eyes at the sheer sensual delight of skin against skin.

"Where'd you get to, dearest?"

The sleep slurred words could barely be heard as Kicker snuggled even closer. "Shhh. I was jus' takin' tea with Lil. Go back to sleep."

She stroked Madelyn's hip gently, and within moments her lover fell back to sleep. As Kicker held her close, she affirmed her vow. She would not give Timothy Bristow the least cause for suspicion. She would be naught but the lowborn stranger who had been foisted upon his kindhearted daughter by a fearful father.

She tried to relax back into slumber, but Kicker could not help remembering her lack of success when she'd tried to lie her way out of trouble the umpteenth time she ran from the detested schoolmaster. All her efforts had earned her was a whipping from her exasperated mother. When Adam had found her, still sobbing down by the creek, he'd offered some sound advice.

"Kicker, you can't lie worth a tinker's damn. Yer face gives you away ever' time. Best thing for you is to jus' own up and take yer licking right off, cuz it's gonna happen one way or t'other. Ma might go easier on you if she don' have to beat the truth outta you first."

Kicker grimaced. Keeping their secret from Madelyn's family was not going to be easy.

"You stride, dearest; ladies glide. Try it once more."

Kicker tried to heed the gentle admonishment. She concentrated on a smoother, shorter gait as she walked across the bedroom floor for what felt like the hundredth time. A faded blue and white striped poplin skirt swirled around her ankles. It had come from the WBU donation box, as had the plain white blouse she wore and three other skirts and dresses that Lil was altering to fit her. They even found a pair of grey canvas oxfords that were only slightly too big.

Privately, Kicker thought that the only thing the sharply pointed toes would be good for was kicking rats out of the barn.

"That's much better. What do you think, Lil?"

Lil glanced up from her perch beside Madelyn on the edge of the bed where she was hemming one of Kicker's new skirts. "With a little more work, she'll be fit for the Queen's court."

Kicker ignored her companions' chuckles and reversed course to glide back across the room.

"Dearest, while you're doing that, tell me again the story you'll offer for my family's consumption."

"My name is Kathleen Stuart, from the village Greenley, an' I'm goin' to Canada to meet my husband, Edward. We was married jus' b'fore he wen' o'er there las' year to stake a claim, an' he's waitin' on me."

They had decided that the more conventional Christian name would be less likely to draw attention in the Bristow household, though Kicker was adamant that as soon as they were at sea, she would reclaim her name.

"Where? Where are you two going to homestead?"

Kicker stopped in mid-glide, frowning as she strove to remember the unfamiliar names. "Manitoba. Aye, that's it. Manitoba, on a farm northwes' of Winnipeg."

"And how did you end up traveling with me?"

"M' da heared you was crossin' by yourself an' asked if you'd take me on as a lady's companion, to see me safely to my husban's side."

"How did he hear about my plans?"

Kicker could hear the undercurrent of concern in Madelyn's voice. This was the most vulnerable part of their story. These details would not bear up under investigation if Timothy Bristow chose to check them out for any reason. "Da's a smith and does some work out at Grindleshire. He heard the talk, asked you, and you said aye."

"Excellent."

Having reached the far side of the room, Kicker spun and almost fell over in her unfamiliar footwear. She glared at her two instructors, who tried valiantly to conceal their smiles.

"Like puttin' party slippers on ol' Cherry, if you ask me." Despite her grumbling, Kicker resumed her determined efforts to master a lady's walk. Earlier that morning, she memorized her putative background with such intensity that Madelyn had frowned in puzzlement. Kicker knew that the change in her demeanour from their joyous first night together confused her lover. But Lil's early morning warning had put the fear of God, and Timothy Bristow, in her, and she was determined not to let Madelyn down.

Lil bit off a thread and nodded at Madelyn, who watched Kicker intently. "And what about you, Maddie, my girl? Let's hear again what your story will be."

Madelyn launched into her recitation with enviable smoothness.

"My beloved husband is Major Kingsley Elliston Bristow, a graduate of Sandhurst, class of '89, now serving with the 12th Lancers under the command of General Sir Redvers Buller. He was posted to India for several years, but I was unable to accompany him for health reasons. He hates that we must be apart, but is determined to do his duty to Queen and country, whatever the personal sacrifice. Naturally, I support him fully, though I miss him desperately and live for those scant weeks when he may return on leave. He was recently sent to Natal, South Africa, but as he wishes to retire and build a new life abroad after the dreadful Boer business has been settled, he is dispatching me to Canada to establish our new home. I'm fearful of the responsibility, of course, but how can I do otherwise when my dear Kingsley is so devoted to his duty? I must not let my husband down."

Lil's eyes twinkled behind her glasses. "And you've no passel of children tuggin' on your skirts because...?"

"We had hoped for many sons to carry on his family's noble line, but sadly, my dear husband was badly wounded in a skirmish in North India, and well—it is as God wills, of course." Madelyn's demure voice trailed off and she let her eyes drop modestly.

Kicker stared at her in amazement and wistfully longed for the same facility with words. If she hadn't known better, she would've believed Madelyn actually had a husband posted in a foreign land—a husband she missed deeply and pined for every day.

"You missed your calling, Maddie girl. The stage is a poorer place for your absence."

Madelyn dropped her pose, and leaned into her old friend with a laugh. "Good Lord, Lil. You know how hard I had to fight just to be a teacher. Can you imagine my father's reaction if I'd wanted to do something as scandalous as the pursuit of a theatrical career?"

Lil gave a melodramatic shudder. "Mr. Timothy would most certainly not abide that. And speaking of your father, do you plan to try your story out on him? Will you send word of a new husband or fiancé once you're safe away in the Colonies?"

"I don't think so, Lil. As it is, I'm sure he leans more to the belief that I am simply after a mad, new adventure, rather than that I actually seek a husband. He equates my desire to leave England with the battle I had to wage to become a teacher. Father has given up on my ever settling down as a normal woman."

"It's best not to complicate your skein of fabrications, I agree. Mr. Timothy would undoubtedly want to check out anyone you planned to marry, so better to let sleeping dogs lie, as it were. Perhaps you can send word next year that you've married. It would be passing hard for him to send his investigators that far away."

Madelyn looked doubtful, and Kicker wondered exactly how far Mr. Bristow's reach extended.

"I'm uncertain, Lil. It might be best simply to let Father wash his hands of me. Truthfully I think he would welcome the opportunity to do just that. Better he attribute a dearth of matrimonial news to the belief that his spinster daughter is not putting any energy into finding an eligible, wealthy landowner. He is accustomed to being disappointed in me, so why do anything to raise his suspicions? I've learned if I am out of sight, I am well out of his mind. As hard a man as he is, I don't think he will go to all the trouble and expense necessary to track my life so far away. However, I do have one problem."

"Only one? You're an optimist, girl, I'll give you that."

Carefully executing her spin this time as she reached the wall, Kicker nodded her agreement with Mrs. Harrington. They faced more problems than there were bees in a hive. Determined that her comportment wouldn't be one of them, Kicker silently retraced her endless path across the wooden floor.

"Lil, I'm serious. I need to find a way to get letters sent from South Africa to our new home, to set the stage for my role as a grieving, resolutely ineligible widow."

"Is that all? I can help you with that. One of my boys is with Colonel Abbot's bunch in the Transvaal. He writes me regular as rain, and he won't mind doing a favour for his old nanny. I'll send my letters to you through him, so they are postmarked South Africa. Don't you worry a bit; I'll take care of that detail for you."

Lil set aside her sewing and stood, resting a hand on Madelyn's shoulder for a moment. "Now, I've just the thing to give your story life."

"Props?"

"Of a sort. Wait here a moment."

Lil left the room and Madelyn beckoned Kicker to her. She wrapped her in a tight embrace and buried her face against Kicker's chest.

Kicker stroked Maddie's hair gently and listened for a sign of what her lover wanted or needed, but Madelyn seemed content simply to have her near. When Lil returned a few moments later, the pair reluctantly parted, their eyes fixed on each other.

Lil sank heavily onto the bed and thrust a paper wrapped package at her one-time charge.

Madelyn glanced at it curiously and carefully unwrapped the thin parcel. It was a silver-framed, sepia toned photograph of a uniformed officer who stood rigidly erect and frowned sternly at the camera. He looked to be in his early thirties. The hand resting on the hilt of his sword bore a wedding ring, and his moustache curled up to an alarming degree.

"That's my Harold, gone these many years now. I don't know if the Lancers' uniforms have changed after all this time, but I doubt any in the Colonies will know either. He can be your Kingsley, proudly displayed on your mantle as you wait patiently for his return."

"Ah, but he never does return, does he? He doesn't even get the glorious death in battle he deserves. Instead, he is struck down by malaria, on the eve of his retirement, mere weeks away from sailing to be with his devoted wife in a new land. It hardly bears talking about."

Madelyn daintily dabbed a tear from her eye with a corner of her wrapper. But the effect was spoiled when a long expanse of thigh was exposed and Kicker drew in a sharp breath.

"Cover up and quit tormenting your girl, Maddie. Here—this will come in handy, too."

Lil dropped something into Madelyn's hand and the would-be thespian turned solemn.

"Oh, Lil, I can't take that. Harold gave you that on your wedding day."

"Take it now or get it once I die, but it is yours, girl. You might as well have it while it will do some good."

Lil closed Madelyn's hand around the simple gold band.

"Harold was a good man, and good to me for the short time we had together, but you know the truth of it, my girl. All I ask of you, if you're here when the time comes, is to make sure I'm buried with this." Lil tapped the tiny silver locket around her neck. "It once belonged to Vivian's mother, and she gave it to me the day we moved in here. Never been off my neck since, and I plan to meet Vi again with it still hanging there."

Madelyn's eyes filled with tears and she flung her arms around Lil's neck.

Moved, Kicker took a few steps away, not wishing to intrude. Without any of them acknowledging it, they all knew the likelihood of Madelyn being present for Lil's passing was slim. Nanny to two score of children, Lil had never had any of her own. With her favourite sailing away, she would have to depend on chance and luck that her last wishes would be carried out.

"Here, no need for that, Maddie. I'd best go check on those girls of mine. Heaven only knows what they'll get up to when I'm not watching their every stitch. I'll call you when lunch is ready."

Kicker glanced over her shoulder to see Lil hurry out of the room, wiping her eyes as she departed. She wondered whether she should allow Madelyn some privacy to collect herself as she peeked cautiously at her. The woebegone look on that beautiful face vanquished any doubts. Kicker hastened back to the bed and fell to her knees.

Kicker gently wiped away Madelyn's tears as they fell. She knew instinctively that words were useless and simply waited until Madelyn was able to give her a wan smile.

"I'm all right, dearest. I suppose it just sank in that I'll never see her again once we leave."

"You'll write 'er, aye?"

"Yes, but letters are a cold comfort when the miles between us stretch so far."

"Are you sure tis what you want, to go to Canada? We could stay around here, or p'rhaps go north, to Scotland?"

Madelyn squared her shoulders and determinedly dashed the tears from her eyes. "No, dearest. You don't know my father. Our only choices are to live apart in England, or to chance the Fates and make a new life together far enough away that we are out of his reach."

The memory of Lil's ominous early morning warning still fresh in her mind, Kicker didn't argue. "Then Canada tis, for I could not live without you."

Overwhelmed by the grateful, loving intensity of Madelyn's expression, Kicker wanted nothing more than to tear the thin silk wrapper from her lover's body, lay her back on the bed, and remind them both why they had chosen this perilous path, but Lil's words haunted her:

"Listen well. You're about to enter the lion's den, and you must beware, child... If you do not hide what you feel for her, if you do not guard your every word and every glance in that house, I fear for what will become of the both of you."

Kicker swallowed hard, then stood and resolutely turned away, intending to resume her perambulations.

Madelyn would have none of it. "You're doing so much better. Shall we take a break now? Lil said she'd call us for lunch in a bit, and we should decide what sights we'll take in this afternoon."

"Jus' a little more. I believe tis comin' to me easier now." Even as Kicker spoke, she stumbled again in the unfamiliar shoes and swore angrily.

"Dearest, please don't be so hard on yourself. You need not learn everything in the next hour. We're not going to my parents' manse for a few days. You have plenty of time. Please, come and sit with me."

Reluctantly, Kicker capitulated in the face of Madelyn's coaxing and sank down on the edge of the bed next to her. She bit her lip as she stared at the offending footwear and furiously wished the oxfords at the bottom of the Thames. An arm slid around her waist and a soft voice sounded in her ear.

"What's going on, dearest? You act like the devil is on our trail, and your learning to walk like a lady is the only thing that stands between us and Hell itself."

"Maybe tis."

"Kicker, please talk to me. What troubles you so?"

The answer came in a half-heard whisper. "What if I fail you? What if your da don' believe we're strangers? I don' know how to act in your world. I'm as unsteady as a newborn foal in these bless'd dresses and fancy shoes. Maybe... Maybe twould be bes' if I await you here. You go on and see your folks, an' I'll be waitin' at the station when tis time to go."

Madelyn's answer was swift and fierce. "No. I'm not leaving you behind."

"But we cannot be t'gether in your da's house."

"I know, but I don't want us to be apart either. Please don't worry so. I can protect you there, I swear it."

"You could not protect Charity."

There was a profound silence. Kicker looked up from contemplating her loathsome shoes to see shock and apprehension in Madelyn's face. Kicker pivoted and wrapped her arms around her lover.

"Bloody tongue! I'm so sorry, love. I ne'er meant to hurt you. Forget I said it."

"You know?"

"Only since this mornin'. Lil tol' me, but she jus' did it so's I'd b'ware and be careful. Sorry I am you went through that, Madelyn, but tis glad I am she tol' me. I know how not to get burnt by the forge, but firs' I gotta know that the forge is lit."

"I—I did intend to tell you about her one day, but...it's not a period of my life that I'm proud of. Charity did not deserve what happened, but there was nothing I could do to stop it, to stop him. I've never in my life felt so helpless, and I swore after that I would never feel so powerless ever again."

"Is that why we're leavin', then?"

"Partly. My father is not a man to be trifled with. I've won a small measure of freedom from him by dint of persistence and willfulness, but he would never accept this—us."

"Then I don' understan' why I don' stay here whilst you're at your parents'."

"You mean other than the fact that I cannot bear the thought of spending one day without you?"

Kicker tightened her arms in unspoken agreement as Madelyn leaned willingly into her embrace.

“I know it would probably be safer. However, I also believe my parents will accept my departure more readily if they see that I shall not be making the journey alone.”

“Hah. They’ll take one look at me an’ send me d’rect to the scull’ry. I ain’t exactly no strappin’ soljer boy.”

Madelyn ran a hand over the strong arms wrapped around her and sent a shiver down Kicker’s spine. “True, they don’t know that you would slay dragons to save me if you had to, but they’ll be pleased by the notion that I have a lady’s companion with whom to travel.”

Madelyn’s gentle strokes made it hard for Kicker to remember what she had objected to. She allowed the sensual wave to sweep away Lil’s warnings, if only for the moment.

“There is one thing, dearest.”

“Mmm?”

“When we are there, I’ll have to treat you as a companion, as less than an equal. If I seem harsh or distant or cold, please, please forgive me. You know that I’m only putting on an act to protect us both.”

“Mmm hmm.”

“Kicker...dearest...what are you doing?”

“You don’ know?”

“I do know that my wrapper appears to be untying itself, and—oh.”

“Oh?”

“Lil’s girls are working downstairs. Do you really think this is the time—Oh, dear God.”

“I’m jus’ explorin’, takin’ in the sights, like you said. An’ I’ll be nice and quiet, I promise.”

“Oh, sweet Mother...”

Kicker gently pressed Madelyn back on the bed and pushed the wrapper fully away from the supple body. As she lowered her head to her delightful task, she heard a whispered, “I do hope you locked the door...”

“I suppose we can always go sightseeing tomorrow, dearest.”

Kicker smiled at Madelyn's languid words as she watched her eyes flutter with fatigue. Lil never called them for lunch, or if she had, her summons had gone unheard, and judging by the long shadows in the room, it was now late afternoon.

"Tis fine, love. Rest now. I'll wake you in a while."

Madelyn murmured something, and gave up the battle to keep her eyes open.

Kicker felt her lover's body slacken and gentled her embrace. Though she felt pleasantly spent herself, her mind, no longer preoccupied by the demands of her body, returned to the topic they had been discussing earlier.

For the next hour, as Madelyn slept in her arms, Kicker reviewed all she had learned of Madelyn's family and made some plans of her own. Despite her distraction, she hadn't missed Madelyn's warning. Kicker prepared herself for how she might be treated in the Bristow household. She was accustomed to being the discounted outsider, but it would be the first time Madelyn treated her as a servile stranger.

Kicker steeled her heart for the emotional pain, and determined to maintain a similarly cool distance from the woman she loved.

"What are you thinking of so hard, dearest?"

"This an' that. Sightseeing, I guess."

Kicker felt Madelyn's chuckle against her chest, and smiled at the sensation as her lover rolled onto her back and stretched luxuriously. It was too warm in the room for even a sheet, so Kicker had an unrestricted view of Madelyn's nude form. With an appreciative gleam in her eye, Kicker rolled to her side and traced a finger down the centre of her lover's body.

"Mmm, that feels wonderful, but if you do any more sightseeing today, I'm not going to be able to move."

Kicker said nothing, but kept her touch light and undemanding as she drew her fingers in gentle strokes and swirls along warm, damp skin. When Madelyn began to undulate under her hands, Kicker whispered, "Jus' cannot keep my hands off you."

With a groan, Madelyn seized Kicker's hand and stilled it over her breast. She turned and backed up against Kicker, not releasing the hand that had been arousing her yet again. "My God, what you do to me. Have mercy, dearest. I've no defences against you."

Kicker chuckled and used her free hand to push aside Madelyn's thick hair so she could nuzzle the soft nape of her neck. "I'll b'have, I swear."

And Kicker did, though it took all her willpower to do so. They lay together in peaceful silence and listened to the distant sounds of activity outside, neither inclined to rejoin the world of busy, purposeful people just yet.

Finally Madelyn asked, "So, what would you like to see tomorrow?"

"The palace."

"Buckingham or St. James?"

"Both."

A soft chuckle greeted Kicker's enthusiasm. "And what else?"

"Big Ben?"

"Of course. And might I suggest St. Paul's Cathedral, Westminster Abbey, the Tower of London, and Trafalgar Square? We'll not be able to do it all in one day, but since this is your first time here, you really should see all the wonders of the city."

"I'll see whate'er you wan' to show me."

"I have so much to show you, dearest. Perhaps we should start tonight. If we went out right after tea, we could cross at least one of those off our list."

Unwilling to leave the haven they had found in Lil's place so soon, Kicker murmured, "T'morrow's good."

"Tomorrow then, my insatiable wench."

The amusement in Madelyn's voice was clear, and Kicker was relieved. This all felt so new and raw that she was not sure of her bearings. All Kicker knew was that the rest of the world could go hang as long as she could stay in this bed, with this woman in her arms.

"I do want to go to the Canada High Commission on Saturday. They're doing a presentation and then having a reception for prospective immigrants afterwards. We'll represent ourselves according to our new histories and see how it goes."

"Aye, a test, then?"

"Exactly. And if you feel ready, we'll go to my parents' house on Sunday."

Unwilling to let the thought of Sunday's trials ruin the moment, Kicker flexed her fingers over the captive breast and pressed herself more firmly against Madelyn's bottom. When a long, slender leg lifted over hers in clear invitation, Kicker's hands began to administer to her lover's growing urgency.

Though hardened and calloused by years of labour, Kicker's hands caressed and worshipped Madelyn's body with infinite tenderness.

Finally Madelyn couldn't stand it any longer and took control of the relentlessly teasing fingers.

"Here?"

"God, yes. Please, Kicker, please..."

Words were lost then in the sound of harsh breathing and low whimpers and pleadings.

At the head of the stairs, Lil stopped and shook her head in wry amusement. It was the second time she had climbed the stairs that afternoon. As a long, low moan sounded from the small room down the hall, Lil turned and began her descent, leaving her guests undisturbed once again.

"I suppose they'll come down for tea eventually. Don't guess they'll let themselves starve." When a high, muffled cry rang out, Lil winced, then chuckled. "Tis well that I gave the girls a half-day off, for I'd be hard pressed to explain that particular noise."

CHAPTER 5

"ONE GROSVENOR SQUARE, DRIVER. THE Canada High Commission."

"Aye, Miss."

The cab driver closed the door firmly and climbed to his seat as Madelyn beamed her approval.

"Well said, dearest."

Kicker smiled in return. Madelyn didn't know it, but she had mentally practiced that very phrase over and over, aware that her lover would expect her to demonstrate her improved diction that evening.

The previous few days had been spent in intensive rehearsals of both speech and manners, even as Madelyn and Kicker took in the delights of the city. The former stable hand now felt moderately confident in her ability to pass as someone she had never been.

Kicker plucked nervously at the rose-coloured tea gown Lil had made for her. She recalled the shock of seeing her image in the mirror an hour earlier. Before her stood a shy, attractive young woman with a wide-brimmed straw hat that served to cover the unconventional shortness of her hair. At that moment, neither Madelyn nor Lil had to work very hard to convince Kicker that she was the perfect image of a young, middle class wife, about to set sail for a new land and a virtually new husband.

Though nervous about the evening's expedition, Kicker felt that, externally at least, she would not raise any comment as Mrs. Kingsley Bristow's young cousin and loyal traveling companion.

"You look wonderful, Kicker."

"Thank you. You look fine yourself." And she did, in her pale green dress and matching hat, but in Kicker's opinion, nothing was more beautiful than Madelyn without a stitch on. She shifted restlessly as her mind filled with the images of what they could be doing rather than going to the High Commission.

"There'll be time for that later, dearest. This won't take all night."

Kicker flushed at being read so easily, but then she suspected it didn't take much effort, given the last several days. Madelyn had taken her everywhere she'd promised, but Kicker found that even Buckingham Palace and the changing of the Guard lost its allure when compared with the intimacies of their small, peaceful bedroom.

"I know. I'll be good, I promise."

"Of that, I have no doubt at all."

Kicker's jaw dropped at her unmistakable innuendo, but when Madelyn started to laugh, she joined in, easing some of the strain of the upcoming performance.

They chatted easily until the driver pulled up amidst the crowd of people in front of the imposing building. More relaxed, Kicker felt ready to take on the first major challenge of their new identities.

As the driver handed the women down from the cab and accepted his fare from Madelyn, Kicker stared at the large number of people milling about the entrance to the building that housed the High Commission. They were a cross section of British society: from the obviously penurious, hopeful of an opportunity to raise their station in a new land—to sturdy workmen and their equally stalwart wives herding noisy children—to well-dressed members of the merchant and upper classes who entered by a side door reserved just for them.

Kicker was about to push her way to the front entrance when a subtle tug on her sleeve changed her direction. Much to her discomfort, she found herself mingled with her betters, hoping desperately no one would address her directly.

Madelyn steered them adeptly through the crowd and they quickly found themselves inside a large hall. It was adorned with posters advertising "Improved Farms at Reasonable Rates", "Healthy Climate, Light Taxes, Free Schools" and "160 Acre Free Farms".

Kicker did not doubt that the latter incentive was the one drawing most of the crowd. During their sightseeing rambles, Madelyn had pointed out posters that advertised a free section of Canadian land to any British male citizen for only the ten pound registration fee. As long as the homesteader lived on his land for three years, cultivated thirty acres and built a permanent domicile, the land was his, free and clear. Kicker was sure that to those struggling to feed families in the overcrowded streets and lanes of the mother country, it must have sounded too good to be true.

Kicker settled into a seat beside Madelyn and prepared to listen to the first of many speakers. She couldn't help imagining the two of them on their very own section of land, but she knew that was unrealistic. While Kicker had worked as hard as any man her entire life and figured to continue doing so, she could not see her well-bred lover as a farm drudge. Madelyn was born for finer things, and if it was within her power, Kicker would give her the life for which she was meant.

"Ladies and gentlemen—welcome. I'd like to get this informative and entertaining evening started by introducing the members of our committee, some of whom have come all the way from Canada to give you the benefit of their firsthand experiences."

"Dearest, I want to have a word with Mr. Russell. Do you wish to come with me or wait here?"

Kicker glanced up from the Magic Lantern. The last in a long line of speakers had used it to illustrate his lecture on the wonders of the Canadian landscape, and it captivated her. The moment Sidney Russell had finished his presentation, Kicker dragged Madelyn up the stairs to the Magic Lantern display to watch the show again.

"Go on. I'll wait here for you."

Madelyn smiled indulgently, touched Kicker lightly on the shoulder, and turned away in search of the evening's main speaker.

Kicker was entranced by the slides that flipped over so rapidly she could almost feel the wind rushing by a train that swept through endless fields of wheat and past roaring rivers as it approached towering mountains. Lost in wonder, she was startled to hear a man's voice from behind her.

"What that doesn't show are the mosquitoes big enough to carry away a horse and winter winds so cold that they'll freeze a jackrabbit in mid-leap."

Recognizing the accent, Kicker turned to the stranger and smiled. "Are you not supposed to be preachin' the virtues of your country?"

The stranger grinned. "That is why I signed on, yes, at least partly, but I do believe old Sidney has done more than enough boasting for all of us. Promise you won't tell Mr. Sifton on me?"

"Mr. Sifton?"

"Mr. Clifford Sifton, our Minister of Interior. His ministry lured me away from my family's ranch and sent me and my brother all this way, along with half a dozen others he pressed into service. Mr. Sifton believes that those of us who've made a success of life in the West are the best ambassadors for our land. If he has his way, he's going to fill every inch of the prairies with homesteaders, and by God, if anyone can do it, he can." The man looked sheepish. "Um, pardon my language, Miss. My mother really did teach me better manners than that. Permit me to start again. I'm Will MacDiarmid of the Steeple Seven Ranch, just northwest of Galbraith's Crossing in western Alberta." He extended his hand, and Kicker shook it.

Kicker liked the friendly, open expression on MacDiarmid's heavily tanned face. A mass of unruly, light brown curls fell over his forehead and almost covered his cheerful, fawn-coloured eyes. She judged him to be in his early thirties, with the rangy, artless look of a man who would be much more comfortable sitting a horse than sitting in the finer salons of London society.

"Kicker Stuart."

Immediately Kicker chastised herself for not using the more conventional "Kathleen", but she rationalized that the name had been created for the benefit of Madelyn's parents, and the slip would do no harm.

"A pleasure to meet you, Miss Stuart. Are you planning to immigrate to our country?"

Kicker glanced over the balcony to the floor below, where she could see Madelyn in animated conversation with Sidney Russell. "Aye, I am. I'm goin' with my—cousin, Madelyn Bristow. She's meetin' her husban' over there. He's a soljer in South Africa right now. She's bin teachin' while she waits his return."

"Teaching? She's a teacher?" Will's eyes gleamed. "Is she looking for a position when you get there?" Then his face fell and his shoulders slumped. "Ah, but what am I saying? Her husband won't allow that. We lose all our teachers to marriage, but then what else can you expect when the men outnumber the women by so many. Can't hardly keep teachers past a year or two, at best. My wife's been schoolin' our three little ones since Miss Carter up and married and left for Minnesota early this spring. We've been trying to get a new teacher in ever since, but all the good ones want to go to Calgary or up to Edmonton. Our little town can't compete with the glamour of the city, and there hasn't been a teacher yet who didn't get five offers of marriage before her first box social."

His doleful look gave way to a conspiratorial grin and Will winked at Kicker. "You know, that's the real reason I'm on this trip—to find my baby brother a bride." He pointed to a young man, his spitting image, who was enthusiastically chatting with three women on the floor below. "My mother told me not to come back until Albert finds himself a wife, but my brother is having way too much fun fishing, and hasn't settled on a catch yet." He looked at Kicker speculatively. "I don't suppose you'd be interested?"

Kicker grinned at the torrent of words that had poured out of the Canadian, and shook her head. "Not right now, thanks, but as to t'other matter, I can tell you that my cousin is one of the top teachers aroun'. She jus' left Grindleshire Academy, and I happen to know they thought she's one of the bes' they ever had. An' I know she plans to teach at leas' 'til her husban' musters out in a year or two."

"Really? She has her husband's permission to teach, then? Does she have an offer pending? Do you know where you're planning to settle? Would he be interested in coming to Alberta? What does he plan to do after he is discharged from service? Does he want to farm or ranch?"

"Um, no, I don' believe Madelyn's got an offer yet, an' her husban' don' mind her teachin', but I think she an' Major Bristow are plannin' to settle in Manitoba."

"Pah, Manitoba. They've got mosquitoes out there can carry off a buffalo. You want to come to Alberta instead."

"Where the winter winds freeze a jackrabbit in mid-leap?"

"I was just joshing you. It's not really that bad, honest. I swear on my sainted grandmother's head that I've never seen a frozen jackrabbit, and I've lived my whole life out there."

Kicker looked at Will sceptically and he responded with an abashed grin.

"All right, maybe I have seen a frozen jackrabbit or two, but never in mid-leap. And the fact is you're going to have to be prepared for cold winters anywhere you go on the prairies. But truthfully, Manitoba is so cold that the ice doesn't come off the rivers until June, and they freeze over again in September. You'd love Galbraith's Crossing, believe me. You look west, and you see the mountains, standing so tall and glorious you think they're reaching right up into heaven. You look east, and you see land so rich that wheat about grows faster than a man can reap it. And we've got the prettiest little town there ever was. You wouldn't want for anything—if the general store doesn't have it, you can order by catalogue or pick it up in the city. River and the railroad flank the town on one side, and the forest is on our back doorstep. We've only got about three hundred people right in town, but there's close to two hundred more homesteading in the area. If your cousin's husband wants to homestead, there's still lots of good land he could lay claim to, all within spittin' distance of Galbraith. Or if he's of a mind to become a merchant, there's lots of opportunity for that, too. One of these days we're going to rival Calgary—just you wait and see."

Kicker wondered if all Canadians were as talkative as Will, but as he spoke, an idea began to grow in the back of her mind. "Does Galbraith have a smith, too?"

"Only one of the best in the whole Northwest Territories. John Blue Wolf is a master of the forge—none better."

"Blue Wolf?"

Will regarded her cautiously. "Yes, he's half Stoney, but John and I grew up together. He's a good man—son of one of Galbraith's founders, actually."

Kicker immediately wanted to allay the man's obvious concern that she not pass judgment on Blue Wolf for him being half Indian. "Soun's like there's a story in that."

Will's face relaxed and he smiled. "Sure is. See, Angus Galbraith came out from Scotland about forty years ago. He was my father's cousin, and what my mother called a restless spirit. He couldn't ever really settle down, but he did stop a while where my father was building the Steeple Seven, long before the railroad made it out that far. Old Angus, he got along with everyone, including the Stoney and the Blackfoot. Met a young Stoney woman out hunting one day and I guess they fell hard for each other, 'cause he kept going back to see her. Eventually he wanted to bring her back to the village that had been taking root by the river, but she wouldn't go, and even my father told him it wasn't a good idea. Best she'd agree to was settling in her own tipi across the river. So, every night, Angus would paddle the river to be with her, and every morning he'd cross back into the village with game, and furs that his woman had cured. Got to be that people started calling the village Galbraith's Crossing, and the name kind of stuck."

"They had a family, then?"

"Yes. John was firstborn, and from the time he could walk, his daddy took him everywhere. Got so you'd never see Angus without seeing John trailing along behind. I swear I never knew them to speak more than two words at a time to each other, but you never saw one without the other, even though John's mama and little brothers and sisters never crossed the river. 'Round about the time John was ten or so, Angus got himself killed. Took on a cougar while he was out hunting, and the cougar won. Young as he was, John went after that big cat, and to this day, that cougar's hide hangs on the inside of his smithy."

Will had the knack of a natural storyteller and Kicker hung on every word. "So what happened with John and his ma?"

"John's mama took the rest of her babies and melted back into the forest. I guess she went back to her tribe, though no one knows for sure, not even John. My father, being blood kin to Angus on their mothers' side, took John in and raised him up with me and my sister and brothers."

"So, he's like your brother?"

Will gave her a serious look. "Miss Stuart, I got one sister, Wynne, and four brothers, Albert, Bruce, Wally, and John Blue Wolf. Every one of them has an equal claim on my love and loyalty."

Kicker's mind flashed to Adam and a lump grew in her throat. She swallowed hard and nodded her understanding. "Aye, I know what you mean. Tis nothin' I would not do for my brother, either."

There was a moment of perfect understanding between the two, and Kicker decided she genuinely liked the friendly, talkative Canadian.

"Are your brothers running your ranch while you're over here findin' Albert a bride?"

Will laughed. "Actually, my sister is running the ranch, just as she's done since my father was crippled up by a nasty tempered stallion about seven years ago. Bruce and Wally left their wives and children behind and headed north to the Yukon last year, lusting after gold. We haven't heard from them since, but they'll come home one of these days. Those two got the same wanderlust that Angus had until he met John's mama."

"Your sister runs the ranch?"

"She sure does, and just about everyone on it, except our father, and not even our mother ever ran him. Why, Wynne can out rope, out ride, and generally out work any man that walks on two legs, believe me."

"An' her husban' don' mind?"

That brought another round of guffaws from the Canadian. "Wynne kicked her sorry excuse for a husband out of the big house about eight years ago. Said it was the last time she was going to make that mistake. The idiot got drunk one too many times, fell into the river during spring run-off and made her a young widow. Many's the men who've come sniffin' around after her, thinking they'd get a piece of the Steeple Seven in the bargain, but they generally only make that mistake once. My sister's a mean hand with her old bullwhip, and she's no time for fools and leeches."

"You don' mind? I mean workin' for your sister and all."

"Miss Stuart, I am many things, but I am not a stupid man. I have my own God-given abilities, but dealing with merchants, fighting for fair market price for our cattle, and overseeing five thousand head of the finest shorthorn you'll ever see, not to mention over a hundred mule-headed hands, is better left in my sister's hands. I work as hard as any man, but I don't need that aggravation. I'd rather take my crew after a bunch of ornery strays than face down a banker after a winter that took nigh on a third of our herd. Wynne's done well by all of us since our father was laid up, and there's none of us fool enough to insist on stepping into her shoes."

"No one says her no, then?"

"Wynne? No one tells her no twice, that's for sure. We're a young country, Miss Stuart, and we're hungry for good, strong people to build her up. You'll find most folks take a newcomer, man or woman, on face value until they prove or disprove themselves. It's not an easy life, and we all know the way to get through it is to pull together. Now, I'll grant you that Wynne isn't exactly your typical boss, but she's kept the ranch intact, and built it up until it's one of the biggest and most productive in the West."

"She soun's amazin'."

"That she is. Ah, I do believe I see your cousin returning. Do you think it would be proper for me to approach her about the position as Galbraith's Crossing's new teacher?"

"Aye, twould."

As Madelyn approached the pair, Will stepped forward and gave a small bow. "Mrs. Bristow, I've been enjoying the pleasure of talking with your cousin, and I'd like to introduce myself. I'm Will MacDiarmid of the Steeple Seven Ranch, just north of Galbraith's Crossing in western Alberta, and I'm pleased to make your acquaintance."

As Madelyn took the hand Will offered, she shot Kicker an inquisitive look. Before she could say anything, however, the irrepressible Canadian launched into his spiel.

"Mrs. Bristow, Miss Stuart told me about you and your husband's plans to settle in Manitoba. I wonder if I might persuade you to consider the town of Galbraith's Crossing instead. We have a teaching position open that we're keen to fill. While I know it would only be for a year or two until your husband could join you, I think we could make it worth your while. We're offering forty dollars a month wages, and we built a schoolhouse only five years ago, so you wouldn't be dealing with too much maintenance and upkeep. We've got between twenty-five and thirty-five children in five or six standards, though the number often changes, depending on new families moving in and whether the older students are needed in the fields.

"Normally our teacher boards with a local woman, but since your husband will be joining you, let me sweeten the deal. We'll throw in ownership of a pretty little piece of land by Shadow Creek on which to build a home. That would put you within easy riding distance of the school, and when your husband arrives, we'll find him a position in town. Unless he has his mind set on homesteading?"

Kicker saw the same amusement in Madelyn's eyes that she was sure was in her own, and she waited to see what her response would be. She was quite taken with Will's persuasiveness and the picture he painted of his town, but she was willing to go wherever Madelyn wished.

"No, Major Bristow has no experience with farming. He's rather set on some sort of administrative work—perhaps in a bank or accounting office, though he also mentioned the possibility of joining the constabulary."

"Excellent. Then we'll have no problem finding him a placement."

Will practically pulsated with excitement, and Kicker covered her smile with her hand as she waited for Madelyn's response.

"Tell me, Mr. MacDiarmid, why should we choose your town over other possibilities?"

"Ma'am, have you ever read *Blackwood's Magazine*?"

Madelyn blinked at the apparent non sequitur, but Will's expression was solemn and she answered him in kind.

"No, Sir, I cannot say I've had that pleasure."

"Well, last year my sister showed me an article titled 'A Lady's Life on a Ranche' written by Mrs. Agnes Skrine. She and her husband settled down by High River, and she's got a mighty pretty way of saying what I feel about Galbraith's Crossing. I never was much for memory work, but this stuck with me. She wrote, 'I like the endless riding over the endless prairie, the winds sweeping the grass, the great silent sunshine, the vast skies and the splendid line of the Rockies, guarding the West.'"

"That's beautiful, Mr. MacDiarmid."

Kicker nodded her agreement.

"Yes, Ma'am, it is. And it describes our land perfectly. Now I'm not going to try and tell you that it's a new Garden of Eden. Summer, we got to fight fires, bugs, twisters, and the occasional hailstorm. Winter, we got to worry about ice and snow, and wolves taking the cattle. It's a land that demands a lot from a man, and a woman, but for those that possess courage and determination and plain old stubbornness, it's a land that rewards them with the opportunity to build a good life. It's a vast land where your neighbour isn't hanging over your shoulder, where you can breathe free and stand close to God."

The two women were silent, contemplating the man's fervent words.

"Now, I know you'll have to talk it over with your husband and all, but if you decide to accept our offer, you just send a telegram care of Will MacDiarmid or Wynne Glenn, Galbraith's Crossing, Alberta, and we'll be waiting for you. What day do you sail?"

"July 24th. We're sailing out of Liverpool on the *Assiniboine*, a Dominion Line steamer."

"I'll be a week behind you, assuming Albert's ready to leave, but I could wire my sister to meet you in my stead."

"Not necessary, Mr. MacDiarmid. We'll be stopping in Manitoba to see an old friend, so if we accept your offer, we wouldn't anticipate arriving in your town until closer to the end of August."

"Just in time to start a new school year after harvest."

Madelyn smiled at his persistence. "Tell me more about this piece of land of which you spoke."

"By Shadow Creek? Well, my family owns it. My sister Wynne and her late husband had planned to build on it at one time because it's so pretty, but you won't pry her and her young son out of the big house now. The creek runs into the Bow River, and we sold the land to the north and south. This is kind of an irregular, sort of pie-shaped section, though—no more than four or five acres, and not practical for homesteading. But you can build a fine home and have enough land for a big garden, as well as run a few head of cows, pigs, and chickens."

"And horses."

Will turned to Kicker with a grin. "Yes, Miss Stuart, and horses. We've got Clydesdales, Percherons, Belgians, Suffolks and Shires in the area, though most homesteaders prefer oxen 'cause they're tougher than horses and better for ploughing. But there's so many mustangs running wild that you can pick one up for no more than fifteen dollars when they bring in a herd, if you don't mind having to break it."

"Fifteen dollars? What would that be in poun's?"

Kicker sensed Madelyn's eyes on her as she asked the question. Between her savings and her final wages, which

Old Thomas had added generously to, she had slightly more than fifteen pounds. She was too frugal to contemplate spending it all, but she was thrilled at the thought that a horse of her own might be within her grasp.

"Roughly three pounds, give or take. You'll find English and American money is used everywhere, so it makes it easier for newcomers."

"My cousin is quite the horsewoman, Mr. MacDiarmid, and I rather enjoy riding myself. It will be something to look forward to."

Will regarded her hopefully. "Are you inclined to take up my offer then, Ma'am?"

"It is certainly worthy of consideration. However, I believe I'd require wages of at least fifty dollars a month, commensurate with my experience, and references."

Will did not hesitate. "Done, but I'll have to see your references."

"Of course. Now, tell me, are you aware of any legal difficulties with establishing land ownership in my name. It is a rather difficult and time consuming process to send papers to my husband for his signature, as his unit is constantly on the move. Naturally, once the Major joined me, we'd get things properly registered in his name."

"I can't see where there'd be any problem, Mrs. Bristow. The Dominion Land Act does specify awarding claims of 160 acres to British males over twenty-one, but I know one woman homesteader who proved up her land just last year, and the deed's free and clear in her name. Mind you, her late husband laid the initial claim, but he didn't make it through their first winter and she's been working the land with her children ever since. Since you're not filing on a homestead, and my family owns the land in question, it should be a relatively straightforward transaction."

"And do you have the authority to offer me both the position and the land? Forgive me for questioning you, Sir, but my husband would be sorely disappointed if I rushed into a decision without confirming these facts."

"I absolutely understand, Ma'am, and the answer is yes, I do have the authority. I don't wish to boast, but my family was the original settlers in the area, and the MacDiarmid name stands for integrity. We are rivaled in size and position only by the Arbuster clan, and they settled around Galbraith more than ten years after my father rode west with Captain Palliser and saw the land of his dreams. My word is good, as is the offer, that I guarantee you. But you should certainly consult with some of the other Canadian delegates if you have any doubts."

Madelyn regarded him steadily and Kicker wondered what she was thinking. She didn't have long to wait.

"Mr. Russell actually spoke very highly of your family in the course of our conversation just a few moments ago. I shall take you at your word, Mr. MacDiarmid. Please have papers drawn up covering the terms of the teaching position, as well as the deed to the land by Shadow Creek of which you spoke, and have them sent to me at 12 Wesley Lane. If we're not in at the time, they may be left with Mrs. Harrington. Leave a returning address with them, and if everything is acceptable, I'll sign and return your copies, along with my references."

"Excellent." Will grinned widely, as if unable to believe his good luck. "12 Wesley Lane. I'll have the papers there within four days. It will be a pleasure to welcome you both to our town. I just know you're going to love it there." He glanced down to where his brother had moved on and was now speaking with an older couple. "If you'll excuse me, I'm going to go tell Albert the good news, then send Wynne a wire."

In his enthusiasm, Will practically bounded down the stairs.

Madelyn and Kicker watched his departure with mutual smiles, before turning quizzical eyes on each other.

"Was that all right, dearest? I didn't sense any reservations from you but I can rescind my agreement if you wish."

"Twere fine. I liked him, an' one place is as good as another, long's I'm with you."

"He certainly did make it sound alluring, did he not?"

"Aye, but he talked about storms and bugs and winter, too. He's not promised us Paradise."

"No, he hasn't. That we shall have to create for ourselves."

"An' we will."

"Yes, dearest, indeed we shall."

It was an easy matter to read the passion in Madelyn's eyes, and Kicker had to restrain herself from moving closer. Aware that she was dangerously close to breaking the ironclad bounds of propriety, she forced herself to speak. "D'you...have you...d'you not wish to stay with your friend Adelaide in Manitoba, then?"

"I do wish to see her as we pass through, but I think it may be fortuitous that we've good prospects awaiting us. With both land and a position, we'll draw less heavily on our funds. When you find work, we'll have added security, and though we may face lean times now and again, we should be securely set."

Kicker thrilled at the way Madelyn spoke of their future, as if nothing and no one would put them asunder, no matter what they encountered.

Madelyn smiled knowingly at her. "And you shall have a horse, dearest."

"Two horses, so we can ride t'gether."

"Two horses, then, but I think our first priority will be raising a house in which to live. If winter is indeed as fierce as Mr. MacDiarmid implies, then we'll want a sound roof over our heads by the time the snow commences."

Kicker cast an anxious look at her companion as she contemplated the thin nature of her own purse. "Can we afford that—a house of our own? I can do a lot of the work myself, but we'll need buildin' supplies. P'rhaps it might be bes' to board with someone for a while."

Madelyn laid a reassuring hand on Kicker's arm, then reluctantly drew it away. "We can afford it, dearest. I want the privacy to be ourselves and though we won't live a lavish life, I'm not without funds."

"Land, horses, a home—'tis more lavish than e'er I thought I'd have. Are you sure you wan'—"

"Don't." Madelyn shook her head at her troubled lover. "What you lack in material wealth, you more than make up for with the love you give so freely—a love like nothing I've ever experienced before. Please don't ever doubt that you are an equal partner in this life we're going to build together. I strongly suspect that your practical knowledge will be of far greater worth to us in that wild, new land than all my poetry and pence."

Kicker accepted her partner's reassurances and pushed her reservations aside, though she knew she hadn't vanquished them. The thought that this incredible creature wanted them to make a life together still awed her. Every morning Kicker woke beside Madelyn, she had to begin anew to believe in them, in their love and in the future this woman offered her. "It'll take us both workin' t'gether to make a go of it, I expect."

"I expect you are absolutely right, Kicker Stuart." Madelyn smiled warmly at her. "Are you ready to leave, dearest? Have you heard enough to have a thorough concept of where we're going?"

"Aye, though doubtless there'll be surprises awaitin' us aroun' e'ery turn."

"I certainly hope so." Madelyn led them down the stairs to the crowded lower level. "What fun would life be without surprises?"

Kicker kept her own counsel on that. She admitted to herself, however, that the previous fortnight had certainly held life-changing surprises, and she would not wish to have missed a one of them.

Will MacDiarmid met them at the base of the stairs. "Mrs. Bristow, Miss Stuart, I'm so glad I caught you before you left. Permit me to introduce my youngest brother, Albert. Albert, it is our great good fortune that these ladies will join our community later this summer, and Mrs. Bristow is going to teach, at least for a year or two."

Albert beamed at them as he held out his hand. "Will told me the good news, and I want to be among the first to welcome you to Galbraith's Crossing. It's a fine town, and I know everyone will be delighted to hear that a teacher's coming."

Kicker accepted Albert's greeting with a smile. Close up, the brothers bore an even more striking resemblance. *No doubt that they're cut from the same bolt of cloth.*

When the pleasantries had been exchanged, Will offered Madelyn an envelope. "This is an informal rendering of what we agreed upon. I'll have the documents delivered as we discussed, but I thought you might wish to have something on paper to refer to when you write your husband. I wrote the name of our hotel in there, too, should you wish to make any further inquiries."

"Thank you, Mr. MacDiarmid. That was very considerate of you. Now, if you gentlemen do not mind, it's been a long day for my cousin and myself, and we're somewhat weary."

"Of course, of course. Albert, go summon a hansom for the ladies. May I walk you to the door?"

Albert darted off into the crowd while Will escorted Madelyn and Kicker at a much more sedate pace. By the time they reached the door, the younger MacDiarmid had a cab waiting, and between the solicitous brothers, they were quickly settled in.

As they pulled away, Kicker glanced through the back window and saw Will slap Albert on the back with a big grin. "They're happy enough, then."

Madelyn followed the direction of her gaze. "I think it will be a good fit for us all. They get a teacher, and we get a home."

"An' if it's less than they claim?"

"Then we'll move on. One of the things I discussed with Mr. Russell is the immense freedom to dictate your own destiny in Canada. I don't claim that there are not rules to be followed, of course. Indeed, I think one of the main attractions is that we'll still enjoy the protection of English law, but from what I gleaned, opportunities abound. He told me several tales of men with virtually nothing who landed on Canadian shores in decades past, and now oversee vast holdings by dint of their own talent and hard work."

"'Tis excitin' to think on."

"It certainly is. A world to shape to our needs, even if we must be circumspect."

"Circum...circ...?"

"Cautious, dearest. We are cousins—devoted to each other unquestioningly, but none must guess the truth that we reserve for behind our door."

"Aye, I know."

"And on that rather serious note, I must ask—do you feel yourself ready to go to my father's house tomorrow? Please speak freely if you do not. You've done tremendously well these last few days, but we can certainly delay for a few more, if need be."

Kicker gave the question serious consideration. Was she ready? She had mastered a more ladylike walk, improved her speech, and taken lessons from both Madelyn and Mrs. Harrington on what to expect and how to behave in the Bristow household. She even had a small wardrobe of respectable clothing, thanks to the talents and kindness of the elderly seamstress.

But would it be enough? Could she mask her feelings well enough to pass muster under the keen eyes of Madelyn's parents? Or would she excite suspicions through an inadvertent look or gesture?

It was time to find out.

"Aye, I'm ready."

CHAPTER 6

KICKER AND MADELYN TOOK ADVANTAGE of the fact that Lil's apprentices were off on Sunday and put their early hours to sensual and quite audible use. It was past mid-morning when they finally descended the stairs to greet their amused hostess.

"I was beginning to wonder if I was going to see you at all today. I'm thinking you'd like some honey tea this morning? You know it's excellent for soothing sore throats."

Kicker turned scarlet, yet from the depth of her embarrassment, she was amused to see that even the usually unflappable Madelyn blushed.

Lil laughed at the pair of them and bustled about setting out a hearty breakfast.

Madelyn tried to demur at the sheer volume of food placed on the table. She protested that they would never be able to do it justice, but Lil shook her head.

"You'll need your strength today, so no backtalk, Maddie. You and your girl eat up."

And as quickly as that, the atmosphere devolved from playful teasing to sorrowful leave taking. Lil tried to conceal her anguish, but there was no mistaking her heavy heart.

Madelyn tried to console her. "I swear, we'll return before we sail, Lil. Remember that we must, at the very least, pick up the papers Will MacDiarmid is sending over."

But Kicker could tell that was of little solace to the former nanny and longtime friend. When they had finished eating and tidied up, Madelyn went upstairs to finish packing while she lingered behind to broach the subject with Lil.

"'Tis sorry I am to cause you such grief. Twas ne'er my intendin'."

Lil smiled wanly. "Though it breaks my heart now, Kicker, please believe that I am truly glad she found you. I'm not long for this world; I know that. And on my last day, as I draw my last breath, I will rejoice that she is finally free and clear of her father's hand. All I ask is that you take good care of her."

Kicker smiled at the echo of the promise Adam had elicited from Madelyn. "I swear." She could feel the intensity of the old woman's appraising gaze.

"She won't always make it easy for you, girl. Many's the time she's jumped before looking and lived to regret it."

"D'you think she's doin' that now?"

"Yes and no. If I know my Maddie, and I do, she plunged full-heartedly into loving you without a thought for the consequences. But that's not necessarily a bad thing, given the nature of the obstacles arrayed against you. Too much contemplation might've given her pause, and that would've been a terrible loss for you both."

Kicker could not disagree with Lil. Madelyn was unquestioningly impetuous, but fortunately had the intelligence and skill and sheer good luck to make her often brash decisions work, at least up until now.

"I see how she looks at you, the tenderness with which she touches you. This adventure you've begun is all happening very fast, but that doesn't make it any less valid. She loves you, Kicker. Of that, I've no doubt at all."

"An' I love her."

"I know you do. The thing is, you'll need to remember and draw on that, no matter what betides. Times will be hard where you're going. There may come a point where she begins to question herself, to wonder what she's gotten you both into. I've seen her do it before. That's when she'll need you most; that's when you'll have to reach deep into your soul and pull up strength enough for both of you. Can you do that? Will you be there for my girl when she needs you most, even if she pushes you away out of fear?"

"Aye. I will."

Lil leaned back in her chair and bestowed a smile on Kicker, who felt like she had passed some test.

"You're a rare one, Kicker. You've got good sense about you, and I doubt not the depth of your love and loyalty for our Maddie. I don't think even I could've chosen better for my devil-may-care girl. Now, off you go. You've still time to...bid each other farewell again."

Kicker ducked her head away from the knowing grin but did as she was instructed, hurrying out of the kitchen and up the stairs to where her lover was supposed to be packing. She swung the door open to reveal a smiling and very naked Madelyn reclining on the bed. Kicker wondered for a second if she had missed some earlier collusion between Madelyn and Lil, but decided not to waste valuable time in pointless reflection.

Their lovemaking was fierce, both of them well aware that this would be the last moment for intimate touches for many days. Despite their activities of the previous night and the early morning, they drove each other on and on until they collapsed from exhaustion. It took a long nap and staunch resolution to finally get them up for good, and even then packing took second place to deep kisses and long, fervent embraces. But finally, sadly, they could not put off their departure any longer.

By late afternoon they bade their weeping hostess an agonized farewell, and with heavy hearts climbed into the carriage.

Kicker worried fretfully at the unfamiliar gold band on her hand. Madelyn had handed it to her without comment after they dressed, and she'd obediently slipped it on. Now, however, as the hansom cab rattled over the cobbled streets of London leading inexorably to the home of Mr. Timothy Bristow, the ring began to feel more like a noose than an ordinary piece of jewelry.

What if...

A hand stole out and covered hers. "We'll get through this, dearest. I swear we will."

Kicker allowed the warmth from the gloved hand to seep into her fingers, which were cold despite the warm afternoon sun. But even that small comfort did nothing to calm the butterflies that fluttered in her belly.

She forced her thoughts from the upcoming ordeal and focused instead on their last few hours at Lil's home, lingering over memories of the pleasure they had given each other.

They were just passing a greensward. Kicker stared out the carriage window and envied the carefree people who enjoyed the gardens, small pond, and paths through the lovely little park. Then something caught her attention. "Madelyn, d'you see that? I ne'er seen the like."

Madelyn glanced past Kicker. "It's a penny-farthing, dearest. I haven't seen one in quite some time. Most riders use bicycles now."

"I seen bicycles 'round the village. I jus' ne'er seen one with such pecul'r wheels." Kicker watched the cyclist avidly and wondered how the woman got up on her vehicle. "Have you ridden one?"

"I did try once many years ago, but I fell off the blasted thing and ruined my dress."

Kicker couldn't take her eyes off the odd contraption with the huge front wheel and tiny rear wheel. "She's not wearin' a dress; she's got pants on."

"Bloomers, actually. Mother told me in her most recent letter that she considers them scandalous, but I think they're very practical for riding and swimming."

Kicker hung out the window as she watched the unusual spectacle, until a tug pulled her back to her seat.

"We're almost there, dearest."

It was like a splash of cold water. Kicker drew back into the seat and unconsciously tried to make herself smaller.

"My dearest love—"

"I'm a'right, Madelyn." The words sounded unconvincing, even to her own ears, and Kicker straightened, determined not to give cause for concern. "Really. Don' let it distress you. I'll be fine."

Madelyn squeezed Kicker's hand tightly then gently withdrew as the carriage rounded another corner. Tension was audible in her voice when she spoke again. "Please remember that I'll be playing a part, dearest. Don't take to heart any of what happens under my father's roof. We mustn't be familiar, but remember that I love you. Oh, please, please, remember that well."

"I will. I promise. An' I won' forget my place, either."

"Your place is beside me, always—as my lover, my partner, and my equal."

The fierceness in Madelyn's half-whispered words warmed Kicker's heart. The fear she had carried since Lil related the dire tale of Timothy Bristow's wrath, and the destruction he had wrought, unexpectedly faded.

Kicker had left behind all that she knew: Adam's unwavering devotion, her parents' often absent-minded love, the rough affection and loyalty of Old Thomas and Cook, even the joy of Banner's whicker as he eagerly greeted her each morning. And she had done it all willingly for love of the woman sitting beside her.

I'll be damned if that mis'ble excuse for a da is gonna cause us grief. Despite her defiant thoughts, Kicker felt like St. George about to brace the dragon, with the wedding ring as a woefully small shield. *But it din't much matter how big and fierce that dragon was. Old George won, din't he?*

The thought amused her, right up until the carriage turned into the cobbled entrance road of a large three-story house. Kicker blinked in amazement. The street across from the park had been lined with elegant, classical buildings, so she had expected that Madelyn's home would be similar, but this house was a testament to excess. From the row of colonnades that fronted the pink stone structure, to the ostentatious carvings and even gargoyles that jutted out from the upper reaches of the house, to the stained glass windows shining from garish gilt frames and the faux Grecian statues dotting the gardens, it all bespoke someone with more money than taste.

"It is rather lurid, isn't it? Father was determined that no one would mistake his domicile for that of any of the lesser divinities. I do believe that Mother hates it, though of course she would never dream of saying so. However, I'm quite convinced that the moment he passes on, her first act will be to put the monstrosity up for sale."

"I'd think her firs' act would be to bury him."

Kicker's dry observation was rewarded with a most unladylike snort from her lover. Madelyn was still chuckling as the carriage pulled to a halt in front of the house.

The driver jumped down, and as he reached to open their door, Madelyn whispered, "Remember to let him bring our trunks in."

Kicker blushed. When they'd prepared to leave Lil's, she'd momentarily forgotten herself and started to carry Madelyn's trunk out to the carriage, until a gentle hand had restrained her.

As they walked up the front steps to the porch, the massive front door swung open. Kicker eyed the somberly uniformed man who stood waiting to greet them. He was an older man, with sparse grey hair, sharp eyes, and thin, pursed lips. Though far too experienced and well-trained to display any condescension, it was clear he was not impressed with the new arrivals.

"Welcome back, Miss Madelyn."

"Thank you, Pruitt." Madelyn's tone was as cool as the butler's as she swept by him into the grand foyer. "Are my mother and father at home?"

"Your father is away on business, Miss, but your mother—"

"Maddie!"

Kicker, who quietly followed Madelyn into the house, looked up the sweeping, mahogany staircase to see an older version of her lover descend the steps, a joyful smile on her face.

"Mother!"

Kicker stood back as Madelyn rushed up the stairs. Her ebullient reunion with her mother was in stark contrast to the butler's frosty reception.

Pruitt directed the carriage driver in the placing of the trunks, paid the man, and firmly closed the door behind him. Then he cleared his throat ostentatiously.

Mother and daughter reluctantly broke their embrace and turned to face him.

"Shall I have your things placed in your room, Miss?"

"Please."

"And this one, Miss? What shall I do with it?"

With evident disdain, he indicated the small, shabby, well-traveled steamer trunk that Lil had bestowed on Kicker the day before. Her meagre possessions took up barely half the trunk and her first instinct had been to decline, but Lil insisted that she didn't need it any longer. It was the thought of bringing something of Lil's with them to their new home that swayed Kicker to acquiesce. However, she was well aware of the stark contrast between it and Madelyn's capacious brass bound leather trunk.

"Oh, Mother, I almost forgot." Madelyn grasped her mother's hand and drew her down the remainder of the stairs. "This is Mrs. Edward Stuart. She's taking passage on the same ship as I, to meet her husband in Canada. He went over last year to set up a homestead for them and is expecting her to join him shortly. Mrs. Stuart's father asked if she might travel with me as far as Manitoba, and I agreed. Do you have a spare room in which we might put her?"

An older woman, who had entered and stood quietly behind Pruitt, spoke up. "Mary's gone to care for her mother this fortnight, Missus. Gertie won't mind sharing her room, if that suits you."

"That is an excellent suggestion, Sylvia. Please put our guest in with Gertie."

Madelyn's mother smiled at Kicker, and the young woman bobbed a small, awkward curtsey. "Thank you for your kin'ness, Missus."

As Kicker followed the housekeeper down the hall, she was keenly aware that she had been instantly assessed and relegated to the servants' quarters, but that was fine with her. In truth, she had worn the oldest, shabbiest dress and bonnet she had, hoping to elicit that very reaction. According to Lil, below stairs was the safest place to be in the Bristow household. Hearing the bright chatter of Madelyn and her mother's conversation fade behind her, Kicker was relieved that the first obstacle had been safely surmounted.

Sylvia was a short, rotund woman about Lil's age, with a mass of white wavy hair escaping from under her neatly starched cap. She led Kicker down a narrow, dark hallway and stopped at the third door, which she pushed open. "Here you go, dearie. Gertie's bed's on the right, so you take the other. Pruitt will have your things delivered to your room. You might as well come down to the kitchen with me. Staff is just taking tea and you can join us."

"Thank you, Missus..."

"Oh, just Sylvia is fine. I been housekeeper to the Bristow's so long that I suspect they don't even remember I have a last name."

Kicker realized that this was Lil's old friend in the household, but she quickly repressed her initial instinct to make known her friendship with the former nanny. Instead, she closed the door and trailed the housekeeper down two hallways to the kitchen. There, under Sylvia's cheerful auspices, Kicker was soon seated with the noisy household staff, a cup of steaming hot tea in one hand and a plate of biscuits in front of the other.

It felt familiar and it felt comfortable, even without Cook's benevolent eyes keeping track and ensuring she got the best bits. As she listened to the lively flow of conversation, Kicker began to relax. For the first time, she believed that she and Madelyn just might get through their stay without incident. Kicker accepted the offer of more tea as her thoughts went to her lover.

I hope she's doing a'right with her ma.

"Goodness, she is a quiet little mouse, isn't she, dear?"

Linked arm in arm, Madelyn accompanied her mother into the sitting room. She quelled the urge to run after Kicker and drag her out of this house, which held so many memories and so many fears. Instead, Madelyn affected the role she knew she had to play. With cool disinterest, she answered her mother. "She appears to be, yes, but that's rather a relief. I couldn't bear to play nursemaid all the way to Canada to someone who never stopped chattering. It would drive me positively insane. At least this girl has the virtue of stillness. According to her father she's not afraid to work, so she may well prove useful on the trip."

Elizabeth gestured her daughter to a seat and sank down in a chair next to her. When a maid appeared at the door, she said, "We will take tea now, Abigail."

The girl disappeared and Elizabeth returned her attention to Madelyn. "I suppose it will be good for you to have some sort of company on your voyage. However did it all come about?"

"Her father's a blacksmith. Now and again he's called to work in the stables at the Academy. I took up riding last year, so I saw him on occasion. I suppose he heard of my travel plans through the domestic grapevine there. He came to me three days before I left and petitioned me to allow his daughter to take passage with me. He's a decent sort, so I agreed to interview the girl. She appeared to be acceptable, so that was that."

"You said her husband is waiting for her?"

"Yes. He departed last year, a mere week after they married. Apparently Kathleen's father insisted that Mr. Stuart establish a home for the two of them before his daughter made the crossing. He's now done so, and sent for his bride."

"Heavens, starting over in a strange place with a husband she barely knows? It must terrify young... Kathleen, was it? Yes, that's right. Well, Kathleen must be very brave to do such a thing."

"You barely knew Father when you married him."

"Yes, but his family was well known to my father, so it was not as if I married a stranger."

Better if you had. Madelyn kept her undiplomatic thought to herself. "Speaking of Father, Pruitt said he is away on business?"

"Yes, he has been gone since the fifth, but we expect him back shortly." Elizabeth got a far away look in her eyes. "It has been remarkably quiet here with him gone." Recalling herself, she smiled brightly at Madelyn. "You are looking forward to seeing him before your departure, I expect."

"Do you really, Mother?"

The conversation ceased temporarily as Abigail returned, carrying a silver tray with all they needed for a hearty tea. They allowed her to serve them without comment. When she left, Elizabeth shot Madelyn a troubled look.

"Can't you let things go, dear? You know how it angers him when you bring up the past, and really, he is a good father. He is a good man, a good husband, too."

The tea tasted bitter and Madelyn set it down. She leaned back in her chair and regarded her mother with pensive compassion. "Do you remember the first time you told me that?"

Elizabeth shook her head in confusion. "Told you what, dear?"

"That he was a good father, a good man, and a good husband. You've used those words to me so many times over the years that I've often wondered whether you were trying to convince me, or yourself."

"I... I don't remember..."

"Father had just whipped me and confined me to my room for breaking his favourite shaving mug. It was more than an hour before you could sneak away to see if I was all right. You found me still crying into my pillows. I was six."

Elizabeth's eyes dropped. "You were so little..."

"And I didn't even break the bloody thing."

"Please, dear, mind your language." Elizabeth sighed deeply. "I know you didn't, Maddie. Roderick came to me later, in tears. He told me how you took the blame and had him hide under the bed so your father wouldn't see him. He was devastated that you had taken his whipping. He wanted to go to your father and confess, but—"

"But what would it have served—two of us beaten bloody instead of one? Besides, it was an accident. Roddy was trying to emulate his hero. He wanted to try shaving because that was what the eminent Timothy Bristow did every morning. He brought the mug and razor in to show me, and when he heard Father coming down the hall, he got scared and dropped it. I didn't have time to pick it all up before Father appeared."

"I'm so sorry, dear. But you bear such resentment, even to this day. That cannot be healthy. Please, can you not let it go? He really is—"

"A good man? I think perhaps your definition of good and mine do not correspond, Mother. In any case, that was neither the first nor last of our confrontations, as you well know."

"Is that why you are going away? Must you run all the way across the Atlantic?"

"I'm not running, Mother; I'm seeking. I want a new life, a new adventure, new challenges, and yes, new people around me."

Elizabeth's eyes were bright with unshed tears. "Your brothers and sisters, all your nieces and nephews—will you not miss them?"

"Very much, but I'll miss you most, Mother—you and Uncle Royce. Nevertheless, I need to make the choices I feel best for my life."

"I'll miss you so much, Maddie. I just do not understand why you cannot choose a nice man and settle down to raise a family here."

"Nice men are hard to find, though I did meet a very interesting Canadian rancher yesterday. In fact, I've accepted a position to teach in the town his family founded, and near which they still live."

"Really?"

Madelyn chuckled at the eagerness in her mother's voice. "I do so hate to disillusion you, but the nice gentleman rancher is already married. However he does have a handsome younger brother who is seeking a wife. Apparently there is a shortage of women in the western half of the country, and wives are keenly sought after."

"Interesting. Though I must admit I am hard pressed to envision you as a rancher's wife."

"I am hard pressed to envision myself as any man's wife, Mother."

Elizabeth carefully set her tea cup down and took Madelyn's hand. "Not all men are as your father is. There are good and gentle men—men like your uncle, men that would make you an excellent husband. Please don't let what has passed between you and your father deny you the life you deserve. I pray every day that you'll know the joy of a family. Do you not long for children of your own?"

"It's not as if I don't have children in my life. In my new school I'll be teaching all ages, from the smallest toddler to the big lads who stay only long enough to learn how to count to ten before they're off to the fields."

"But they will not be your children, dear. It's not the same thing."

"I don't rule it out, Mother. I cannot foresee the future, and there may well be marriage and babies along the way. But I won't wed just anyone and endure a loveless marriage."

The unspoken "as you did" hung in the air between them, and Elizabeth pulled away. She took some time to collect herself, then spoke softly.

"You've always been so different from the others, Maddie. Perhaps it's my fault. When Roderick died, I know I wasn't there to comfort you in the loss you also felt keenly. You must have felt so abandoned. I blame myself for...well, that incident."

"No, Mother. The conflict between Father and me started long before Roddy died, and none of it had anything to do with Charity."

Elizabeth winced at the mention of the forbidden name. "The conflict between you and your father started when you were still in diapers."

Madelyn laughed; she could not disagree. "You see? We were born to combat each other, and there was nothing you could've done about it."

"I should've protected you more."

There was anguish in the soft words. For a second, Madelyn felt the old hurt that her mother had not done so, but she was determined they would not part on that note. "You did your best. Roddy and the others were easier to protect. They, at least, listened to you."

Elizabeth accepted the absolution with grace and gratitude. "You were somewhat headstrong, dear, but I never loved you one whit less for it. I want you to believe that, if nothing else."

"I do. I'll carry that with me, Mother."

Elizabeth rose to her feet and crossed the room to a massive mahogany and copper armoire. She extracted something from a drawer, returned, and handed her daughter an envelope.

Madelyn cocked her head inquiringly.

"I want you to have this to give yourself a good start in Canada. It's part of your grandmother's legacy to me." Elizabeth's chin lifted defiantly. "I kept it hidden these many years. I knew there might come a time when I or one of my children would need it. I believe that time is now."

Madelyn opened the thick envelope and stared in amazement at the number of hundred pound notes within. "Mother, I can't take this."

"Yes, you can, dear. He does not know about it, and he does not need to know. This is between us, and must remain so."

Madelyn suspected she was looking at money her mother had carefully hoarded in order to escape one day. "But what if you need this?"

"I will not."

Elizabeth's voice was grim, and Madelyn wondered what underlay her certainty. She knew her mother was a strong, intelligent woman, but the callous force of her father's personality had always overshadowed the beautiful girl he married when she was merely seventeen. Timothy Bristow brooked no defiance and required no consultation—from his wife, his children, or his business associates. That her mother had kept the inheritance a secret these many years indicated an unanticipated resourcefulness. If this was what had kept her going, if this money was meant to buy her way out of the bleakness that was her marriage, how could Madelyn accept it?

Before she could object again, her mother cut her short. "You have to trust me, Maddie. I don't need this money now, and I want you to have it."

"How is it that you're so sure? You can't know what the future holds. You may well need it in another year or two."

Madelyn was shocked to see the bleakness of her mother's smile.

"Believe me. I shall not. My future security is assured."

"Mother, what have you done?"

"It is not what I have done, Maddie; it is what your father has done. He crossed a line he should not have, and angered someone that has the power to terminate Timothy's vaunted position in London society. The evidence of his indiscretion is now at my disposal, should I require it. Your father is unaware of this, but he is walking a tenuous tightrope at the moment. I will no longer brook his hurting any of my children."

Madelyn stared at her mother and tried to discern the meaning of the incredible statement. All her life, her father had loomed in her mind as an omnipotent figure, but now her mother's calm assurance began to undercut that image.

"Do not gawk, dear; it's rude."

"It's Uncle Royce, isn't it? He's the one who gave you information."

Madelyn always thought that her mother should've married her favourite uncle, a gentle, considerate man—the diametric opposite of his overbearing older brother. She knew there was a deep affection between her uncle and her mother, though she was fairly certain there had never been any impropriety between them.

Royce, who had never married, was one of her father's partners in a business that often dealt with sensitive government matters. Madelyn wondered if Royce had caught his brother in some illegal machinations and, aware of Elizabeth's vulnerable status, had conveyed that knowledge to her as insurance.

"I would rather not say. This whole matter stays strictly between you and me, is that understood?"

"Absolutely. And thank you for the money. I accept with gratitude. It shall certainly make my life easier, though I do have some savings of my own."

"You will probably need those to establish yourself in your new home. Look at that money as your future, in case..."

"In case I never marry?"

"Yes, dear. But I will never stop praying that you do find the right man. No one should go through life alone, and I just know you would have the most beautiful babies."

"As if you do not have enough grandchildren."

Joy returned to Elizabeth's eyes. "There is no such thing, Maddie. And speaking of which, the whole family will gather for dinner on Saturday. Your father will be back by then, and I thought it might be easiest for you to say goodbye to everyone at once. I've no doubt the next few days will be busy ones as you gather everything you need to take with you. I've had Sylvia set aside several boxes of household goods that I think would be appropriate for the establishment of your new home, and I want to go through those with you tomorrow."

"Thank you, Mother, for both the dinner and the house wares. We'll look at them in the morning, shall we? Oh, I wanted to ask you about something else, too."

"What is that, dear?"

"I don't mean to—I mean, this may be a delicate subject and I don't wish to bruise your feelings..."

Elizabeth looked at her daughter curiously as she began to fill two plates from the assortment of pastries and sandwiches. "What is it, dear? Please speak freely."

"Well, I was thinking that Mrs. Stuart and her husband have so little. From what she has told me, Mr. Stuart is quite a slight man, and I wondered if perhaps you might still have some of Roddy's things that you'd be willing to part with?"

Madelyn held her breath as Elizabeth froze. Her brother had died over a decade before, but she doubted that her mother would ever stop grieving for her youngest. Madelyn would not have brought the subject up, but she knew that Kicker would shed the hated dresses as soon as she could. Madelyn hoped to acquire some high quality clothing that she wouldn't mind wearing. Fifteen-year-old Roddy had been about the same size as Kicker, and chances were good that the clothes would fit with few alterations, if her mother could be persuaded to part with them.

Finally Elizabeth passed one of the plates to Madelyn with fingers that trembled just slightly. "I suppose it is time, isn't it? It is very kind of you to think of Mr. Stuart, and I can do no less. I believe Roderick would be pleased to know that his clothes were going to someone less fortunate. We will look them over in the morning too."

Madelyn released the breath she held. She had taken a chance, but it would be worth it to see Kicker outfitted in warm, thick clothes when the cold winds began to blow. It was time to switch to a less sensitive subject.

"Did I mention that I saw several cyclists riding in Brower Park, Mother?"

"Those ridiculous contraptions should be outlawed in the name of public safety. Honestly, whoever invented those deathtraps had no regard for life and limb. I say we should..."

The initial few days flew by for Kicker, and she was surprised to find herself settling into a comfortable routine. On her first day, the Bristow's cook, a formidable woman named Hannah, found out that she knew little about preparing meals. Aghast that the young woman would go to her new husband so ill-prepared, Hannah took it upon herself to instruct Kicker in some of the basics. Kicker was put to work beside Olivia, a shy, pretty kitchen maid who served as Hannah's assistant.

Though Kicker missed Madelyn with a palpable ache, she enjoyed the kitchen routines, and struck up friendships with Olivia and Gertie, her erstwhile roommate.

The only time she saw Madelyn was the morning of the third day, when her lover appeared at the door of the kitchen and summoned her imperiously.

"Mrs. Stuart, a word with you, if I may."

Kicker glanced at Hannah, who jerked her head to indicate that the new kitchen helper should step lively.

Kicker wiped her hands on a towel and went to the door. "Yes, Miss. You wanted t'see me?"

"My mother has very graciously decided to donate some men's clothing for you to take to your husband. You are to come along with me; I'll take you to her."

Kicker nodded obediently and trotted after Madelyn, who did not pause to ensure her order was heeded.

When they turned the corner away from the kitchen and passed her room, Madelyn grabbed Kicker's hand, swung open the door, and pulled her inside.

Madelyn pressed Kicker against the door and kissed her hungrily while her hands roamed feverishly over her lover's breasts. "God, I've missed you so. I think I may go mad before it is time for us to leave. I think of you, sleeping only two floors away, and it's all I can do to force myself to stay in bed."

Kicker didn't waste time protesting, even though she knew they were unwise to take such a chance. She had suffered their separation every bit as much as Madelyn and arousal instantly drove any thoughts of caution from her mind. Aware this interlude would have to be quick, Kicker forewent any subtlety and swiftly tugged the front of Madelyn's dress high enough that she could get her hand underneath.

"Oh, God, oh, God!"

"Shh, love. You don' wan' anyone to hear us."

Madelyn whimpered and leaned her head next to Kicker's as nimble fingers worked past soft cloth to silky flesh. She heeded the admonition, though, and while her breathing was ragged and harsh, and her hips jerked frantically, she let out only a quiet moan when she reached her climax.

Madelyn allowed herself just seconds to recover, then she sank to the floor and pushed up Kicker's skirt. Suitable underwear had not been among the gifts bestowed from Lil's capacious Women's Benevolence Union donation box, and Kicker was suddenly very, very glad about that.

There were no soft touches, no gentle build-up, just a raw hunger that overwhelmed both women. As Kicker willingly spread her legs wider, she tried desperately to abide by her own warning. When the inevitable happened, and happened fast, Kicker was forced to cover her mouth with her forearm and bite down, so intense was the sensation and the urge to scream.

Madelyn withdrew and rose to hold her. They stood in an embrace that lasted longer than their frenzied lovemaking.

Finally, Kicker gently pushed Madelyn away. "We mus' not be missed, love."

"I know. Dearest, Father will return tonight. We dare not do this again, but I had to—"

"An' tis fair grateful I am that you did. Bless'd Jesus, am I ever."

Madelyn laughed softly and Kicker joined her. Then, without a word, they fell back into their distant personaes and left the room.

Kicker had not seen Madelyn since, though her small steamer trunk was now packed full with a young man's clothes—everything from pants, shirts, vests and boots, to another warm winter coat. She'd thanked Mrs. Bristow profusely, and played up how grateful her husband would be for the woman's largess. Kicker had thought the lady uncommonly quiet—quite melancholy even—but was delighted with her unexpected treasure trove.

It was late Friday evening, and the kitchen staff had been hard at work for two days preparing for the Bristows' dinner party on the morrow. Kicker volunteered to be one of the cleanup party. Well past midnight and the last one out of the kitchen, she wearily stumbled to her room. She knew she would be needed early the next day, too.

Kicker threw on a nightshirt and grinned at the snores emanating from Gertie's side of the room. She had grown used to her roommate's nightly chorus and it no longer kept her awake. She sank onto her cot gratefully, sure that she would be asleep within moments.

When something woke Kicker, she was confused—uncertain as to how long she had slept, and puzzled over what had woken her. She lay quietly and listened to the noises of the night, then realized that the sound came from next door—Olivia's room. The shy kitchen maid was one of the few staff with a room of her own, if such a tiny cubbyhole could be called a "room", and Kicker was surprised to hear any noise from that direction.

She was more taken aback when she discerned the nature of the sounds. Growing up in her large family, with space at a premium, such sounds often emanated through the thin walls of her parents' bedroom, but it was a shock to hear them now. Olivia was the last person Kicker thought would entertain midnight company, but she wasn't about to judge her new friend. Instead, she pulled the pillow over her head in an attempt to block out the noise.

However, now awake, Kicker was aware that the salt pork they'd eaten for dinner had left her with a decided thirst. She checked the pitcher and found it bone dry. With a scowl in the direction of the sleeping Gertie, Kicker lit a candle. She left the room and trudged down the hall to the kitchen, idly curious about the identity of Olivia's visitor. Though several of the young men on staff clearly had eyes for the pretty kitchen maid, Kicker had not noticed Olivia return anyone's interest.

Once her thirst was slaked, Kicker started back to her room, only to collide with someone as she rounded the corner to her hallway. Startled, she almost dropped her candle.

"Who are you? What are you doing here?"

The words were snarls, and Kicker instinctively stepped back. She could see the man's face clearly in the candlelight; it was no one she recognized from the staff. She decided she had best play it safe.

"Only Kathleen Stuart, Sir. I jus' finished in the kitchen and was goin' to my room."

There was a silence and Kicker could tell she was being evaluated.

"Get on with it, then." The man turned and stalked away, tugging his suspenders up over his shoulders as he went.

Kicker stared after him for moment and then trotted down the hallway. She stopped at her door, but hearing a sound from Olivia's room, made an instant decision. There were no locks on the doors in the servants' quarters, and she slipped quietly into her friend's room.

Huddled on the bed sobbing, Olivia gasped at her entry, but Kicker quickly reassured her.

"Shhh, 'tis jus' me, Livvie. Are you a'right?"

The girl's voice was barely distinguishable. "Yes. Please..."

Please what? Does she wan' some privacy, then? Should I leave? Instinctively, Kicker rejected those thoughts and went to Olivia's bed. She set the candle down on the floor and took the girl's hands. They were cold so she chafed them.

"Who was he?"

Olivia's head dropped in shame.

"'Tis a'right, Livvie. 'Tis not your fault. We can make this better. I can tell Miss Madelyn for you, if you—"

"No! No, Kathleen, you can't do that. I'd be fired, and my family can't survive without my wages."

"Fired? But—Bless'd Jesus. Was that...?"

"The Master, yes."

"He cannot do that."

"He can do anything he wants." Olivia's voice was bitter, and oddly old. "Everyone knows anyway. I was here when Nancy left. They said he'd gotten her in a family way, but all I know is that Pruitt sent her packing and moved me to this room."

Stunned, Kicker tried to think of something to say, but words of comfort, or suggestions for surcease, failed her. Only one thing occurred to her. "D'you think the Missus knows?"

"I doubt it. They've had separate rooms a floor apart since before I came to work here. It's only common knowledge below stairs, and everyone knows better than to talk about it. Pruitt has ears everywhere, and if he heard any gossip, it would go badly for the one doin' the telling."

"But what if you end up like Nancy? Livvie, you'd be sent packin' anyway. Would it not be better—"

There was such a vehement anger in the girl's coarse laugh that Kicker unconsciously recoiled.

"No need to worry, Kathleen. He's smarter this time. He's figured a way to avoid getting me with child. He says that he should've thought of it sooner. Ain't I the lucky one?" Olivia rolled over, drew her legs to her chest and pulled the covers up. "Go back to your room. Sometimes he returns for seconds, and you don't want to be here if he does."

Stunned, Kicker stumbled to her feet and picked up her candle. It was clear there was nothing she could do for her friend tonight, and she needed to think things through.

Mostly, she needed to decide whether to tell Madelyn.

CHAPTER 7

"WHAT DO YOU MEAN, OLIVIA's sick?" Sylvia glared at Gertie, the unfortunate bearer of the bad tidings. "She can't be sick. We have to start serving dinner in less than an hour."

"Well, she says 'less you want 'er heavin' all over the guests, you'd bes' excuse 'er for t'night." Having delivered the news, Gertie sidled out of range as the housekeeper twisted her apron in exasperation.

"Now what?" Sylvia's gaze roamed the busy kitchen, where every member of the staff appeared to be working double time, until her eyes fell on Kicker, who was quietly washing a tall stack of dishes.

"Kathleen."

It had become second nature over the week to answer to the unfamiliar name and Kicker turned, dripping bowl in hand.

"Have you ever served at a formal dinner?"

Kicker's eyes widened. *Bless'd Jesus! Go in there, where she an' her da will be? At the same time? Bloody hell!* "I...uh, I ne'er..."

"That's all right. Don't you worry, dearie; it's not difficult. You can wear Olivia's uniform. It'll be a bit big for you, but no one will pay any mind. I'll teach you the basics, and you just follow along with Gertie and the others. Do what they do, and try to stay out the way. And for Heaven's sake, don't drop anything. Nothing angers Mr. Bristow more than clumsy servants."

Forty-five minutes later, Kicker found herself second in line behind Gertie, carrying a large tureen of soup and waiting at the dining room entranceway for Pruitt's signal to begin serving. The housekeeper's instructions had been simple enough, and although Olivia's dress fit her like a sack, that didn't bother Kicker either. She only wished she'd had time to warn Madelyn of her new role. Madelyn's aim had been to keep Kicker and the Bristows far apart, and though her lover was quick on her feet, the newly minted table servant worried about Madelyn's initial reaction when she entered the hall.

Kicker decided there was little to be done about it. She would simply have to perform her unfamiliar duties as competently as possible. While the servants waited, she studied the large group of people gathered around the table. Though she knew little of Madelyn's family, she tried to assign names to the siblings, their spouses, and the oldest of the nieces and nephews.

Kicker thought she was doing well until she came to an older man seated between Madelyn and Mrs. Bristow. Both women looked at the man with undisguised affection and laughed at something he'd just said.

"Gertie, who's the bloke nex' to Missus Bristow?"

"Tis Sir Royce, the Master's younger brother."

Pruitt frowned at the unauthorized whispers, and Gertie fell silent.

Kicker ignored the butler's glare, well aware that she would soon be out of this house and that he had no real authority over her, no matter what he seemed to think. Instead she studied the man who was so clearly a favourite of Madelyn and her mother.

Sir Royce was a lean, balding man, with a homely, albeit kind face, and eyes that twinkled in amusement as he chuckled at one of his niece's ripostes.

Kicker's gaze moved between Royce and Timothy Bristow, amazed that they were brothers. The man she had encountered in the hallway the night before sat imperiously at the head of the table. The fine cut of his dinner jacket could not disguise the corpulent body beneath. A starched white collar cut deeply into the excess flesh of his thick neck, which segued into his jowls with little break. His face was an unnatural shade of red under a full head of white hair. He was handsome in a coarse fashion, and Kicker judged that he had been much the more attractive of the brothers in his youth. But whereas Royce exuded a calm, gentle bearing, Timothy projected domineering arrogance. On either side of him, his sons, though much less substantial in bulk, were clearly cut from the same cloth, minus the haughty air.

She watched as one of the men hastened to refill Mr. Bristow's glass. It struck her that neither son spoke unless directly addressed, though both were glued to every word their father said. They even ignored their wives if one of the bejeweled women beside them dared to interrupt.

Lost in contemplation, Kicker missed Timothy Bristow's signal to Pruitt to begin serving. It was only when the woman behind her trod on her heels that she realized Gertie had stepped out into the dining room. Kicker tried to remember to glide, while not spilling the soup. She quickly caught up with the other woman and fell into line two dutiful steps behind. Her assignment was to carry the tureen as Gertie served each guest, beginning with the Master, and Kicker was determined not to disgrace herself.

Kicker concentrated so diligently on being in the right position for Gertie to smoothly fill a bowl and replace it on the table that she forgot to look at Madelyn. It was only as they drew near the far end of the table that she dared steal a glance. She was acknowledged by a slightly lifted eyebrow and an almost imperceptible frown, but Kicker maintained her stoic façade.

When they reached Mrs. Bristow, at the far end of the table, the Mistress of the house smiled at the servants.

"How very sweet of you to fill in for Olivia, Mrs. Stuart. Sylvia tells me that you have been a tremendous help this week in Mary's absence, and we certainly appreciate it."

"Thank you, Missus," Kicker mumbled. She kept her eyes lowered as she followed Gertie to the other side of the table, where Sir Royce thanked them politely as he accepted his bowl. Madelyn gave a bare nod, and Kicker worried for an instant that she was angry at her unexpected appearance. Though she wished she could whisper an explanation, she pushed her concerns aside for the moment and concentrated on her task.

When they reached the last guest and she hadn't spilled the soup, tripped over anyone's feet—including her own, or in any way drawn the Master's wrath, Kicker felt as if she had won a victory of sorts.

As they exited the dining room, Kicker heaved a big sigh of relief, but there was no time to relax. She and Gertie hurried back to the kitchen, and returned in short order with the trays they would need to remove the soup dishes as two more staff served the next course. That went on all evening, until finally the family departed the dining room and the entire staff set to work cleaning up.

Kicker had been much too busy to do more than cast an occasional glance Madelyn's way. Her lover, after the initial unspoken acknowledgement, took no further note of the novice servant.

From the disjointed bits of conversation that Kicker overheard, she gathered that Madelyn was entertaining her mother, uncle, and sisters with anecdotes of her days at the Grindleshire Academy, though there apparently had been no mention of Merrick and his proposal.

As she stacked dirty dishes and folded soiled linens for laundering, Kicker longed for a chance to speak with Madelyn privately. She had been unable to decide whether to reveal Timothy Bristow's perfidious behaviour to her. Kicker had argued with herself though a near sleepless night, but she was sure that if she could just talk things over in general terms with Madelyn, she would be able to decide.

The sounds which emanated from behind the big glass doors separating the dining room from the drawing room, indicated that the Bristow family party would not end soon. There would be no opportunity for a chance meeting in a quiet hallway.

Resigned to carrying her secret at least one more night, Kicker picked up a heavily loaded tray and wearily followed

Gertie back to the kitchen as she wondered how long it would be before she could finally retire.

Madelyn watched Kicker's departure through the glass doors, dismayed by how tired she looked. It was never her intention that her lover should end up as a part of the Bristow domestic staff during their brief stay. She had been startled by Kicker's appearance in the dining room that evening. Since Madelyn had effectively established her disinterest in the woman, however, it was much too late to raise a fuss or insist that their houseguest be treated as such.

Madelyn was momentarily worried when she overheard her father question Pruitt about the new member of the kitchen staff the morning after he returned from his business trip. However, he appeared satisfied when he learned that she was temporary and would depart shortly. Her father had demanded background information on his daughter's traveling companion, but again, seemed to accept Madelyn and Elizabeth's explanations at face value. His grunt was as much as she could expect in the way of approval, but he apparently dismissed her travelling companion as a matter of no import.

"You are really looking very well these days, my dear. You have always been my loveliest relative—well, you and your mother, of course, but I am not sure I have ever seen you so...robust."

Madelyn turned away from the doors and smiled at Royce. "It must be all the time I've spent in the countryside, Uncle. I quite enjoyed riding, and I'm looking forward to owning my own mount once I get established in Canada."

Royce tucked her hand into the crook of his arm and gently drew her out of the crowd to a quiet corner, where he seated her on a sofa and took the chair at right angles to her.

"I think it must be more than that, Maddie. I do believe this proposed adventure of yours has invigorated you. Your eyes sparkle and your whole face lights up when you speak of your forthcoming journey. Do you feel no trepidation at all?"

She leaned forward and took his hand. "None. I think perhaps I should have done this long ago."

Royce glanced reflexively across the room to where his brother was bullying one of the Bristow sons-in-law. He turned back to his niece with a sad smile. "Perhaps you are right. Your mother will miss you terribly, though. I shall miss you, too, but I admire your courage. If I were young, I might be tempted to join you, but as I am practically in my dotage, I shall simply enjoy your adventure from afar. You will write often, will you not?"

"Of course." Madelyn was about to go on when she realized she had lost her uncle's attention. He was looking past her shoulder with a warm smile that could only mean one thing.

"There you are, my dear." Elizabeth approached and smiled at her daughter and brother-in-law. "I wondered where you'd gotten to."

Madelyn suppressed a knowing grin and made a space for her mother, manoeuvring so that Elizabeth sat closest to Royce.

"Did you enjoy the dinner, Maddie?"

"It was wonderful, Mother. Your dinners always are."

"That's absolutely true, Elizabeth. Do you remember your reception to welcome Sir Rycroft home from his African expedition in '82? That one established your reputation, my dear. You set the standard, and few have ever equalled you."

Elizabeth laughed and shook her head at Royce. Madelyn sat back and enjoyed their mock argument as she took the opportunity to observe them. They, along with Lil, had redeemed her youth with their love, kindness, and—when disaster struck—their understanding and compassion. She could tell that they communicated in the affectionate shorthand usually reserved for longtime lovers, and Madelyn wondered briefly if they had ever crossed that line. She certainly would not have blamed either of them, though it was not something she wished to dwell on.

It was only hours later, when her sister Sarah came to bid her goodnight, that Madelyn realized she had been so lost in conversation with her mother and uncle that she had not noticed the party drawing to a close. Younger children and governesses were collected from the third floor nursery, carriages were summoned to convey guests home, farewells were made and tears were shed.

Madelyn was to depart in two days, and she was well aware that it would be years before she saw her sisters and brothers again, if ever she did. When the last sibling waved goodbye, Madelyn stood tearfully in her mother's embrace as Royce awkwardly patted her shoulder.

A looming presence joined them. "Oh, for Christ's sake, buck up, girl. It was your decision to flee to some Godforsaken land, so don't go blubbering about it now."

Madelyn glared at her father, who staggered as he tilted his head back and drained yet another snifter of brandy. Before she could snap back the retort that sprang to mind, her mother steered her away and into the lower parlour.

"Come now, dear. Why don't we finish the evening with some tea, then it's off to bed for a good night's sleep."

Timothy, however, had other ideas, and he followed the women into the room. A worried looking Royce tried to stop him, but he contemptuously shook off his brother's arm.

"Pruitt!"

The butler obediently appeared at Timothy's elbow with a full crystal decanter on a silver tray. He silently refilled the Master's empty glass.

"Leave it here."

Elizabeth, sat as far from her husband as she could and spoke at the same time. "Pruitt, we will take tea."

"Yes, Madam. I will return promptly."

Pruitt set the decanter on a side table and backed out of the room. Madelyn, still seething, followed her mother's lead in taking a seat on the far side of the room. She noticed that her uncle took up a position between his brother and the women.

"Don't you have to get home, Sir Royce?" Timothy sneered at his brother, who remained calm.

"In a while. I thought I would join the ladies for tea first."

"Now why doesn't that surprise me, brother Sir?"

Oh, dear God. He is on about that again. Madelyn could feel her mother stiffen beside her, and didn't doubt that their thoughts ran in the same vein. Timothy had never stopped resenting his younger brother for being awarded a knighthood for distinguished diplomatic service to the Queen, twenty years earlier.

When Royce later left the Queen's service without explanation and joined his brother in business, Timothy lost no occasion to needle him about his apparent comedown. He well knew, however, and was deeply aggrieved that his knighted brother wielded much more influence and moved in social circles considerably higher than his own.

Madelyn and Elizabeth exchanged glances. Timothy was a mean drunk, and while Royce was more than capable of defending himself, the situation had the potential to detonate quickly.

Heeding her mother's slight nod, Madelyn stood and addressed her uncle. "On second thought, I think I'll say goodnight for now. I hope to see you again before I leave."

Royce rose to his feet, took Madelyn's hands and kissed her cheek. "I will most certainly be there to see you off, even if I don't make it over before, my dear."

"What's the rush, Madelyn? One of the serving girls waiting in your bed?"

Madelyn whirled to face her father, who regarded her smugly. Feeling her uncle's hands squeeze hers, she choked back her initial response. "That does not warrant the dignity of an answer, Father. Perhaps you might think of retiring soon yourself. It's been a long night."

"What, and leave these two alone?" Timothy's slurred voice was mocking, and he leaned against the fireplace mantel as if it alone was holding him erect. "They would be so lonely without me, dear daughter." He pinned an ashen Elizabeth with a bleary stare. "Wouldn't you, dear wife?"

Elizabeth stood with consummate dignity. "If you will excuse us, Royce, Madelyn and I are retiring."

"Of course. Please sleep well."

"Oh, she'll sleep well. I'll make sure of that, brother dear."

Royce scowled at his drunken sibling. "That is more than enough, Timothy. I will not have you—"

"You won't have me what? You have no rights in this house, Sir Royce. You are merely an invited guest, who can be disinvited any damned time I wish. And by the way—she's *my* wife. You would do well to remember that."

Madelyn stood frozen at the abrupt fusillade of hostility as she vacillated between the urge to flee and the need to protect her mother. Elizabeth, too, stopped. She stood next to her daughter and glared at her boorish husband.

Timothy was either unaware or uncaring that he was the focus of three sets of angry eyes. In truth, as he smirked at his family, he seemed to enjoy the tableau his innuendo-fraught words had provoked.

"Timothy, there is no call for this. Why don't you and I share a nightcap while the ladies take themselves to bed, then it will be time for me to leave, as well."

The Master of the house sneered at Royce's obvious attempt to defuse the situation. "The time for you to leave, brother dear, is right now. Your presence is neither required, nor desired. I have business with my family. Pruitt!"

Instinctively, Madelyn stepped forward and faced her father head on. "You have no right to speak to Uncle—"

"Silence. I have every right. This is my house, my family, and my wife—not his!"

Stunned, Madelyn realized for the first time how deeply jealous her father was of his brother.

"You all think I don't see how you dote on His Lordship's every word? How you rush to welcome him into my house, and hang on him like moss from a tree? Pruitt! Where the hell are you, man?" Splashing more brandy into his glass, Timothy glared at the door as the butler hurried into the room. "My brother is leaving. Send for his carriage."

"Of course, Sir. Right away."

Madelyn glanced at her mother and saw her concern echoed in Elizabeth's eyes.

"Tell me, brother dear, while I was away, did you drop over to pay your respects? And once installed in my house, did you even bother to go home? Or did you just bed down with my wife for the night, taking my place between her legs?"

"That is enough!"

Madelyn had never seen her uncle so furious, and for a moment she thought he was going to strike his brother.

"You will not insult your wife, Sir! She has done nothing to deserve such grave calumny, and I insist you withdraw your insinuation."

Timothy laughed maliciously. He clearly enjoyed the confrontation he'd engendered. He licked his lips and cocked his half-empty glass at Madelyn. "Perhaps you would rather we conversed about my daughter, then. Shall we discuss this tribade that I begot?" He stopped and tapped a forefinger against his lips mockingly. "Or did I? Elizabeth, do please tell us. Is she my spawn? I've not seen anything of me in her, but both she and your darling Roderick have my brother's eyes; wouldn't you agree?"

Pruitt reappeared at the door, but none of the Bristows paid him any heed until Elizabeth said stiffly, "That will be all for tonight, Pruitt. You may retire."

With a quick glance at Timothy, Pruitt nodded and began to withdraw, halting when the Master of the house bellowed at him.

"Damn it, man! Is my brother's carriage here or not?"

"Yes, Sir. It is waiting out front."

"Then get thee gone, brother dear. There's nothing more for you here."

"Dismiss the driver, Pruitt." Royce's voice was calm, but Madelyn could tell he was livid. "I'll walk home later."

Pruitt stopped, obviously in a quandary over whose orders to follow.

Timothy opened his mouth to say something but Elizabeth cut him off. "That is enough. This all ends now, tonight." She turned and faced Pruitt calmly. "You are dismissed, permanently. You are to be out of this house by breakfast tomorrow. I will no longer tolerate you bullying my staff or toadying to my husband."

"What the bloody hell!" Timothy straightened as best he could in his state and stared at his wife in outrage.

Madelyn was almost as shocked as her father. Though technically her mother did run the household staff, everyone knew that Pruitt was an extension of her father's will. As such, he was untouchable, no matter how often he encroached on Elizabeth's authority.

Elizabeth dismissed the ashen-faced butler, who belatedly stumbled away after one beseeching glance at his sputtering, dumbfounded master. Elizabeth returned her attention to her husband. She was icily calm, though Madelyn trembled at both her father's accusatory insults and the dramatic turn of events.

"June fourth, southeast of Calais at the Chateau of the Marquis de Girondon, you met secretly with representatives of General Count von Schlieffen, Chief of the German General Staff. In exchange for a substantial payment, you agreed to deliver certain papers pertaining to the aftermath of the Fashoda crisis and the state of Anglo-French relations. You thought to acquire those papers through your affair with Eleanor, wife of Lord Lansdowne's chief of staff."

Madelyn's head reeled. She recognized the name of Lansdowne, the former Viceroy of India and current War Secretary under the Salisbury government. And she knew that the Fashoda crisis in the Sudan the previous fall had imperiled the already shaky state of relations between England and France. From what her mother said, it sounded as if her father had benefitted financially from activities perilously close to treason. It was obvious from the way that Timothy's florid complexion paled, that he was stunned that his actions had been discovered.

"You are such a fool, Timothy. Long before that meeting, and in fact as soon as Eleanor realized your true intentions, she confessed all to her husband and begged for his forgiveness. She may be a trollop, but she is a loyal Englishwoman. He forgave her, but he will never forgive you. You were followed by agents of the War Department from that day on."

Royce picked up the narrative as Timothy sank into the nearest chair and gaped at his accusers. "Luckily, Lansdowne's intermediary approached me first, before the extent of your perfidy became public knowledge. Because of my long personal history with His Lordship, I was able to protect Bristow Brothers Ltd., and your family, from the potential consequences. But Timothy, the sword hanging over your head is hanging by the proverbial thread; the threat has not been removed. Should you put the slightest foot wrong henceforth, I shall, without qualm, facilitate the unleashing of Lansdowne's wrath upon your head."

"You would not dare..."

"I would. And believe me, Timothy, I do not speak only of future political missteps. You have tyrannized all those about you for the last time."

Madelyn stared in fascination and watched the stark unmaking of a bully as her father quailed before his brother and his wife. Timothy threw back the last of his brandy and refilled his glass with a shaky hand before he spoke.

"The Germans..."

"Will no doubt be quite angry when you fail to deliver on your end of the bargain, but that is not our concern."

"They will want their money back."

"I rather imagine they will," Royce agreed neutrally.

"I don't have it anymore. I used it to meet certain... debts." There was panic in Timothy's voice. "I will have to secure a loan."

It was Elizabeth's turn to speak. "Only if you can do so without involving our home or the business. You no longer have authority over either. With the knowledge and approval of the board of directors, Royce has already taken steps to limit the company's liability. Further, you will sign the documents tonight transferring full title of this house to me."

"Goddamn it! Would you throw me to the wolves, woman? Do you have any idea what could happen?"

Madelyn saw the sadness in her mother's eyes, but nothing in her expression or posture hinted at any possibility of relenting. "It did not need to be like this, Timothy. There was a time when you were well satisfied with the bounty with which we were blessed, and would never have considered such actions as those that have laid you low. You brought this upon your own head, but I will not allow you to disgrace our family. If you go down, you go down alone. I will divorce you with ample cause, and have the children sever their relations with you, as well."

"And no doubt marry Royce the moment the decree is final."

Elizabeth ignored her husband's bitter charge and took Madelyn's arm. "Come along, dear. It's time for bed."

Madelyn allowed herself to be led out of the room. She stopped when her mother paused outside of the doors. Without turning around, Elizabeth said clearly, "And from this moment on, all bedrooms in this household, without exception, are now and forever off limits to you, Timothy. I trust that is perfectly understood."

Without waiting for an answer, Elizabeth regally mounted the stairs. As Madelyn followed in her mother's wake, she heard Royce close the parlour doors, leaving him alone with his brother. For one brief moment she felt a twinge of pity for her father's devastation, then it was gone and she felt nothing—no anger, no bitterness, no fear—nothing. Timothy Bristow was no longer relevant to her life.

The kitchen was in an uproar. Pruitt had been seen leaving early that morning with all of his possessions, and Sylvia was summoned to a meeting with Mrs. Bristow. Rumours and idle speculation flew thick and fast as the staff gathered to discuss the possibilities and what the implications would be for them.

"I 'eard as 'ow 'e got caught pinchin' the silv'r."

"Pruitt? No bloody way. That prig's ne'er so much as pinched a girl, let alone the silv'r."

"Mebbe the Mast'r got tired of Pruitt bein' stuck to his arse and finally wiped 'im off."

Roars of laughter greeted that theory, and Kicker didn't try to suppress her smile. She had no idea what was actually going on, but it was clear that the unpopular butler would not be missed.

"'Allo, d'ya think Miss Madelyn had a hand in it? She and Pruitt have hated each other for years."

Nods and murmurs of agreement swept the staff.

"Well, good on 'er if she finally done 'im in. 'E deserv'd it, ta bluidy bastid."

"That will be enough, people." Sylvia entered the kitchen and swept her excited staff with a stern gaze. "I want you to listen to me, and then get back to your duties. Am I understood?"

Everyone immediately quieted down and stood listening eagerly.

"As many of you have speculated, Pruitt has been dismissed from service."

A muted cheer went up and Sylvia indulged the celebration briefly. "I'm not at liberty to tell you why, but suffice it to say he was let go with references."

Even Kicker knew that indicated the man at least had not been dismissed in disgrace.

"I am told that a new butler will be installed shortly, but until that time, I will be responsible for the staff. Ethan, you're to go at once to see Mrs. Bristow. She'll have directions for you, as you are to fill in for Pruitt as butler until further notice. Come back and talk to me when you're done."

The thin, quiet footman nodded briefly and left the room.

"All right then, back to work, and keep the idle chatter to a minimum."

The staff scattered and Sylvia walked over to Kicker, shaking her head in amusement. "As if that will have any effect. They'll be gossiping on about this for months, I'm afraid." She smiled and handed her an envelope. "Mrs. Bristow asked me to give you this. It's your wages for a week's work."

Startled, Kicker protested, "But I—"

"Now, now. I told her how hard you've worked this week, and she said you were to be given what Mary would've earned, plus a wee bit extra since you'd been pressed into duty." Sylvia held up her hand when Kicker tried to return the envelope. "No, dear. You'll need that where you're going, and you really did earn it. I don't know what we'd have done without you, especially with Olivia out sick. Thank heavens Mary returns tomorrow night."

The housekeeper turned to leave just as Madelyn appeared at the door. "Ah, Miss, were you looking for me?"

"Actually, Sylvia, if Mrs. Stuart is free for a few minutes, I have some travel instructions for her."

"Of course, Miss." Sylvia gestured Kicker forward, then she caught sight of two of the housemaids halfway down the hallway with their heads together, giggling. "Gertie! Edith! What did I just tell you?" Sylvia strode off and left Madelyn and Kicker to a semi-quiet corner of the kitchen.

With a quick glance around to ensure there were no eavesdroppers, Kicker asked softly, "What's goin' on?"

"I guess you could call it a palace coup, dearest, but don't worry—everything is going to be fine."

"You're a'right? Your ma, too?"

"I am, as is Mother. I'll tell you about it later, but for now, I need you to get away after breakfast tomorrow. Can you do that?"

"Aye."

"Meet me at Brower Park—where we saw the penny-farthing." Kicker nodded her understanding. "I told Mother I'll need the carriage to run some errands. I'll pick you up at the south end of the park about ten and we'll spend a few hours with Lil. Does that sound acceptable?"

Kicker straightened. "Aye, Miss. An' what time would the train be departin' on Tuesday mornin'?"

With instant understanding, Madelyn replied coolly as Sylvia swept back into the room past them. "Seven a.m. You're to have your things in the foyer and be dressed and ready to leave by five-thirty, no later. Is that clear?"

"I understan' the instructions, Miss. I'll be on time. An' thank you."

Kicker saw a ghost of a smile on Madelyn's lips, and knew she had received her message. She would be waiting in the park at ten the next morning.

Madelyn left the kitchen and Kicker turned to scrub the huge cutting block that she had been working on before all the pandemonium over Pruitt's departure began. It struck her that in less than two days they would be on a train traveling to the coast. And within three days, they would steam out to sea, leaving behind everything familiar.

For a brief instant she was overwhelmed with fear—of leaving the known, sailing into the unknown, and of the magnitude of settling in a vast, harsh new land. There were so many unanswered questions, so many chances for failure...

"An' for success an' happiness, so quit your whingin', you feckless whelp."

"Did you say something, Kathleen?"

Kicker raised her head from her furious scrubbing and smiled at the cook. "No, Hannah. Jus' talkin' to m'self."

"Phttt. You don't want to be doing that, girl. I had an uncle once talked a blue streak to hisself. Ended up in Woodshall Sanatorium before he was forty. Now come on over here and let me see if you remember what I taught you about making biscuits."

Kicker gratefully abandoned the cutting block and joined Hannah for one last lesson. She allowed the cook's cheerful, non-stop guidance to allay her worries, at least for the moment.

CHAPTER 8

THE FINAL MORNING OF THEIR stay, Elizabeth, Madelyn, and Kicker left the house early; Timothy Bristow was conspicuous by his absence. Since Madelyn spent part of their all too few final hours together briefing her and Lil on all that had transpired the night of the family gathering, Kicker was not surprised that Bristow didn't show up to bid his daughter farewell. She was certain that no one, including Madelyn, would miss him.

Their feelings were still raw from saying good-bye to Lil the evening before when Madelyn and Kicker faced another emotional leave taking at the train station. They'd barely arrived at the station when siblings and in-laws, nieces and nephews descended on them from a multitude of cabs and carriages. Even Madelyn's brothers, Percy and Edgar, made an appearance.

The mood was sombre and subdued as Madelyn stood between Sir Royce and her mother, accepting hugs and kisses and earnestly promising to write.

Eighteen-year-old Beatrice, Madelyn's newly engaged niece, stepped forward. "I really was counting on you being at my wedding, Aunt Maddie. Won't you please reconsider? Our parties are never as good when you're not there and I cannot bear to think you'll never join us again—that my children will never know their great-aunt."

Confused by Beatrice's words, Margaret, the youngest of the Bristow offspring, tugged on her aunt's skirts. "You will be home for my birthday, won't you, Auntie Maddie?"

Madelyn knelt down to the seven-year-old's level and took her hand. "I'm afraid not, sweetheart. Canada is a very, very, long way off, and I'm not sure if...when I will be back."

"But you have to come back." The child's eyes welled with tears. "When you went away to that school, you promised that you'd always come back for my birthday. You promised."

Madelyn glanced helplessly at her sister who had moved to stroke her daughter's hair. There was no help from that quarter, however, as Sarah too had begun to cry quietly.

"Sweetie...sometimes things happen and adults have to change their plans, even break their promises, though it makes them very sad to do so. Sometimes they must go far, far away—"

"But you promised." Margaret stopped short and stared at her aunt as if stunned by a sudden realization. "Are you never coming back?"

It seemed as if the whole family collectively held their breath, waiting for her reply. Kicker watched Madelyn struggle for a comforting answer.

"Auntie Maddie," Margaret's gaze dropped toward the ground, and when she looked up again, her eyes were filled with hurt and tears overflowed, "don't you love us anymore?"

Kicker felt a lump rise in her own throat. She doubted that Madelyn would be able to respond to the child's plaintive question.

Madelyn gathered Margaret in an embrace and buried her face in the girl's hair.

Edgar's son Harry spoke up seriously. "You'll be all alone, thousands and thousands of miles away. Who will you celebrate Yuletide with, Aunt Maddie?"

Ten-year-old Peter wheedled, "Why can't you stay, Aunt Maddie? You promised you would teach me to row this summer." Adding weight to his plea, he said solemnly, "There are wild Indians in Canada, you know. They might scalp you, and we would never see you, ever again. You would end up buried in a strange land, so far from home that none of us could ever visit your grave."

Margaret's renewed sobbing was heart wrenching and Sarah lifted her daughter into her arms.

Madelyn stepped forward and gently caressed her niece's face. "Please understand." She looked pleadingly at each family member. "I hate the thought of leaving you all, but I simply have to go."

Harry's eyes narrowed in anger. "It's Grandpa, isn't it?" He was instantly hushed by his nervous father. Edgar automatically glanced around, as if expecting the baleful patriarch to appear from thin air.

Elizabeth, who had witnessed her grandchildren's heartbreak, spoke up at last. "Listen to me, all of you. Maddie knows that we love her, that we'll miss her terribly, and that she'll constantly be in our hearts and in our prayers. None of us wants to see her go, but as this is something she feels she must do, I know that we don't want to make it more difficult for her. You must give her a chance. Perhaps she may find it not to her liking, and come home." Elizabeth's voice broke, but she took a deep breath and managed a wan smile. "But first, she must make this journey. We should all regard it as a wonderful adventure, and wish her Godspeed."

Kicker heard the wistful undertones and knew that Elizabeth Bristow, at least, had not given up hope of her prodigal daughter's return.

With forced bravery, Clara, Madelyn's middle sister, stepped forward and gave her a hug. "We'll be fine, Maddie. Travel well, and write as soon as you arrive. None of us will sleep truly soundly this next month until we hear that you're safely at your destination."

Madelyn looked at her sister gratefully. "Thank you, Clara. From what I understand, it takes only three weeks for a letter to travel the distance that will lie between us. I swear that I'll write every week, once we...once I get settled in."

Standing well back from the mass of Bristows, young and old, Kicker saw Sir Royce and Elizabeth exchange glances as Madelyn bent to embrace Harry, who found that eleven was not too old to cry after all. Kicker would have given anything to know what they were thinking at that moment. However, as neither so much as glanced her way, she had little from which to divine their thoughts.

It in no way affected the warmth of their behaviour towards Madelyn. Elizabeth kept one arm around her daughter's waist and Royce frequently patted his niece's arm, as if comforting, and seeking comfort, from her presence.

"All aboard for Northampton, Coventry, Birmingham aaaaannnd Liverpool."

Madelyn turned and fell into her mother's arms as her sisters crowded around, apparently convinced that this was the last time they would ever hold one another.

Weeping children picked up their parents' distress and stood howling like a pack of baby wolves while their teenaged siblings looked alternately distressed and embarrassed.

Percy and Edgar stood back with their clearly discomfited brothers-in-law and tried to pretend that they were barely affected—a façade shattered when Percy pulled out a large handkerchief and blew his nose so loudly that it competed in volume with the sound of the train's warning whistle.

It was Sir Royce who finally loosened Elizabeth's embrace and coaxed Madelyn away from her anguished mother and sisters.

Kicker, who had fiercely fought every instinct to go forward and comfort Madelyn, was grateful for the man's innate sensitivity as he led his niece to the door of their carriage. She was certain there was no way Madelyn could have seen her way safely across the platform through her tears.

Kicker mounted the stairs, and turned to watch as Madelyn stopped and spun to face her family. Waving, she called, "May God watch over you. I love you all so!"

Seeing the sorrow on Elizabeth's face, Kicker feared that the distraught woman might collapse. Obviously the same thing occurred to Madelyn's sisters as they gathered around to support their mother.

Madelyn flung her arms around Royce and buried her head against his chest as she wept.

He glanced over her head at Kicker, gave her a stern look, and mouthed, "Look after her."

Kicker nodded solemnly. He may only have meant on the upcoming journey across the ocean, but she took it as one more promise she made to care for Madelyn, promises that she honoured as she would vows sworn before the Queen.

"I can hardly bear to let you go, sweet Maddie, but your train is departing." Royce kissed her forehead and assisted her up the stairs.

Madelyn stood beside Kicker and looked back at him. "Promise me you'll look out for Mother, for all of them?"

"I swear it, Maddie. I will never let him hurt her—hurt any of them again, of that you may have no doubt."

"I love you, Uncle."

Royce's eyes, twins of Madelyn's own, teared up again. "I love you too, my dear. You are the daughter Fate chose not to give me, and I am so grateful to have had you in my life. If you need anything...anything at all, you write me. Promise you will?"

As Madelyn nodded, the train whistle sounded again and the carriage jerked. When the train began to move, Royce walked alongside, obviously unable to relinquish the last sight of his niece. As the train picked up speed, he jogged alongside. Madelyn reached out, and they touched hands briefly just as the platform ended and she moved beyond reach.

Kicker trailed her weeping lover into the car and took a seat opposite her in the first available compartment. It tugged at her heart to see how Madelyn twisted in her seat to try and keep her family in view as long as possible.

An hour northwest of London, an occasional tear still rolled down Madelyn's cheeks to be caught and absorbed with an already sodden lace handkerchief. Kicker watched her closely, unsure what might comfort her, but Madelyn shook her head and gave her a pallid smile.

"Forgive me for being so maudlin, dearest. I promise I'll do better."

"Tis a'right. I do know how you feel."

"But you were so much braver—and with so little time to bid your family farewell, too. Here I've had days and days, and I still weep like a babe in arms."

Lost in thought, Kicker looked out the window at the passing scenery, then back at Madelyn. "P'rhaps twas easier my way—less time for thinkin', less time for grievin'."

Madelyn held out a hand and Kicker took it, crossing the small space between benches to slide in next to her. Her voice soft, though they were the only occupants of the compartment, Kicker tried for words of solace. "I don' think you'd recovered from saying goodbye at Lil's yesterday. Then to have to say goodbye to your ma and the res' of the family... tis fittin' to weep. I'd ne'er think the less of you for it."

A hand caressed her cheek and dropped away as the conductor appeared at the end of the aisle. "Surely I am the most fortunate among women."

"Many would argue on that."

"Only because they don't know you as I do."

Their hands disengaged and they moved apart from each other before the conductor stopped at the door of their compartment. He tipped his hat and smiled at Madelyn.

"Looks like we'll be making Liverpool right on schedule, Miss."

"Thank you."

He nodded and moved on, but his words reminded Kicker. She took the wedding ring off her finger and wordlessly extended it to Madelyn. She accepted it, tugged her glove off and slid the ring into place.

"But Mrs. Stuart, surely your Edward will be sorely disappointed to see you arrive with an unadorned finger."

Kicker was relieved to hear a note of teasing return to Madelyn's voice. "I'm as glad to be droppin' Edward as I am to forego the Missus. I swear it was odder to be called that than to answer to Kathleen."

Madelyn regarded her fondly. "My Kicker."

"Aye, and right glad to stay that way. Now if I can jus' doff these rags..." Kicker twitched impatiently at the skirt that covered her legs. She longed for the freedom and comfort of her trousers and boots.

"Soon, dearest. We'll be stopping for an hour or so in Birmingham, but we should reach Liverpool by six. We'll have our trunks stowed and be aboard the *Assiniboine* by nightfall. Once we're safely on our way, you may change if you like. I do think you should resume wearing the dresses when we disembark in Montreal, though." Madelyn patted Kicker's hand. "Just think, dearest, tomorrow we sail with the morning tide."

Kicker was unable to interpret the underlying emotion in Madelyn's words. It was an odd mix—excitement, sorrow, anticipation, trepidation; she was unsure exactly how her lover felt.

She considered again something that had been on her mind since learning the previous day of Timothy's downfall. Kicker had decided to withhold her information on what the master of the household had been up to in the servants' quarters. She reasoned that sharing it with Madelyn would serve no good purpose, but now she weighed other considerations.

"What troubles you, dearest?"

Kicker bit her lip as she sorted out her answer. "You tol' me your da is no more a threat, right?"

"True. I believe Mother and Uncle Royce have him contained for the moment. Though I suspect the shock will rapidly wear off and he'll begin scheming anew."

"So if he cannot hurt us, do we still need to flee? If it hurts us both so to leave our families behin'..."

"I do understand your implication, but in my heart, we are leaving for many reasons, only one of which was fear of my father's retribution should he learn of our love for one another." Madelyn looked out the window, then back at Kicker. "I'm not sure if I can explain what I mean, but I'll try. When I was young, Roddy and I were very close. The others were so much older than the two of us. My sisters all married early, and for as long as I can remember, Percy and Edgar were Father's shadows. There was never any doubt that they would follow him into his business and live exactly as he dictated. But my younger brother was cut from another cloth. Roddy dreamed big dreams—of adventure, of exploring, of conquering new worlds—and he swept me up in those dreams."

Watching Madelyn closely, Kicker saw a far off look appear in her eyes and a wistful smile on her lips.

"I remember going to Mother when I was about nine and telling her in great excitement how Roddy and I were going to explore the wilds of Africa as soon as we were old enough. Do you know what she said to me?"

Kicker shook her head.

"She told me that perhaps Roddy would go to Africa one day, if that was his destiny, but I shouldn't entertain such notions. For my destiny was to marry, settle down, and raise a good man's children. Mother thought to console me by telling me that perhaps one of my sons would then go to Africa, or that someday I might accompany my husband on a tour. All I could think of was how terribly unfair it was. I could run faster than Roddy; I could throw farther, and beat him at all manner of games. Why then could he go to Africa, or anywhere he chose, and I could not? I don't believe the injustice of that notion ever left me."

"So we're goin' to Canada...because we can?"

"That does sound terribly trite, doesn't it? No, dearest. We're going to Canada because, despite what anyone insists to the contrary, you and I have the right to choose our destiny. I believe we'll find the freedom to exercise that right more readily in the New World than in the Old."

Kicker considered Madelyn's words. It wasn't that she too hadn't had to fight battles to live in her preferred manner, but she was content with her station and prospects by the time Madelyn entered her life. It occurred to Kicker that despite their disparate social and economic circumstances, Madelyn's life had actually been far more restrictive than hers. In the bedlam that was the Stuart home, it had been easy, for the most part, to slip away with Adam and escape the strictures placed on her more pliable sisters.

"I took it for granted."

"What, dearest?"

Kicker smiled at Madelyn. "Freedom—I took it for granted, an' I do understan'."

Madelyn closed her eyes, then opened them and gave her a look of relief. "So you are in agreement then?"

"Aye."

With a quick glance around, Madelyn lifted Kicker's hand and kissed it. "To freedom."

"Aye. To freedom."

They emerged from the Lime Street railway station in Liverpool, trailed by a porter with their trunks. Kicker stared in amazement at the crowd which swirled around her and Madelyn. Before she had time to take it all in, a seedy looking man with a ragged moustache and a cigar hanging from his mouth rushed up to them.

"You lydies lookin' for a transit 'otel, are ye? I know just the place. It's a fine, temperance 'otel—clean an' upstandin', just for lydies like yourselves, and I kin see your luggage to your ship, lickity split."

"'ere you! Git the bloody 'ell away from 'em." A cabbie dismounted from his carriage and shook his buggy whip at the disreputable hotel agent. "Ne'er you mind that blighter, lydies. I'll git you safely where you need to go. Let 'im put 'is hands on your trunks and ye'd ne'er see 'em agin, believe me."

Madelyn regarded the cabbie searchingly. "We're bound for the *S.S. Assiniboine*, Dominion Steam Line. Do you know of it?"

"Ain't a ship lining the docks I don' know, Missus." With that assurance, the cabbie directed the porter in loading the trunks. By the time Madelyn's three large trunks and Kicker's small trunk were loaded, the carriage sagged dangerously low, but the women eagerly got inside, grateful to be out of the crowd.

When they reached the quay in front of the long, black-hulled steamship with the bright red funnels, Kicker realized that there was no escaping these crowds. She had never seen such a noisy mass of humanity.

"Ha' you e'er seen the like?"

Madelyn inclined her head and Kicker realized she had not made herself heard. She tried again, with voice raised. "Ha' you e'er seen so many people in one place?"

Madelyn shook her head as she lowered her mouth to Kicker's ear. "Rarely, dearest. It's terribly cacophonous, isn't it? Please don't stray from my side. I would despair of finding you, should I lose you in the multitude."

The cabbie hopped down and poked his head in the window. "Ye'd bes' stay with the carriage, Missus. I'll be back straightaway wi' a porter."

He vanished into the crowd, and the two women emerged to stand beside the carriage. Madelyn retrieved a dainty handkerchief from her handbag and pressed it to her nose. Kicker smiled understandingly. Even accustomed as she was to the smells of the stable, the stench of unwashed bodies, rotting garbage, and diesel fumes, permeated by the pungent musk of the ocean, made for a powerful funk that hung over the quay.

Kicker patted Madelyn's arm comfortingly and stared about the crowd in open-mouthed amazement. *Surely all these people cannot be travelin' to Canada wi' us. Twill be no room to e'en turn about on board.*

The faint sound of lively music above the din of the crowd sidetracked Kicker's wonderment, and she turned to locate the source. Two men, one perched on a barrel and the other standing next to the barrel, played for the crowd and accepted the occasional pence thrown into a hat with a nod of thanks. Kicker eyed them closely.

They were undoubtedly brothers—twin thatches of bright orange-red hair marked them as such—but the resemblance ended there. The fiddler was a lean, pale man with a melancholy expression, and the drummer, who switched to a flute as she watched, was a husky, ruddy-faced man with a cheerful grin for all, even those who stood to enjoy the music and didn't contribute to the hat.

Kicker couldn't help smiling as the flautist jumped to his feet and tapped out an accompaniment on the top of the barrel. Enjoying the music, she nevertheless heard Madelyn gasp and spun in time to see her blanch and clutch at the carriage for support.

"What? What's the matter?"

When Madelyn appeared unable to answer, Kicker followed her line of sight to where a blowzy woman in a tight, dirty red dress was obviously conducting a negotiation with a couple of sailors in the shadow of a warehouse. The trio apparently came to an agreement, as one sailor handed over a coin, which the woman swiftly tucked into her bodice before jerking her head at them to follow her. As they did so, one of the sailors dropped his hands to the whore's buttocks and fondled her. She didn't bother to shrug him off as they disappeared from sight between buildings.

Though the scene was lewd, it certainly was not out of place on the overcrowded pier. From where she stood, Kicker saw several whores linger in the shadows and importune potential customers. She wondered what had upset Madelyn so.

Before she could ask, the cabbie returned with a uniformed porter who dragged a large wheeled cart with him. He wore a cap that announced him as one of the *Assiniboine* crew. The two men quickly unloaded the trunks, and Kicker tugged subtly at Madelyn's arm as the cabbie stood, awaiting payment.

Still pale, Madelyn fumbled in her bag and extracted a generous amount, which elicited a large grin from the cabbie. He tipped his hat and swung up onto his carriage as the porter began to push his way through the crowd, using the loaded cart to clear a path. Kicker, worried about her companion's silence, kept one hand firmly on Madelyn's arm as she fought to stay directly behind the porter and not get separated in the unruly crowd.

It was not until they finally mounted the gangplank and stepped onto the deck of the steamer that Madelyn roused herself. She pulled their tickets out of her bag, and handed them to the purser who greeted them.

"Ah yes, Mrs. Bristow. Welcome aboard. You and your companion are in saloon class, cabin number twelve. If you'll just point out which trunks you'll require for the journey, I'll have the others stowed until we reach Montreal. Louis here will show you to your cabin. I'm sure you'll find everything you need there, but if there's anything at all that we can do to ensure a smooth and comfortable voyage, please don't hesitate to ring for one of my staff."

Madelyn wordlessly pointed out Kicker's trunk and the smallest of her own three, then the women followed their escort to their cabin.

Louis opened their door, handed them the key and promised to see to their trunks immediately.

Kicker thanked him and closed the door, leaving her alone with Madelyn. "Maddie? What's goin' on? What's upset you so?"

Madelyn turned to look at Kicker, who flinched at the bleakness in her eyes. "I think that is the first time you've called me Maddie."

"An' doubtless won' be the las'. C'mon, love, what's goin' on?"

Madelyn sank onto one of the berths and stared at her hands. When she did not answer, Kicker grew increasingly worried.

"Was't the sailors that disturbed you, love? Or the woman they went with? Did you not know that kin' of thing goes on? E'en in my village we knew of such women and their ways."

"I... I never thought much about it one way or another, but that woman in the red dress, that—"

"Whore?" Kicker saw Madelyn flinch and shiver. Her voice softened. "D'you know her then?"

"I think... I am almost certain...it was... Charity."

Kicker took a moment to connect the name with Madelyn's past. "The one your da—"

"Ruined, yes. That one. Oh dear God, Kicker. What have I done?"

Kicker dropped to her knees and took Madelyn's hands in her own. "You did nothin' wrong, love. Your da did. You're not responsible for her bein' a..."

"A whore. She's a whore, Kicker. If she'd not met me, she'd live in a fine house and want for nothing. Instead she...sells herself to any man that will have her for half an hour, just to exist another day."

"Can you even be sure, Maddie? Tis many a year since you las' saw her, right?"

Madelyn met Kicker's gaze squarely. "I'm not absolutely sure, dearest, but it certainly looked like her. Remember, Charity was my first love. There was a time I lived for the sight of her face, the touch of her hand. The woman I saw was obviously hard used by life, but the resemblance was striking."

The sound of a knock on the door silenced them, and Kicker went to admit Louis with their trunks. Once he left, she locked the door, drew the curtains over the portholes, and returned to her anguished companion. She gently pressed Madelyn back onto the narrow bed and crawled up next to her. Kicker wrapped her in an embrace and rocked Madelyn softly as she tried to think of something to say. Words, never her strong suit, failed her, but as time passed Madelyn's body released some of its tension and softened against her.

"She did not deserve this, Kicker."

"Aye, I know."

"If I'd never...if I'd said no that first time..."

"An' if you had, then no doubt, there'd have been others. An' if not your da, then p'rhaps another's. She'd still have come to ruin through her own imprudence. Did she press you, that firs' time?"

"Maybe a little, but I was willing."

"Tell me?"

Madelyn snuggled closer, burying her face against Kicker's chest. When she finally spoke, her voice was muffled but the sadness in it was unmistakable. "We met when I was seventeen and she was twenty-three; we grew to be good friends. One day when I was over at her house, she invited me up to her room to see a new book she'd just acquired. We often read to each other, so I thought little of it and readily agreed. Charity said a friend had given it to her, and bade me sit beside her as she read to me. It was a tale of romance, but unlike any I'd ever read. It was very...blatant, leaving little to the imagination, and the illustrations—I blushed to see them. But Charity read on as if nothing were out of the ordinary. Finally she closed the book and turned to me. She asked if I'd enjoyed it, and when I was unable to answer, she laid a hand on my chest to feel the pounding of my heart. She teased me about being such an innocent, and challenged me to examine what I felt."

Madelyn shook her head and Kicker stroked her back soothingly. "I didn't know what I was feeling. I was in a great state of unease, but didn't wish to leave her. Then she kissed me. She told me that she had many things she wished to show me and teach me, things that would bring me much pleasure. I couldn't say no, nor did I wish to. For the next few months, at every opportunity, we would retire to her room or mine, and she would instruct me in the ways of love. I was a willing, eager student, until the day..."

"When your da came upon you."

Madelyn shuddered and strained to be closer to Kicker, who tightened her arms around her. "It was horrible. I begged him not to hurt her, but he threw me back into my room and had Pruitt bar the door to me. The last I heard of Charity was a terrible scream. I never saw her again—until today."

"An' maybe not today, either." Kicker had no wish to be unkind, but she could not bear to see Madelyn blame herself for things not within her control. "If twas her, love—an' I'm not sayin' twas—then she brought herself to this place. Maybe your da had a hand in it, tis true, but there was naught you could have done to stop him." Kicker gently tugged Madelyn upright and sat beside her, one arm wrapped around her waist. "You spoke on the train of our right to choose our own destinies, did you not?"

"Yes."

"An' if tis our right, then surely your Charity had the same right."

"The right, yes, but what if she had no options? What if my father ensured all respectable avenues were closed to her? What if destiny took her straight from our relationship to where she finds herself now?"

"Truthfully, Madelyn—was there anythin' you could have done to stop your da?"

Madelyn shook her head bitterly. "I couldn't even leave the house alone for over a year. By the time I was released from his prison, I had no idea where Charity was."

"Then tis naught you need regret."

"Except saying yes in the first place."

"Tis foolish to chafe yourself for that, Maddie. From what you say, Charity was both older and more schooled in her desires. You were an innocent, and you were in love."

"She didn't take advantage of me, dearest."

Kicker smiled at Madelyn's firm denial. "Nor have you taken a'vantage of me, though you be older and wiser and more learned in what has passed between us."

Madelyn gave Kicker a startled look. "I never thought of it like that."

"Then you should. The only blame here is your da's—not yours, not Charity's. An' if that were Charity on the dock, then I sorrow for her, but you may not grieve for what has passed. I would not have blamed you had we been caught lovin' each other in your da's house, no matter what the outcome."

Kicker could feel the shiver go through Madelyn's body but she kept silent, allowing her time to absorb the alternative viewpoint. When she finally heard a deep, assenting sigh, she stood and held out her hand.

"Now, let's explore a bit."

Madelyn took her hand and stood, then drew her close. Bending to kiss Kicker, she whispered, "Thank you, dearest. I may be the older and more experienced, but I believe you may be the wiser."

The ship barely cleared the mouth of the Mersey estuary the following morning when it became apparent that Madelyn was not a natural sailor. She retreated to their cabin, and by nightfall, Kicker was alarmed enough to summon the ship's doctor.

After a cursory examination, he pronounced judgment. "I'm afraid your mistress has fallen prey to mal de mer, Miss—common seasickness. It may well be that only time and a return to terra firma will cure her, but in any event, give her a few drops of this when things are at their worst. It won't stop the nausea completely, but it will allow her to sleep through most of it." He handed over a small brown bottle from a leather satchel that seemed packed with similar bottles.

"That's all, then? Tis naught I can do to help her?"

"I'm afraid not. Try to get Mrs. Bristow to take some water when she can, and call me if she gets much worse. For now, if you'll excuse me, half the ship seems to be suffering the same affliction and I must see to my rounds. God help us all when we get out on the open seas and the waves really start to roll."

There was a deep groan from the bed, and Kicker hastily grabbed the basin as the ship's doctor took his leave. By now Madelyn had nothing left to expel but that seemed to make little difference in her convulsive retching.

As the hours went by, they settled into a routine with Kicker coaxing Madelyn to take water, and a little broth supplied by the ever helpful Louis, whenever she could. She gave her unhappy patient the doses of laudanum the doctor prescribed, and quickly became competent at bathing, changing, and reading to her miserable lover.

By the evening of the second day out at sea, Kicker was fairly certain she had things under control. A very pale Madelyn was propped up on pillows as she listened to Kicker read *Wuthering Heights.*

"It's a rough journey, and a sad heart to travel it... We've braved its ghosts often together, and dared each other to stand among the graves and ask them to come... But Heathcliff, if I dare you now, will you venture?"

"It has indeed been a rough journey, dearest. I'm so sorry to put you through this."

Kicker looked up from the book. "Tis not like you planned it, love. In another few days we'll reach land, and you'll be fine."

"I'm sure I will, but you need to get out of this cabin and take some air."

"I'd rather not leave you."

"I'll be all right, I promise. I feel like sleeping anyway, so bid Miss Bronte farewell for now and off you go."

Kicker could not deny the restlessness that afflicted her after two days of being cabin bound, but she hesitated to leave Madelyn, even for a short while.

"Truly, dearest, I'm just going to sleep for a bit. There is nothing for you to do here but watch me. It will make me feel much less a burden if I know you've gotten out on deck."

Kicker marked her place and set the book aside. "A'right, but I'll be back b'fore you know it."

Madelyn gave her a weak smile.

Kicker bent to kiss her forehead before she tucked the coverlet around her and left. At the door of the cabin she turned to glance back; Madelyn had already closed her eyes.

Kicker stepped out of the cabin and breathed in deeply as the scent of sea air filled her lungs. She gloried in the freshness of it after days of stale cabin air. She wished Madelyn was up to a walk, for she felt it would do her much good to be outside. Then the ship rolled into a deeper trough and Kicker smiled ruefully. It was probably best, after all, that Madelyn sleep away most of the next seven or eight days until landfall.

Having gotten her sea legs in her first hours aboard, Kicker rambled down the windward side toward the stern of the boat and enjoyed the stiff breeze that tossed her hair. She had abandoned the dresses and bonnets their first night out, and reveled in the freedom of her customary garb. The few passengers she passed took little note of her and she was grateful for that, especially after the shocked look on Louis' face the first time he saw her in her trousers, shirt, and boots. The steward readily adjusted, though, and his help in caring for Madelyn was invaluable.

Kicker only meant to take a quick walk around the deck and then return to their cabin, but the faint sound of a fiddle drifted up to her from the steerage deck and curiosity compelled her to follow the music. She soon found herself perched on a ladder, looking down on the red-haired fiddler and his brother. They were alone on a deserted section of deck, barely visible in the gathering dusk but for the weak light of a lantern around the bulkhead from where they sat.

His eyes closed, the fiddler was lost in his music, and Kicker was enthralled with the air he was playing. She had never heard it before, but she ached at the sadness that echoed in the notes drifting up and out across the water. Captured by the music, Kicker didn't notice the other brother watching her with a smile until finally he spoke.

"You're right welcome to join us, lad."

The fiddler stopped and looked at his enraptured audience. "Pudge, you're daft. That's no lad." He stood and touched his cap. "He's right, though. You're very welcome to listen, Miss, any time."

Pudge glanced at his brother sharply, then back at Kicker, who self-consciously descended the rest of the stairs to stand even with them on the deck. He jumped to his feet and whipped the cap off his head. "Ain't I the blind one then? I do most humbly apologize, Miss." He stuck out a hand. "Michael Eamon Kelly, at your service, though all who knows me calls me Pudge." He jerked a thumb at his brother. "This melancholy musician is my brother, Seamus. We're pleased to meet you."

Kicker shyly shook hands with both brothers and instantly felt the difference between them. Pudge had the rough, calloused hands of a working man, much like her own, whereas Seamus' hands were much smoother.

"Kicker Stuart. Jus' Kicker."

"Well, Kicker, can I offer you a seat?" Pudge indicated the pile of sacks on which he had been perched, but Kicker shook her head and leaned against the ladder.

"That song—what was it?"

Pudge chuckled as Seamus answered, "It has no name, Miss Kicker. Just something that flowed from my heart to my strings this very night."

"He's always doing that. Sometimes we'll be in the middle of an old song and he'll go off on one of his fancies, expecting me to keep up."

Seamus smiled at Kicker. "And he always catches up and does me proud."

"Are you two professional musicians, then?"

Pudge laughed and Seamus examined his brother with quiet good humour. "I'm not sure what you would call us." He returned his attention to Kicker. "We're not above adding to our purses when people enjoy our music, but it will be thin gruel this winter if we rely merely on our musical talents."

"So you're goin' to homestead?"

Pudge reached behind him and pulled out a lumpy burlap sack. "We are, but we've brought a little magic with us." Reaching into the sack, he flourished a small object with pride.

"Potatoes?"

"Not just potatoes, lass. Our great-grandfather kept our family alive during the blight with these. Now they're going to sustain me and Seamus in the New World."

"But is it not late in the summer to plant?"

"That it is, but we'll get them in the ground right away and hope to have enough of a harvest to have seed potatoes in the spring. It'll be a near thing, but we have faith." Pudge glanced quickly up at Seamus, then tossed the potato back in the sack and knotted it closed.

Kicker suspected there was more he would have said, but it was not her place to ask. "Which part are you headin' to?"

"Not a clue. We just plan to board the train and see the country. We'll know when to stop."

Kicker smiled at Pudge's cheerful admission. "It doesn't soun' like much of a plan."

The two men laughed together.

"The Kellys are not noted for planning, Miss Kicker."

"I didn't even know Seamus intended to go. Our family home is in County Carlow, a little outside of Clonegal. A week ago, I'm out working in the garden and I sees Seamus coming up the road with his fiddle under his arm and a sack over his shoulder, so I ask him where's he going. 'To America,' he says, so I says, 'Hold up a minute... I'm going with ya.' I toss him a bag and tell him to dig up some spuds whilst I grab some of my things. Then we hit the road, take the ferry to Liverpool, and here we are."

Kicker frowned. "But we're goin' to Canada."

"The *Assiniboine* was the first ship leavin', so we took that as a sign and booked passage. If we don't like where we end up, we'll move on til we do. So where are you and your mister headin' for, Kicker?"

"No husban', jus' me and my cousin, Mrs. Madelyn Bristow. She's a teacher, and she's got a position in a town called Galbraith's Crossing, in Alberta—the Western Territories. Her husban's gonna meet her there when he musters out in South Africa."

"Galbraith's Crossing? What's that like?"

Kicker repeated what Will MacDiarmid had told them of the town, including his glowing description of the land and the tale of how the town had gotten its name.

Both men hung on her words attentively, then Seamus tucked his fiddle back under his chin and drew his bow over the strings.

Initially it sounded like a random tune, but Kicker quickly heard the sigh of the wind over the prairies and the sweep of the mountains to the sky in the notes Seamus played. Then the tempo picked up and soon Kicker couldn't keep her toes still.

Seamus ran through three more lively tunes before Kicker became aware that she had been gone much longer than she had intended.

"Thank you for the music, Seamus. Pudge, twas nice to meet you. I should get back now. My cousin's been ill."

"Sea sickness?"

Kicker nodded.

"That's brought down over half the folks in steerage. It's cut into our earnings considerable."

Seamus poked his brother's broad shoulder with the bow. "That is not very compassionate, Pudge."

Kicker turned to climb the stairs, amused at the genial argument that now ensued between the two over practicality versus charity. As she reached the top of the ladder, she heard Seamus call after her.

"It was a pleasure to meet you, Miss Kicker. Come back anytime."

Kicker did go back, every time Madelyn told her to go get some air. The Irish brothers always welcomed her with laughter and music. The night that was to be their last at sea, she again descended to the corner of the steerage deck the brothers had claimed for their own. However, Pudge was missing from his usual perch.

"Don' tell me Pudge has succumbed to the seasickness?"

"My brother, with his cast iron stomach? Not a chance. No, young Michael Eamon is off courting."

"Courtin'?"

"Yes. He found a likely lass who, for some unknown reason, has not yet thrown anything in his face, so he's wooing her with all the traditional Kelly charm."

Kicker grinned at that thought. "An' d'you think he'll be successful?"

"Depends what you mean by 'successful'." Seamus smiled. "Pudge wooed many a lovely lass in County Carlow, but he is notoriously fickle. I suspect one of the reasons he was so eager to join me on this trip was that Father O'Brien had had enough of his romantic shenanigans. Rumour was that the good Father was working with Bernadette Shanahan on getting Pudge to the altar."

"An' what about you? Was Father O'Brien after you to wed, too?"

Seamus grimaced and Kicker instantly regretted posing the question. "I am afraid I gravely disappointed the good Father, Miss Kicker. He would have nothing to do with me."

"Why?"

Seamus was quiet a long time and Kicker silently chastised herself for blurting out intrusive questions. Finally he sighed and lifted his gaze from the deck planks to her face.

"It is not an uplifting tale, though common enough, I suppose. I was to be a priest. When I was a boy, I was Father O'Brien's devoted acolyte. As I grew, he hammered the lessons into my thick head and prepared me well for the seminary. This spring I was only two months away from being ordained when I left, and I do not think he will ever forgive me. My family was very displeased with me, too, all except Pudge. I think he was the only one who really understood."

"Un'erstood what?"

"That no matter how long lived their expectations, or how proud they would've been to see me ordained, it was not the right path for my life."

"Twas not your destiny."

Seamus nodded solemnly. "Exactly."

"D'you think any of us e'er really knows our destiny?"

"Some lucky souls, yes. For most of us, though, I believe it is a process of elimination, with perhaps a modicum of luck thrown our way by powers both benevolent and just."

Kicker grinned. "You soun' a lot like my cousin."

"Ah, and how is Mrs. Bristow today?"

"Maybe a little better. I was hopin' to bring her to hear you an' Pudge play, but she's as weak as a newborn foal right now."

"Well, I am not sure when Pudge will return, but perhaps I might serenade your cousin."

Kicker jumped up. "Would you do that? Would you play for her?"

The fiddler stood and swept her a bow with his tweed cap. "I would be delighted to."

As Kicker started to scramble up the ladder, Seamus cautioned, "They frown on steerage passengers mixing with our betters, so we had best tread discreetly."

Kicker stopped and glanced back with a frown. She could not dispute what he said. She herself had endured the wrath of a righteous steward who tried to prevent her return to saloon class the evening before. Fortunately, Louis had come upon them and quickly settled the matter, but the incident still stung. Kicker knew she could avoid such things if she dressed conventionally, but it was not her nature to bend her will to conformity.

"Let them in'erfere, if they dare. Tis a mission we're on."

Seamus chuckled quietly. "Then lead on. I can show no less courage."

They did not encounter any stewards as they quickly made their way back to the cabin. Kicker bade Seamus wait while she checked on Madelyn and ensured her cousin was ready to receive a visitor. Stepping into the cabin, she was pleased to see Madelyn awake, though no less pale.

"How're you feelin', love?"

"Somewhat improved, dearest. Did you enjoy your walk?"

"Aye, an' I brought you back a gift."

Madelyn raised herself up on the pillows and regarded Kicker curiously. "A gift? Where would you find a gift on board?"

"In steerage. Tis a musician—a friend—and he offered to play a while, should it please you."

Madelyn glanced down at her rumpled bedding and wrinkled dressing gown and frowned. "I'm not dressed for a concert or to entertain strange men, dearest."

"Oh... Perhaps he could play outside your window then. Would that be a'right?"

Madelyn studied Kicker for a moment. "You say he is a friend?"

"Aye. I've been listenin' to him an' his brother play for days now. They're very good. Twill take your min' off your illness, love, I swear. He knows you've been ill, and he only wants to help...truly."

"All right, bid him come in, but don't wonder if he runs screaming from the cabin at the sight of me."

Elated, Kicker yanked the door open and gestured Seamus inside. He snatched off his cap, stepped in, and gave Madelyn a small bow.

"Seamus Kelly, at your service, Mrs. Bristow. I am sorry to hear of your protracted affliction, Madam. Miss Kicker thought perhaps my music might prove a suitable distraction."

"Thank you for coming, Mr. Kelly. I appreciate your thoughtfulness...and hers." Madelyn threw a warm smile at Kicker. "Won't you take a seat? I do apologize for my dishabille, but I wasn't expecting company."

"It is I who must apologize, Madam. I do not generally barge in upon ladies, but I hope I am not too much of an intrusion."

Kicker rolled her eyes, unseen by her two earnest companions. "Seamus, you sit and play. Madelyn, jus' listen. Tis like the sounds of angels, I swear."

Obediently, Seamus dropped into a chair on the far side of the cabin. Madelyn held out a hand to Kicker, who perched on the edge of her berth and settled in to listen.

Seamus played for over an hour without pause. He never repeated himself, and captivated the women with a wide diversity of music. He culminated his performance with an air that Kicker quickly recognized as the one she had first heard him perform, the music he claimed as his own heart's composition.

When the final notes faded, Madelyn clapped enthusiastically and Kicker beamed at Seamus.

"Well done, Sir. My cousin did not exaggerate your talent, and I thank you most dearly for entertaining us. Kicker, will you get my purse?"

Seamus held up his hand. "No, please, Mrs. Bristow. There is no need for that. Miss Kicker has greatly enlivened this tedious voyage for my brother and me. I am simply returning the favour. It was a pleasure to play for you, and that is reward enough."

"But surely—"

Seamus just shook his head and picked up his cap as he turned for the door. Kicker bounded across to open it for him.

"Thank you, Seamus. I'll come see you t'morrow then. Do tell Pudge to stay out of trouble, a'right?"

That got her a smile and an unexpected wink. "My brother and trouble have been twinned since his birth, but I shall certainly tell him of your caution." With that, he stepped out of the cabin and closed the door behind him.

Kicker turned to find Madelyn studying her. She cocked her head in silent enquiry as she returned to her lover's bedside.

"He reminds you of Adam, doesn't he?"

Kicker hadn't thought of that, but gave it consideration as she sank down beside Madelyn. "I suppose, in a way. He carries a sadness in him that Adam ne'er did. An' my brother can scare the birds outta the trees when he tries to be musical, but I do like the way Seamus looks out for Pudge."

"The way Adam always looked out for you."

"Aye." Kicker wriggled around until she had Madelyn propped against her body. "Did you enjoy the concert, love?"

"Very much, dearest. He's a gifted musician and a very nice gentleman indeed."

"He and Pudge are quite the pair."

"I'm glad you found friends aboard. I know this hasn't been a very good start to our adventure."

Kicker tightened her arms and felt Madelyn's head settle alongside her own. "Shhh, tis fine. Tomorrow we see land, and soon we'll be off this bloody ship."

Madelyn turned to nuzzle Kicker's neck. "It won't be a moment too soon. We had better be content with our new home, because I swear you'll never get me on a boat again."

Kicker watched with worried eyes as Madelyn wavered on her feet. "Are you sure about this, Maddie?"

"Absolutely, dearest. I refuse to arrive in our new land flat on my back." Madelyn took one tentative step, then another.

"Then at leas' hol' tight to my arm."

Madelyn took Kicker's arm gratefully. "That will be a pleasure."

Kicker steered Madelyn out of the cabin and toward the bow where a number of people already sat. They watched the land loom ever larger as the steamer made its way deeper into the Gulf of St. Lawrence. The ship had passed through the Cabot Strait several hours earlier, and they could see the Isle d'Anticosti ahead in the distance on the starboard side.

"Pudge tol' me one of the sailors said they sometimes see whales around here. D'you think we might see one?"

Madelyn accepted Kicker's help to settle in a deck chair and smiled as her solicitous lover tucked a warm robe around her legs. "Perhaps, if we're lucky. I don't know too much about their habits, so I'm afraid I cannot help on that account, but why don't you see if you can spot one?"

Kicker alternated her time between keeping Madelyn company and standing at the rail, searching the dark waters for the fabled maritime creatures. Aware of Pudge's penchant for exaggeration, she doubted his tales at first, but Seamus assured her that whales did indeed haunt the Gulf waters and Kicker believed him. As it was, a boy who stood beside her was the first to spot the giant cetacean, white flesh dipping and rising through the water's surface as it seemed to pace the steamer.

Open-mouthed, Kicker stared at the beluga as cries went up all around her, then she urgently beckoned Madelyn to the rail. "Quick, Maddie! You have t'see this!"

People crowded the rail trying to see, but Kicker fiercely held her spot and reached back to pull Madelyn forward when she approached.

Madelyn clung to the rail as Kicker kept one arm around her waist and pointed with the other hand. "D'you see it?"

"I do see it. It's truly magnificent, isn't it?"

Kicker was pleased to hear the awe in Madelyn's voice, for she felt the same way and was thrilled that they were able to share the experience. When the whale finally angled away from the ship, Madelyn wilted, as if it had taken all of her diminished strength to witness the beluga's passage. Kicker quickly helped her back to the chair and knelt as she tucked the robe around her.

"Are you a'right? Did it weary you too much? D'you wish to go back to the cabin?"

"I'm fine. Just a little tired. And no, I'd rather stay out here." Madelyn patted Kicker's hand reassuringly. "Go and visit the Kellys if you wish, dearest. I'll just wait here."

Kicker shook her head. She hoped to see Seamus and Pudge again before they left the ship, but not right now. "No, tis fittin' to see this all with you." It was the best she could do at an explanation of how she felt: awed, overwhelmed, and deeply grateful that they had made a successful crossing to their new land. She wanted to share that with the woman she loved.

Tired eyes shone with renewed zest as Madelyn smiled at Kicker and squeezed her hand. "Do you think perhaps the whale was a sign, dearest?"

"A sign?"

"To welcome us to our new home."

Kicker set aside thoughts of all the miles they had yet to cross and returned Madelyn's smile. "Aye—home."

CHAPTER 9

KICKER EXTENDED A HAND TO halt their faithful steward's passage across the deck. "Louis, d'you not come from Montreal?"

"Oui, Mam'selle. I was born and raised on the North Shore."

"D'you think you could recommen' a good place to stay? Missus Bristow isn't up to any more travelin' just yet. A few days rest is what she needs b'fore we go west."

Louis glanced over Kicker's shoulder to where Madelyn reclined in the deck chair, her eyes closed. He nodded gravely. "Madame did not weather the ocean well, I am sorry to say."

"Aye, you're right about that. An' after nine days of nothin' but broth and water, she needs time and some good food to rebuild her strength."

Louis straightened and looked squarely into Kicker's eyes. "The best inn in all of Montreal belongs to ma famille—L'Auberge de St. Christophe. You will taste Maman's cooking and believe you have truly ascended to heaven."

Kicker smiled at Louis' obvious pride. "That soun's wonderful. How d'we get there?"

"Anyone on the docks will know the way, but tell your driver it is on Rue Saint Paul, just off Boulevard St. Laurent, and he cannot possibly get lost."

Kicker concentrated on memorizing the unfamiliar names. "L'Auberge de..."

"St. Christophe. He is the patron saint of travelers, and will see you safe until Madame Bristow is well enough to go on. I would take you myself, but I will not be off duty for many hours after we dock. However, I will give you a letter for Maman. She will tell Papa to give you the best room he has available. She will not cheat you like the swine who dishonour my people by lying in wait for helpless innocents like yourselves. You wait here. I will be right back."

Kicker had heard many stories during their nine days on board of scoundrels who gouged and preyed on naïve immigrants, so she was grateful to the obliging steward. As he scurried off, she knelt down beside Madelyn.

"I think we have a place to stay for a few days."

Madelyn opened her eyes. "I know. I was listening."

"You're not angry with me?"

"For finding a place where I may put this awful experience behind me? Not at all. I can hardly wait to set foot on solid land and rest my head once again on a pillow that doesn't move. If ever I thought that going to sea sounded romantic, I've been thoroughly disabused of that notion."

Kicker grinned. Madelyn had improved steadily as the ship made its way down the calmer inland water of the St. Lawrence. Though she was far from the picture of health even yet, Kicker no longer feared for her wellbeing.

"Don' you love the way he says 'Montreal?'"

"It does roll off his tongue, doesn't it?" Madelyn sat up slowly and waved Kicker away as she leaned in to help. "No, I'm fine, really. Why don't you go bid farewell to your friends while I await Louis' return? We have less than an hour until we dock. Once there, it may be hard to locate the Kellys in the crowd at the immigration reception centre."

"Are you sure you'll be a'right alone?"

"Go."

Kicker grinned and jumped to her feet. "I'll be back soon."

"Take your time. The trunks are packed; I've coaxed you back into a dress—however temporarily, and I believe we are more than ready to disembark. I want to press Louis for more details about the arrival procedure anyway, so off you go."

Kicker tried to remember to glide as she made her way through the saloon class crowds that lined the rails to watch their arrival. It was equally crowded in steerage as families and individuals clustered around boxes, sacks, and a vast assortment of household possessions. The din was overwhelming as mothers screamed at restless youngsters, and men, trying to assemble families and goods, cursed each other for getting in the way. The air of anxiety, excitement, and tension was as palpable as the aroma of sweltering, unwashed bodies.

For the first time Kicker was glad of Lil's excellent handiwork, as both men and women stepped aside for her in her finery. She knew she would not have been accorded such respect in her usual garb, and however false it felt, was grateful for her unimpeded passage.

Kicker finally picked her way through the chaos to find Seamus and Pudge guarding their usual corner of the deck against the encroachment of the throng. The men failed to recognize her at first under the brim of the fancy, wide brimmed hat with rose-coloured silk trim that matched her dress. It was the most elegant garment she owned. Though Kicker suspected she might never wear it again, she hadn't protested overly much when Madelyn cajoled her into putting it on. It seemed fitting to put her best foot forward in her new land.

"Well, Holy Mother! If it isn't our little Kicker!" Pudge stared at her in amazement while his brother swept her an elaborate bow.

"Miss Kicker, that is a truly beautiful dress, and you most certainly do it justice. Surely a prince must await you in a golden carriage."

Kicker blushed at the obvious admiration on the faces of her friends, even as she missed the easygoing camaraderie that had developed between them over the past week. They were treating her like a lady, and she was not at all sure she liked it.

Seamus, keenly attuned as always to permutations of mood, addressed her gently. "Forgive us, dear Kicker. You have been such a boon companion on our journey that we long ago mislaid our manners, and have only now rediscovered them. We meant you no discomfort."

Meanwhile, Pudge gallantly snatched a wobbly stool out from under the gaze of a distracted matron, and ostentatiously dusted it with his cap. He offered it to Kicker, who eyed it dubiously but sat gingerly in appreciation of his efforts.

"Are you ready to land, then?" Kicker asked the Irishmen as she tried to balance on the stool.

Pudge beamed. "Seamus gave the ship's master all our immigration information, though we couldn't tell him for sure where we plan to settle. We're healthy enough to pass the doctor's exam; and we've got more than our five pounds apiece to land, so I'd say we're ready."

Kicker was instantly worried. If there was a medical examination that they needed to pass, Madelyn, in her current state, simply wasn't fit.

Again, Seamus appeared to read her mind. "You needn't be concerned. Saloon class passengers are not subject to the same prerequisites as steerage immigrants. I doubt that you will be detained long in the immigration hall. You will probably be halfway to Galbraith's Crossing before Pudge and I see the inside of the colonist train."

"No. We'll be stayin' in Montreal a few days til my cousin is able to travel."

Pudge's expression saddened. "As soon as we're processed, we're going to jump the first train west. I'd hoped you and your cousin might be on the same train. I guess this'll be goodbye, then."

Kicker nodded, but was unable to speak past the lump in her throat as Seamus gave her one of his infrequent smiles.

"It has been a true privilege for both of us to have met you. We wish you well in your journey. And who is to say? Perhaps, God willing, we will meet again."

"God willin'," Kicker said fervently and hoped the words were more than just an expression. "P'rhaps when we do, you an' Pudge'll be the Potato Kings of the West, an' have a golden carriage of your own."

"Then if we do, we shall come and take you and your cousin for rides in the countryside every Sunday."

"Well, maybe not every Sunday," Pudge countered with a twinkle in his eye. "I'm thinking a golden carriage would be mighty handy to impress the ladies."

Kicker laughed at her irrepressible friend. "Have you given up so quickly on the girl you jus' met?"

Seamus leaned forward to whisper confidentially, "It was not so much that he gave up on her, Miss Kicker. It was more that her father threw him out on his impudent ear."

Pudge grimaced and rubbed his jaw.

Kicker noticed a shadow under the thick red stubble that covered the Irishman's cheeks. She bit her lip and tried not to laugh, but when she noticed the merriment in Seamus' eyes, she could not repress a giggle. "You'd bes' be keepin' him away from the ladies if you're goin' to get out west in one piece."

"Hey, it's not like I can help it—the lasses just can't resist me. What's a man to do?"

Seamus shot his brother a glance. "If you do not find a good answer to that question, one of these days you are going to find yourself standing before an altar at the business end of a shotgun."

Kicker was surprised to hear the sternness in his voice. She wondered how many times Seamus had bailed his younger brother out of romantic trouble. She suspected he would be glad to see Pudge settle down and marry a good wife. She'd caught Seamus looking at her speculatively early in the week, though he apparently abandoned any such marital notions when Pudge continued to treat her as a sibling.

Kicker wanted to erase the solemnity that had settled over both their faces so she made a request. "Would you play for me, one las' time?"

Pudge dug into his bag for the pipe as Seamus picked up his ever ready fiddle. Without a word the brothers launched into *Carrigfergus*, moving seamlessly into *Roisin the Bow*, before ending their brief concert with Pudge's favourite—*Eileen Aroon*.

Pudge set his pipe aside and Seamus began to play the music that had come to inhabit Kicker's dreams. She marveled at how he had taken the notes she first heard only a week ago and woven them into a powerful, haunting melody. Spellbound, Kicker had to shake herself when he finished and slowly lowered his instrument. "That is the mos' beautiful thing I e'er heard. Did you name it?"

Seamus looked at her gravely. "I believe I will call it *Kicker's Journey*. Whenever I play it, I will think of the voyage we all took together to a new and unknown land."

This time Kicker could not stop the tears that welled up in her eyes. "But tis so sad. D'you foresee such sorrow ahead for us?"

Seamus looked past her, his eyes distant and almost transcendent, as if he contemplated things imperceptible to others. For an instant Kicker pictured the Irishman as one of the mystics that populated Madelyn's favourite book of British legends. Then her gentle friend was back.

"I think sorrow is a part of everyone's life in some measure, Miss Kicker, but that is not necessarily a bad thing. In some instances only pain will serve to steer us away from potential disaster, whether physical or spiritual. In the end, we are measured by the strength and wisdom we acquire on our journey. Surely if a man encounters nothing but ease and plenty in his life, he will lack the steel that hardship tempers within each of us. And when adversity does descend, as is inevitable, he will shatter beyond repair."

Kicker considered Seamus' words. She was braced by his lyricism and momentarily visualized the priest he would have become if he had not abandoned his training. She wasn't sure she completely understood his meaning, but the affection in his voice was clear, and she was glad for that. "I wish I could take your music with me."

"You can. It is all up here." Seamus touched the side of his head. "It will come to you whenever—"

The rest of his sentence was cut off by the blast of a horn, and Kicker bolted to her feet. "We mus' be gettin' close. I'd bes' get back to Maddie."

"Godspeed, Kicker." Pudge gingerly gave her a hug, and she smiled at him.

"Keep outta trouble, Pudge." Turning to Seamus, Kicker held out a hand.

He took it and raised it to his lips. "Be well, dear Kicker. I believe we will meet again some day."

Kicker stepped forward, wrapped her arms around him and gave him a brief, fierce hug. Then without another word, she climbed the ladder up to her deck and hurried back to Madelyn.

The immigration officials who greeted the saloon class passengers were deferential and welcoming. The only information those passengers were asked to provide was their name. Where the forms required information such as occupation, age, birthplace, destination, and reasons for traveling, the officials simply entered "gentleman" and waved the new immigrants through.

Last in line, Madelyn, leaning heavily on Kicker's arm, explained that her husband would be along later, as she gave her name and that of her traveling companion. The immigration official nodded politely and offered to assemble their trunks and secure a cab for the ladies traveling alone. They accepted, and followed the man through the crowded hall along a roped off aisle reserved for the first class passengers. As Madelyn's pace was slow, Kicker had plenty of time to look about in search of Seamus and Pudge.

The hall was huge and starkly lit by lamps suspended from the high ceiling. The wooden benches that lined the walls were crowded, and hundreds of people simply sat on the floor or on their possessions until their names were called. The piercing babble of a dozen different dialects rose from the crowd, only stilling momentarily each time a family name was hollered from the front processing desks. A small canteen in one corner did a booming business, and

Kicker thought for an instant that she saw the distinctive Kelly hair in the lineup there, before her view was obscured by the mass of people.

Sighing, Kicker accepted that she simply was not going to be able to pick out her friends in the maelstrom of humanity that eddied about the hall.

They had drawn even with the admissions desks when an unfolding incident caught Kicker's eye. A shabbily dressed man pleaded with a Canadian official, while his thin, pale wife, three young girls holding tight to her skirts, cradled a baby in her arms. Kicker was too far away to hear what was going on, but judging by the desperation and dawning anger on the man's face, the sullen resignation on the woman's, and the stubbornness on the official's, the family was being turned away for some reason.

Kicker glanced around and realized she was not the only one caught up by the small drama. It wasn't difficult to read the apprehension in many of the faces of the would-be immigrants, nor the relief in those lucky ones who looked back from beyond the processing tables.

Suddenly Kicker was overwhelmed with sadness for these people whose lives and futures hung on the decision of an overworked official. They were her true peers—not the woman who paced slowly next to her, listening politely to their obsequious guide. By rights, Kicker should be clustered with the mass of unwashed and overburdened humanity, sharing their fears and desperate hopes for a better life. Her family would never have been given the preferential treatment Kicker now enjoyed. It was not difficult to imagine her brother Adam standing in the place of the hapless would-be immigrant, pleading for entry into Canada. She could easily picture her small nephews—Jeremiah and Elijah—holding tight to their mother's skirts as her sister-in-law Anne rocked their baby daughter, Jane, in her arms.

Kicker's infant niece had been sickly since her birth the previous winter. If she were feverish when it came time for the family to be checked by the Canadian physician, would the family be denied entry solely on that basis? Kicker shivered as she imagined Adam's torment after having sold all he owned to pay for his family's journey, only to be turned back in the shadow of the promised land with no way to go forward and no means to go back. How many of these immigrants would even have enough to pay their way home if they were rejected? And who could they turn to for help in a strange land? Kicker knew that societies existed to assist new immigrants with information, temporary shelter, and even hot meals, but what happened to those who never made it past the immigration officials?

Kicker's eyes filled with tears as she watched the rejected immigrants turn away from the table. She had a clear view now of the man's devastated face as he stared blankly across the hall. His wife looked up at him expectantly, his children fussed, and the baby started to wail, but he said nothing to any of them. He simply slung a large canvas bag over his shoulder and trudged off, disappearing into the crowd with his family in his wake.

After sending a silent prayer for their safety after the unfortunate family, then adding one for all the immigrant hopefuls, especially Seamus and Pudge, Kicker reluctantly turned her attention to the official who steered them through the hall.

"It is very brave of you to travel without your husband's protection, Mrs. Bristow, but you must be wary of boosters. Sadly, though the police do closely monitor the docks and railway station, too many new immigrants fall prey to these confidence men. I don't expect that to happen to you, of course, but you must guard your purse well. Many a gentleman and lady have lost their wallets to a skillful dip."

"Thank you for the advice, Sir. We will indeed be on our guard."

The official beamed as Madelyn graced him with a warm smile. "They should have given you a voucher for your trunks while on board, Madame. If you will give it to me, I will see to their recovery."

Madelyn handed the man the paper. As he hurried off, Kicker steered her to a bench outside the noisy hall. Though the pier was almost as crowded as the hall, few people lingered after making it through the immigration gauntlet, and the benches there were mostly clear.

"Sit for a moment, Maddie. You're lookin' a bit pale."

"As compared to what, dearest? I don't think Uncle Royce would be much impressed with my constitution at the moment."

Kicker sat beside her. "P'rhaps not, but according to Louis, a few days of his ma's cookin' and you'll be good as new."

Madelyn patted her small grip. "We'll know soon enough. I have his letter of introduction, and I do hope he was not exaggerating out of familial conceit. I would dearly like a quiet place to recuperate for a few days. We need to write our families of our safe journey, and I must send Adelaide a telegram to let her know our expected arrival date in Winnipeg. I did write her once I booked our passage, but I've not heard from her in four months. I expect she's been very busy. They had their sixth child last fall, and I know that she and Charles have their hands full with the farm."

Kicker regarded Madelyn with amusement. "An' when you write, will you tell your family of how you spent the crossin'?"

"Not in great detail, no. I'd hate to disillusion them about the joys of ocean travel."

"I kinda liked it. Oh, not the part where you suffered, mind."

"I know, dearest. You took to the sea like Lord Nelson, himself. I do believe there is no force in nature that could knock you off your stride."

Kicker blushed and mumbled, "You do it so easy—e'ry time you look at me."

"Ah, but I'm not a force of nature."

"You changed my course as surely as the wind tosses a leaf. If that ain't a force of nature, I don' know what is."

Madelyn's response was cut short by a noisy crush of immigrants that spilled out of the hallway, boisterous in their excitement and relief. Kicker counted at least twenty in the large, multi-generational family. She couldn't help but smile as the white-haired matriarch issued instructions in a thick Yorkshire brogue. Even the smallest toddler got his marching orders while the family organized themselves for the next stage of their journey.

The women were silent, watching the family's energetic, if less than efficient assembly of goods and members. Finally the gaggle moved off across the pier and a relative calm resumed.

"What are you thinking about so deeply, dearest?"

Kicker, who idly watched the activity on the pier while her mind was on the plight of rejected immigrants, shrugged. "He said we were brave to travel without your husban's protection."

"Yes, he did. You don't agree?"

"They're the brave 'uns, Maddie." Kicker nodded at a young couple who had just exited the hall and staggered under a load of bags and boxes. "You got money, position, prospects, and your family name to protect us. What have they got? Dreams? Hopes? A few shillin' in their pockets? That's real courage—to step out into the unknown with so little."

"I agree that we're starting out with many more advantages, but surely you can acknowledge that it's at least somewhat courageous of us to have made the same journey to an unknown destination."

Kicker heard the underlying hurt in Madelyns voice. "Aw, I din't mean it like that. I jus' meant...well, say we'd been turned back for some reason. We'd jus' get back on the boat and go home, right?"

"Perish the thought. You would have to tie me in chains to get me back on that ship."

Kicker was amused at the horror in Madelyn's voice. "Maybe sea travel's like birthin'. Ma says you forget the pain once tis done, so you don' min' doin' it again."

"Trust me, dearest, I'll never forget this journey."

"I know, and God willin', you'll ne'er have to make it again. But what I meant was that if any of these people get turned back, maybe they cannot jus' get back on the ship. Maybe they got no money for passage or maybe they got nothin' to go back to. Maybe they put all their courage into jus' gettin' here in the firs' place and got nothin' lef' inside to go anywhere else and try again."

The arrival of the official with their trunks in tow ended their conversation. He saw them into a carriage, and, having ascertained their destination, issued a stream of instructions in rapid fire French. Kicker decided he must have impressed on their driver the need for swift and direct transport, because within twenty minutes they pulled up in front of a small, but tidy inn.

"Would you wait here with the trunks while I ensure that Louis' family has room for us?"

Kicker eyed Madelyn with concern. "Are you sure you can make it inside a'right?"

Madelyn patted her arm. "I'm sure. I'd just rather one of us kept an eye on things until we are safely settled. Here, take this to pay the driver once I've ascertained that our arrangements are in order."

Kicker accepted the coins and watched Madelyn slowly make her way inside.

The letter of introduction proved effective, for within moments, three young men swarmed out of L'Auberge de St. Christophe. They hustled around the carriage unloading trunks, while Madelyn beckoned to her from the doorway.

Kicker hastily paid the driver and joined her. She barely had time to greet Madame Gagnon before she and Madelyn were led up to their room.

When the door closed behind them, enclosing them in a pleasant, sun-lit corner room with their trunks neatly piled in the corner, Kicker and Madelyn blinked at each other.

"They're a remarkably efficient lot, aren't they?"

"Aye, that they are." Kicker took Madelyn's arm and gently pushed her towards the bed between the front and side windows, where a pleasant breeze could be felt. "Why don' you lie down a bit and rest?"

"Will you lie with me?"

Kicker stopped short and eyed her closely.

Madelyn chuckled at the scrutiny. "No, dearest. I don't think I'm quite up to what you have on your mind at the moment, but I would enjoy feeling you near."

Kicker blushed at how easily she was read. She latched the door before joining Madelyn on the edge of the bed. Madelyn turned to indicate the row of buttons on her dress, and Kicker, by now well used to the delicate fasteners, made quick work of undoing them. Then she allowed Madelyn to return the favour and enjoyed the feel of her lover's hand trailing over the back of her neck and shoulders. Shivering at the feelings that touch engendered deep within, Kicker decided the wisest course was for them both to leave their chemises in place.

Seeing the fatigue on Madelyn's face strengthened her resolve. Kicker laid both of their dresses carefully over the dresser before she stretched out next to Madelyn on the narrow bed.

Madelyn tucked her head on Kicker's shoulder and was asleep within moments. Kicker, who had been convinced she was not the least bit sleepy, was lulled by the steady hum of street noises coming in through the open window and soon joined her in slumber. It was dusk when they woke to the sound of a knocking on their door.

"Aye?"

A high pitched, young voice answered. "Maman sent up some food. She said to tell Madame Bristow not to bother coming down tonight, but to rest and feel better. Oh, and Louis is home. He said to say he would see you tomorrow, too."

Madelyn, now full awake, responded, "Thank you. Please leave the tray by the door." She kissed Kicker's shoulder. "Would you mind bringing in Madame Gagnon's bounty, dearest? I'll light the lamp so we can see what we're eating."

They made swift work of the consommé and tourtiere. Kicker was delighted to see Madelyn take a small second helping of the pork pie. She thought her lover looked better, though it was hard to be certain by lamplight.

Once the dishes were set aside, Madelyn brought out her silk covered handkerchief box and took cream coloured paper and two pens from within. She fetched an inkwell from her trunk and set the items on the small desk that had served as their table.

Kicker frowned as she was handed a pen and a sheet of paper.

"None of that, dearest. I promised Adam that you'd write, and write you shall."

"You said once a month, an' I wrote him from London."

Madelyn smiled at Kicker's protest. "By the time your letter arrives, it'll be well past a month since you bade him farewell. Do you not think he will be hungry for word of your wellbeing?"

"I suppose." Kicker pulled a chair up and regarded the paper glumly. Though her studies with Madelyn had made her literate, she far preferred reading to writing, and if given a choice, would select riding over either. However, Kicker really did not want Adam or her family to worry, so she set to work. Three brief paragraphs later, she signed her name and looked up to see that Madelyn was already at the bottom of her second page.

She took a moment to admire Madelyn's swift hand and the elegant script that covered the page, when something occurred to her. "Maddie?"

"Yes, dearest?"

"Will there not be a problem if your letters come addressed to 'Miss' Bristow? Will the people of Galbraith's Crossing not question why your family addresses you so?"

Madelyn stopped short. "Good heavens, that never occurred to me." She tapped the end of the pen against her chin as she considered it.

Kicker waited, confident that Madelyn would swiftly solve the problem. She was not disappointed.

"I have a solution. What if I simply tell my mother that I've assumed a married persona to avoid the persistent advances by the multitude of men seeking a wife over here? Naturally I shall drop such a charade immediately, should a likely seeming gentleman enter my life, but in the meantime, she and my family could assist me in this innocent deception by addressing all letters to me as Mrs. M.E. Bristow, c/o Galbraith's Crossing. What do you think?"

"I think you'd better change the Major's name from Kingsley."

"Of course. It will have to be something with an M..."

"Pudge's real name is Michael. Would that do?"

Madelyn smiled. "Michael, it is. I am now the wife of Major Michael Elliston Bristow, of the Queen's 12th Lancers. I must remember to tell Lil when I write her." She yawned, and Kicker set her pen aside.

"Why don' you finish up your letter? I'll take the dishes down, and you get yourself back to bed."

Madelyn looked at her gratefully. "I promise I'll make this up to you, dearest. I'm already feeling so much better, though oddly the floor still seems to sway now and then."

"Aye, I felt it too, back on the pier. I suspect twill pass."

Kicker gave Madelyn a quick kiss before she dressed and gathered the dishes. By the time she returned from the kitchen, Madelyn had returned to bed and was sound asleep.

Wide awake, Kicker extinguished the lamp and sat at the window, watching the streets below which bustled with horses, carriages, and pedestrians until well past the midnight toll of church bells. The long nap had rested her body, and her mind was far too active to sleep.

Between caring for Madelyn and enjoying the companionship of the Kelly brothers while at sea, she had barely taken time to contemplate the remarkable turn in her life. Now, bathed by the warm, humid night air, Kicker marveled at the fact that she was sitting half a world away from everything she had ever known. As a child, even a trip to London would have seemed like an exotic endeavour. Content with her life, Kicker never once considered leaving the confines of her small village or Grindleshire Academy. Until Madelyn came into her life.

Kicker glanced over her shoulder and a smile touched her lips. Madelyn's face was serenely illuminated in the moonlight and peaceful in sleep.

"What have you done, my love? Where will we end this a'venture you've set us on?"

Madelyn stirred at the murmured words then settled back; her steady breathing marked the depth of her slumber.

Kicker watched her a few more moments, then rose and stretched to ease muscles stiffened by long hours at the window. She disrobed and set her dress aside as she crossed to Madelyn's bed. Kneeling, she gently brushed back some strands of hair before she kissed a pale brow.

"Matters not, does't, love? As long as where e'er we end, we're t'gether." The words barely made a sound in the dark room.

Kicker caressed Madelyn's shoulder before crossing to her own bed. Eschewing a nightshirt because of the heat, she pushed back the covers and settled into the soft bed. Though the sea voyage had not bothered her, Kicker too relished the comfort of a bed that didn't move, and within moments she drifted off.

The women looked up from their dinner to see Louis approaching their table. Both smiled to see him, and Madelyn invited him to join them.

"Merci, Madame, but no. I must return to the *Assiniboine*, as we sail on the evening tide. Before I go, I wanted to wish you well on the rest of your journey."

"You're leavin' a'ready? You've only had three days here."

"Oui, Mam'selle." Louis nodded to Kicker. "We will 'ave longer after the next voyage, but Capitaine 'arvey does not like to waste time. I will miss Maman's cooking, though."

"It is every bit as good as you promised, Louis. It was so kind of you to facilitate our stay here. It's readily apparent that your parents run an extraordinarily busy inn, yet we couldn't have asked for better or more considerate treatment. Thank you very much for telling us of L'Auberge de St. Christophe, and for the lovely letter of introduction."

Louis fidgeted at Madelyn's praise. "It was my pleasure, Madame. I know Maman has enjoyed having ladies such as yourselves here." He leaned closer and jerked a thumb at the table behind them, where two rough looking men sat devouring their meal with no semblance of couth. "They're the more usual patrons, and the reason Papa keeps an axe handle under the check-in counter." He winked at them.

Kicker had noticed during their three days at the inn that they were the only unaccompanied women in the place, but they had encountered no problems from fellow guests. Madame Gagnon had made it her personal mission to see that they were not bothered, and any man who crossed their path was watched like a hawk. The few who dared approach the women were instantly swarmed by the innumerable younger Gagnons who did everything in the inn from sweeping, to serving, to chopping wood and making up rooms. Kicker had been unable to determine exactly how many siblings Louis had, but she could testify to the effective way in which they ran interference under the direction of their all-seeing mother.

"We wish you a wonderful voyage, Louis, however you'll forgive me if I would rather not travel with you again."

Louis laughed. "Mais oui, Madame. I understand perfectly. Not everyone is meant to go to sea. One of my brothers also 'ired on with the Dominion Line, but 'e suffered from such severe mal-de-mer that 'e never made it past the mouth of the St. Laurent before 'e 'ad to quit. I wish you a smooth journey to your destination. May St. Christophe see you safely on your way." He gave them a little bow and left them to their excellent dinner.

The women were quiet as they finished their ragout de boulettes and warm, crispy bread. A loud belch caught their attention, and though Madelyn determinedly ignored the louts at the table behind them, Kicker couldn't help eavesdropping on the men's conversation.

"Are you headin' back to Saskatoon tomorrow?"

"Yeah, my damned brother is runnin' the business, and no doubt skimmin' my profits til I won't have a dollar to my name."

"Good money to be made then?"

"Hell, yeah. Those greenhorns arrive by the trainload, and half of 'em don't know one end of a horse from the other. You tell 'em what they need to have to homestead, and they're so bloody grateful for the advice that they don't even care that ya charge 'em triple." The men guffawed in unison as Kicker frowned.

"Hey, mebbe you kin tell me. I heard that some of those damned fools won't buy a horse unless he's already harnessed, cuz they don't know which end is which."

"It's true. I seen 'em draw chalk lines along the horses themselves, just so's they'd know where to put the harness the next mornin'. No word of a lie."

The second man snorted, and out of the corner of her eye, Kicker could see him shaking his dirty mane of hair.

"God save us all from 'gentlemen' immigrants. Can't say I got much use for the Irish, but at least they ain't afraid to get their hands dirty and they know how to work the land."

"You ever read the employment ads out in the Territories? Half of 'em say 'No English need apply', and I don't blame 'em one bit. Nothin' worse than some cocksure bastard who thinks the rest of us should kiss his ruddy boots on account of his family name. And ain't nothin' I love more than seein' one of them conceited know-it-alls run cryin' home to England cuz the winter's too cold and the land's too harsh."

"You said it."

A touch on her hand drew Kicker's attention back to her own table. Troubled, she said, "They don' seem to like us much, Maddie."

"I believe we should pay more heed to men like Will and Albert MacDiarmid, dearest. I'm sure some Englishmen have not acquitted themselves proudly, but I'm equally sure that many have. Otherwise the Canadian government would not be going to such lengths to inveigle prospective immigrants. These men may hardly represent the views of those we'll encounter in Galbraith's Crossing."

"Maybe you're right." Kicker finished up her last few bites of the meatball and pig's feet stew. But, even after they left the dining room, she could not shake the echo of gleeful malice in the men's voices.

Both women declined the blueberry tart Madame Gagnon pressed on them and bade the warm, motherly woman goodnight as they left the table and returned to their room.

Kicker automatically shed her skirt and shirtwaist as soon as they were back in their room. She had reluctantly accepted the need to cater to Madame Gagnon's traditional sensibilities while they were under her roof, but dispensed with the hated garb the moment they were away from critical eyes. Clad only in her chemise, Kicker stood off to one side of the window, hidden by the curtain. She resumed her observation of the fascinating and unending pageant of Montreal street life that had enthralled her the last three days.

She was so absorbed in the spectacle that she didn't notice Madelyn's approach until she felt arms circle her waist and firm breasts push against her back. Kicker leaned back into the welcome embrace and her eyes widened as a low voice sounded behind her ear.

"Might I draw your attention away from the street this one night, dearest?"

Whatever answer Kicker might have made was stillborn as hands rose to firmly cup her breasts while mischievous fingers teased her nipples.

"Bless'd Jesus!" Kicker's knees almost buckled. She wanted nothing more than to give in to her instant rush of desire, but she forced herself to ask, "Are you sure?"

"That I love you? That I want you? That if you do not touch me very soon, I shall die of deprivation? Absolutely."

There was not the least bit of doubt in the throaty growl that caressed her ears, and Kicker spun to face her sweet tormenter. Without a word, she took a step back, slowly drew her chemise up over her head and thrilled to the amorous expression on Madelyn's flushed face.

Still not speaking, Kicker dropped the garment to the floor and deliberately crossed the room to Madelyn's bed. She lay back on the bed and watched with mingled lust and merriment as her lover's suddenly clumsy fingers fumbled to undo her dress.

"You could help here, dearest."

"Aye, I could."

Madelyn glanced up at the amusement in Kicker's voice and shook her head as she shed the first layer of clothing. "What happened to that shy innocent who feared to even lie beside me the night I confessed my love?"

"You taught her well."

Tearing at the laces holding her stays, Madelyn groaned. "God in Heaven, did I ever." She glanced up and froze as she watched Kicker run one hand deliberately over a hardened nipple and down the centre of her belly. As nimble fingers provocatively explored their path and slowly dipped between outstretched legs, stays, chemise, drawers and shoes flew off in rapid succession to land in haphazard array on the floor.

Kicker was well aware that Madelyn's fevered gaze was locked on her, even as she knelt to strip off her stockings. Deliberately she tilted one knee away from the other and ran a hand up her inner thigh. Her lover's deep, almost anguished moan was her reward. Within seconds Madelyn stood at the foot of the bed, breathing as hard as if she had just run a race.

Madelyn lifted her gaze from where Kicker's hand moved languidly between her legs and the women stared at each other, hardly breathing. They had not made love since their hasty encounter in Gertie's bedroom prior to their departure. Kicker hadn't wanted to rush Madelyn in her recovery, but the ache for her touch never abated.

It was very apparent Kicker was not the only one eager to end their illness-enforced abstinence. As Madelyn deliberately lowered herself to the bed, Kicker felt the touch of her lover's mouth. She soared into an immediate orgasm, choking back the sounds that fought to spill from her throat. She was shocked at her instant response, but had little time to consider it. Madelyn allowed her no respite and her body quickly rose again to meet her lover's urgency.

A long while later, finally forced by sheer exhaustion to desist, both women rested in quiet contentment. Kicker half lay across Madelyn, her head on her thigh and her lower legs tucked under Maddie's arm and hanging off the edge of the bed.

She could hear an almost inaudible hum of satisfaction from Madelyn as she slowly stroked Kicker's body. She caught herself drifting, and forced herself to open her eyes. Her lover's adoring gaze was fixed on her, and Kicker smiled at the joy therein.

"I guess you're ready to travel then?"

Madelyn tilted her head teasingly against the pillows as if considering the matter, then nodded. "I settled our account with Madame Gagnon this afternoon when young Luc was showing you the stables. We'll be on our way in the morning."

"Good." Kicker had no desire at all to move to a more conventionally comfortable position, so she allowed her eyes to drift shut again. After a long moment she felt Madelyn's hand trace a path up the back of her thigh and come to rest between her legs. It was not a demand, simply an unspoken assumption of intimacy, and Kicker smiled as she heard Madelyn's breathing begin to deepen.

Kicker was unable to summon enough energy to consider what must be done in preparation for their departure in a few hours. Finally, utterly content, she allowed the pleasant lassitude to overwhelm her and joined Madelyn in sleep.

CHAPTER 10

MADELYN DABBED AT THE SWEAT on her upper lip with a handkerchief that was now a mottled grey. The rocking of the train car, while not as oppressive as that of the *SS Assiniboine*, still left her feeling queasy. Though they had only departed Montreal four days earlier, it felt like forever that they had been traveling on the rough tracks. Hour after interminable hour they chugged on through the small, familiar-feeling towns and villages of English Ontario, the thick forests and daunting granite of the Canadian Shield, and for the last hour or two, the endless prairie vistas of Manitoba.

In Montreal, Madelyn took one look at the standard immigrant cars that ferried would-be homesteaders to their western destinations and rebelled. She immediately upgraded them to first class tickets, despite Kicker's protests that they should conserve their funds where they could. Though the smells, sounds, and service in the first class car were immeasurably better than in the immigrant cars, little could be done to alleviate the heat, soot, and boredom of the long journey.

Now, four days out from Montreal and nearing Winnipeg, even Kicker's unrelenting fascination with the passing landscape had become a source of irritation. Madelyn found she was hard pressed not to snap at her innocent companion.

"Look, Maddie." Kicker pointed out the open window toward an odd-looking structure just north of the tracks. The slow moving train gave ample time to consider the house, but Madelyn barely glanced at it. "Tis almos' like tis made of earth."

The gentleman seated across the aisle from them smiled. "It actually is, Miss. They're called 'soddies', and they are in fact constructed using sod cut from the ground. Timber can be scarce in these parts, so if available at all, it's usually reserved for framing, then sod bricks are piled up for the walls and roof, and plastered with clay. They call them 'prairie shingles', and when it rains, sometimes it rains two days longer inside."

Madelyn frowned at the eager way Kicker hung on the man's words, but her lover was heedless of her annoyance and picked up the conversation.

"Why would it do that?"

"The sod absorbs the moisture as it did when it was in the ground, and with no other place for it to go, sheds it slowly within the cabin." The man leaned forward, a twinkle in his eyes. "But that's not the worst drawback of living in a soddy."

"Tis not? I'd think havin' it rain on your table would be pretty annoyin'."

"True, Miss, but how would you feel if a snake crawled out of your ceiling and joined you for breakfast?"

Kicker's eyes widened, but before she could respond, the gentleman's wife tapped him sharply on the arm with the fan she had been using energetically, but to little effect.

"Herbert. For heaven's sakes." The matron leaned around her husband and looked at the two women. "Please don't let him discourage or mislead you. The vast majority of us live in perfectly respectable homes, and the only sod you'll find on our property is out in the pastures. What you saw there was probably no more than a relic of some settler's initial attempt at shelter, or perhaps a storage shed."

Kicker turned to the window to watch the odd shelter recede in the distance. Madelyn could tell by the thoughtful expression on Kicker's face that the lady's words had not entirely convinced her. *And knowing her, she probably thinks a snake crawling through one's ceiling is an adventure.*

Aware that her sour mood was no fault of her companion, Madelyn resolved not to take it out on Kicker. She turned her thoughts instead to the upcoming reunion with Adelaide and Charles. She had a great affection for her old friend, and knew that she could depend on Adelaide to lift her spirits and cajole her into a more positive frame of mind.

Adelaide had always been one of the most lively, charismatic driving forces behind the nascent Suffragette movement. Her energy and enthusiasm were contagious. Despite the fact that Adelaide was the mother of four young children at the time, she always seemed to be in the thick of planning and strategizing. Her amiable husband, Charles, came in for his share of criticism for allowing his wife so much independence, but their relationship thrived on their diverse interests. Madelyn was shocked when Adelaide announced that they were moving to Canada, but her friend's relentless optimism and fervent descriptions of their new home-to-be had planted the seed of her own departure.

Since Adelaide arrived in the new country, her letters were sporadic but positive, at least until the previous fall when her sixth child was born. The last letter Madelyn received several months earlier spoke of the newborn's uncertain health. Although Adelaide closed with her usual sunny invitation to come and join them in building the young country, Madelyn had not heard from her since.

Indeed Madelyn's current querulous mood, though aggravated by the hardships of the long train trip, was underpinned with worry. She sent letters to Adelaide from London informing her of their plans to visit, and had followed up with a telegram from Montreal giving their arrival date, but Madelyn had heard nothing in return.

She tried to convince herself that delivery of Adelaide's response must have missed them in passing or been delayed until past their departure date. Perhaps Addie was simply too busy—between her children and the demands of their family farm—to write. But the closer the train drew to Winnipeg, the more concerned Madelyn became. She began to make contingency plans in case she was unable to find her old friend once they reached the city.

As the train began to mount a small rise, a laugh from Kicker drew her attention. Her companion was watching several young men from the immigrant cars who ran alongside, then dropped back to jump up on the train again. A scowling conductor marched past the ladies toward the rear of their car. His efforts to discourage the train racers with threats and curses had thus far produced little result, and Madelyn couldn't help feeling sympathy for the young men. *If I were restricted to those foul cars, I'd seize any opportunity to get off for a few minutes, too.* Then she noticed the sparkle in Kicker's eyes.

Madelyn fixed a stern glare on her. "Do not even consider the possibility."

"Wasn't." Kicker's assurance was belied by her sheepish expression.

Madelyn leaned forward and patted Kicker's hand. "We'll be in Winnipeg in less than an hour. You'll have at least a week of being on solid, unmoving ground again. If you find yourself in need of some exercise, I'm sure that Charles would be delighted with any assistance you could offer him around their farm."

Despite Kicker's fascination with the landscape, Madelyn knew it had to be hard on her to be sedentary for so long. They hadn't dared to find surcease from the boredom, even in the illusionary privacy of their sleeper compartment, and had contented themselves with the briefest of stolen kisses. Madelyn decided that if Adelaide and Charles were not waiting for them at the Winnipeg station, they would take a room in the city, at least for a night. Once they made their way out to the farm, they would be even less likely, in the household of eight, to find the privacy to indulge their desires.

The thought of a night alone with Kicker finally put a smile on Madelyn's face. When the train slowed and crawled into the Winnipeg station, she found herself hoping that their hosts would not be waiting.

Those hopes were dashed soon after disembarking, when they were approached by a serious young man, his wide-brimmed straw hat in hand. "Ma'am, would you be Miss Bristow?"

"Indeed. Why, Charlie Jr, is that you?"

"Yes, Ma'am. Father couldn't get away, so he sent me to pick you up."

Madelyn squelched her disappointment and gave the boy a smile. "Thank you, Charlie. That was very good of you." She signaled the porter who had manhandled their trunks out of storage, and he trailed them with the cart as they followed Charlie past the station to the street beyond. "Goodness, you've grown since I last saw you. But then I guess it has been a few years."

"Yes, Ma'am."

Charlie stopped by an old buckboard, which had wisps of hay protruding between slats and over the tail. Without a word, he helped the porter lift the trunks to the bed of the wagon, and solemnly assisted Madelyn to the plank seat. Kicker jumped lightly into the back and took a seat on the largest trunk. Charlie didn't glance at her before he untied his horse and took a place beside Madelyn. She realized belatedly that she had not introduced Kicker to the taciturn young man.

Charlie concentrated on guiding the horse around other wagons and through the noisy crowd of mostly men, who were gathered in the streets around the station and the adjoining grain elevators and shops.

With an apologetic look over her shoulder, Madelyn addressed their driver. "I'm sorry, Charlie. I neglected to introduce you to my cousin, Kicker Stuart. She's accompanying me out west to Alberta."

That got a reaction, and Charlie shot a look of surprise over his shoulder. Madelyn realized that he had assumed Kicker—in her trousers, boots and wide-brimmed hat—was a young man. His was not an uncommon confusion, as Kicker had insisted on changing back to her familiar, comfortable garb as soon as they began their train journey. But the fact that Kicker now wore Roderick's high quality, if somewhat outdated clothes at least gave her a semblance of respectability.

Charlie awkwardly tipped his hat to Kicker, who nodded soberly in response.

Madelyn could tell the boy was uncomfortably aware that he had consigned a woman to the cargo section while he sat up front, so she attempted to distract him. "How are your parents? I'm so looking forward to seeing them again. I've missed your mother terribly since you all moved away."

"Father is doing well. It's been a good year for Red Fife, and he's already getting ready for the threshing. He thinks we'll be able to start harvesting within two weeks. Might even make a decent profit this year if the bloody freight rates aren't raised again." Charlie punctuated his comment by spitting contemptuously over the side of the wagon, then he shot Madelyn an apologetic look. "Sorry, Ma'am. That was rude."

Madelyn stifled a smile. "I take it the freight rates are a bone of contention in this part of the country?"

That set Charlie off, and for the next hour as they left the city behind and drove briskly over progressively narrower dirt roads, he vented passionately about the perfidy of the Canadian Pacific Railroad, the corruption of its rapacious agents, and the arrogance of Eastern economic interests that exploited the poor, hardworking farmers of the West. By the time they turned into the long driveway that led to a wooden frame house, Madelyn had been given a thorough primer in Western politics and culture.

A woman and two young girls hung laundry on a line at the side of the house. They stopped working as the wagon rolled down the driveway and pulled to a halt at a hitching post in the yard. Madelyn waved as her old friend walked quickly toward them, her daughters tucked behind her wide skirt and peering out curiously.

"Adelaide!" Madelyn waited impatiently for Charlie to tie off the horse and help her down from her seat. "Adelaide!"

"Charlie, your father is in the barn with your brother. He wants you out there immediately." Only after her son had nodded his acknowledgement and set off did Adelaide give Madelyn a terse smile and a quick hug. "Well, Maddie, you made it. Wasn't sure you would." She addressed her daughters, who stared openly at Kicker. "You girls finish up with the laundry while I get these two settled."

Madelyn and Kicker exchanged baffled looks before falling in behind Adelaide as she led the way to the front door of the house. Madelyn was shocked—both by the physical changes in her friend and the coolness of her greeting. Adelaide was thin to the point of gauntness, and her clothes flapped on her as she walked. Though only a decade older than Madelyn, deep, new lines had carved themselves into her weary face, and eyes that once sparkled with the excitement of life were now jaded and wary.

"The boys will sleep in the barn and you two can have their room." Adelaide opened the bedroom door and gestured them inside. "Should be water in the pitcher. Go ahead and wash up, then meet me in the kitchen. I'll have the boys fetch your things when they come in for dinner." With that, their hostess disappeared through another doorway that apparently led to the back of the house.

Madelyn stared after her until Kicker gently tugged her inside and closed the bedroom door. Dazed, Madelyn looked around. She surveyed the contents of the tiny room without awareness until she felt Kicker wrap her hands around a tin cup.

"Here. Drink this. Twas a long journey and you mus' be dry."

Madelyn numbly drank down the lukewarm water. Then she handed the mug back to Kicker and sank down on the edge of the room's only bed. Helplessly she looked up at her companion.

"I don't know what's happened to her, dearest. I swear she and I've been the best of friends. Her letters continually urged me to consider joining her and Charles in their new land. Now it's like we're the most unwanted of intruders."

Kicker sat beside her. "P'rhaps tis me she cannot abide."

Madelyn shook her head. "I don't see how that could be, dearest. All I told her in advance was that my cousin had joined me on this adventure, and I was grateful for the company. She would have no reason to take umbrage at that."

"Then this, maybe?" Kicker tweaked the material of her trousers.

"Adelaide was the first in our set to adopt bloomers for swimming. Heavens, she even named her firstborn daughter Amelia, after Mrs. Amelia Bloomer. I'm sure that your clothing isn't it, either. No, there's more to this than first meets our eye, dearest, and I intend to find out what it is."

Madelyn's distress evolved into a determination to discover what lay behind the dramatic changes in her friend. However, when they made their way to the kitchen, they were immediately put to work helping with dinner preparations, and any questions beyond the immediate and practical were forestalled.

Detailed to slice apples for a pie, Madelyn was startled anew when she witnessed how deftly Kicker made biscuits that drew a nod of approval from their gruff hostess. When she raised a questioning eyebrow at Kicker, all she got was a wink and a grin. However that small mystery was lost in the bigger one, which began to unfold with an innocent question Madelyn addressed to Adelaide.

"Is the baby asleep now? I've been looking forward to meeting the latest member of your family. I imagine Georgie is quite the little man now, too. The last time I saw him, he was still in swaddling clothes."

Adelaide barely paused as she rolled crusts for the pies. "Georgie and Eliza both passed this spring, gone not long after the snow melted."

Madelyn gasped. "Oh, dear Lord! Adelaide, I am so, so sorry." She reached out an arm to her friend, but before she could say anything further or offer a hug, the two girls came in the back door.

"We finished hanging the clothes, Mama."

"Then the chickens need to be fed and the eggs haven't been collected yet. And tell Benjamin that he needs to bring in more carrots from the cold cellar. I haven't enough for company." Adelaide ignored the stricken looks from her guests as she pulled a bowl from the cupboard. "Amelia, tell your brother to fill this to the top and bring it to me right away."

The older girl took the bowl. "Yes, Mama." She stopped before they reached the back door. "Can me and Joanie play after that?"

Adelaide shook her head. "You two still have to do the mending that you didn't finish yesterday. Get that done and then you can play until dinner."

The two girls pouted but did not protest, and as they left the kitchen, Madelyn tried again.

"Adelaide, I'm so sorry for your loss—"

"The Lord giveth and the Lord taketh away—isn't that what they always say?"

The bitterness in Adelaide's voice was so pronounced that it stopped Madelyn in her tracks. It was not until hours later that she finally got her old friend alone to talk. Charlie and Benjamin had gone to make up their pallets in the barn, Amelia and Joanie had been sent to bed, and Kicker was assisting Charles—over his initial protests—to straighten out several bent tines in the thresher in the long summer twilight. Madelyn, helped clean up the post-dinner leavings, then coaxed Adelaide into taking a cup of tea to the porch. They sat in twin rockers, and Madelyn let Adelaide sit, sip, and rock for many long minutes before she braced her friend.

"Adelaide, why didn't you write me about Georgie and Eliza?" Madelyn had turned her chair so that she could see her friend in the dwindling light, so she saw the flash of misery pass over Adelaide's tired face.

"What good would it have done, Maddie? Nothing could bring them back. What would be the point of fruitless caterwauling?"

Madelyn rocked slowly as she considered her words. "So you gave yourself no time to grieve? Surely that's not healthy. You were always the one who asserted that we women listen to our own minds and bodies, rather than the voices of those who declared how we must think and behave."

That was met by a derisive snort, but Madelyn was sure she could hear an underlying wistfulness, too. "I mean it, Adelaide. Your babies died..."

"Many do in this cursed land."

"Cursed?" Madelyn leaned forward and laid a hand on her friend's forearm. "But you always spoke of this as if it were the land of milk and honey."

"The land of bugs and blight is more like it." Adelaide's rocker picked up speed. "You've made a mistake, Maddie, and I'm sorry that I did not tell you true and advise you against leaving England. This is a fierce, harsh land. The summers burn the crops, and the winters sear your lungs. Every day is a struggle to live—to see your children live—while a vengeful God sits on His throne and laughs at your best efforts."

The caustic words began to flow faster and Madelyn sat quietly and listened.

The more Adelaide spoke, the faster her chair rocked, as she ignored the perilous plight of the tea which ricocheted violently in her cup. "When you need rain, you can count on it drying up. When you pray for sunny days to bring in the harvest, an early freeze will surely lay the crop to waste. The flies and mosquitoes torment you until you think you'll go mad. If the drought and the cold don't destroy you first, summer lightning ignites the land, and flames race unchecked, burning everything in their path. And if, by the beneficent disregard of a neglectful God, you do beat all those odds, He'll roll the dice with smallpox and measles and typhoid and polio..." Adelaide's voice broke and her words ended as tears flowed freely down her weathered cheeks.

Madelyn rose and, setting aside her tea, knelt beside Adelaide. She took her weeping friend in her arms as the woman finally gave voice to her grief. When finally the deep, guttural sobs slowed and quieted, Madelyn urged softly, "Tell me."

Adelaide mopped her face on one sleeve and leaned back in her chair. "Eliza was poorly from the start. She always seemed to be sickly from one week to another, but Georgie was a sturdy boy, solid as an English oak even as a babe. So when Georgie came down with the pox first, I was sure he would recover. But the doctor took him away from me. Said he had to be in the isolation hospital so he wouldn't infect anyone else. Two days later Eliza showed the pox and I didn't want to tell anyone. I begged Charles to let me look after my baby myself. I said we'd go stay in the shed so we weren't a danger to anyone, but he wouldn't let me. He said we couldn't chance the other children catching it, and he took her to the hospital himself." Adelaide closed her eyes, and Madelyn was shaken at the depth of grief on her face. "I hated him for that. She was less than five months old, and all alone."

"Surely there were doctors and nurses to look after the patients?" Madelyn whispered.

"There were so many took sick this spring. The Grey Nuns did all they could, but most of their charges died. Many of the nuns did, too, and bless them for trying, but they couldn't save my Georgie, or my baby girl. Eliza and her big brother were dead before week's end. They died abandoned and forsaken, surely wondering where their mama was—and I couldn't get to them, couldn't tell them how much I loved them or how sorry I was for bringing them to this Godforsaken land."

At a loss for any words that might comfort her friend, Madelyn simply held her until the tension left Adelaide's body and a calloused hand wrapped around her arm.

"I'm sorry, Maddie. I've not been able to find any joy since my babies were taken, and it was a poor greeting today for a friend who came from so far." Adelaide set her tea aside and seized Madelyn's hands, staring at her feverishly. "Go back, Maddie. You listened to me and came here, now I'm begging you to go back. I would go home to England myself, only Charles won't go, and I won't leave my babies."

Madelyn wasn't sure whether her friend meant her surviving children or those lost that spring, but she was deeply shaken by the unbending conviction in Adelaide's voice.

"I know you well, Maddie, but it's not grand adventure you'll find in this land. Only tears and regret and futility await you, and I cannot bear to have that on my head, too. I beg you to set aside your pride and return to the gentle land of our birth. There is no escape for me, but the trap has not yet closed over you. You can go back."

Madelyn gently extricated herself from Adelaide's painfully tight grasp. "I really can't go back." She rose and determination supplanted the compassion in her eyes. "I'm so terribly saddened by what you and Charles and the children have gone through, but my cousin and I are bound to chart our own course. I've a position waiting for me, a life that I anticipate with great eagerness in a place that is fresh and new and offers all manner of possibilities."

Madelyn's words caused Adelaide to sag and turn to stare back out over the yard. "It's an illusion. What this land really offers is cloaked in the splendid words of the men who lured you here, in the bright promises that will, when they are broken, also break your heart and crush your spirit." Adelaide gave a harsh, soul searing cough. "What will you do when the fever strikes, your cousin dies, and you are left alone in your new home?"

Madelyn shuddered at the bleakness in her friend's voice, unable to contemplate how losing Kicker would devastate her.

Adelaide didn't pause for an answer, expecting none. "What will you do when the icy winds and howling snows of January blind you mere feet from your front door? When you know if you choose the wrong direction between house and barn, it will be spring before they find your frozen, lifeless body? What will you do when you have eaten the last tin of pork and beans in the house and nothing now stands between your children and starvation? When they cry and beg for something you don't have to give them? What hope can you offer them in a land so unrelentingly fierce that no future is secure and no child may be sure of their next meal, let alone that they will live long enough to have children of their own?"

Madelyn knew that Adelaide was dealing with her own demons. She wanted to flee her friend's misery, yet was held by old bonds of affection and loyalty. Adelaide's next words, however, chilled her, despite the warmth of the summer evening.

Adelaide rested a hand on her stomach as her voice sank to a murmur. "Even now this one grows—waiting to take his turn, waiting to see if he might survive this game of chance. His mother cannot protect him; his father does not care how many of his children will abide in the churchyard before they're barely weaned. I swear if I could turn this babe back, I would. There is nothing here for him but sorrow unending."

Stymied for words of comfort, distressed by her utter inability to break through her old friend's pain, Madelyn retreated. In the shadow of the front door, she watched Adelaide's monotonous rocking until, unable to stand her helplessness any longer, she entered the house. Eyes filled with tears, she stood irresolute, unsure where to turn. Then she noticed Charles. He leaned against the wall beside the fireplace and stared at her.

"She thinks I don't care." The pain in Charles' voice was palpable. "She thinks I don't mourn for my little ones."

"Charles, I'm sure she doesn't—"

"No, she does. She blames me for bringing us here, but she forgets that we made that decision together. We had such dreams for our new home, such hopes for the lives our children would make and the land that would be ours alone." Charles pushed himself off the wall and crossed the room. He stopped where he could see his wife through the front window. "It has been a bad year, but we had three good years before that. We even proved up on our land before the deadline. But there are things I cannot control no matter how hard I work and how much I plan—she has to accept that."

"I... I don't know what to say to her, Charles."

"No more do I. She's not been herself since Eliza's birth, and after the babies passed, it got so much worse." Charles turned to face Madelyn, a look of grim determination on his face. "No matter what she says, we cannot go back. We've sunk everything we had into this life, and we have to make it work. There is no other choice. I know it's hard on a woman, being so far from her own kind with none but the children for company all day. I try, but there's so much work to be done that there is little time or energy at day's end for aught but sleep."

Madelyn laid a comforting hand on his arm. "I'm sure she's aware of that. She'll come around. The woman we know won't stay down for long."

"The woman we used to know, Maddie. I'm not so sure I know this woman." Charles turned to watch Adelaide again. They were quiet for long moments, then Charles grunted. "Your cousin is an unusually competent woman."

Madelyn smiled at the backhanded compliment. "Yes, I suppose she is."

"She was a big help tonight, and she offered to assist me and the boys with getting things ready for the harvest." Charles looked at Madelyn. "Will you be staying?"

His voice was neutral, and Madelyn knew he had steeled himself for her request to be taken immediately to the train station. Conflicted, she was torn between her desire to escape Adelaide's misery, and the feeling that would mean abandoning her old friends when they needed her most. Madelyn gave brief thought to what Kicker would say, and knew what side she would come down on.

"We'll stay for a few days, if that's all right with you."

He nodded curtly, but some of the tension seemed to leave him. "You'll be good for her." Charles took a step toward the door. "Your cousin has retired; you might wish to do the same. We rise early here."

Madelyn nodded as the front door swung open and Charles stepped out on the porch. Before she turned away, she saw him kneel beside Adelaide.

On her return from the outhouse, Madelyn paused to stare out over the prairies at the sunset, which limned the few clouds lingering over the horizon in shades of brilliant orange and gold. The immensity of the landscape and the splendour of the heavens took her breath away. When she shook herself out of her reverie, she hastened back to the house.

Noting that Charles and Adelaide were still out on the porch, she slipped quietly into her room.

Kicker was already in the bed, but her eyes opened as Madelyn began to shed her clothes. She remained quiet, until Madelyn turned off the lamp and pulled back her thin sheet. Kicker had worn a nightshirt, for propriety's sake, but she'd left her buttons unfastened.

"Wise woman," Madelyn murmured. She pushed the shirt aside and her hands moved urgently over her lover's body. Kicker seemed to understand the depth of her need, and made no move to slow or direct the pace. Even the distinct creak as the front door opened, then closed, did not give Madelyn pause.

She was grateful, though, that Kicker's quick response to her frenzied lovemaking was silent except for her ragged breathing. Only the sound of the bed's overstressed slats signalled her furious ardour as she drove herself against Kicker again and again. And when finally Madclyn collapsed on Kicker's body, more exhausted than satiated, she began to cry.

Kicker wrapped her arms around Madelyn and stroked her back while Maddie's tears soaked her shoulder and the pillow. She did not try to coax Madelyn to talk, nor did she tender any facile platitudes. Kicker had offered the solace of her body; now she offered the comfort of unspoken understanding, unstinting support, and unflinching strength.

CHAPTER 11

THE TRAVELERS HAD FINALLY PASSED beyond the unbroken flatlands. Though there were still many wide open areas between the booming city of Calgary and their destination nearer the mountains, they had clearly left the prairies behind and entered the hills, gulches, and forests of the foothills. Now, three days after their departure from Winnipeg, the sound of the train's whistle and the squeal of the wheels as they began to brake signalled their arrival into Galbraith's Crossing.

Kicker glanced quickly at Madelyn. She hoped she would share her excitement at finally reaching their new home, but Madelyn had been withdrawn since their departure from Winnipeg and merely nodded acknowledgement. Troubled, Kicker returned to perusing the town as they pulled into the station.

From what she could see, it was not much different from the dozens of other towns through which they'd passed on their journey across the prairies. The ubiquitous grain elevator stood next to the brick railroad station, and a general store, hotel, and livery stable were among the wooden buildings that lined the dirt main street. Two small churches with low white fences surrounding adjoining cemeteries anchored the east end of the thoroughfare with an equally small schoolhouse next to them. Kicker was much more interested in the several corrals filled with horses and surrounded by men near the livery stable.

Once the train stopped, Kicker led the way out onto the wooden platform and turned to offer Madelyn a hand.

Her companion stepped down and looked around. Kicker tried to read her countenance, keen to know if their new home made a good first impression, but it was impossible to interpret Madelyn's impassive expression.

A small boy stepped out of the shade next to the station and approached them. He swept off a ragged cap to reveal a mass of straw coloured hair that stuck out in all directions.

"Excuse me, Missus. Are you the new schoolteacher, Mrs. Bristow?"

When Madelyn nodded, his bright blue eyes dimmed in disappointment. "Aww, four more days and I'da had enough for my new wagon."

Kicker was relieved to see Madelyn regard the child with amusement. "Excuse me?"

Their welcomer looked embarrassed as he twisted his cap in his hands. "Mrs. Glenn was paying me to wait here for you. If you'd been four days later, I'da earned enough for my new wagon."

"Well, I do apologize for our precipitous arrival, Mr...?"

"Hanford William Donnelly, Ma'am, but everyone calls me Billy, except my ma. She says she christened me Hanford and that's what she's gonna call me." The boy scowled at the obvious indignity of his mother's intransigence.

"Well, Billy, perhaps you could tell me where we could find Mrs. Glenn. We should notify her immediately, as she apparently has been awaiting our arrival."

The boy turned and whistled sharply. A black and white border collie sprang from under a bench and dashed toward him. "Brander will go get her, Ma'am. That's why he's with me instead of with Mrs. Glenn. Normally you can't get him away from her side, but she told him to go with me while I waited." Billy whipped a dirty bandana out of his pocket and knotted it around the dog's neck. "Go find the boss, Brander."

The dog whirled and shot off around the station and down the street, his body low to the ground as he streaked around the few people in the road.

Madelyn turned to Kicker and nodded at a cart resting next to the door of the station. They were the only passengers who had disembarked from the train, which was already building up steam for its departure. "I see our trunks are off, so we may as well wait here for Mrs. Glenn."

Billy raised his hand and Kicker stifled a smile as he fidgeted eagerly.

"Yes, Billy?"

"Ma'am, Mrs. Glenn gave me money to buy you and... um..." The boy stared at Kicker with puzzlement in his eyes, as if unable to determine quite how she fit with the new teacher.

"This is my cousin, Miss Stuart, Billy."

Kicker extended her hand to the boy, who took it and returned her handshake with enthusiasm. "Call me Kicker."

"Mrs. Glenn said to buy you some lemonade over at Mrs. Thatcher's, and she'd be in as quickly as she could."

"Well, I suppose since she is the boss, we'd best go along with you," Madelyn said.

"Yes, ma'am. Mrs. Glenn will look after you—she looks after everything."

Madelyn and Kicker exchanged amused looks before the teacher addressed the boy again. "Mrs. Glenn sounds like a redoubtable lady." Billy frowned at the unfamiliar term and Madelyn clarified with a smile. "Well respected, influential..."

Billy nodded vigorously. "Mrs. Glenn and her family own the Steeple Seven. Her son Laird is my best friend, and my pa's the foreman of the Steeple Seven. It's the biggest an' oldest ranch in the district, an' everyone knows not to mess with the MacDiarmids...well, 'cept Rupert Arbuster, an' he's just a mean, jealous git, he is."

"Billy," Madelyn admonished. "It's not nice to speak spitefully of people behind their back."

Amused at how easily Madelyn dropped into her teacher persona, Kicker saw the boy blush and felt sorry for him. "Hey, Billy, what's goin' on down at the corrals?"

Billy shot her a grateful look. "My pa sent some of the hands in with a bunch of mustangs today. They were moving the herd to a new range this week. They didn't want the mustangs interfering with the grazin' of the cattle, so they rounded 'em up and brung 'em in."

Kicker's eyes brightened with excitement. "They're sellin' them?"

"Oh yeah. Well, some of them, anyway. My pa says that that some of the mustangs are just too wild to ever be broke, so they'll probably send those ones to slaughter." When Billy saw the look of outrage on Kicker's face, he hastened to assure her. "They have to, Miss...um, Kicker. They found mange in another bunch of mustangs, and if they don't catch it fast, it can spread to the cattle. They put down a bunch of the horses, but I guess these ones was healthy enough to sell. My pa says they're gonna hafta do a mange round-up and run a dip for at least two hundred head. I think that's what Mrs. Glenn's overseeing today. They were hoping Mr. Will and Mr. Albert would be back by now to help out, but they ain't due in until the weekend."

Kicker's indignance at the fate of the mustangs subsided, even as her interest in the horses grew. Despite her intention not to consider buying a horse until they were settled and she found work, she felt an overwhelming urge to take a look at the wild herd. She glanced up to find Madelyn watching her.

"Go ahead, Kicker. I'll have Billy escort me to Mrs. Thatcher's. Once Mrs. Glenn arrives, we'll seek you out."

"Thanks, Maddie. See you later, Billy." As she trotted away, Kicker touched the small leather bag that she had tied inside her trousers for security. It held a little over sixteen pounds—all the money she had in the world. But if Will MacDiarmid was right, three pounds of it would buy her a horse of her own. Not just any horse, though. It had to be one with the intelligence, nobility, and bearing of Banner, and that might take a while to find.

When Kicker arrived, the holding corral was still full of horses milling about nervously. The smaller cutting corral was almost completely surrounded by men and boys hooting and laughing at a cowboy on foot inside. He was trying to rope a small sorrel mare, so quick on her feet that she had danced away from every throw of his rope.

Kicker slipped into an open space beside the only man who watched quietly. She noticed the wild eyes and flared nostrils on the mare, and ached for the animal's obvious fear.

One of the men perched on the top railing hollered at the hapless cowboy. "You rope worse than my grandmother, Bullard."

The frustrated cowboy whirled and flung his coil of rope at his tormentor. "If you're so goddamned good, Rupe, then you do it."

There was a flash of anger across the catcaller's face, but as the crowd momentarily fell silent, he dropped to the dirt and scooped up the rope. Taking his time, he coiled it in one hand and shook out a loop with the other as he began pacing after the mare.

Kicker could see the mare's muscles bunch as she prepared to dodge, and she cheered internally when the cowboy's first two casts missed the mark. The taunts started up again, louder now as the cowboy's movements became less controlled. After the third fruitless cast, he spun and swore at his audience, but that only made their insults more creative.

"This is not good."

Kicker heard the man's quiet words and turned her head to look up at him. With a start, she realized he was a native, even though he was virtually indistinguishable from the others under his wide-brimmed, sweat-stained hat. She also noticed that he was wearing a leather smith's apron and had soot stains on his bronzed face and thickly muscled forearms. Kicker was suddenly certain that she was looking at John Blue Wolf, Will MacDiarmid's adopted brother and the town's blacksmith.

Noticing Kicker's appraisal, the man looked down at her.

They gazed at each other for a long moment with guarded curiosity and an instant mutual recognition of their manifest outsider status. Their unspoken acknowledgement was intruded upon by a roar of laughter, and they both turned to see the cowboy sprawl in the dirt as the cornered mare bolted past, knocking him down.

Furious, the cowboy staggered to his feet. "August, get me my goddamned rifle! I'm going to blow this nag's bloody brains out!"

One of the men scrambled down and jogged over to where a number of saddled horses were tied to a hitching post.

Wide-eyed, Kicker saw August pull a rifle from its boot and hurry back towards the corral. Without thinking, she launched herself up and over the fence, landing lightly on her toes. She walked slowly toward the mare.

"What the hell? What do you think you're doing? Get the hell out of there!"

The cowboy's indignant shout, the noise of the crowd, the whinnies of overexcited mustangs in the holding corral faded into the background. Even the distinct sound of a horse's hooves pounding an approach failed to register. Kicker focused solely on the mare who watched her nervously and shifted hooves as she prepared to bolt again.

"Shhh, tis a'right. Don' pay them any mind. Tis jus' you and me now. I won' let them hurt you. Shhhh, quiet now, pretty lass."

As she advanced to within a couple of yards of the mare, Kicker kept her voice soft and her hands down at her sides. As soon as she saw the horse's muscles bunch, she stopped, maintained eye contact, and spoke soothingly. "Tis all strange, tis it not? All this noise, all these people throwin' ropes at you. I don' blame you for bein' scared. No, not one little bit, but you gotta believe in somethin', right, pretty one? Believe in me, lass. I swear I won' hurt you. I'd ne'er hurt you, lass."

The crowd had gone quiet as they watched Kicker inch closer to the mare. Still she did not raise her hands, and the mare settled into a watchful stance.

"You remin' me of Ol' Cherry, lass. Not that she was ever as lively as you, but she's much the same colour. Such a pretty red, you are. So pretty. You don' wan' to give anyone an excuse to shoot you, do you, sweet one? That's it...jus' be easy. You're a'right. Everythin's gonna be fine. Believe, lass."

There was an angry hiss from behind Kicker. Simultaneously, she heard a rifle cock and a commanding voice sound from near where John Blue Wolf stood.

"Put that down, Rupert."

It was a woman's voice; her hushed but stern tone radiated authority and the expectation of obedience.

"Goddamnit, Wynne! She's too bloody wild. She'll be useless, even as a pack animal. I'll be doing everyone a favour to shoot her."

The woman's voice took on a note of amusement as Kicker finally came within range of the mare and slowly raised a hand to settle on her neck. "I believe you may be mistaken there, Rupe. Looks like the girl's about got the mustang eating out of her hand."

Kicker did not dare look around, but she was grateful for the woman's intervention. She gently stroked her fingertips along the horse's sweating neck and listened. Rupert sounded so angry that she wasn't sure he would heed the woman's order, so as quickly as the mare would allow, Kicker slipped around to the side and put herself between the horse and the immediate threat from the infuriated cowboy. She continued to calm the animal as she ran gentle hands over her heaving sides with long, slow strokes.

Kicker heard an audible gasp from the crowd, and the woman's steely voice ripped across the corral.

"I said put that down, Rupert. She came off the Steeple Seven, not the Triple Flying A. You shoot that horse and I'll have you arrested for destroying my property."

Kicker dared to glance over at the rails and saw a woman sitting easily on a tall roan, staring past her with narrowed eyes and an implacable set to her mouth.

Bless'd Jesus. If I were Rupert, I'd pay her heed.

As if in answer to her thoughts, Kicker heard the cowboy curse and stomp over to the rails, where he angrily swung up and over, disappearing into the now subdued crowd.

Wynne leaned down to say something to John Blue Wolf and he nodded in acknowledgement.

Kicker closed her eyes in relief, even as her hands continued to soothe the mare. She had no idea what would happen to the horse, but she was certain that Wynne hadn't stepped in to save the small mare only to have her put down.

Kicker heard the creak of the rails and felt someone approach from her left. She opened her eyes to see John Blue Wolf extend a short length of rope. With a nod of thanks, Kicker took the rope, slipped it gently around the mare's neck and knotted it, soothing her as the sorrel reared half-heartedly.

Following the blacksmith, Kicker led the horse over to the gate, which swung open. As she walked away, a man's voice rang out.

"C'mon, boys. We got work to do. Jim, cut out another one and let's get this show back on the road."

The men filled in behind Kicker, and the business of buying and selling the mustangs picked up again. She led the mare over to where Wynne Glenn was watching her approach. Kicker made up her mind as the mare softly bumped her shoulder. "I thank you, Ma'am, an' I'd like to buy this mare from you, if we can reach an agreement on her price."

Wynne swung off the horse, the border collie instantly at her side. "First things first." She held out her hand. "I'm Wynne Glenn, and I guess you're the new schoolteacher's cousin."

Kicker flushed at her lapse in manners and shook the woman's hand. "Aye, Ma'am. I'm Kicker Stuart, and Madelyn Bristow is my cousin. She's waitin' for us at Mrs. Thatcher's."

No longer pre-occupied with the mare's survival, Kicker noted the woman's distinct family resemblance to Will and Albert MacDiarmid. Wynne's long, light brown hair was tied back in a single, thick plait, and her eyes, while more serious than Will's, were the same fawn colour. Her skin was unfashionably tanned, and her features far too strong to be called pretty, but Wynne Glenn had a striking presence, with a gaze that bespoke little patience for fools. Everything from her dusty boots, to well-worn chaps over wrinkled dungarees, to the negligent ease with which she had sat her horse indicated that, like her brothers, this was a woman better suited to saddles than salons.

"Then why don't we walk that way." Wynne looked past Kicker and smiled warmly. "Thanks, John. Would you bring a wagon down to Mrs. Thatcher's for me? And could you pick up their things at the station on the way?"

"I'll be there in a few minutes." The man started to walk away, then turned back to the women. "That little mare moves like a jackrabbit, Wynne. With proper training, she'd make a great cutter."

Wynne nodded acknowledgement as her brother strode away.

Kicker turned to express her gratitude, but the blacksmith's long legs quickly widened the distance between them. He disappeared into the nearby livery stable before she could open her mouth. Instead Kicker fell into step beside her benefactor and quickly controlled her horse as it shied away from Brander.

Wynne whistled her dog away from the mare and the collie obediently paced on her far side. "She's a feisty one, isn't she? Are you sure you want her?"

The doubt in Wynne's voice was clear, but Kicker was adamant. "Aye, Ma'am. She wasn't what I was lookin' for, but I believe she'll do."

"Perhaps. She looks a lot like a mare my brother Albert tried to bring in not too long ago. First night in the corral, she kicked over a railing and jumped the fence, followed by half a dozen other mustangs. They were long gone by the time the boys got out of the bunkhouse. I suspect she'll turn out to be more trouble than she's worth. Are you sure you can hold her?"

Kicker considered that seriously as she eyed the mare. "If I can convince her she wants to be held."

Wynne laughed and shook her head. "That will be a sure and certain miracle, Miss Stuart."

Kicker did not respond until they neared Mrs. Thatcher's boarding house, which was near the schoolhouse and church. "Ma'am, you still ain't said what price you'll put on her."

Wynne stopped and eyed Kicker shrewdly. Just as she opened her mouth to answer, her voice was drowned out by the sound of several horses galloping down on them. They pulled their horses to the side as Rupert and four of his men pounded past without a glance at the women.

When the dust settled, Wynne shook her head in disgust. "Miss Stuart, you'll want to watch out for that one. He's been a spoiled, irresponsible brat since the misbegotten day he arrived in this world. You made him look like a fool back there. He won't forget that."

"Billy doesn't think too highly of him."

"Not many do. His brothers shun him, and even his father thinks he's a waste of rations, but he's an Arbuster, which means something in these parts, so he coasts on the name." Wynne stopped and laid a hand on Kicker's arm. "Miss Stuart, in this land a man can make his fortune with luck, hard work, and the quality of his mind and body. No one need tug their forelock to another by reason of birth. But put money and a bully together and there will always be those who scrape and bow and do his bidding. All I'm saying is to watch your back."

"Mus' you watch yours, too?"

Wynne gave Kicker a grim smile. "Not even Rupert is fool enough to take on me or my family, especially given that our fathers are good friends."

Further discussion was cut off as they reached the boarding house and saw Madelyn, Billy, and a grey haired, squarely built woman emerge from the building. Kicker saw her lover's smile as she spied the mare now ambling docilely alongside Wynne's big gelding.

Kicker gave Madelyn a sheepish grin, but said nothing as Wynne tied her horse to the hitching post and stepped up on the boardwalk. Pulling off a leather glove, she offered her hand to Madelyn.

"Mrs. Bristow? It's a pleasure to finally meet you. You're a very welcome addition to our town, I can tell you that. Will was downright effusive about finding you—more so even than about Albert getting engaged."

Madelyn shook Wynne's hand with a smile. "Then Albert's search was successful?"

Wynne laughed heartily. "Well, we're not really sure, to tell you the truth. Will's last telegram said that Albert had proposed to several women in the hope that at least one of them would say yes. If I know my baby brother, he'll have found some way to complicate matters beyond belief. With his luck, they'll all have accepted, and several furious fathers will be out for his blood. They're due home in a few days, so I suppose we'll find out then."

Wynne turned to Billy, who practically danced with impatience. She took a couple of coins from her vest pocket and flipped them to the boy. He caught them with a wide grin. "Well done, Billy. Now I believe Laird hopes you'll go fishing with him this afternoon."

"Yes, Ma'am!" Billy ran off in the direction of the livery stable, quickly dashing by John Blue Wolf who was stopped, with his horse and wagon, at the railroad station.

The older woman now spoke up. "I'm sorry I don't have room for these two, Mrs. Glenn. I wasn't expecting the constable until next week, but he changed his patrol route this time around, and will be stopping here for a couple of nights. I can take them in as of Saturday, if you'd like."

"No need, Mrs. Thatcher, but thank you. We'll put them up at the ranch until Mrs. Bristow's place is ready. Mrs. Donnelly already has everything ready. Will we have the pleasure of seeing you Saturday night for the party?"

"Indeed. I wouldn't miss it for the world."

"And may we count on some of your wonderful mince pies? It simply would not be a proper celebration without them."

Mrs. Thatcher beamed at the compliment. "I've already got the filling made, and if I can just keep the men out of them long enough, I'll have two or three ready for Saturday."

Turning to Madelyn, Mrs. Thatcher said, "It was lovely talking to you, dearie. I just know you're going to like it here fine." She gave Madelyn a friendly pat on the shoulder and bustled back into her boarding house.

Madelyn looked at Wynne curiously. "Excuse me, Mrs. Glenn, but you mentioned 'my' place?"

"First of all, please call me Wynne, and secondly, I hope I'm not being presumptuous. When I got Will's telegram about the terms of your agreement with him, I took the liberty of assigning some of my men to start building a small house on your land."

Kicker and Madelyn exchanged surprised looks. "Mrs. Glenn..." Madelyn began.

"Wynne."

"Wynne. We're very grateful, but..."

"I know. No doubt you and your husband already had the design of your home in mind, but the way I saw it, there's not a lot of time before the cold starts setting in. From what Will told me, your husband won't be here for quite some time. Now you're free to board with Mrs. Thatcher if you like—that's what the schoolteachers have done up to now, but Will indicated that you were looking forward to setting up your own place in preparation for your husband's arrival. It's nothing fancy that the boys are putting up, but it'll be snug and comfortable for the winter. Plus you'll be able to add on quite easily, depending on how many additional bedrooms you need in the future."

Madelyn lowered her gaze and Kicker had to stifle a grin at the melancholy look on her face. "I'm afraid the Major and I are unable to have children as a result of injuries he sustained in Africa." Wynne murmured sympathetically as Madelyn continued, "So the size of the house is not at issue, but payment—"

"Don't you worry about that, Mrs. Bristow. We'll work it out fairly, and in whatever fashion would be best for you. I won't charge you for the men's labour. I wasn't able to assign a full crew to the task. This is one of our busiest times of year, what with haying and fattening the herds up for the winter. I'm afraid I'll have to pull two of them off now, too. We've got to run a mange dip in the next few days and I'll need all available hands. I can leave you with a couple of the newer hands, since they wouldn't be much use with the dip, and they can finish it up. We should have you in your house inside of a week, ten days at the outside."

John Blue Wolf pulled the wagon up next to the boarding house, and Kicker took a firmer grasp on the mare as she shied away from the new arrivals. That drew the other women's attention and Madelyn smiled at her.

"I see you couldn't resist temptation, dearest."

Kicker glanced up from soothing the mare, in time to catch the casually inquisitive glance that Wynne directed between her and Madelyn.

"Your cousin has a good eye for horse flesh, but I hope she hasn't taken on more than she counted on with this one, Mrs. Bristow."

"Please call me Madelyn, Wynne. And I wouldn't worry about Kicker when it comes to horses. She has a natural way with them." Addressing Kicker, Madelyn asked, "Have you chosen a name for her?"

Kicker gave Wynne a worried look. "I don' know that she's mine yet, Maddie. Mrs. Glenn has not set a price."

"I haven't, have I? Tell me, Miss Stuart, does your cousin speak true? Are you indeed gifted with horses?"

"Don' know's you'd call it a gif', but I worked around them for many years. They seem to listen to me, right enough."

"My cousin practically ran the stables at Grindleshire Academy when I arrived to teach there. The stable master, Old Thomas, told me once that he'd never seen anyone as good with horses, or a forge."

There was no mistaking the loving pride in Madelyn's voice, and Kicker worried anew over the speculation in Wynne's eyes as she looked between the two women.

"You've had experience with a forge, then?"

At the sound of John's voice, Kicker turned to face him. "Aye, Sir, I have. Da's a smith, an' I learned at his knee for many a year, b'fore I wen' to work for Ol' Thomas."

"John, didn't you tell me your assistant left a few days ago?"

The blacksmith frowned at Wynne's question. "Small loss, that boy. Eight months, and he never did learn the meaning of a full day's work."

"I know the meanin'," Kicker interjected quickly. "If tis a hard worker you're lookin' for, I'd be grateful for the chance to prove it." She looked hopefully at the blacksmith, who regarded her steadily before speaking.

"It's hard, dirty work, not fit for a woman."

"P'rhaps not mos' women, no." Kicker stood defiantly erect and met the man's gaze directly. She had almost lost hope when she detected a glimmer of approval in his dark, impassive eyes.

John gave Wynne an almost imperceptible shrug. "We'll see how it works out."

Wynne smiled broadly. "All right then, Miss Stuart. John will be out at the Steeple Seven shoeing all next week. You work with him, and if he tells me you've lived up to advance billing, that little mare is yours."

Kicker didn't ask what would happen if she didn't live up to expectations. She just leaned into the mare's neck and closed her eyes. *She's mine.* When she finally opened her eyes, she found the other three looking at her with varying degrees of amusement. Blushing, Kicker tugged her hat lower and stared at the ground.

"So about her name then, Kicker...?"

Kicker only considered Madelyn's question for a moment. "Rabbit." She glanced at her new boss and basked in his quiet nod of approval.

Wynne laughed, drew on her glove, and offered her hand to Madelyn to assist her into the wagon. With the teacher settled, the rancher tied her horse to the rear of the buckboard and climbed up to the seat, gathering the reins in her hands.

Kicker seated herself behind the trunks, legs dangling as she knotted the mare's lead beside the roan's reins. She heard the other two chatting as they pulled away, but she ignored them as she watched Rabbit.

The little mare seemed to accept her current lot, but Kicker didn't miss the way she eyed her surroundings as they followed a rough trail that paralleled the river and headed westward out of town. She wondered whether Rabbit was plotting her escape, and reminded herself to watch the mare closely.

When they reached a small tributary of the river, the wagon turned north. Paralleling the creek banks, they began to climb a series of gently sloping hills.

Wynne called back, "This is Shadow Creek, Miss Stuart. Your cousin's land is only a few minutes up the trail. When the weather is good, she'll be able to reach town in ten to fifteen minutes."

Kicker raised a hand in acknowledgement. From her vantage point, she had caught glimpses through the trees of the town, now below them and backed by the river and the railroad, but within moments, the town was out of sight. The creak of the wagon, the soft murmur of women's voices, the sound of the horses' breathing, and the chatter of squirrels and birds engaged Kicker's senses as she took in her new home.

"Kicker," Madelyn called back, "Wynne says we're going to stop at our property to look over the house, then continue on to the Steeple Seven."

"Soun's good." Kicker answered, then addressed Rabbit. "You're not thinkin' of makin' mischief now, are you, pretty lass? I want you on your bes' behavior. No kickin' o'er railin's or leadin' t'other horses in an escape, or the boss lady will throw the both of us off the ranch." Kicker knew her words meant nothing to Rabbit, but she wanted the mare to grow accustomed to the sound of her voice. "Now we'll be stoppin' for a bit, so you be a good lass." She jerked her thumb at the big roan, plodding placidly behind the wagon. "You watch him, and pay 'tention. He's a gen'leman, he is."

The wagon turned off the trail and rolled to a stop. Kicker jumped off, and after rechecking the knot in Rabbit's lead, rounded the horses to see Wynne help Madelyn down from the buckboard. Drawing even with the women, Kicker saw a long, narrow, log cabin under construction in a deep clearing between the trail and the creek, which she could hear, but not see. Nearby, to one side, a deep hole, big enough for a man to enter standing up, had been cut horizontally into a hillside. Kicker could see that the interior had been half-shored up with small logs, and guessed that was to be their root cellar. An outhouse and a small storage shed flanked the unfinished cellar, and a couple of horses were tethered to a tree near a work wagon, the bed of which was littered with a variety of tools.

In the cabin itself, walls were up and chinked, the roof was more than half done, and the framework was in place for two doors and several windows. She could see one man toward the rear of the roof, working on a stone chimney, and another on the ground, shaping shingles with an adze. Two other workers dragged a tree from the brush. As they emerged into the sunlight, Kicker's mouth dropped open in surprise.

There was no mistaking those twin thatches of bright orange-red hair, lit by the early afternoon sun. Joy exploded within and Kicker let out a wild whoop. "Seamus! Pudge!"

Kicker tore across the clearing and skidded to a stop in front of the men, who met her with delighted grins as big as her own. "What're you two doin' here? I thought I'd ne'er see you again." It was all Kicker could do not to tackle her friends into the dust. "What happened to homesteadin', and plantin', and becomin' the Potato Kings of the West?"

"Those plans haven't changed, Miss Kicker. We just decided on our way west that you had made this idyll sound so inviting, we would stake a claim here. Our homestead is no more than an hour distant, and our potatoes are even now taking root in the ground." Seamus' eyes glowed with quiet pleasure as he regarded her. Then he nodded over her shoulder and doffed his hat to the approaching women. "However, our empty purses dictated that we find work for the winter. Mrs. Glenn was good enough to take us on as general labourers."

"And I certainly haven't regretted it, Mr. Kelly. You're both excellent workers." Wynne kept a hand under Madelyn's arm as they crossed the rough ground. "Miss Stuart, I assume you're acquainted with my newest hands?"

Kicker nodded, unable to take her eyes off her friends for the pure delight of being with them again. She had been so certain that she had seen the last of them in Montreal, and had mourned the loss of their easy humour and affectionate company. "We met on the boat comin' o'er. Their beautiful music passed many a long hour."

Wynne raised an eyebrow as she regarded the brothers. "You're musicians? You didn't mention that when you applied for work."

Pudge's eyes gleamed with pride. "We were pretty sure you'd have more need of our muscles than our music, Ma'am. But if you ever need a fiddler, my brother was about the finest in Ireland."

Seamus elbowed him, and Kicker grinned to see the familiar dynamic between the two. "Pudge, do not exaggerate."

Turning to their boss, Seamus addressed her respectfully. "Between the two of us, we can turn a tune, Mrs. Glenn. If indeed you have need of music, we would do our best to oblige."

Madelyn had been observing with a smile. "I've had the pleasure of listening to the senior Mr. Kelly play, Wynne. I can vouch for both his talent and his wide ranging grasp of traditional and classical genres. I'm afraid I've not heard his brother play, but Kicker has repeatedly enthused about their joint musical abilities."

"Excellent. Then if you're of a mind, Mr. Kelly, we would love to have you both play on Saturday."

Turning to Madelyn, Wynne explained. "My brothers are due in on Friday, and we decided to combine a welcome home party for them, with a welcoming party for you two. With any luck, we can call it an engagement party for Albert, too."

Wynne addressed the Kellys with a smile. "When you return to the ranch this evening, see Mr. Donnelly and he'll give you the details for Saturday."

Wynne patted Madelyn's hand where it rested on her arm. "Come, my dear, and I'll show you the interior of your new home. If you see something you'd like to change, I'll have my foreman make the arrangements."

As the women turned away, already discussing the cabin's design, Kicker leaned in, eyes sparkling with excitement, and whispered to the brothers, "I have a horse. Can you believe it—me with my own horse?"

"Kicker," Madelyn called from the doorway, "I'd appreciate your opinion too, please."

"Go," Seamus said. "You will have lots of time to show us your mount, Miss Kicker. We're not going anywhere."

Unwilling to take her eyes off Seamus and Pudge, Kicker backed away toward the cabin until she stumbled and almost fell. Then, with a sheepish grin at her friends' laughter, she spun and dashed over to join the women, who had already entered the cabin.

As Kicker crossed the threshold, she decided there could not have been a more auspicious omen for their future. Friends were building her and Madelyn's new home.

CHAPTER 12

In her bedroom on the second floor of the MacDiarmid manor, Madelyn heard the sound she had been listening for. She crossed the room and opened her door in time to see the door of the room directly across the hall close. Kicker was finally back. Madelyn left her room and tapped softly on her partner's door.

"Come in."

Rolling her eyes in affectionate exasperation at the bellowed words, Madelyn opened the door. "Dearest, ladies do not raise their—" Her admonition stumbled to a stop as she stared at her bedraggled lover. "Kicker! What in heaven's name happened to you?"

Kicker shook her head in disgust and looked down at the half-dried mud on her clothes. "Rabbit and I had a partin' of the ways—jus' as we were crossin' Shadow Creek. Bloody hell! I ain't bin thrown from a horse since I was three. I swear that damned mare was laughin' at me, too." She brushed at a clump of grass embedded in the knee of her trousers. "Good thing I din't cross Mrs. Donnelly comin' upstairs, or she'da had my head for messin' her floors."

Madelyn tried to conceal a smile. Over the past few days, Kicker's efforts to civilize the mare had been an up and down proposition...more often down than up. "Are you quite sure you want to keep her, dearest? I'm sure Wynne would let you out of your deal, if you'd rather." She was stopped short again, this time by the horror on Kicker's face.

"Not keep Rabbit? Are you daft?"

"Well, you could certainly obtain another horse. I'm just suggesting—"

Kicker's snort was eloquently dismissive. "Twould be no other like Rabbit."

It was clear the topic was not open for discussion, so Madelyn changed tacks. "I had a bath drawn for you, Kicker. Even before I saw the results of your tumble, I thought you would wish to clean up before the party." She gestured at the large iron tub in the corner, a tin cover over it to hold the heat in the water.

Kicker nodded and started to unbutton her filthy trousers.

"Perhaps you should step behind the screen to disrobe."

There was absolute silence, and then Kicker crossed to the wooden tri-fold by the tub and stepped behind it. As the sounds of undressing could be heard in the quiet of the room, Madelyn sighed. Kicker really did not understand the need for total discretion, even though the likelihood of anyone walking in on them was slight.

Madelyn didn't feel like getting into another discussion as heated as the one they'd had the night they arrived when Kicker had come to her door, late. She felt terrible, but had to turn her away. Madelyn saw the light fade in Kicker's eyes as the door closed on her, but she knew it was too risky to allow Kicker to stay.

The next morning Madelyn knocked on Kicker's door, intent on explaining the need to maintain a proper distance while they abided in the MacDiarmid's home, but the room was empty. She felt a stab of panic until she descended the stairs and encountered Mrs. Donnelly. The housekeeper passed along a message that Kicker had taken Rabbit out, and would be back later.

Mrs. MacDiarmid, the family matriarch, was an expatriate Briton with whom Madelyn quickly struck up a rapport. Immediately after breakfast, they set out on a tour of the neighbouring ranches to introduce the new schoolteacher to the leading families in and around Galbraith's Crossing.

As a result, it was many hours before Madelyn was finally able to have a talk with Kicker, and in the end it was singularly unsatisfying. Her arms crossed and an inscrutable expression on her face, Kicker listened silently to Madelyn's lecture on the dangers of anyone even suspecting their true relationship. She had been impossible to read.

The past few days had been a whirlwind of activity, as Mrs. MacDiarmid was determined that her grandchildren's new teacher would be well integrated into the community. The older woman had hosted teas, offered advice, and helped Madelyn shop for necessities for her new home.

Kicker disappeared every morning before Madelyn arose and returned long after dinner, thwarting Madelyn's desire to try anew to explain her caution.

Now, Madelyn wavered. She wanted to escape the oppressive silence but was reluctant to leave matters as they lay. She saw Kicker drag the screen around the tub and heard her slip into the water. With another heavy sigh, Madelyn took a seat facing the hidden bather. "Will and Albert got in on the morning train."

Kicker grunted an acknowledgement.

"They didn't make it last night because they stopped in Calgary for the night. I could tell Mrs. MacDiarmid didn't know whether to box their ears or give them a hug, but at least the party can go forward now with the guests of honour present. Oh, and Albert's new fiancée should arrive before the end of the year. Apparently Will and Albert were delayed in their departure from London because her father was slow to give his permission, and insists that she needs much more time to prepare before leaving England." Madelyn waited for an answer, but heard only the sound of water slopping against the sides of the tub. "Were you over at the cabin today?"

"Aye."

It was an answer, grunted or not, and Madelyn tried to build on it. "How is it coming along? Do you think we'll be able to move in soon?"

"Roof's finished. So's the root cellar."

"That's wonderful. So they'll finish up the interior next?"

"I got 'em buildin' a small barn firs'." There was a clear note of defiance in Kicker's voice. "We'll need it, an' not jus' for Rabbit."

"Of course, dearest," Madelyn soothed, though she felt like she was dealing with her own Rabbit. "You know I'll defer to your judgment in these matters. As I told you before, your experience will be of far more value in the Wilderness than mine. I'm not so blind as to think some small skill at playing the piano or a familiarity with Chaucer and Shakespeare will be of much use when the snow begins to fall."

"Ain't like I had much experience with snow, either."

Had Kicker's voice softened a little, or was it wishful thinking? Madelyn chose to believe the former. "Then we shall have to learn together. You'll be pleased to know that under Mrs. MacDiarmid's guidance, I placed a rather large order at the general store yesterday."

"For what?"

"Things that we were unable to bring with us, items that Mrs. MacDiarmid assured me we would need. And of course some furniture—a table, chairs, bed, that sort of thing."

"Twas a waste of money. Seamus and me could've made mos' of those things."

The coolness was back in Kicker's voice and Madelyn almost groaned aloud. "With you working for Mr. Blue Wolf all next week, you wouldn't have had time to finish those things before we move in. Really, we cannot take advantage of the MacDiarmid's hospitality for too much longer."

A splash almost covered the sarcastic snort from behind the screen, but not quite. Grimly, Madelyn ignored the unspoken accusation. It was true that she was enjoying her time at the Steeple Seven. Mrs. MacDiarmid had proven an extremely gracious hostess and Mrs. Donnelly had seen to their needs before they could even voice them.

Much to Madelyn's amazement, the impressive MacDiarmid house was a sprawling, two story Victorian manor that would not have looked out of place in Mayfair. A capable domestic staff kept the interior sparkling—with polished oak banisters, Chippendale furniture, gleaming silver tea sets, Nottingham lace curtains, and thick velvet carpets. Mrs. Donnelly ran her uniformed staff with a stern hand; not a mote of dust escaped her eyes. Even Wynne was not allowed into the parlor with dusty boots on.

Outside of the main manor, smaller, but no less attractive homes were perched on the western banks of the ranch's small lake. These housed Will's family, as well as the wives and children of Bruce and Wally, the brothers who had gone north to the Yukon the previous year. Albert, Wynne, and her son, Laird, lived with Mr. and Mrs. MacDiarmid in the big house, and the Donnellys resided in the adjacent foreman's house. Large bunkhouses sheltered the ranch hands, and corrals, barns, and various buildings covered acres of the Steeple Seven. The ranch was far more like a large English estate than the simple farm that Madelyn had envisioned.

Having briefly seen the cabin that she and Kicker would soon inhabit, Madelyn was determined to enjoy the luxuries offered at the Steeple Seven, even if it meant being extra cautious not to give offence to her hosts. She was prepared to guide Kicker through the intricacies of polite society, but her intent was moot. Though Mrs. MacDiarmid made it clear that Madelyn's cousin was welcome to accompany them on their social rounds, Kicker politely declined all invitations.

Alternately relieved and disturbed by Kicker's absence, Madelyn rationalized that her lover was much happier with Seamus, Pudge, and Rabbit. She salved her conscience by including a new saddle, bridle, and tack in her general store order to replace those loaned to Kicker by Wynne. She even went to Wynne to solicit advice on which saddle to order, justifying it as an early Yuletide gift.

Madelyn found herself angered by Kicker's apparent unwillingness to understand. *Why can she not see what I am feeling?*

She was emotionally battered from the upheaval of the past several months. *Fending off unwanted advances, losing my job, torn from the bosom of my beloved family, tossed about on that wretched voyage, hopes and spirit dashed by the bitter experiences of my old friend. Why is it so hard for Kicker to empathize?* Madelyn ignored the small voice that added to her litany—*All while falling in love with the most obstinate, intransigent...*

In a crisp voice, Madelyn issued instructions. "You'll need to dress appropriately tonight, Kicker. I set out your rose dress. I think it will suit the occasion." She brusquely forestalled the expected protest. "This is the first chance many will have to meet you, and the last thing we need is for you to give offence by wearing Roddy's trousers. Whether you believe it or not, it's important to immediately establish a good reputation and a positive impression. I've laid the groundwork with our neighbours this week, but you must do your part, too."

"Tis groun'work, eh? An' how do you explain your horse breakin', house buildin', smithy of a girl cousin?" Madelyn was startled to hear amusement in Kicker's response.

Madelyn shifted nervously as she heard Kicker stand up. "It helps immensely that Wynne's broken the ground for...eccentricities. They could not very well criticize you for unladylike ways without slandering the head of one of the richest and most powerful families in the province."

A non-committal murmur greeted Madelyn's words. She stood and paced as she continued. "From what I've observed this week, as long as we're sheltered by the MacDiarmid's good will, we'll be left alone. That's why it's so important not to offend them, dearest. It won't be long until we're in our own home, and free, for the most part, to live as we choose. There will be time then to make up for the distance we must maintain now."

Kicker stepped from behind the screen and Madelyn forgot what she had been saying. As Kicker deliberately crossed the space between them, all Madelyn could focus on was the way drops of bath water rolled down her sleek, naked form. Discretion was instantly irrelevant, caution was abandoned, and reticence had no place in the room. Madelyn stepped into Kicker's open arms and met her kiss with eyes closed and good sense vanished.

Only the sound of a discreet tapping on the door wrenched Madelyn back to propriety. She had been moments away from breaking her own rules, but now, instead of pushing Kicker on to the bed, she propelled her toward the dressing screen with all haste.

The knock came again as Wynne's voice sounded from the hall. "Miss Stuart, are you in there? I'm looking for your cousin and wondered if you knew where she was."

With a quick glance at the screen, Madelyn answered. "I'm in here, Wynne. Come in, please."

Wynne opened the door. "Ah, Madelyn, there you are."

"Yes. I've been talking to my cousin as she gets ready for the party. She'll be out of the bath momentarily, if you want to wait."

Stepping inside, Wynne shook her head. "I've no wish to interrupt you or your cousin's preparations, Madelyn, but I wanted to let you know that Will has added his signature to Father's and mine on the deed. All that's needed now is your signature, and the title to your property can be registered. Our solicitor has arrived from Calgary, so perhaps you could join us in the study and we'll complete the formalities."

"Thank you. I shall join you in a few minutes."

"Of course. But no doubt you'll need time to dress for the party, so we'll expect you in about fifteen minutes, shall we say?" Addressing the screen, Wynne added, "John is here too, Miss Stuart, and he wanted a word with you, so if you could look him up?"

"Aye. I will." Kicker's voice was muffled, as material rustled behind the screen.

Wynne smiled, nodded at Madelyn, and slipped out of the room so smoothly that it was only when the door closed that Madelyn realized what she had said.

Change for the party? I've already... Madelyn glanced down at her clothes and blanched. Her grey silk tea gown had distinctive wet patches where Kicker's nude body had pressed against her. "Oh, dear Lord!"

Kicker stepped out from behind the screen as she tugged fabric up over her shoulder and shrugged into the other dress sleeve. "What's wrong?"

Madelyn looked at her in shock. "My dress. How can I possibly explain how this happened? Wynne will know..."

Frowning, Kicker regarded the blatant water stains and shook her head. "It don' matter."

Madelyn stared in disbelief at her cavalier dismissal. "What do you mean it doesn't matter? Haven't you heard a word I said?"

"Aye, but you needn't explain a thing. If Wynne noticed, then she did you kindly by pointin' it out and savin' you from shamin' yourself in front of t'others."

"If she noticed? How could she not. She might as well have caught us naked, rolling on the bed." *And two seconds later, she would have.* The thought was no consolation to Madelyn as she chastised herself furiously for her lack of self-control.

"P'rhaps. But does it not give you comfort that she made no fuss, nor asked any questions? If she suspects anythin', she's keepin' it to herself."

"Why would she do that? Why not expose us and send us packing?"

A speculative look came into Kicker's eyes and she started to say something, before she cut herself off and started again. "An' if she did sen' us packin'? Did we not count that a possibility when we set out? Did we not say if this spot din't suit, we'd move on to find one that did?"

Madelyn sank into the chair and covered her face with trembling hands. "I don't wish to move on, Kicker. I'm tired. I feel safe here. Please, please..." Her words faded away as the tears began to fall.

Kicker knelt and wrapped her arms around Madelyn. "Shhh, why d'you weep, love? What's wrong? Tell me."

Madelyn tried to explain what she herself couldn't quite understand. "It's so...overwhelming, dearest. We're so very far from everything that was familiar to us, with nothing to fall back on but our own resources. What if those resources fail? What if we're not brave enough, or strong enough, or wise enough to navigate the treacherous waters around us? Oh, Kicker. What if I made a mistake bringing you here? What if, in wanting to make a new life with you, I destroyed your old for naught? I didn't ask you first. I didn't discuss it with you. I just made my plans like I always do...like I always have, but this time it's not only me who suffers if those plans go awry. What have I done to you?"

Madelyn was startled to hear Kicker's soft chuckle.

"What have you done to me? You've given me a world I ne'er e'en dreamed of, an' made me happier than I could e'er imagine. Maddie, I've learned much from you, but I'm no child to be led by the han'. You did not bundle me into your trunk and kidnap me away. I came willingly, eagerly. Whate'er happens, I'll ne'er regret settin' sail with you to this land. I gave up Adam, an' the Academy, an' all my frien's, and would do so again tomorrow, to be with you, where'er that takes us. Do you not know that, love?"

"But, what if—"

"No, Maddie. If bad times b'fall us, so what? Bad times may well have b'fallen us back home, too. As smart as you are, you cannot know what awaits us—here or if we was still back there. No one can, so it jus' don' matter. We'll deal with what happens when it happens, as all mus'."

Madelyn felt Kicker's hands gently smooth her hair and rub her back. As she let the pleasure of touch soothe her misgivings, the fears began to subside. "I'm sorry, dearest. I don't know what came over me."

"Miss Adelaide an' her troubles, maybe?"

Sitting up, Madelyn took Kicker's hands and kissed them. "In part, dearest. I cannot deny that hearing her despair made me question so many things, but I can't place the blame fully on that. I think my doubts began on the pier in Liverpool and simply escalated from there, but I should've shared them with you."

Kicker nodded somberly. "Aye. You said we'd be equal partners in this journey, so don' carry the load by yourself no more. An' I promise I'll give no cause for worry t'night."

Madelyn managed a smile. "I know you'll do your best. I'm sure everything will be fine." *Oh, my darling, you really have no idea how poorly you blend with the crowd, but then that's one of the many things I love about you.*

"Twill—I swear twill." Kicker rose to her feet and brushed her skirt into place. "Now, if you could please help me with these bless'd buttons b'fore you go change. Saddlin' Rabbit takes less time than doin' up these bloody things."

She turned her back and Madelyn began to fasten the long row of buttons. But before she closed the last two, she leaned forward and kissed the nape of Kicker's neck. Then looking past her, she noticed their image in the mirror and saw how seriously Kicker watched her. Fastening the last two buttons, Madelyn whispered, "It really is all right, dearest. I'll be fine."

"Aye."

But there was little conviction in the single word.

Kicker stood in the shade of a tall ash and mentally reviewed her performance over the past few hours as she surveyed the large crowd scattered across the lawns and gardens of the MacDiarmid home. She had been introduced to countless people, and, concentrating on her diction, limited herself to brief pleasantries, allowing Madelyn and their hosts to carry the conversations. Kicker was certain that she passed muster, or at least sailed beneath most people's notice, which suited her fine. As quickly as possible, she retreated to a quiet sanctuary to observe and listen.

As always, Kicker's gaze rarely left Madelyn for long. Watching her effortlessly charm their new neighbours under the attentive auspices of Mrs. MacDiarmid, Kicker could not help remembering Lil Harrington's cautionary words.

She won't always make it easy for you, girl. Many's the time she's jumped before looking, and lived to regret it.

Madelyn's behaviour since their arrival at the Steeple Seven disturbed Kicker more than she would acknowledge to herself. She trusted her own instincts. Once the decision to cast her lot with Madelyn's was made, Kicker never second-guessed herself. Judged by Madelyn's tears and words, though, the same could not be said of her partner. Kicker wondered if Madelyn now regretted her impulsive choice to leave England with a lower class lover in tow. She desperately wished she could ask someone for counsel, but as that was impossible, she strove instead to remember every word of Lil's advice.

There may come a point where she begins to question herself, to wonder what she's gotten you both into. I've seen her do it before. That's when she'll need you most; that's when you'll have to reach deep into your soul and pull up strength enough for both of you. Can you do that? Will you be there for my girl when she needs you most, even if she pushes you away out of fear?

Aye, I promised I would, din't I?

Lost in thought, Kicker didn't notice anyone approach until a man stopped and stood silently beside her. When she realized that she wasn't alone, she looked up to see John Blue Wolf soberly watching the crowd, too.

"I looked for you, Mr. Blue Wolf. Missus Glenn tol' me you wanted to see me?"

He nodded but said nothing, so Kicker resumed her surveillance. They stood together silently for long moments, before John said, "Do you see the man to Rupert Arbuster's right?"

She had been keenly aware of the arrival of Rupert Arbuster and his entourage less than an hour before. With Wynne's words in mind, Kicker kept well clear of the man. Now she studied the tall, thin man next to Arbuster.

"Aye. I see him."

"His name is Rick Biggart, Miss Stuart, and you would be wise to stay well out of his way. He is an indefatigable, remorseless bloodhound once set on a trail. He has no mercy, qualm, or conscience at carrying out his master's bidding."

Certain she knew the answer, Kicker nevertheless asked, "An' his master is?"

"Rupert Arbuster." John Blue Wolf looked down at Kicker. "Arbuster is a fool about many things, but he knows how to cover his foul tracks. Biggart, though by far the more intelligent, has done his bidding since they were children."

Kicker shivered, despite the heat of the August afternoon.

"You stung Arbuster's pride, and although he is a blowhard, Biggart is not. Rupert is sheltered by the Arbuster name; Biggart lives by his wits. Of the two, Biggart is the more dangerous, but only when Rupert sets him loose."

"An' he's set him loose on me?"

"So I've heard."

They were silent again as Kicker absorbed his warning. *Bless'd Jesus. How did I get in trouble so quickly? An' how can I possibly tell Maddie?*

"Are you sure of these things, Mr. Blue Wolf?"

John smiled grimly. "I grant you that it may only be the talk of men with too much whiskey and too little sense, but I would nonetheless give it heed."

"Did you o'erhear them yourself?"

"I am not allowed in the hotel bar, Miss Stuart. Their words were relayed to me by a friend, who has no stake in the matter one way or another."

Not allowed in the bar? For a moment Kicker wondered if her initial instinct about the man was mistaken for some reason. Then understanding set in, and along with it, increased misgivings. If the power of the Galbraith and MacDiarmid names were not enough to protect John, to give him access to a common hotel bar despite his native birthright, would it be enough to protect her and Maddie?

"Are you familiar with the game of mumblety-peg, Miss Stuart?"

Kicker's eyebrow shot up at the odd segue. "Aye. I played with my brother, Adam, when e'er Da was lookin' elsewhere."

"Are you good at it? Is your aim accurate?"

"I could pin a fly to a stump at twen'y paces."

"Good. We will play the game when work is done next week." John did not elaborate. "Your cousin placed a large order at Godwin's General Store last week, but failed to include a rifle in your provisions. It would be wise to do so, given where you will live. I recommend a Spencer pump action repeating shotgun with a five shell magazine."

With those cryptic suggestions, John Blue Wolf walked away and left Kicker to stare after him as he disappeared in the direction of the stables.

"Was that John?" Wynne's voice sounded behind her and Kicker nodded. "Blast. I'd hoped to catch up with him. Father wanted to discuss something with him."

Kicker turned to face Wynne. She immediately found it disconcerting, even with Brander in his customary spot at her heel, to see the ranch boss dressed indistinguishably from all the other ladies in their finery.

Wynne gave her a wry grin, as if reading her mind and invoking a bond of mutual discomfort.

"P'rhaps you can fin' him later. The party will go on for hours, yet, won' it?"

"Yes, but John wasn't attending for the party. My father's favourite stud threw a nail and he came to make repairs, or he wouldn't have been here at all today. He's probably already past the gates and on his way home to Esther by now."

"Esther?"

"His wife. She's Métis, and doesn't feel comfortable mixing with all these people. She and John will socialize only when it's just the family."

Kicker added that information to the mental portrait she was building of the blacksmith. She momentarily thought to tell Wynne of John's warning, but, worried that word would get back to Madelyn that way, decided against it.

"Will you walk with me a bit, Miss Stuart?"

"If you'll call me Kicker, I'd be pleased to."

Wynne smiled. "Then I must be Wynne to you, Kicker."

Linking her arm through Kicker's, she began to stroll slowly across the grounds, steering them adeptly as she warmly greeted friends and neighbours.

It was only when they concluded their perambulations at the food tables that Kicker realized what Wynne had done. A quick glance to see Arbuster scowling in their direction confirmed it. Like everyone at the party, he had gotten the message—it was clear to even the most oblivious observer that Madelyn had found immediate favour with the matriarch of the Steeple Seven. But Wynne's actions clearly signalled that Madelyn's misfit cousin was not to be left out in the cold. Kicker, too, was under the MacDiarmid aegis.

Kicker grinned inwardly at Arbuster's pique, but was distracted when two small boys ran up to them.

"Mama. Can me and Billy go down to the lake with Grandpa and Mr. Donnelly? We're going to catch frogs."

A dark eyed miniature version of his uncles, Laird looked hopefully at his mother.

Wynne ruffled his hair. "All right, but don't go in any further than up to your knees. And make sure Grandpa doesn't forget his canes down there this time."

The boys chorused their thanks and dashed off. Wynne looked down at the border collie. "Brander, stay with Laird."

Instantly the collie was in hot pursuit, and Wynne smiled affectionately after the trio. "I never have to worry about Laird or his grandfather if Brander is around, but I swear when he isn't there to shepherd them, you'd never know whether my father or my son is the seven-year-old."

Turning back to Kicker, Wynne gestured to the lavishly spread tables. "I do believe your friends are getting ready to play. Shall we get ourselves a plate and find a place to listen?"

As Kicker filled her plate from the abundance of food set out for the guests, she pondered Wynne's actions. Had John already told her about Rupert's threats, or was she simply being a gracious hostess by including Kicker in the celebration?

Though grateful for her tacit support, Kicker resolved not to rely on it too heavily. They were probably perfectly safe while in residence at the Steeple Seven, but they would soon be isolated and vulnerable at the Shadow Creek cabin. John was right; she needed to be prepared.

"Miss Stuart!"

Kicker turned to see Will MacDiarmid bounding up to her with a wide grin.

"Miss Stuart. It's so good to see you." Will pumped Kicker's hand enthusiastically as she tried to keep her over-filled plate balanced with her left. "I can't begin to tell you how happy I was to find that you and your cousin had already arrived."

"Will, for heaven sakes, you're going to make her spill her dinner all over the grass." Wynne gave her brother a mock scowl as he sheepishly released Kicker's hand. "Kicker, please forgive my brother. I think he's just a little exuberant about being home again."

Will slung his arm around Wynne and hugged her. "Damn right I am. Oops, sorry, Miss Stuart. I do apologize for my language, but honestly, you can keep that London town of yours; I'll take this little piece of paradise any day."

Wynne winked at Kicker. "He says that now, but you should see him complain if he's got to be out on the range when it's twenty below."

"Ah, I'm not that bad. Albert's the one who really hates to leave a warm bed and no doubt will be twice as bad once he's married." Will ignored his sister's derisive snort. "So, Miss Stuart, what do you think of our home?"

"'Tis ever' bit as beautiful as you said, Mr. MacDiarmid," Kicker assured him. "I believe twill make a fine home for my cousin and me."

"And the Major, of course. Any word yet on when he'll be able to join you?"

Kicker shook her head. "You'd have to ask Madelyn for details, but I don' believe he's musterin' out til late next year."

Will looked around at the crowd. "Where is your cousin, by the way? My wife's been tending our youngest that's been sick all week, and hasn't had a chance to meet our new teacher yet. I'd like to introduce them."

"Find Mother and you'll find Mrs. Bristow, Will. Mother hasn't let her stray two inches from her side since she got here."

Will tipped his hat to Kicker and Wynne, and hurried off.

"I hope my brother didn't overwhelm you in London, Kicker. When you're not used to it, his enthusiasm for our land can be a little off-putting." Wynne again linked arms with Kicker and guided them to seats which overlooked the makeshift stage where Seamus and Pudge were warming up. "I do hope too that your cousin hasn't been wearied by Mother's attention. It's just that she so rarely gets to talk to someone from her old world. When she does get the opportunity, she tends to go overboard. Mother and Will are much alike in that."

Kicker shook her head as they settled into their seats. "Truly, Wynne, Maddie and I are grateful to have met your brothers. Until then we had no clear idea where we'd settle. Twas a comfort to set sail, knowin' our destination."

"And Major Bristow is fine with these arrangements?"

Wynne's question was casual, but Kicker didn't dare look up from her plate. "I guess so. I know Maddie's written him about it." The music started as Pudge and Seamus let loose with a lively air, and Kicker silently blessed them for their opportune timing.

It wasn't until the Kelly brothers took a break an hour later that Wynne initiated further conversation with Kicker.

"They are every bit the fine musicians that you and your cousin proclaimed them."

Kicker beamed with pride in her friends. "Aye, they are wonderful, ain't they?"

"Indeed. They would not be out of place in the Calgary Opera House, should homesteading not pan out for them."

"Seamus and Pudge are gonna be the Potato Kings of the West," Kicker declared with the certainty of absolute faith in her friends. "Jus' wait an' see."

"I believe you, my dear." Wynne smiled warmly at her. "And you, what are your dreams, Kicker? When the Major returns to his wife, what do you plan to do? Will you stay in this area, or will you and Rabbit head out for horizons unseen and opportunities unknown?"

Kicker hesitated. She and Madelyn hadn't covered that question in laying their groundwork. She was unsure what her lover would want her to say. "I... I don' really know. I guess I'll jus' wait an' see."

"A good choice. For who knows—by that time you may be settled and have babes of your own, perhaps with a Potato King of the West?"

Kicker did not know how to decipher Wynne's gently teasing tone. It made her nervous, so she just shook her head and mumbled, "Not har'ly. They're jus' good frien's."

"But, my dear Kicker, all the best relationships begin as friendships, don't you think?" Wynne looked up at the sky, where the light of the long summer day had begun to fade. "At least, so I've heard. I'm not exactly a paragon of experience in that area. I threw Laird's father out on his drunken, no good ear before my son was even born."

Kicker had no idea how to respond to that revelation, but the sound of several gunshots and men hollering from the direction of the barns cut off any need.

Wynne frowned and rose to her feet just as one of the hands ran across the grounds and up to her. "Franklin, what's going on over there?"

The man, breathing heavily, stumbled to a stop. "Come quick, boss. Someone's been messing with the horses."

Instantly Wynne gathered up her skirts and rushed off toward the barns.

Cursing the skirts that slowed her pace and the dainty boots that made her footing dangerously uncertain, Kicker tried to keep up, but fell behind. By the time she arrived at the barns, several men were milling around, all talking at once.

Wynne's voice rang out over the commotion. "Enough! Peters, tell me what happened here."

"I was comin' down to check on the piebald, boss, you know—the one we thought was limpin' yesterday? Well, I get down here and I see someone openin' the corral gate. I yelled and the bastard shot at me. I hit the ground, and he fired a couple more times into the air. Spooked the damn horses so much they took off running like the devil 'imself was after them."

Franklin chimed in, "Some of the boys went after them, boss, but they had a helluva lead on 'em."

Wynne scowled. "Did you see who opened the gate, Peters?"

"No, Ma'am. He was in the shadows, an' then the horses were in the way."

"Plus, Peters was eatin' dirt at the time."

A couple of the men chuckled at Franklin's gibe, but quickly subsided under Wynne's glare.

"There was only half a dozen horses in there, Ma'am, and I'm sure the boys will bring 'em back," Franklin said reassuringly.

"I want the rest of you in the saddle and after them. Peters, not you. You're coming with me. I know you didn't get a good look at him and no doubt he's long gone now, but maybe you'll recognize someone up at the house."

Wynne strode off through the crowd of people who had gathered. Peters jogged along behind her as the other men hastened to their horses.

Kicker stared at the empty corral as tears filled her eyes. The sound of her voice was barely audible as she whispered into the warm night air.

"Rabbit."

CHAPTER 13

"DEAREST?"

Kicker sat on the edge of the back porch and gazed north at the cloudless morning sky.

"Won't you come in and have some breakfast?"

Kicker shook her head, her eyes never leaving the distant horizon. "I'm not hungry."

Madelyn stooped and laid a hand on Kicker's shoulder. "She may still be found. Don't give up hope."

"She's long gone, Maddie. If I'd had more time with her, maybe..." Kicker's voice trailed off disconsolately.

"Did you not tell me that the ranch hands found four of the runaways?"

"Aye, but Rabbit will not be tak'n. She's jus' gone."

With a sigh, Madelyn changed the subject. "The whole family is going into town for church after breakfast. I thought it wise for us to join them."

"Why?"

Madelyn stood and twitched her dress into place. "Because it behooves us to adhere to local custom. From what Mrs. MacDiarmid tells me, attendance at St. Mark's is not only expected, it's an excellent way to meet and get to know our neighbours."

Kicker had no desire for the company of strangers or the illusory comfort of religious ritual, but a thought occurred to her. "D'you think Wynne would min' droppin' me at the cabin on the way to town?"

"I wouldn't mind at all, Kicker." Wynne's husky voice sounded from the doorway. "Madelyn, Mother sent me to ask if you'd like to join her in the library. She enjoys reading and discussing biblical passages before breakfast on Sunday mornings, and she's long given up on my participation. You'd be doing me a great favour if you would shoulder this burden for today."

"It's no burden at all, Wynne. I'd be delighted to keep your mother company." Madelyn gave her lover's shoulder a quick squeeze and left the porch as Wynne came out to sit beside Kicker.

"The boys tell me they haven't seen hide nor hair of your Rabbit, Kicker. I'm real sorry about that."

The gloom that had enveloped Kicker since the previous evening was barely dented by the sympathy in Wynne's voice.

"We can easily drop you at the cabin, but if you like, I'll loan you one of our horses, just until Rabbit is found."

Even as she shook her head, Kicker gave Wynne a grateful look. She knew that the head of the Steeple Seven could not possibly believe the mare would ever be found, but she deeply appreciated the woman's optimistic words. However, Kicker's heart simply wasn't yet ready to give up on the small, feisty mare, and as foolish as it might be, it felt disloyal to ride a replacement so soon. "Thanks, but if you jus' drop me, I'll catch a ride back with Seamus and Pudge."

Wynne nodded her understanding. "All right, but the offer stands. If you change your mind, just come see me or Mr. Donnelly. Also there's a bay gelding I'm willing to sell. I want you to come take a look at him as soon as you can."

Kicker instantly bristled, but Wynne patted her leg soothingly.

"No, I'm not trying to replace Rabbit. Your cousin is going to need transportation to the schoolhouse, and this gelding is a gentle five-year-old. Laird learned to ride on him, and the horse is steady with a wagon or a rider. I think he might be perfect for Madelyn, but I know she'll want your opinion."

Kicker subsided sheepishly and gave her hostess a nod. "Well, at least you're not tryin' to sell us an eight-year-old."

Wynne laughed at Kicker's savvy. Too many disreputable horse dealers had an excess of eight-year-olds to sell because the age of a horse could not be determined accurately by its teeth after the age of eight.

"No, I wouldn't do that to you. Galahad was bred right here on the Steeple Seven."

"Galahad?"

"My father was in his romantic period at the time. Hell, poor Will ended up with King Arthur. Luckily my roan, Ballantrae, was foaled the following year, when my father had moved on to Robert Louis Stevenson. Ballantrae's fellow foals weren't so lucky. We've got a Long John Silver and Mr. Pew, not to mention a Dr. Jekyll and a Mr. Hyde, all from that year."

Kicker couldn't help but smile at Wynne's recital, and that earned her an answering grin.

"Yes, my father does enjoy naming the new foals, but I'm a bit worried about next spring's crop."

"Why?"

"Because he's been reading the collected works of Edgar Allen Poe this year."

Kicker laughed outright. "Well, I guess Rav'n or Tam'rlane wouldn't be so bad."

"You've read Poe?"

"Some. Maddie taught me how to read when she came to teach at Grindl'shire, an' she likes me to read to her, too. She says the more I practice, the better I'm gettin'."

"Your cousin sounds like an excellent teacher."

Kicker nodded, and immediately worried that she had said too much. Though the educational differences between the putative cousins were obvious to anyone who had heard them both speak, she was trying not to draw too much attention to it. *Surely Wynne'll wonder why we're so diff'rent, Maddie an' me.*

Wynne, however, simply picked up her earlier thread. "So, anyway, Galahad's dam drew my mother's carriage for a lot of years, and Galahad himself is a real gentleman. Speaking of carriages, there's an old wagon behind the south seed shed. It's not very big, and it's not worth anything—one wheel's broken and it needs a lot of repairs, but you'll have to have something with which to haul goods. If you and John want to take a look at it this week, and you think you can fix it, I'll throw it in with Galahad for an extra dollar."

Kicker suspected that even with a broken wheel the wagon was worth much more than a dollar, but she accepted Wynne's now familiar generosity at face value. "Soun's like a fair deal. An' I'll take a look at Galahad t'night, if that suits you."

"Good. We'll go down to the stables after dinner."

Rising to her feet, Wynne held out her hand. "Now why don't you come on in for breakfast? I happen to know that maple oatcakes are on the menu, and you really don't want to miss those. The leftovers will make a good lunch for you, too."

Wynne's matter of fact manner succeeded where Madelyn's sympathy failed. Kicker felt the crushing depression ease, and she accepted Wynne's hand up.

As the two women walked into the house, Wynne whispered, "Don't tell Mother that you're not going to church. Just hang back and make sure you're in the last wagon with Will, me and the boys." Her conspiratorial wink elicited an answering smile from Kicker.

Wynne earlier warned Kicker not to tell the MacDiarmid matriarch that she was working unchaperoned alongside the bachelor Kelly brothers. On the rare occasions she came to Mrs. MacDiarmid's notice, Kicker quickly learned to give evasive answers about her daily activities. She counted on the matriarch's patent delight in Madelyn's company to shield Kicker's less than ladylike behaviour, and thus far, her strategy had worked.

Less than an hour later, three carriages and a buckboard rolled down the Steeple Seven's long access road. Kicker was comfortably ensconced in the bed of the buckboard with Billy, Laird, and five of his male cousins, all fidgeting in their Sunday best. She watched the ranch recede from view as the MacDiarmid caravan entered the forest, en route to Galbraith's Crossing and St. Mark's Anglican Church.

When the procession neared the clearing where sounds of hammering and song could be heard, Kicker slipped quietly off the back of the wagon, a wrapped packet of cold oatcakes in one hand and a canteen in the other. As one of the cousins opened his mouth, a stern look from his aunt quelled any potential protest. Sullenly, the small boys looked enviously at Kicker as she strode down the path toward the cabin.

Kicker grinned to herself. She had not forgotten the many times in her childhood that she had been forced inside the village chapel when all she wanted was to take to the fields and woods at a dead run. On beautiful warm mornings like this, long services had seemed an early harbinger of the Hell pastors thunderously predicted for the errant of their flock. Kicker was well aware that Laird and his cousins would have given anything for the freedom to jump off the buckboard with her and head straight for Shadow Creek to go swimming or fishing.

As it was, Kicker felt her spirits lift when she saw Seamus and Pudge working on the walls of the barn.

"Miss Kicker." The delight in Seamus' voice was clear as he lowered his hammer and waved. Pudge yelled a greeting, and took advantage of the break to dip water from the nearby bucket. "I did not think we would be graced with your presence on the Lord's Day."

"An' I wasn' sure you'd be here, either," Kicker answered Seamus as she tossed her lunch on the back of the work wagon. She grabbed a hammer and a handful of nails and joined her friends. "Is't not a sin for you to skip Mass?"

"No doubt God has many worse sins etched beside my name." Seamus' sad smile momentarily quelled Kicker's resurgent spirits, but he read her easily and shook his head. "Do not let my hereafter give you pause." He swung his arm in a slow circle, encompassing the forest and sky surrounding them. "I believe God dwells more easily here than in any structure created by man."

"Pagan," Pudge muttered around the nails hanging between his lips as he raised his hammer.

"Perhaps," Seamus agreed. "But I think not profane."

The friends settled down to work in earnest, and by the time they broke for lunch, three sides of the barn were completed.

Kicker grabbed her lunch and joined the men in leaning back against the wall on the shady side of the barn. She traded them two of her sweetened oatcakes for half of one of their thick beef sandwiches, and settled down to eat with an appetite honed by a morning of hard labour.

Little was said until the meal was done and Pudge had pulled out his rolling papers and bag of tobacco. As he tamped down his tobacco, Kicker addressed Seamus.

"You two sounded wonderful las' night. I overheard a lot of the guests talkin' about your music."

The men grinned, clearly pleased.

Pudge elbowed Seamus. "Maybe we should draw up some playbills and hang them in town. Could be some extra shillings in it for us."

"Dollars," Seamus corrected. "But yes, your suggestion has merit."

Kicker nodded vigorously. "The las' one you played had me bawlin' like a babe, though that coulda been 'cause of what happened with Rabbit."

The brothers looked at her in puzzlement.

"Something happened to Rabbit? To what are you referring, Miss Kicker?"

It was Kicker's turn to regard them with confusion. "You mean you don' know?"

"I suspect there are many things we don't know, but in this case, we are completely in the dark," Seamus assured her gravely.

Kicker related the events of the night before, omitting her suspicion that Rupert's attack dog was responsible for the opening of Rabbit's corral.

"We must'a bin on break when it happened. Me and Seamus didn't know anything about it." Comprehension spread over Pudge's broad, freckled face and he poked his brother's arm. "That explains why we saw Rabbit this morning—"

"You saw Rabbit? Where?" Kicker leapt to her feet and scanned the woods around them as if that would make her missing mare appear by sheer force of will.

"Easy, Miss Kicker. She will return. We saw her off and on for about an hour, very early this morning. When Pudge tried to approach her, she departed rather rapidly."

Angry, Kicker shouted, "Why din't you tell me when I got here? I coulda been out lookin' for her!"

Seamus rose to his feet and laid a calming hand on Kicker's arm. "Truly, we thought she had thrown you during a morning ride, and assumed she would return to you as she has done before."

"An' did you not think it odd that she bore neither bridle nor saddle?" Kicker's wrath ebbed and her shoulders slumped. "I'm goin' down to the creek."

As she walked away from her friends, Kicker heard Pudge's indignant words to his brother. "We've seen her ride Rabbit with naught but a bit of rope. How were we to know?"

Seamus' quiet response was inaudible as Kicker walked into the forest and took the path down the short, steep hill. Squatting on the mossy shore and staring into the crystal clear stream, she castigated herself.

"Bloody fool. Turnin' on the bes' frien's you got like that. Where's your damn sense?" Gloomy, Kicker trailed her fingers in the cool water then leaned over and dunked her face in the stream.

Though warmer than the glacier fed Bow River, the slow moving waters of the tributary were still cool enough to give Kicker a start, and she reared back, wiping her face with her sleeve.

She'd turned to start back up the hill when a nicker from the other side of the stream made her whirl about. Rabbit poked her head above a copse of thick bushes and watched her with what Kicker swore was amusement.

"Rabbit! You vixen." Despite her euphoria, Kicker determinedly kept her voice low and even as she cautiously waded out into the broad creek. "D'you have any idea how much you stressed me, runnin' away like that? Aye, lass, I got nary a wink o' sleep las' night, and tis all your fault."

Knee deep in the water, she stopped well short of the mare. "So are you about finished playin' games? Ready to come home?" As she lacked rope, Kicker simply held out her hand to Rabbit. "C'mon, lass. Come with me."

For an instant Kicker did not think Rabbit would emerge from the brush. Finally, with a defiant shake of her head that said it was all her own idea, the small mare stepped daintily out and ambled into the water. Kicker promptly grabbed hold of her mane and swung up on her back.

Kicker felt the mare's muscles bunch, then relax. She leaned forward to wrap her arms around Rabbit's neck. "I missed you, lass. Please don' run away again."

With a gentle nudge of her knees, Kicker coaxed Rabbit in the direction of the cabin. By the time she arrived back in the clearing, the brothers had resumed work. They stopped hammering as soon as they saw horse and rider emerge from the woods. Without a word, Seamus picked up a long length of rope and approached.

Kicker slid off the mare and accepted the rope with a shamefaced glance at her friend.

After tying Rabbit to a tree distant enough that the mare wouldn't be bothered by the noise but close enough to keep an eye on her, Kicker left her horse to graze and returned to the barn. Squaring her shoulders, Kicker addressed her friends forthrightly. "I'm sorry. I misspoke and I should not have said what I did. Twas wrong to blame you, and I'm 'shamed of myself."

The brothers exchanged looks. Pudge picked up Kicker's hammer and handed it to her while Seamus looked thoughtfully at the space behind the barn. "It occurs to me that we should begin on a paddock next, so you needn't worry about Rabbit when you're here."

Kicker knew that she would hear no more about the incident, and her heart swelled with affection for her big hearted friends.

When the MacDiarmid caravan passed by less than an hour later, on the way back to the Steeple Seven, Kicker wanted to run out to tell Madelyn the good news. But her partner sat in the lead carriage with the senior MacDiarmids, and Kicker was loath to attract their attention. Instead she stayed behind the barn until the three carriages had passed, then trotted up to the buckboard.

Will pulled the wagon to a halt and Wynne leaned around him to speak. "You didn't miss anything, Kicker. The pastor was particularly and obnoxiously loquacious today."

Will nodded in rueful agreement. "I was beginning to think he was going to preach right into Monday."

A small hand reached forward to tug on Wynne's sleeve. "Mama. Can I stay here and help build?"

Wynne patted her son's hand. "Not this time, Laird. You're in your Sunday clothes, and neither Grandma nor Mrs. Donnelly will be happy if you ruin them." She winked at Kicker. "Besides, I'm not sure the builders could handle much of your kind of help."

Kicker couldn't restrain herself any longer. "Rabbit's here, Wynne. She showed up down by the creek a while back. Seamus and Pudge said she'd bin comin' 'round since early t'day."

"Excellent." Wynne beamed. "I guess that little mare knows who she belongs to then."

"I expect she thinks I b'long to her, not t'other way 'round. Would you tell Maddie the good news?"

Wynne's answer was interrupted by a holler from the carriage ahead of them. Will shook his head and clucked the reins. "Guess we'd better catch up with them, Miss Stuart. We'll see you later at the ranch."

As the buckboard started off with its load of bored little boys shoving and jostling in the back, Wynne called over her shoulder, "Don't forget to come by and check out Galahad tonight."

Kicker acknowledged her with a wave. "I won'."

By the end of the afternoon, the small construction crew had completed the exterior of the barn and the roof. When Kicker announced that she needed to get back to the ranch, the men accompanied her to the creek. Pudge stretched out on the bank and dunked his head in the water while Seamus untied his neckerchief and used it to wash his face and neck.

As had become her custom, Kicker took off her socks and boots, which were almost dry from their earlier soaking, and waded right in.

Welcoming the coolness on her hot feet, Kicker splashed water liberally on her arms and face, getting much of her garb wet, as well.

"Don't know why you don't just lie down and float around," Pudge teased with a grin. "Don't they ever wonder up at the big house why you always come back dripping like a fresh caught trout?"

Kicker kicked a small geyser of water at Pudge, who quickly retaliated.

Seamus sat back on a downed tree and watched his brother and friend with amusement. Both Pudge and Kicker were swiftly soaked and yelping from the cool water. However, when they eyed Seamus and took off their hats to fill, he quickly scrambled back up the hill.

Laughing, Kicker and Pudge followed at a slower speed.

By the time they reached the clearing, Seamus had brought Rabbit over to the cabin. "Will you be able to manage her with just a rope, Miss Kicker?"

Kicker nodded at Seamus and accepted his hand up onto Rabbit's back. "If she wanted to bolt, she'd ne'er have come back." She laid an affectionate hand on the mare's neck. "We may take the long route back to the ranch, dependin' on what Rabbit has in min', but we'll get there." Looking down at the brothers, Kicker asked, "Are you headin' back soon, yoursel'?"

Seamus shook his head. "We've decided to bide out here for now, Miss Kicker. We have our bedrolls and we shall make use of the barn in case of inclement weather. It is much quieter and we can get right to work in the morning."

"Smells a helluva lot better than the bunkhouse, too," Pudge asserted.

"You know, you're welcome to use the cabin. You don' have to sleep in the barn."

The brothers shook their heads in unison. "The barn is luxurious compared to some of the places we stopped during our journey here. Please do not concern yourself with us. We will be fine."

Kicker frowned at Seamus, but he held up his hand before she could speak.

"The cabin will be your home—you and your cousin, of course. It would not be proper for us to occupy it first."

"It'd be bad luck," Pudge agreed.

"What's that? An ol' Irish curse?"

"Nah, just the ancient wisdom of Grandmother Kelly."

Seamus added his support. "And you would not want us to go against our sainted grandmother's ways, would you, Miss Kicker?"

"I guess not. If you're sure you'll be a'right."

"We have food and drink—"

"Drink?" Seamus raised an eyebrow at his brother. "Is that what I heard clinking in your bedroll this morning? And you did not offer me any last night?" He swept off his hat and swatted Pudge with it.

Kicker laughed at the brothers. "Like I tol' you, I'll be working with John Blue Wolf smithin' this week, but I'll get over when I can." She raised a hand in farewell as she nudged Rabbit into a trot.

The last thing she heard as she left the clearing was Pudge's voice. "Sainted? Grandma Kelly? Are you crazy, Seamus? That woman could single handedly out drink, out curse, and out brawl the entire Royal Irish Constabulary."

Seamus' response was inaudible, but Kicker began her trip back to the ranch with a smile on her face. After the anguish of the previous night, all was again right with her world.

While Kicker waited in the ranch's smithy for John Blue Wolf's arrival Monday morning, she stoked the brick fire pot with coal from a large exterior bin. She was well aware that the quality of fire and how well she packed the green coal to cook into the more valuable, clean carbon coke would shape the smith's first opinion of his new helper. She was determined to make the best impression possible, not only for the sake of her future employment, but also to secure clear title to her mare.

Kicker had built forge fires since she was old enough to distinguish a poker from a slice, but this forge was equipped with the latest in factory made blower fans. Her father could never have afforded one, and Old Thomas insisted that the traditional wooden bellows had been good enough for his father and were good enough for him. Kicker's only familiarity with the modern blowers was from the lengthy and loving description of a visiting smith at Grindleshire, but she quickly determined how the blower forced oxygen through the tuyere into the base of the fire pot, and got the fire going.

As the fire grew hotter, Kicker laid out hammers and tongs next to the vise on the blacksmith's bench. She hesitated over laying out the new rod stock, as she could see factory-made horseshoes in a keg against the wall. She decided she would wait to find out John's preference.

She began to collect the accumulation of cut off ends, and bits and pieces of metal from the floor around the anvil, sorting out those that still had some worth and adding the rest to the scrap pile outside the back wall of the smithy.

Finally back in her element, Kicker rejoiced as she worked. *Maddie can keep all that high-falutin' nonsense. This is where I b'long.* The heat of the fire as it caught and burned steadily; the feel of familiar tools in her hand, and even the flies lazily buzzing around the stables were deeply comforting in their familiarity.

Kicker was relieved to see by the horn of the cast iron anvil that John Blue Wolf was also right handed. Old Thomas was a lefty, and it had complicated her work immensely.

She filled the slack tub with water and was rounding out a small nick in the anvil's edge when John arrived two hours after dawn. His nod of approval was all the recognition he gave her efforts, but it was enough for her. Neither her father nor Old Thomas had been effusive men, and while working the forge, Kicker preferred silent efficiency to gregarious fellowship.

As the morning progressed, Kicker was very conscious that despite the blacksmith's quiet manner, she was being thoroughly tested on her knowledge and skills. John didn't use a shoeing stall, as her father had, so when she brought the first horse up from the barn, she tied it off next to the three legged, metal clinching stand. John watched closely as she efficiently removed the old shoes, cleaned the sole and frog, then pared, trimmed, smoothed and levelled the first hoof.

John directed Kicker to use the rod stock rather than the pre-made shoes for the first horse, and she understood he wanted to watch her proficiency at shaping and sizing. Hiding a smile, she fell easily into the rhythm of the work.

When Kicker finished pounding in the last nail of the fourth shoe and let the horse's hoof drop back to the ground, he gave her a simple, "Good."

They quickly established their routine, each alternating between anvil and John's old wooden shoeing box. Kicker initially deferred to the older man, but he quickly made it clear he wanted her to work as independently as possible, and she gladly accepted the responsibility.

Their toil had been solitary at first, but as the ranch hands began their work day, a growing number of them dropped by the smithy. Kicker knew they were curious about a woman smith but she ignored them, having long ago grown immune to sometimes hostile male scrutiny. It wasn't until she was turning a stubborn toe caulk that she heard John growl impatiently at the onlookers.

"This isn't a circus. Get out of here before I tell Wynne what a worthless lot she's paying wages to."

Invoking his sister's name was enough to disperse the crowd, and the two smiths were left in a silence broken only by the ring of the hammers and the sound of the mechanical blower. By the time the lunch bell rang from the cookhouse, they had shoed eleven horses between them.

John finished the hoof he had been working on and straightened up. "You might as well go on up to the big house and get something to eat."

Kicker shook her head. She wasn't comfortable eating with the family at the best of times. Having the clear evidence of the day's labours on her body and clothes made the situation even worse, so she had brought a lunch down to the smithy with her. After she washed the dirt and coal dust off her hands, Kicker joined John under a tree and took a seat on the grass.

They ate in silence, then John stood up, took a heavy bladed hunting knife from the sheath at his side, and cut several small x's in the bark of the tree under which they had been sitting. He moved fifteen paces back, beckoned Kicker to his side, and extended his knife to her. "Work down from the top, and waste no time."

Kicker hadn't played mumblety-peg in years, and she was accustomed to throwing at a target drawn on the ground, but she accepted John's knife and began to cast. It took her half a dozen throws to shake off the rust, but she finally earned his grunt of approval.

They stopped and went back to work. Later, when they finished the day's work, he had her throw again at x's he carved into the railings of a corral.

Once Kicker demonstrated her proficiency with the new targets, John had her turn away from the railings and, on his mark, whirl and throw the knife.

Between the day's heavy labour and the target practice, Kicker was certain her arm would fall off.

When John finally called a halt, his faint praise made it worthwhile. "You did well. I'll see you tomorrow."

With a growing grin, Kicker watched him saddle his horse. John didn't look back at her, but he did raise his hand in a silent farewell as he cantered down the road.

Her body aching but her heart light, Kicker walked quickly back to the big house. She could hardly wait to tell Madelyn about the small triumphs of her day.

"I don't wish to interrupt you, dearest, but it's a beautiful evening. Would you care to go for a walk down by the lake before we retire?"

Kicker looked up from the letter she had been laboriously writing to Adam and saw Madelyn in the open door of her bedroom. "Yes!"

Madelyn smiled at her eagerness. "You know you'll still have time to finish that when we get back."

Kicker set the half-finished letter aside. "Mrs. Donnelly said she'd take it when she goes into town day after t'morrow, so there's no hurry. I got lots of time."

"Mrs. MacDiarmid and I are going tomorrow, so I can take it if you like."

Grabbing her hat, Kicker kept her fingers crossed that they would be out of the house and gone before Mrs. MacDiarmid noticed. Just this once she wanted Madelyn to herself.

"If you're goin' to the gen'ral store, don' forget to add my list to your order, a'right?"

"I'll do so, though I'm at a loss as to why we're arming ourselves like soldiers."

Kicker waited until one of the housemaids passed them on the stairs before answering. "Wolves, bears, cougars. I'm not tryin' to frighten you, Maddie, but if we keep chickens like we planned, we're goin' to have to be able to shoot at predators."

Madelyn paused at the back door and regarded Kicker curiously. "And the hunting knife?"

"Good for lots of things. Cuttin' rope, cuttin' meat, cuttin' the head off a chicken..."

"All right." Madelyn surrendered with an amused smile. "You've convinced me, but just remember that when it comes time to decapitate Sunday dinner, you're in charge."

Madelyn pushed the door open and stepped out on the porch.

Following her, Kicker gave a relieved but inaudible sigh. She needed to be able to protect Madelyn from all manner of predators—animal and human, but she didn't want to worry her. A debate about whether to mention the threats presented by Rupert Arbuster and Rick Biggart had raged inwardly for days. Thus far Kicker had come down on the side of not alarming Madelyn.

Plus, you don' wan' to confess to her how you got in so much trouble so fas'.

Kicker studiously ignored her nagging conscience and offered Madelyn her arm as they crossed the lawn and began to stroll along the uneven beach of the small lake. They headed for the eastern shore, away from the houses of the MacDiarmid brothers. As she paced slowly across the sand and small pebbles, while water lapped near their feet, Kicker felt her earlier stress ebb.

"It feels a little cooler tonight, doesn't it, dearest?"

"Aye. John said he thinks winter will come early this year."

"Did he now?" Madelyn pressed closer to Kicker. "The new school term begins next week, so I suppose that means autumn at least is almost upon us."

"Is that why you're goin' into town t'morrow with Mrs. MacDiarmid?"

"Yes. We're going to open up the schoolhouse and see what needs to be done in preparation."

They left the open beach behind and navigated around driftwood and deadfalls in the half light. Kicker took a firmer hold on Madelyn's arm, only to find herself pulled away from the beach and up to the tree line.

"D'you wan' to turn back, love?"

"No, dearest. This is what I want." Safely in the cover of the trees, Madelyn drew Kicker into her arms. "I've missed you so."

Her face buried against Madelyn's breast, Kicker mumbled her heartfelt agreement.

"I know it's been terribly hard on you. I know—"

"Shhh. Tis hard on both of us, Maddie, but we'll soon be in our own home."

"It can't be soon enough."

Kicker looked up in surprise. "But I thought—"

Madelyn shook her head. "I was wrong, dearest. None of life's luxuries can compare to the pleasure of feeling your body next to mine. There is little joy if I cannot touch you like this..." Her hands slid over Kicker's body, then cupped her head and pulled her into a fierce kiss.

Kicker lingered blissfully in the embrace, content to let her lover lead as Madelyn's fingers fumbled with buttons and tugged urgently on her shirt.

As the last button separated from fabric and Madelyn pulled Kicker's shirt open, the sound of a distant call could be heard floating through the still evening air, down from the big house.

"Maaaaadelyn! Mrs. Bristoooooow! Where are yoooouuuu?"

Kicker could not help but chuckle. She'd never heard Madelyn emit quite so anguished a whimper.

"No, no, no!" Madelyn groaned and banged her head on Kicker's shoulder while her hands lingered on her breasts.

"Tis a'right, love. There'll be time enough for that soon." Kicker gently disengaged Madelyn's hands and began to button her shirt. "We'd bes' get back b'fore she sends the dogs after us."

Once again decent, Kicker took Madelyn's hand and led her back to the beach. "I thought you liked Mrs. MacDiarmid."

Madelyn gave a deep, frustrated sigh. "I do, dearest, truly, I do. She's been incredibly kind and generous to me. I've no doubt that without her auspices I'd have found it much more difficult to fit in. But..."

Despite dusk's fading light, Kicker could see the hungry way Madelyn looked at her. "But if she'd jus' waited ten more minutes, eh?"

"Five."

Kicker laughed at Madelyn's flat assertion. She contemplated suggesting a midnight rendezvous after the house was settled for the night, but didn't want to tempt Madelyn when her resistance was so obviously low. Instead she contented herself with a mental promise to ensure that their first night in their own home would be a memorable one.

Reluctantly roused from an enchanting erotic dream which featured Madelyn and a very soft, very large bed, Kicker tried to ignore the unusual and intrusive sounds that came through her open bedroom window. But the shouts of men and the sound of people running through the hallways quickly dispersed the last of her cobwebs.

Kicker hastily threw off her nightshirt and pulled on her clothes and boots. She tucked her shirt in just as her door swung open. Madelyn, still clad in nightclothes with a robe draped haphazardly over her shoulders, called fearfully to her. "Kicker?"

"Maddie? What's goin' on?"

"I don't know, dearest, but it seems as if there's a grave emergency."

The women fairly flew down the stairway and followed the sound of tumult out to the front porch. Most of the household was gathered there. Mrs. MacDiarmid hastened towards them as soon as she saw Madelyn. Her agitated voice was drowned out by the clangour of the ranch emergency bell being struck again and again. Kicker was unable to distinguish her words.

Fighting her way to the edge of the porch, Kicker saw men running down by the stables. *Rabbit!* Before she could jump down and join the rush, she saw Wynne dashing back up to the house from the direction of the bell. A distinctively acrid scent in the air caught her attention.

Fire!

Kicker leapt to the lawn and scanned the horizon. Her breath caught as she saw a telltale glow in the night sky from the southeast.

Bless'd Jesus!

The clatter of the ranch's fire wagon as it thundered down the road, a stream of mounted men in its wake, confirmed Kicker's fears. And as Wynne skidded to a halt on the damp grass and looked directly at her, she knew what the ranch boss would say.

"Your cabin, Kicker. It's on fire."

Kicker heard Madelyn's horrified gasp from the porch behind her, but her thoughts flew immediately to her friends. "Seamus! Pudge! Are they a'right? Wynne! D'you know if they're a'right?" Dread consumed her, and Kicker wasn't even aware she had grabbed Wynne's arms until comforting hands settled on her forearms.

"I'm not sure. I've only got a few details, but I've sent all my available men and equipment."

Whirling, Kicker reached out for Madelyn and clutched a handful of her robe. Her lover stared down at her fearfully, but nodded.

"Go, dearest, but be careful. For God's own sweet sake, be careful."

Sparing a quick nod, Kicker ran for the stable and Rabbit. Wynne caught up with her just as she finished securing a bridle on her jittery mare.

"I'll come with you."

Kicker nodded, but ignoring a saddle, she vaulted onto Rabbit and kicked the mare into a gallop. She was halfway to the cabin before she heard the sound of Wynne's roan race up behind her.

Well before the women reached the scene, they could hear the sounds of men shouting and flames crackling. Still, the sight of the cabin in a towering blaze tore the breath from Kicker's lungs.

Spooked by the smells and the sounds, Rabbit and Ballantrae reared and danced as they neared the fire. Their riders were forced to stop and tie them off far from the clearing.

Kicker frantically scanned the crowd of men who had formed two bucket lines from the creek to the inferno, but nowhere could she see Seamus or Pudge. She grabbed a man running past and blurted, "The men who were here—the Kelly brothers, d'you know where they are?"

When the man tried to shake off Kicker's frantic grasp, Wynne snapped, "Hillier! Do you know if the Kellys are all right?"

The familiar voice halted the man's attempt to wrestle free. "I'm not sure, boss. Someone said a man had been badly hurt. Don't know who, but they'd already rushed him into town on the work wagon by the time I got here. Sorry."

Stunned, Kicker released the man and he ran toward a stack of shovels and picks. Feeling as if she would be ill, she stumbled toward the fire, only to have strong arms halt her progress.

"No, Kicker."

"They were in the barn, Wynne. I have to know..."

"The barn's not on fire, and they wouldn't be in there now, in any case. Whoever is hurt must be one of my men, and I'm going to check on him. We don't have a town doctor, so they'll have gone to John's wife, Esther. Come with me."

Wynne led the way back to the horses. Ballantrae took the lead as Kicker blindly gave Rabbit her head, trusting the mare to follow. As they galloped towards town, two names tumbled over and over in her mind.

Seamus. Pudge.

CHAPTER 14

KICKER REINED RABBIT IN AS Wynne's horse slowed. They were rapidly approaching the west end of Galbraith's Crossing. Most of the town was dark, except for a light in the train station.

Wynne twisted in her saddle and motioned Kicker forward. "When we get to John and Esther's, let me go in first. It's not unusual for Esther to be called out in the middle of the night—she serves as the midwife around here—but I don't want to scare their children by roaring into the house."

Though frustrated by any delay, Kicker reluctantly nodded. As they neared the livery stable, she eyed the two story, wood frame house which adjoined the smithy. A light could be seen in a ground floor rear window. The work wagon, its team absent, had been pulled around the side.

Kicker and Wynne drew up at the hitching post and dismounted. As Kicker knotted the reins, she realized there was someone on the porch watching them. Startled, she peered into the darkness, only to sigh with relief as she heard John's voice.

"I figured you'd be in before long, Wynne." John unfolded from the bench on which he sat. He approached them and nodded at Kicker.

"They're here then?" Wynne mounted the two steps to stop in front of John.

"Yes."

"Are they a'right?" Before Kicker could bolt for the door, John held up a cautionary hand.

"Whoa, there, Kicker. My wife doesn't need you bursting in on her right now. She's got enough on her hands."

"But I could help..." Kicker knew she was pleading; the urge to see her friends was overwhelming.

Her companions shook their heads, and Kicker's heart sank as John addressed her.

"It looks like your horses have been ridden hard tonight. Why don't you take them to the stable while Wynne and I have a talk? There's a lantern inside the door on a bench to the left. It just needs to be turned up. The last two stalls on the right are empty; you can put them in there. There's water in the trough and hay in the loft. By the time you get back, Esther might be done and you can go in to see your friends."

John's tone was mild, and for a second Kicker contemplated ignoring him. Then reason triumphed and she drew in a deep breath. The last thing she wanted was to interfere with Esther's treatment and so cause her friends harm.

Reluctantly, Kicker gathered up Rabbit and Ballantrae's reins, aware that the other two watched her from the porch. "Can you at leas' tell me—which one's hurt?"

"Neither looked in very good shape when they got here, but the thinner man seemed more shaken up than anything. The other one, his brother..." John shook his head soberly.

Pudge. Oh, Pudge, what happened to you?

With lowered eyes, Kicker led the horses to the stable. Within moments she had unsaddled Ballantrae as her mind whirled around the meagre information John provided. She was ashamed of her involuntary relief when she found out that Seamus was not the one badly injured. Though she cared deeply for the reckless, good natured Pudge, it was Seamus who had slipped effortlessly into the space that the absence of her brother Adam had opened in her heart.

Kicker scrambled into the loft and pushed hay down to Rabbit and Ballantrae, ignoring the hopeful whickers of the stable's other residents. Then she sat at the top of the ladder and dangled her feet, suddenly reluctant to return to John and Wynne. Kicker was afraid to see Pudge, afraid to find out how severe his injuries were. Mostly, she was afraid to face Seamus with her overwhelming guilt.

Tis all my fault.

Head bowed, Kicker tried to determine how she could have prevented this disaster. From the moment she learned of the fire, she was certain that her friends had gotten caught in the backlash of her split second decision to stop a bully from killing a small mare. But she knew that given the same circumstances, she would do the same thing again. What filled Kicker with terror, even more than the thought that Pudge might die, was that Madelyn too might get caught up in the same lethal current.

Finally, with a deep sigh, Kicker pushed herself off the edge of the loft and dropped lightly to the stable floor. She gave Rabbit a quick pat on the flank and left the mare munching contentedly.

Tense, lowered voices sounded as Kicker approached the porch, but Wynne and John stopped talking as she drew near.

John rose from the bench. "I'll go check with Esther to see if she'll let you in yet."

He vanished into the house and Wynne patted the bench beside her. Kicker accepted the invitation. They waited in silence for long moments, and Kicker began to grow nervous at John's failure to return.

"It doesn't necessarily mean anything, Kicker. Esther may simply need his help with something. Give him a few more minutes."

Her mouth dry and her thoughts increasingly frantic, Kicker sought for something to distract herself. "Esther... is she a nurse?"

"Not formally, I suppose, but she was trained by the Grey Nuns. She's Métis, from up north. Her entire family was wiped out by typhoid when Esther was small. The nuns took her in and raised her at St. Albert's. So it just seemed natural that she would study nursing under them when she grew up."

"How'd she end up here?"

Wynne chuckled softly. "I guess I can sort of take credit for that. About six years ago, John and I went into Calgary. He'd been kicked badly a few weeks before, and he was still limping. I nagged him into going to the new Holy Cross Hospital to have it looked at. Esther was working with the doctor that day, and I swear it was like magic from the moment they saw each other. For five months John found every excuse imaginable to go into the city, until finally I told him to stop being a fool and propose to the girl."

"An' he did?"

"He did, and here they are."

Kicker glanced back at the door, but it remained ominously shut. "So she does all the doctorin' around here?"

Wynne's voice hardened. "Yes and no. A lot of folks won't come see her by day, but they're quick enough to show up at her back door after sunset if they're sick or hurting."

Kicker's next question was cut off by the sound of the door opening as John stepped out. She jumped to her feet and stared at him hopefully.

"You can both go back. He won't be awake, but Esther said you can have a few minutes with him. She also said you should try to convince the brother to go back to the ranch and get some rest."

Kicker shook her head. "Seamus won' leave Pudge. Ne'er. No more would Pudge leave him."

"That's pretty much the sense that I got, too." John stepped aside and pushed the door wide. "I'd ask that you keep your voices down so the babies don't wake up."

Kicker nodded and let Wynne lead the way down the narrow hall to the back of the house. A slender, dark-haired woman washing soiled cloths and dressings in a tin basin looked up as they emerged into the large kitchen.

"Hello, Wynne."

"Esther, this is—"

Esther held up her hand. "I know. You're both welcome."

Kicker eyed the curtained off area next to the stove and almost missed Wynne's question to her sister-in-law.

"Is he all right?"

"Barring complications, Mr. Kelly will live." Esther's voice was tired. "You may see him for a few minutes, but then I want him to rest."

No sooner had permission been given than Kicker darted to the curtain and drew it back. Barely able to stifle an involuntary gasp, she stared at the sight before her.

Pudge lay on a narrow cot, with dressings over most of the right half of his face and upper chest. The skin that could be seen at the edge of the dressings had clearly been burned. A crisp white sheet covered him from the waist down. Kicker grasped for hope and found some relief as she noted that his hands appeared unaffected.

Seamus sat in a wooden chair by his brother's bedside, his head down and eyes closed. Clearly exhausted, he too bore the marks of the night's misadventures. His shirt, burned and ragged, hung in tatters over the clean dressings that covered half his torso. More dressings were wrapped around the palms of his hands, which dangled limply between his knees.

For a fleeting second, Kicker wondered if Seamus was asleep, or praying. Then he lifted his head with an effort and met her horrified gaze.

Kicker's shock at the bleakness in his eyes propelled her to his side. Without hesitation, she knelt beside him and draped a comforting arm around his shoulders. His head slumped toward her, and she rested her forehead against his.

"I'm so terr'bly sorry, Seamus. Bless'd Jesus, if I could'a stopped this..."

Seamus' hollow voice nearly broke Kicker's heart. "I promised my mother I would take care of him. When we left home, the last thing I swore to her was that I would put my brother's welfare ahead of my own, always. Now look at him... She would not forgive me; no more will I forgive myself."

Kicker's arm tightened around the grieving man, and she sought to comfort him. "There's naught to forgive. Twas jus' an accident."

"No, it was not." Seamus raised his head, anger on his strained features. "It was attempted murder, plain and simple."

"What do you mean?"

The sharp question came from behind Kicker and she glanced back over her shoulder to see Wynne, John, and Esther watching them.

Wynne spoke again. "Mr. Kelly, what happened out there tonight?"

With a visible effort, Seamus sat up straighter. Kicker's arm slipped from his shoulders, but she kept it solidly around her friend's back as he began to tell his story. "We had been asleep in the barn for what I am sure was hours, when all of a sudden we heard a great commotion from the horses outside. We ran out to see what was going on, and saw that the cabin was on fire. I grabbed the water bucket and Pudge grabbed the tin box in which we had been storing our gear. We ran back and forth to the creek, fighting the fire. I thought we were getting ahead of it. Pudge picked up an axe to try knocking down some of the burning timbers, while I went for more water. I was just about down to the creek when I heard Pudge cry out—a strangled cry, like someone stopped his voice cold. I scrambled back up in time to see Pudge laid out on the ground and a man pulling him toward the fire."

Seamus stopped and accepted the glass of water Esther pressed on him. "I shouted and ran at him. The fellow went for his gun, but I threw my bucket and seized upon him, knocking it out of his hand. We rolled around the ground, exchanging blows..."

He paused and looked ruefully at Kicker. "I am not much of a fighter, as you may imagine."

"But you were fightin' for Pudge."

Seamus nodded at Kicker's words. "I was. But if I had been faster, if I'd fought harder... If I'd kept my eye on where Pudge lay..."

"Stop it," Kicker admonished. "'Tis not your fault."

"Just as I thought I'd overcome our assailant, I heard this terrible cracking of timber and saw part of the cabin crash down near Pudge. I hastened to him, but..." Seamus stopped and swallowed hard.

"Shhh." Kicker felt hopelessly inadequate as she tried to alleviate his anguish. "Tis over, Seamus. Pudge is here. He's right b'side you."

"He was on fire, Kicker." Seamus clenched his injured hands into fists and slammed them down on his thighs. Kicker seized his hands to stop him from hurting himself further. "On fire!"

"But you pulled him out."

"Yes, I pulled him out. I rolled him in the dirt and smothered the flames as quickly as I could. At the same time, I heard some men yell as they rode up fast..."

Wynne glanced at John. "Those would be some of the boys coming back from town."

"Let me guess, Whitford, Tyler, and Milos."

"Who else?" Wynne shrugged. "But for once I'm glad they can't stay away from the Windsor's bar. If not for them, we might not have found out about the fire until it took half the forest."

Kicker stole a quick glance at Seamus' burnt and tattered shirt. She had a pretty good idea of how he had tried to save Pudge. She knew without asking that he had thrown his body over his brother's without a second thought.

Wynne spoke up. "And the assailant, Mr. Kelly? Did you get a good look at him? Would you be able to identify him?"

Seamus closed his eyes for long moments, then shook his head. "I can tell you no more than that he was a tall man of exceedingly lean build, with fair hair and no beard. Other than that, I'm afraid I could not be certain if I saw him again."

Biggart. I knew twas that bastard! Though Kicker's certainty was reinforced by Seamus' accurate description of the man, she knew that if he were unable to identify the arsonist with surety, she would have no grounds to accuse Biggart outright.

"There was one thing, though... I just cannot..." Seamus' eyes had a distant look as he struggled to remember. "His gun."

"His gun, Mr. Kelly?"

"Yes. When I was rolling Pudge over in the dirt, I remember stumbling over something hard, something metal. I didn't take time to examine it, but as our assailant ran off when the Steeple Seven hands came on scene, I believe he may have left his gun behind."

John whispered something to Wynne, but though Kicker strained to hear, all she caught was something about a pearl handle. Frustrated, she wanted to scream at them to acknowledge that they knew who had done this terrible thing, but as she opened her mouth, Pudge uttered an agonized groan.

Esther was instantly at his side, shooing the others away. Kicker barely had time to hug Seamus again before she was chased off. John drew the curtain around his wife and her patients, and gestured to the women to follow him back outside.

The cool cleanness of the night air suddenly made Kicker aware of the acrid miasma that had hung in the kitchen. Though partly medicinal, she realized that much of the stench emanated from Pudge's seared body.

Kicker retched and bolted for the edge of the porch. A hand settled on her back and offered her a handkerchief to clean up. Shaken, she sat back, only to have Wynne gently push her head lower.

"Give it a few moments, Kicker."

Kicker heard John leave the porch, and by the time she was able to rise shakily to her feet, he returned with their horses in tow.

"I'm sorry."

Wynne shook her head at Kicker's mumbled apology. "Forget it. I was half inclined to do that myself."

John handed Ballantrae's reins to Wynne and pulled Rabbit alongside the raised sidewalk. Kicker acknowledged his consideration with a grateful nod, and slid onto her mare's bare back.

"Wynne, are you going to stop and see if you can find that gun?"

"I think so, John. If you're right, and it is...unique, then maybe we'll get some answers." Wynne glanced at Kicker as she answered her brother's question. "Might not be easy, though. There were a lot of men running around there tonight; a gun could have ended up anywhere."

John shrugged. "You can only try."

He raised his hand as the women reined their horses out onto the street, and Kicker called softly to him, "I'll see you in a couple of hours."

Wynne looked at her curiously. They trotted their horses down the road, and quickly left the town behind. "You're coming back to see the Kellys?"

"When the work's done, aye."

"Work?"

Kicker nodded tiredly. She wasn't looking forward to a long day of shoeing horses, but she had no intention of shirking her second day of work.

"I'm not sure that John will even be out at the ranch today, Kicker."

"Matters not. I can keep workin' whether he's there or not."

"I'm sure he would understand, given the circumstances."

"Aye, I'm sure he would, but I'll be there."

Kicker heard Wynne's incredulous grunt, and was glad when her companion let the subject drop.

As they followed the river, Rabbit slowed to a walk and Ballantrae followed. Too tired to argue, Kicker let her mare set the pace and the women rode in silence until they turned north.

"Kicker..."

Kicker had been dozing, but she opened her eyes at the sound of Wynne's cautionary tone.

"I don't want you to do anything foolish."

Kicker snorted sourly. "Like what?"

"Like trying to get revenge on whomever you think was behind this fire." Worry was clearly apparent in Wynne's voice.

Kicker gave her a sidelong stare. "D'you think me a hothead, then?"

"I think you just saw people very dear to you terribly hurt by the deliberate hand of an enemy, and I think you may wish to avenge them."

"Bloody right!" Kicker was startled at the rage that erupted with those words. She did not just want justice; she wanted vengeance of biblical proportions. Kicker wanted to heap plague and pestilence on the heads of Biggart and Rupert Arbuster, and consign them to the flames they had so callously brought down on Pudge and Seamus. She wanted to—

Wynne grabbed Rabbit's reins, pulled the mare to a halt, and wheeled Ballantrae to come up beside Kicker. "Listen to me. I know who you think did it—"

"You know who did it! You know what bastard's foul hand lies b'hind this cowardly—"

"Kicker." Wynne grabbed Kicker's arm in a firm grip. "I need you to think right now. I need you to set aside the anger and the exhaustion, and I need you to think clearly. If you go off half cocked, you'll hurt your friends, you'll hurt yourself, and you'll hurt Madelyn. Do you want that, Kicker? Do you want to destroy Madelyn with what you're thinking of doing?"

The sound of her lover's name was like a bucket of cold water. The rage evaporated, leaving a bitterly hollow emptiness behind. "So he'll jus' get away with it—both of them, no price to pay for what they did?"

Wynne squeezed Kicker's forearm. "He won't, I swear. But the reality is that Rupert is protected by his family's wealth and position. Folks around here may know that he's a scoundrel, but he's our scoundrel. His roots are here. He belongs here."

"An' we don'. Seamus and Pudge are jus' a coupl'a immigrant Irish, an' I'm jus' the misfit cousin of the new teacher. Who'd stan' for us?"

"I would. And my family would. You're not without friends, but we don't wish to ignite a range war, either. We must tread carefully where Rupert is concerned."

"An' Biggart?"

Wynne released Kicker's arm with a grim laugh. "Now him we might be able to do something about, particularly if we can locate his gun at the cabin." She wheeled Ballantrae and the horses picked up their pace again. "If we could find solid evidence to implicate Biggart, we might be able to de-fang Rupert in the process. That's something that every law abiding citizen in this territory would get behind."

Kicker considered that as they followed the well traveled trail through the forest. Convicting Biggart alone would not satisfy her need to see both culprits punished, but it was a start. At least she might be able to rest easy where Madelyn's welfare was concerned.

Lost in thought, Kicker did not notice the sound of a horse rapidly approaching until Ballantrae and Rabbit stopped. She looked up to see a lone rider galloping toward them. Before her tired mind could process the rider's identity, Madelyn pulled Galahad to a stop and ran to her side.

"Kicker! Thank God! I've been out of my mind with worry."

Without a moment's thought to Wynne's presence, Kicker slid off Rabbit and into Madelyn's embrace. They clung to each other, murmuring nonsensical reassurances until they both laughed at the sounds.

"I couldn't wait a moment longer, dearest. I had to come find you."

"Shhh, I know. I'm fine, Maddie. Jus' fine."

Madelyn drew back enough to look at her face. Kicker had no doubt that the night's fear and rage must have left their mark, because Madelyn's expression melted from relief to profound compassion. "Oh, dearest, what is it? Are Seamus and Pudge hurt?"

Kicker nodded, and tears overflowed her eyes. "Twas ghastly. Pudge is... Pudge is so ...he's hurt bad, Maddie."

Wynne, who had moved Ballantrae to a decorous distance as her companions embraced, quietly filled in the details as Kicker sobbed.

For the first time that night, Kicker felt anchored. Warm, familiar arms held her tightly and a soft voice whispered loving assurances in her ear. Safe at last, she released all that she had been feeling in an uncontrolled and cathartic outpouring. When the tears finally ebbed, she rested her head on Madelyn's shoulder until her lover coaxed her up onto Rabbit's back.

"Come, dearest. Let's get you back to the ranch. I think a hot bath and a soft bed are just what you need."

Kicker felt drained as they set out again, three abreast where the trail would allow, two where the trees encroached too much on their way. She was never allowed to ride alone; one of the other women was always beside her. Kicker was grateful that neither Madelyn nor Wynne seemed to expect her to talk, and she listened to their conversation as if from a great distance.

"Did you see the cabin, Madelyn?"

"I stopped only long enough to find out where you two had gone, but from what I saw, it's been completely destroyed."

"I'm so very sorry."

"Thank you, Wynne. And thank you, too, for sending men and equipment so quickly. The barn and the outbuildings are still standing, and I know that's because of their efforts."

"We would do no less for any neighbour. Fire is the terrible leveler out here. All of us know how rapidly it can spread and what a horrific toll it takes. Less than ten years ago, a prairie fire rolled in from the east and took half of the town before we could stop it. Many a settler has lost everything and been driven out by our annual summer scourge."

"It could've been worse, I suppose. We'd not yet filled the cabin with our furniture and possessions. We can rebuild."

"There may be a problem with that. From what I saw tonight, the Kellys are not going to be up to hard, physical labour any time soon, if ever. And I'm afraid I won't be able to spare another crew now for at least a month. If John's prediction is right, and I've never known him to be wrong about this, winter will be upon us early this year. I don't know that we'll have time to reconstruct your home before the bad weather makes it impossible."

We can live in the barn. I can make it liv'ble for winter by myself. Kicker wanted to voice her thoughts, but lacked the energy.

"But look, it's not as bleak a picture as it might seem. Mother would be delighted to have you stay at the ranch for now, and I have an idea that might solve several problems at once. I just need to talk it over with Father before I say anything more."

No. We cannot stay at the ranch.

"Wynne, I cannot even begin to thank you and your family for the kindness and hospitality you have shown Kicker and myself, but we really mustn't impose on you any longer. We'll find our own accommodations now, and begin to rely on ourselves again."

If Kicker hadn't been so exhausted, she would have cheered the determination in Madelyn's voice.

"I understand. And as I said, I think I do have a solution that will satisfy everyone, except perhaps Mother, but allow me until this evening before I present it. Perhaps we can all gather after dinner and discuss it."

But I have to see Pudge and Seamus. I don' wan' to waste time arguin' all night. Too weary to utter her protest, Kicker decided she would simply slip away after her duties at the smithy had been performed.

"Kicker, I won't hold you up for long, but this will also concern your friends, so you may wish to sit in with us before you go into town."

Kicker looked at Wynne in surprise. She was quite sure she hadn't voiced her objection aloud, but both of her companions smiled knowingly at her.

Madelyn leaned over and patted Kicker's hand where it rested on her thigh. "There's a reason I've not tried to teach you bridge, dearest."

Any retort Kicker might have summoned died as they approached the clearing.

Even in the scant pre-dawn light, the destruction was evident. The ruins of the cabin still smoked, and only the stone chimney remained intact.

Several men had stayed at the site to tear apart burned timbers and shovel dirt on stray embers. One of them raised his hand as he noticed the women's approach.

"Mr. Donnelly," Wynne called as she swung off Ballantrae and handed Kicker his reins. "May I have a moment?"

The soot streaked foreman strode forward. "Hey, boss. How are the Kelly boys?"

"Not so good, I'm afraid, though they will live."

One of the other men swore at the bad news and swung his axe viciously at the remnants of the north wall.

Donnelly shook his head in dismay. "Damn, I'm sorry to hear that. They were good men, especially that Pudge. Always up for a laugh or a song, that one was."

"I know, and we'll make sure they're well taken care of," Wynne assured him. "Look, Seamus Kelly told us that whoever set the fire and attacked them may have left his weapon behind. Do you know if any of the boys reported finding a pistol near the fire?"

Donnelly frowned. "Not that I know of, but I'll ask around."

"It's pretty important, Jake. If the culprit is who we suspect, that gun could pin him to the crime."

The foreman looked at her doubtfully. "Dunno about that, boss. Most of these boys don't carry anything fancier than an Eaton two dollar special."

"That's not what we expect to find."

"What're you expecting to find?"

Wynne lowered her voice to where Kicker strained to hear her. "One of Colt's newest double action .32 cal., with a pearl handle and a particular set of initials carved into the base of the stock."

Donnelly stared at her with instant understanding. "Sonovabitch! You telling me that snake—"

Wynne held up a cautionary hand. "This is just between you and me. Don't give the boys any ideas, but do see if you can find that revolver."

"You got it, boss. I'll go look around right now."

"But remember, just between us." Wynne regarded him warningly. "I don't want anyone going off half-cocked before we have proof."

Donnelly's expression was grim but he nodded. "I understand."

The two began to discuss the coming day's work assignments, so Kicker let her attention drift. She stared at the smoking ruins of what was to have been her and Madelyn's first home. The optimism of the previous evening, when all had appeared right with her world, now seemed to be something in the distant past, but she was almost too weary to care.

"We'll build again, dearest."

Kicker acknowledged Madelyn's soft words with a scant nod.

"And we'll find a place where we can live this winter, where we can be alone together. I promise."

Kicker's gaze turned to the barn and she pointed at it. "I could make that liv'ble, Maddie. When the new stove comes, we could put it in there, an' I could build 'nother fireplace for warmth. Twould only be one room, but it could be done."

A momentary silence preceded Madelyn's noncommittal response. "Perhaps, dearest. Let's first see what Wynne has in mind, shall we?"

That was a no, if e'er I heard one. Kicker knew she was too tired to construct a logical argument for converting the barn into their winter residence, so she let it rest, though she didn't abandon the idea.

Wynne concluded her discussion with her foreman and retrieved Ballantrae's reins.

As they departed, Kicker looked back once, then turned her gaze to the path leading ahead.

Kicker was quite sure she had never been so exhausted in her life. Against Madelyn's protestations, she spent nine hours shoeing horses with John. Grimly determined not to show any weakness, she stopped only when John packed things up early with the excuse that Esther required his help back in town.

The unexpected early end to the work day left Kicker enough time for a quick bath and a change into respectable clothing. In anticipation of the gathering, she donned a plain dress without being coaxed, much to Madelyn's delighted surprise.

Now that the meal had ended, Kicker was seated in a straight chair tucked into the corner of the parlour as she listened to Wynne address her parents, Will, Albert, and Madelyn. Despite her interest in the topic under discussion, Kicker had difficulty staying upright and alert as Wynne succinctly recapped the events of the previous night. Kicker's eyes were fluttering closed when she heard her name uttered.

"...and Kicker believes that the barn, which was undamaged, could be converted to suitable living quarters—"

Wynne's summation was abruptly cut short by her mother's loud protestation. "Absolutely not, Wynne. It would be totally unacceptable for Madelyn to reside in a...a barn, for mercy's sake. What on earth would people think of us, providing such barbaric quarters for our new schoolteacher? It is simply not done. She will remain here at the Steeple Seven for the winter, and I'll hear no more about it. And of course her cousin is welcome, too."

Despite her weariness, Kicker almost chuckled aloud at being a hasty afterthought to Mrs. MacDiarmid's impassioned expostulation.

"Mother, please just listen for now. As I was saying, although the barn is standing..." Mrs. MacDiarmid's loud harrumph left no doubt as to her opposition. "...we have another option, aside from our guests continuing to reside here. And yes, Mother, they are more than welcome to do so."

Wynne turned to her brothers. "Will, while you and Albert were away in England, we had a near uprising against Horace Mackey."

"Still trying to cheat the little guy, is he?" Will shook his head in disgust. "We oughta run that sniveling weasel out of town on a rail."

"Believe me, it's been suggested," Wynne assured her brother. "However, the Landowner's Association wants a less...violent solution, though they do acknowledge the farmers have a valid complaint. Everyone knows that Mackey is so deep in the railroad's pocket that he couldn't find his way out with a compass and a map."

"He's just an Eastern lackey in a Stetson," Albert chimed in. "Damned if I know how he even got the job as railroad agent. Must be some politician's bastard spawn."

"Albert!" Mrs. MacDiarmid glared at her youngest son. "Watch your language."

"Sorry, Mother."

Will snickered at his brother's chagrin, then quickly quieted as he, too, fell under their mother's reproving glare.

"As I was trying to say," Wynne scowled at her brothers, "we passed a motion at last week's meeting to convince Mackey it would be in his best interests to find a job elsewhere...before the farmers hereabouts lynch him for cheating them on the freight and grain rates."

Kicker found her second wind and tried to absorb the nuances of her new culture. She glanced at Madelyn and found her partner equally engrossed in the conversation. Obviously Charlie Jr was the rule, not the exception when it came to common disgust with the railroad's monopoly and business practices.

"So who gets to try and make him see the light?"

Wynne grinned at Will. "That selection was unanimous. We voted for you."

"What?"

There was a round of chuckles at Will's indignant squawk.

"Yup, you're it, my brother. And assuming you're successful, Mackey's departure opens up a spot for a stationmaster and railroad agent." Wynne looked directly at Kicker. "Which is where your friends come in."

Kicker cocked her head in query.

"Tell me, can your friends read and write?"

"I don' know about Pudge, but Seamus was almos' a priest. He tol' me he lef' the sem'nary only two months short of ord'nation."

Wynne nodded in satisfaction. "He struck me as an intelligent and well educated man. I suppose he wouldn't necessarily know telegraphy..."

"He could learn quick," Kicker asserted loyally, then she frowned. "But what about their homestead? They're t'be the Potato Kings of Western Canada."

Wynne approached Kicker and knelt before her. "I'm not sure you realize how badly the younger Mr. Kelly was injured. He lost most of an ear; Esther isn't sure he'll still have sight in the affected eye, and the fire partially fused the upper part of his right arm to his body. It may be years before he can even handle moderate activity, and he certainly will never be capable of homesteading. It is my belief that Seamus will need work with which he can not only support his brother, but also have time to tend to him."

Kicker sucked in a horrified breath. Esther's clean, white bandages covered the worst of Pudge's wounds, and she'd convinced herself that it would only be a matter of time until he was completely healed.

Wynne took Kicker's icy hands in her own. "It's not an unmitigated tragedy, Kicker. Pudge will live, and this opportunity will allow the brothers to forge a livelihood in their new home. Seamus strikes me as an honest, incorruptible man, and that's what we need here."

Kicker wasn't listening; her mind was filled with nightmarish images from her youth. She recalled a child whose face was badly burned and deformed by a cooking fire. The boy suffered such unrelenting taunts from scornful village lads that he eventually threw himself in the river to drown. Imagining a similar social ostracism for the amiable Pudge broke her heart.

Oblivious to the depth of Kicker's anguish, Wynne stood up and addressed the others again. "Assuming Mackey takes Will up on his gracious offer to relocate anywhere else..."

"Hell, maybe," Albert muttered, not meeting his mother's resultant glower.

"Then his house will be empty, and I thought it might be ideal for Madelyn and Kicker."

"Good heavens, Wynne. That is almost as bad as consigning them to that barn." Mrs. MacDiarmid's voice was shrill with indignation. "Bless me. Everyone in town knows what a filthy little hovel Mr. Mackey lives in. It is simply not possible to expect a lady to inhabit such a...such a..." Lost for words dire enough to express her outrage, the matriarch abruptly switched tacks. "Why, what will the Major think if he arrives to find his wife living in squalour? He will be appalled. Appalled, I tell you. He will think we are nothing but a bunch of godless savages—no better than those he has been fighting in Africa."

"Mother. Please, Mother. We'll clean it out first. We'll apply a couple coats of whitewash, too. It'll be just fine. And it's only a few steps from the schoolhouse. It's perfect, really."

There was no sign of Mrs. MacDiarmid's outraged protestations diminishing, until a commanding voice rang out over the room, "Agnes! Enough!"

All eyes swiveled to fix on the usually quiet patriarch, who tapped his cane vigorously on the carpet.

"Wynne has come up with an excellent suggestion for solving a number of difficulties. I do believe we should listen to her with an open mind."

"But, Andrew. The Major... What will he say? What will he think? It is not only the filth, but there is barely room enough to turn around in that..." Unable to bring herself to describe the Mackey residence as a house, Agnes MacDiarmid sputtered to a halt.

Madelyn, seated next to her hostess on the chesterfield, addressed her calmly. "Dear Agnes, please don't worry so. My husband foresaw such possibilities when he sent me on ahead. He knew that there would be times that I would encounter difficulties with accommodations and such. That's why he entreated my cousin to go with me to Canada."

Mrs. MacDiarmid cast a doubtful glance at Kicker, who sat stone faced in the corner. "He did?"

Madelyn slid closer and linked her arm with the matriarch. "He did, indeed, Agnes. He knew that by virtue of Kicker's unusual birth and background, she was quite suited to making much out of little. Had she been unable to accompany me, he'd never have allowed me to make the journey, and you and I might never have met. Please have faith. We'll be just fine. After all, it's only for the winter."

The whole room seemed to hold its breath until Agnes capitulated with a reluctant nod. "I suppose...under the circumstances. But you must promise to visit often."

Madelyn nodded.

"And celebrate Yuletide with us?"

"Of course, Agnes. We'll see each other every week."

"And Wynne, I want that place scrubbed with lye."

"I promise, Mother. We'll put Mrs. Donnelly in charge of cleaning. You know nothing escapes her."

Mrs. MacDiarmid appeared to take comfort from Madelyn and Wynne's assurances, and the gathering broke up. Albert followed Will from the room, teasing him about his diplomatic assignment. Andrew MacDiarmid hobbled out the door with a parting comment about finding Laird and going down to the stables. Mrs. MacDiarmid did not appear willing to allow Madelyn to depart anytime soon, so Kicker left the parlour on her own. Wynne caught up with her before she reached the bottom of the stairs.

"Kicker, did you want to tell Seamus the news when you see him tonight, or do you think it better to wait until we can make him a formal offer of the job?"

Kicker turned to face Wynne, devoid of expression. "I don' know. I'm awf"ly tired. I think I'll jus' retire."

Without waiting for Wynne to respond, Kicker climbed the stairs, well aware that despite her exhaustion, guilt and fear would make sleep an elusive companion that night.

CHAPTER 15

Tormented by her conscience, Kicker spent the night pondering how matters had gone so wrong and how to put them right. She spent hours staring out her window into the darkness, but her vigil brought no answers, and no surcease of guilt. Finally, wearied from incessant tossing and turning, she rose well before dawn.

By the time John arrived, Kicker was on her third horse. She disdained the pre-formed shoes, preferring instead the demanding rhythm of shaping the iron by hand. The sweat that rolled down her body could not wash away her misery, but the piercing, ceaseless clanging of her hammer brought temporary respite.

John made no comment when he joined her, but throughout the morning Kicker sensed him studying her. She studiously disregarded his obvious concern and drove herself fiercely as she sought to repress her remorse through sheer exhaustion. As quickly as one horse was done, Kicker was back to the stable for another. And as the morning hours passed, the animals she loved blurred one into another.

When the noon bell rang, Kicker continued working until John spoke.

"That will keep. Come with me."

Kicker briefly considered ignoring his order, but as she met his implacable gaze, she saw that he would not allow it. She reluctantly followed him to their usual lunch spot, though she had not brought anything with her from the main house. Wordlessly he offered her part of his lunch, which she accepted in like silence.

When they had eaten, Kicker stood and held out her hand. John handed over his knife and watched quietly as she swiftly spun and threw. The knife buried so deeply in a trunk that when she went to retrieve it, she had to wrestle it free.

Rather than stopping Kicker after a dozen throws, John allowed her to go on until she exorcised whatever demon she had pinned to the tree. Barely able to lift her arm, she returned the smith's knife to him. As he re-sheathed it, Kicker could have sworn she saw a glimmer of amusement in his dark eyes. He said nothing, however, and they returned to work.

An hour later, as Kicker finished with a mean tempered bay, John led Galahad up the hill from the stable.

"This is the last one, Kicker."

Kicker looked up in surprise. She had not been keeping count, but knew John had expected their task to take all week. Instead, they had finished in less than three days.

"You've done well. Finish up with your cousin's horse and call it a day. You've earned your mare, and you've earned the job. You can start on Monday. We'll get going on repairing that old wagon too, so you and your cousin can haul your goods once you start rebuilding the cabin."

Kicker knew she should be grateful for John's thoughtfulness. She knew she should feel some sort of joy at accomplishing two of her goals—a job and a horse—in such a short time, but she couldn't seem to work up the energy to feel anything at all.

John began to collect his tools. "I expect you'll have lots of time to get into town and see your friends this afternoon. I'll tell Esther to expect you early on."

Kicker froze. Oppressive guilt instantly resurfaced and her throat closed. She tried desperately to inhale without alerting John to her distress; it was useless. After a sharp glance at his assistant, he quickly took her arm and led her to where their water bucket stood in the shade. John handed her a dipper of water and watched sternly as she drank.

The terrible constriction eased, and Kicker drew in deep breaths as she accepted a second dipper. This time she dumped the water over her head. She closed her eyes against the image of Pudge, laughing and teasing as he splashed water at her in Shadow Creek. That barely formed memory had already taken on the lustre of days lost so long ago in time that they acquired an artificially golden patina.

Kicker wondered if she would ever again feel such innocent, affectionate, and natural companionship as she had enjoyed with the Kelly brothers.

"I'll finish up Galahad. You've done enough for today."

When Kicker started to protest, John held up his hand. "No. You've nothing to prove to me; you did that on your first day. Take some time to spend with your friends. I'll expect you at the town forge early Monday morning."

My frien's. If they knew I was the root of their sorrows, Seamus and Pudge would curse the day I blackened their lives.

"It wasn't your fault, Kicker. You have to believe that or you'll be useless to yourself and your friends."

John's quiet reassurance fell on deaf ears. Kicker trudged away, head lowered, as the litany of her morose thoughts, pushed aside for so many hours, returned to haunt her.

What do I do? How can I face them? Seamus will hate me.

Inside the main house, Kicker encountered only one of the young maids as she mounted the stairs to her room. She was grateful for the absence of the family, but more so, for that of her lover. Madelyn had come to her room late the night before, but Kicker feigned sleep and Maddie quietly slipped away without trying to rouse her.

Kicker was not ready to face the woman who knew her best, the woman who could see right through her; the woman who did not know what danger she was in because of Kicker's actions.

Sins of omission crushed Kicker. Though she'd told Seamus and Pudge of her encounter with Arbuster, she had not told them of John Blue Wolf's warning, or Biggart's role in driving Rabbit away, or cautioned them to be wary as they worked alone in the woods. And after the destruction, she had not confessed her responsibility to Madelyn, who, along with Mrs. MacDiarmid, had assumed the fire was accidental. None had told the ladies otherwise, though

Kicker had half-expected Wynne to voice her suspicions. However, the rancher apparently thought discretion the best course, at least until all the evidence was in.

I didn't e'en tell Maddie the danger may well still hang o'er our heads. Tis a gutless cow'rd I am.

An overwhelming sense of helplessness compounded Kicker's guilt. If Rupert was as untouchable as Wynne implied, how could she possibly protect her loved ones? The scales appeared too heavily weighted in Arbuster's favour, and the only defence she could conceive of was to leave Galbraith's Crossing immediately. However, Madelyn had already made her opinion of that option abundantly clear, and Kicker had no desire to leave Seamus and Pudge behind in any case.

It was a toxic emotional cesspool, and unlike anything Kicker had ever had to deal with before in her once blessedly uncomplicated life.

Uncomplicated, hah. Maybe b'fore Maddie, but not now. Not since that firs' kiss...

Despite her rueful thought, Kicker was too honest to place the blame anywhere but squarely upon her own shoulders. She had willingly left the mundane safety of her old life behind to follow the woman she loved. If her new life was one of tumult and danger, it was not because of anything Madelyn had done.

Tis my fault, all my fault. She did nothin' to call this upon our heads.

Kicker decided not to call for a maid to bring up heated water from the kitchen. Instead she filled the copper tub from the cistern and stoically lowered herself in, unable to prevent a small gasp as her hot flesh met cold water.

Stop your whingin', you witless fool. You're growin' soft as a babe.

With that reproach, Kicker picked up the rough sponge. She deliberately bypassed the perfumed Castille soap that so delighted Madelyn, and selected the carbolic acid soap she normally used only on her hands. She took a perverse satisfaction in fiercely scrubbing her flesh until her skin was red and stinging.

Finally, Kicker tossed the soap aside and slipped under the water. Eyes open, she welcomed the sting of residual soap as she viewed the world from beneath the wavelets that rippled over her face. She forced herself to stay down until the last vestige of oxygen left her lungs, then surged upwards, gasping for air.

Filling her lungs, Kicker ducked under again. As the seconds ticked by, she began to appreciate the serenity of the muted aquatic environment. She focused on the solitude and the rhythmic thumping of her own heartbeat in her ears and finally found a measure of tranquility that moderated her desperation. This time she rose and sank again peacefully.

The blurring of her external vision sharpened Kicker's inner vision.

You have to tell him, and take your jus' dues. You owe that an' more.

Her resolution solidified and when next Kicker surfaced, she propelled herself up out of the tub. Calm settled over her as she dried her body and dressed in Roddy's clothes. She no longer tormented herself by picturing Pudge's hellacious ordeal, or imagining the revulsion in Seamus' eyes when she confessed her role. Kicker could not change what had happened but she meant to take responsibility, even though she knew it would cost her the friendship that had come to mean so much. On the way into town, Kicker heard the approach of horses and carriage, and the sounds of women's voices from around a bend. She was unwilling to be bothered with wearisome social niceties before she faced up to Seamus so she pulled Rabbit off into the forest.

She watched as Madelyn, Mrs. MacDiarmid, and Mrs. Donnelly, deep in conversation, drove past. Once safely alone again, Kicker nudged Rabbit back onto the trail. She grimly turned her eyes away from the ruins of their cabin as they passed the deserted and desolate site.

Kicker did not contemplate the finer points of evidence and guilt. She had no doubt Biggart, and by extension, Arbuster, were the culprits. It was irrelevant. Seamus and Pudge were all that mattered, or more specifically, how Seamus would react to her confession. Physical violence from the gentle almost-priest seemed unlikely, but she knew harsh words would hurt every bit as much. Nonetheless, Kicker was determined to accept his justice without flinching.

By the time Galbraith's Crossing came into view, Kicker's plans had solidified. Certain her encounter with Seamus would go badly, she would retreat to the countryside and seek solitude to lick her wounds.

Kicker decided she would give Billy a note for Madelyn to let her lover know that she would be back by Sunday. Then she and Rabbit would ride toward the mountains, and maybe, for a few days, find the peace she craved.

John don' expect me 'til Monday. No one will miss me 'cept Maddie, an' she'll unnerstan'.

Kicker's musings about a solitary wilderness journey came to an abrupt end as she pulled Rabbit up in front of the Blue Wolf home. Dread, reborn with a vengeance, mounted steadily as she tied the mare off. With queasy stomach and uncertain steps, she made her way past the open side windows where curtains fluttered, stirred by the incessant prairie breezes.

Kicker rounded the corner of the building and halted as she saw Seamus sitting on the edge of the back porch. Several books were piled next to him and he held a pen and a sheaf of papers in his hands. He raised his head at her approach and his tired smile caused Kicker's resolution to wither.

Stop it. You knew twould be hard, and damned if you're backin' down.

Kicker strove to push her misgivings aside as she approached her friend.

Seamus pushed the books aside and patted the porch beside him. "You are a sight for sore eyes, Miss Kicker. Please do me the honour of joining me."

Kicker sat down awkwardly, grateful only that she did not have to meet his gaze as she stared out over the abundant garden. She stalled for time to find the words for her confession, as she glanced down at his hands. "Do they hurt fearsome?"

Seamus regarded his palms, still wound neatly with bandages that had lost some of their pristine whiteness. "A little, but my fingers are sound and I am still able to wield the pen, if not the sword."

"How's Pudge?"

"Miss Esther is currently tending to my brother's dressings; she kicked me out of the house whilst so engaged. She informs me that I am far too emotional to be of any use to her, and I cannot disagree."

Kicker was at a loss as to what to say, and though she had a sickening feeling that she should not ask, still she said, "D'you think he's any...better t'day?"

Seamus was silent for a long time. Kicker hung her head and stared at her dusty boots, but her friend's words were calm when he finally answered.

"I think it will be a long time before Pudge is better, but he did recognize me when he woke briefly. I think he may even have tried to smile at me..." Seamus' voice cracked and he cleared his throat. "But we have to have faith, do we not, Miss Kicker?"

"Faith? In what?" Unable to stem the raging emotional flood any longer, Kicker bolted to her feet and spun to face her friend. "Faith in what, Seamus? In God? D'you not think He has abandoned us, jus' like you—" She stopped herself, horrified at what she had been about to say.

Seamus regarded her mildly. "Like I abandoned Him?"

"No. I ne'er meant..."

Seamus extended his hand, but Kicker couldn't bring herself to take it. She wanted to fall to her knees and scream at her friend that it was all her fault; that it wasn't God who had failed to protect Pudge, it was her.

"Kicker..." Seamus let his hand drop and regarded her keenly. "Kicker, what happened was terrible, and I hope one day to exact an accounting from the one responsible, but for now—"

"Twas me, Seamus." The words were barely whispered, so Kicker raised her head and spoke more clearly. "Take your vengeance on me. Tis my fault your brother lies in that bed, my fault your dreams ended that night."

Tears flowed freely, blurring Kicker's vision, but she could see Seamus' confusion. Words began to trickle from her, then erupted in a torrent as she recounted how she had inadvertently angered Rupert Arbuster and thereby become the target of Rick Biggart. How Rupert's attack dog, seeking to punish her, had accidentally entrapped Pudge and Seamus. "He mus' ha' meant to cov'r his tracks, when he tried to burn Pudge." Kicker raised anguished eyes, only to drop them at the sight of Seamus' frozen face and furious eyes. With sickened heart, she mumbled her remorse. "I'd gi' anything if twere me an' not Pudge lyin' in that bed, Seamus. I swear it."

"So... Asmodeus is named."

Kicker did not understand the reference, but she shivered at the icy hatred in the words. It took desperate determination to remain standing before him. Seamus shot to his feet, papers scattering like late autumn leaves. Kicker flinched, but stood her ground and awaited her punishment.

"I will see him dead."

It was not a threat; it was a blood chilling, flat statement of fact. Kicker had no doubt that this gentle man, whose music sang with the sad compassion of the angels, meant every word.

"He?"

"Biggart."

On Seamus' pale lips, the name was a curse. Kicker saw her friend's body shake, as if with ague.

"Seamus."

Seamus looked at Kicker as if he did not recognize her.

She laid her hand on his arm and shook him hard. "Seamus, Seamus."

He stared down at her hand, and Kicker could see him fight to calm himself. She steered him back to the porch and urged him to sit. When he settled on the edge, she scrambled to pick up the papers scattered about them, then extended the lot to him. Seamus accepted them and stared at the words he had written as if they were foreign to him.

How do I reach him? I cannot let him go after that bastard on his own. Biggart would kill him. E'en if Seamus somehow succeeded, they'd hang him.

Kicker set aside her own anguish for the moment and focused on her friend. He had passed judgment, and if Kicker could not dissuade him, he would carry out the inevitable sentence, dooming himself as surely as he doomed Pudge's assailant. *What do I say now?*

"Seamus, I know what you're thinkin', but you cannot do it. Who'll look after Pudge if you're tossed in jail, or worse, danglin' from a nearby tree?"

Seamus glanced uncertainly over his shoulder at the back door, then he looked at Kicker with tormented eyes.

She pressed her advantage. "You promised your ma, 'member? You tol' her you'd look out for him, right?"

"And I have done such a superlative job, have I not?"

Kicker ignored the bitterness and mustered all the urgency that consumed her. "We cannot change what's happened, but we gotta look after Pudge now. He needs us. We cannot let him down."

"We?"

Kicker nodded solemnly. "We...if you'll let me help." She had to force herself to not look away. "I unnerstan' if you don' want me around. It is my fault—"

"No, it is not." Seamus had regained some colour in his face and his eyes had lost their wildness. "You bear no responsibility for this evil; its consequences can only be laid at the feet of the men who set it in motion. They alone must answer for what they have done." Grimly he added, "And they will. If not immediately, then when God wills it."

"So you'll leave it to God and the law? You'll not take your own revenge?" Kicker looked at her friend hopefully. She knew how hard it was to resist the ache for retribution, the need to retaliate against Arbuster and Biggart, but she desperately did not want Seamus to endanger himself.

Seamus regarded her gravely, and she was relieved to see that he had control of himself again. "I will not make you any promises on that account, Miss Kicker, but I will swear to put my brother's welfare first in all decisions."

Kicker mulled that over. It would have to do for now. "Wynne says that they may be able to tie Biggart to the fire, by way of his gun. If so, we may yet see him b'fore the law."

His eloquent scoff was the most cynical sound Kicker had ever heard, but she doggedly pressed on.

"Has Wynne tol' you about her idea?"

"Her proposal that I take the position as railroad agent?"

Kicker nodded, encouraged to see a glimpse of a smile from her friend.

"Mrs. Glenn and Mr. MacDiarmid came around late this morning to offer me the placement, and on very equitable terms, I must say. I am to take up my duties as soon as I can demonstrate an adequate grasp of telegraphy." Seamus gestured at the books piled next to Kicker. "In fact, I spent several hours in study today, and only paused to write my mother shortly before you arrived."

Kicker looked at the papers she had thrust back into Seamus' wounded hands, and a lump came to her throat. She tried to imagine writing the formidable Mrs. Bristow to tell her that Madelyn suffered such a devastating injury. The thought was too terrible to bear. "I'm so sorry. If only—"

"No, Kicker. It does neither of us, nor Pudge, any good to tread that path. As you so wisely said, we cannot change what has happened, so we must wrest what triumphs we may from the maw of despair that threatens us."

"I don' think I used exac'ly those words." Kicker's lame jest elicited a small chuckle, and she counted it a victory. "So where'll you live, then?"

"There are a couple of rooms in the station for the use of the resident agent. The wife of the current agent would not deign to live there—apparently the rodent population is quite lively—but Pudge and I are used to the company of field mice and their assorted cousins. We find they are much less critical of our music than many of our two legged audiences."

Kicker felt a fresh rush of anguish. *Music. Can Pudge still play? Can Seamus?*

As if reading her mind, Seamus patted her arm reassuringly. "Do not count my brother out, Miss Kicker. I swear he was making music while in the womb; we will find a way to play together again."

The sound of the door opening behind them cut off Kicker's response, and the friends turned to see a weary looking Esther standing in the doorway.

"Your brother is sleeping, Mr. Kelly, and will not wake for several hours. Why don't you go for a walk? It will do him no good for you to sit around and yourself much good to move about." Her black eyes settled on Kicker, who responded to the silent command with a nod.

"Aye, Missus. I'll make sure he gets some air." Kicker took Seamus by the arm. She barely gave him time to tuck his letter between the books before she led him away.

He protested mildly, "There is plenty of air right here, you know."

"I know, but it'll be cooler down by the river."

They walked out the back gate and quickly reached the shaded shores of the Bow River. By unspoken consent, the two friends sauntered west along the bank of the river and stopped occasionally to pitch a stone into the tumbling waters. They had left the town well behind by the time Seamus broke the comfortable silence.

"So what are your plans, now?" He looked at his bandaged hands. "By the time I am fit to help you rebuild, we will be well into winter."

"Aye, and I'm deeply grateful for all your help—yours and Pudge's. But we'll not be livin' out there this year, I'm afraid. We're to abide in the railroad agent's house, once he and his missus move on." Disconsolate, Kicker launched a pine cone out of her path and into the shallows of the river. "I wanted us to stay in our barn til spring. I could'a made it winter ready, but no one would e'en listen to me."

"Highly frustrating, undoubtedly," Seamus consoled her. "I think people underestimate the extent of your capabilities."

"E'en Maddie, sometimes." Kicker was surprised at her own words. *Tis not Maddie's fault that Mrs. MacDiarmid had a fit at her livin' in a barn.*

"And that bothers you?"

Kicker gave that some consideration, instinctively seeking an answer that would deflect any blame from Madelyn. "Aye, I guess." She stopped and turned to face Seamus. "It's jus'...well, when we came here, I thought we'd be free."

"Free? Do you feel yourself constrained?"

"Why do we have to do what e'eryone else thinks we mus' do, Seamus?" Kicker's frustration boiled over and her voice rose. "Will tol' us in London that we wouldn't have neighbours hangin' o'er our shoulder, and we could breathe free. Then Wynne tells me, our firs' day, that you're judged here by your hard work and qual'ty of min' and body. So why do we have to do what Missus MacDiarmid says to do, buy what she says to buy, go where she says to go? Bless'd Jesus, why ain't we free to live in a barn, if we want?"

"My dear Kicker, you are longing for a land that has never existed. In all places and in all times, there will be those who count themselves better than others. These benighted individuals labour under the delusion that they have the God given right to dictate to those whom they consider lesser than themselves."

"I jus' wanna be free," Kicker mumbled. *I jus' wan' me an' Maddie to be t'gether.*

"Kicker, listen to me." Seamus' voice was very serious, and she turned to face him. "Of all the people I have ever met, yours is the most unfettered spirit I've encountered. You blithely break every convention of your gender, and allow no man's censure to sway your path. Can you escape all the onerous customs of the world in which you live? Unlikely. I suspect even the railroad barons, who sway Parliament at will, must conform in many ways. Yet you have carved out a life that suits you." He lowered his voice. "A life that allows you and Miss Bristow more freedom than many in your situation find. This is no small achievement, dear girl."

Kicker stared at Seamus in shock, holding her breath. *Does he mean... Can he know?*

Seamus gave her a warm smile then briskly changed the subject. "Let's turn back to town, shall we? I thought we might inspect your new abode before I return to Pudge's side and resume my studies."

He turned to walk eastward along the shore and Kicker followed in his wake, turning over his words. Suddenly a thought made her stumble. *He called Maddie* "Miss" *Bristow.* With anyone else it might have been a slip of the tongue. From the scrupulously precise Seamus... *Was he signalin' me he knows our secret?*

Kicker considered that as they wended their way back to town. There was nothing in Seamus' attitude and behaviour, past or present, to indicate that he was or ever would be any threat. She longed to ask him why that was, but could not overcome her innate caution. *He knows, or he don'. If he does, he seems not to min', and I'll leave it at that.*

Shortly the two wanderers reached the western end of the main street. They ambled down the boardwalk, past the hotel, general store and post office, bakery and confectionary, print shop, and railroad station, and finally stopped in front of a small house next door to the schoolhouse and St. Mark's Church.

Kicker looked at it critically. Wind, desiccation, and time had beaten the raw clapboards into a dull, mottled grey. The two tiny front windows were caked so thickly with dirt that she doubted sunlight could even penetrate. She was also dubious about whether there was space for more than two modest rooms within. The privy out back had a precarious lean to it, and an outbuilding that was almost as big as the house looked like it, too, had seen much better days. At length, Kicker rendered her verdict.

"Tis a hovel."

"It is rather unprepossessing, is it not?" Seamus looked over the property, and Kicker was certain he was looking for something positive to say. "It has a large yard, though. There would be plenty of room to grow a garden, and the fence is in reasonable condition."

Seamus was right. The fence looked sturdy enough, but the front gate hung haphazardly on its hinges. Kicker shook her head in disgust.

"An' they think tis better for us to live here than in that beaut'ful barn you built? Bloody fools."

She turned away and Seamus followed her. "I would be pleased to assist you in any way I can. Perhaps between the two of us we can make your situation tolerable. And remember, it is only temporary. When spring comes, we will resume work on your real home."

"Aw, Seamus, you're a prince among men, you know?" Kicker bumped against him affectionately, then winced as he grimaced. "Damn! I'm so sorry. I forgot."

"Do not let it give you a moment's pause. My injuries are minor and I am recovering swiftly. Mrs. Blue Wolf is a skilled and tireless healer, though I confess I am not familiar with the curatives she employs. Nonetheless, they give Pudge great relief, and I am deeply grateful she is at his side."

"I am too." When the severity of Pudge's injuries had finally become clear to her, Kicker had been troubled that his care might be inadequate in a town without a doctor. She was relieved that Seamus was satisfied with his brother's nurse.

When Seamus stopped next to Rabbit, who was still tied up in front of John and Esther's house, Kicker looked at him in surprise. "I was gonna ask if Miss Esther would let me in t'see Pudge."

Seamus shook his head. "I think it is better if you give my brother a few days before you visit him." His voice was kind, but firm. "I will tell him that you have been here, and are anticipating him being well enough to see you."

Kicker regarded her friend curiously as she opened her mouth, and closed it. She had been about to ask him if he was more worried about her or Pudge, but decided it didn't matter. She would abide by his wishes, aware he was most likely protecting them both. "Tell him...well, jus' tell him I'm prayin' for him."

That got her a bemused smile, and Seamus leaned closer as he lowered his voice. "From one pagan to another, I will tell him that we both are."

By the time Kicker got back to the Steeple Seven, it was late afternoon. She rode Rabbit to the main barn and dismounted wearily, feeling buffeted by the endless emotional storms of the previous few days. Kicker longed for nothing more than to find Madelyn and some privacy for them to share, though she acknowledged to herself that even if she found the former, the latter might be difficult to come by.

Kicker finished grooming Rabbit and had just released the mare into the paddock when she heard the sound of horses approaching rapidly. She looked up and saw Wynne and Will riding toward the stable. She swung up on the top rail of the corral and waited for them.

As they neared, Kicker could see their frustrated expressions. When they pulled up, a ranch hand hustled out of the stable to meet them and take their horses.

Wynne and Will handed off their reins, then Wynne beckoned Kicker to accompany them as they walked back toward the main house. "Join us, Kicker. You'll be interested in hearing how we spent the last couple of hours."

Will shook his head in disgust. "Yeah, you'll be bloody fascinated by how the Arbusters closed ranks around the family weasel."

Kicker had to move quickly to keep up with their long, agitated strides. "They're protectin' Biggart?"

"No. I was referring to Rupert, Miss Stuart. Ralston and Willa insist there's no way their precious son could've done something like set fire to your cabin and risk the entire forest in the bargain."

"Well, what did you expect, Will?" Wynne asked her brother ruefully. "It's not like we have any solid evidence. Besides, Rupert never does his own dirty work, so his folks probably were telling the truth about him being with them Sunday night."

"Goddamnit, Wynne!" Will exploded. "Did you see the cocky look on that sonofabitch? The way he sneered at us behind his parents' backs? And it ain't like his old man doesn't know the cut of Rupert's jib, either, even if his mama thinks her precious baby is an angel."

Impatient, Kicker interjected, "But what about Biggart? Did you fin' his gun? Is he t'be charged?"

Wynne stopped and looked at Kicker with a grim smile. "Biggart hightailed it. No one's seen him since Sunday evening. Word in the Arbuster barn is that he took off for Montana, but no one can or will say for sure."

"But his gun," Kicker persisted. "Did you fin' it?"

Will shook his head. "A couple of the men said they came across a gun, but they were too busy fighting the fire to stop and pick it up. Middleton said he remembers kicking it aside, but didn't see again. Donnelly had the site thoroughly searched under his supervision, but his men didn't come up with anything."

Kicker's shoulders slumped in disappointment.

Wynne patted her back. "Look, I know you were hoping we could nail Biggart that way, but look on the bright side. At least he's gone...for now."

"D'you think he'll come back?" Kicker saw Wynne and Will exchange glances.

"We can't say for sure, Miss Stuart. Technically there are no grounds for charges against him, and undoubtedly Rupert will let the bastard know when it's safe to return. Those two have been joined at the hip since they were boys, and they won't be easily sundered."

"Don't give up hope, Kicker. I suspect one of the men found the gun and has it hidden."

"Why?" Kicker was genuinely puzzled. Surely the ranch foreman had made it clear how important it was that the gun be found and turned over to the law.

Wynne snorted. "Some of these guys are like squirrels: they see something shiny, they pick it up and stash it. Whoever has it probably hopes he'll be able to sell it once things calm down. There's a few of these boys who would sell their own mothers for another bottle of whiskey, believe me."

The siblings resumed their course to the main house and Kicker followed. She tried to console herself that Biggart was no longer an immediate threat, but Wynne's words, with their ominous codicil, echoed in her mind.

At least he's gone...for now.

It was another long evening of enduring Madelyn's monopolization by Mrs. MacDiarmid. Kicker finally gave up hope of getting her alone and went upstairs to her room. There, she found some consolation in a newly arrived letter Mrs. Donnelly left in her room. Adam had written her, or more accurately, he had dictated a letter to his more literate wife.

Dear Kicker,

I hope you are well. We received your letter from London telling us where you were to settle. I hope Galbraith's Crossing is to your liking, and that you and your friend are happy there.

Anne and the children are well, as am I, though Preacher Dodd's horse, Toby kicked me hard in the leg two days ago. Perhaps it is because I have not gone to church lately.

I told everyone where you had gone, though not why. Ma cried and Da shrugged. He said you had better be good and not disgrace our family name. I told him you were the best among us, and would do us proud. We all miss you. I miss you most of all.

There was a most scandalous incident at your old school a week ago. The headmaster's son was caught...

Kicker chuckled, as several words had been heavily crossed out.

...in rather indelicate circumstances with Sir Phillip Twitchell's youngest daughter. They were hastily married the following day, and vanished from town, but it is still the talk of the parish.

We hope to hear from you soon. Your nephews want to know all about the cowboys and Indians. Jeremiah asked if his favourite aunt could send him a buffalo hat, but I told him no.

Please write soon. Love from all of us.

Your brother, Adam

Kicker re-read the letter and gleefully anticipated telling Madelyn of her erstwhile suitor's fate. She wanted to run downstairs immediately to relate the news, but knew that Madelyn would still be in the velvet clutches of her benefactress.

Kicker settled on the window seat and leaned against the sash. As she watched dusk give way to darkness, she contemplated the year that had gone by since she picked up a beautiful new teacher from the train station.

By the time Kicker heard Madelyn's light step on the landing and the sound of her bedroom door creak open, she had come to some conclusions. She was fed up with others coming between her and Maddie, even when the interference was well intentioned. It had to end. It was time they took control, time they made their own decisions about what was best for them.

They had set out on this adventure into an unknown future together, linked by love, faith in each other, and optimism. The journey was ultimately theirs—not Mrs. MacDiarmid's, not Wynne or Will or John's, not even Seamus or Pudge's. Together they would rejoice in their victories, and confront their challenges.

They had been forced apart far too long, denied the comfort of a spontaneous embrace, a reassuring touch, a spiritual as well as physical intimacy. Kicker knew how much she needed these things, how much she missed them, and she was certain Madelyn felt the same. Though she never doubted that the love between them was stronger than ever, she also sensed that their love had to be shored up with the common intimacies of partnership.

After waiting a few moments to ensure the corridor was empty, Kicker crossed the hallway and tapped lightly on Madelyn's door.

"Come in."

Kicker slipped quietly inside and eased the lock closed behind her back before she crossed to where Madelyn sat on the bed, unlacing her high shoes. She handed her the letter and knelt to finish the job, tugging the shoe off just as Maddie chuckled. Kicker finished with the second shoe, then gently rubbed her calves as Madelyn smiled down at her.

"Mmm, that feels wonderful, dearest. Sometimes I swear I envy you Roddy's boots, though they would look very odd with my dresses." Madelyn continued to read the letter and broke out in laughter. "So, I see Merrick has finally incurred the righteous wrath of an aggrieved father. It was really only a matter of time. He was a most importunate young man."

"Did he try to take a'vantage of you, Maddie?" Kicker's face darkened at the thought.

"Let us just say he tried to seal his marriage proposal by taking liberties he was not permitted." When Kicker's hand clenched convulsively on Madelyn's ankle, she murmured soothingly, "Don't fret, dearest. My most unladylike response convinced him that his attentions were unwelcome and he quickly desisted."

"Bastard." Kicker couldn't help a laugh at the smug look on Madelyn's face. "Did Lil teach you that move?"

"Actually no, it was my mother, of all people." Madelyn's face lost its satisfied expression. "I believe she was afraid that my...well, let's just say that she did not wish me to go out into the world entirely unarmed."

Kicker had no wish to pursue anything that put such a look of sadness on Madelyn's face, so she changed the subject. "Did you receive mail t'day, too?"

"I did. Missives arrived from both my mother and uncle. I'll read them to you, if you wish."

"Later. When you wen' to town, did you see the house we're to live in?"

Madelyn grimaced. "I did, but Mrs. Donnelly assures me that she'll send her girls in there and have it shipshape forthwith. Mind you, they must wait for Mr. and Mrs. Mackey to leave the premises. That could be a week or two, depending on how quickly Mr. Kelly is ready to assume his duties. However, since Mrs. Mackey cannot wait to shake the dust of Galbraith's Crossing from her feet, I expect they'll vacate soon, whether Mr. Kelly is ready or not."

Kicker's hands slid slowly up slender legs and came to rest above the knees. She saw Madelyn swallow hard as calloused hands began to stroke gently over soft inner thighs. She watched desire and caution war in her lover's eyes.

"Dearest, we cannot..."

"Shhhh," Kicker whispered as her hand eased inward.

Madelyn shivered as an insistent finger found its mark beneath bunched fabric. "You know we must not..." But her protest lost impact as her legs involuntarily shifted apart.

Kicker projected all that she felt for Madelyn into her voice. "You need this, my love. We both need this. We need t'be us again."

When Madelyn did not object further, Kicker rose to one knee, extracted one hand from beneath the skirts and laid it softly upon her lover's breast. Both hands began to move in slow circles.

"Oh, dear Lord!" Madelyn's eyes closed, then flashed open. "Kicker, the door..."

"Tis locked. But you mus' make no noise, not e'en the smallest soun', my sweet love."

Kicker's hand moved from Madelyn's breast to the long row of buttons that ran from her collarbone almost to her waist. One set of buttons, then laces fell open under Kicker's nimble fingers, and she parted the dress and corset over smooth, pale flesh.

A finger traced slowly up the centre of Madelyn's body, then Kicker slid Maddie's dress from her shoulders.

Maddie whimpered as Kicker's hands moved in an erotic dance on her body.

"Shhhh, love. Would you have them all see you like this, exposed to the whole world, writhin' on your cousin's han'?" Kicker's voice was sensuous and teasing.

"Please, Kicker..."

In response to Madelyn's whispered plea, Kicker intensified her actions. "No noise, b'loved. Not a single soun'..."

Madelyn froze as the sound of footsteps could be heard in the hall walking past, but Kicker focused only on her. Her free hand cupped Maddie's breast and teeth closed over a hardened nipple, shaking it lightly. The other hand moved more firmly and drew Madelyn deeper into their connection.

Though Madelyn struggled not to make noise, her breathing sounded like a bellows in Kicker's ear. Her own excitement at fever pitch, she felt Madelyn begin to thrash uncontrollably as she leaned back on arms that trembled and offered feeble support.

Suddenly Madelyn stiffened and a strangled sound erupted from her throat. Her climax was so intense that Kicker had to strain to keep her hands in place until at length Madelyn crumpled to the bed, gasping for air.

Kicker gently worked her hand out from beneath Madelyln's dress. Crawling up beside her lover, she rested her head on heaving breasts. They remained like that for long moments, until Kicker heard Maddie's whispered words.

"Wicked wench."

Kicker chuckled softly and raised her head, propping it on her hand. Madelyn's eyes were half lidded, but the expression on her face was equal parts amusement and satisfaction.

"I'd return the favour, dearest, but I appear to be somewhat trapped."

Shifting her body, Kicker tugged Madelyn's dress free, rising so Madelyn could shuck her garments onto the floor before resuming her position.

"You're evil, you know that, don't you?"

Kicker leaned forward to nuzzle the damp flesh of Madelyn's naked body. "Not evil, love. Jus' so very, very eager to touch you. I don' think I e'er needed you as much."

"Mmmm, nor I, you. Thank you, my darling. Thank you for having the courage I lacked. That was...exquisite." Madelyn's hand caressed Kicker's hair, then slid down to bunch her shirt as she coaxed her into a kneeling position.

Maddie reached for the buttons of Kicker's trousers, and Kicker could tell by the devilment in her eyes that she was about to pay for the delicious torment she had inflicted.

"Remember, dearest, not a sound." Madelyn urged Kicker onto her hands and knees and slipped the trousers out of the way as she wriggled into a more opportune position. "Not one single, solitary sound, no matter what. If the Queen herself bursts into this bedroom, you will not move. Understood?"

Kicker murmured her understanding and shivered in rapturous anticipation as she heard Maddie's husked words.

"My God, how I love you."

CHAPTER 16

The lovers parted shortly after midnight and Kicker slipped silently back to her own room. Madelyn mourned the loss of the lithe, naked body that had snuggled into hers for far too brief a time, but she reminded herself that soon there would be no need for stealth. If all went as planned, they would retire and rise together for the rest of their lives.

Madelyn stretched in utter satisfaction and pulled up the light cover. As she drifted into that pleasant state between wakefulness and sleep, images of their lovemaking filled her mind. Even as she cautioned herself of the continued need for discretion, Madelyn marvelled anew at Kicker's audacity.

"Prudence be damned, dearest. Much longer without your touch and surely I'd have sought you out for a liaison in the stable or the woods."

Madelyn smiled at her own murmured confession before finally allowing the lassitude that had followed their ardent lovemaking to overtake her.

When she awoke the next morning, Madelyn was pleasantly surprised to find that Kicker had not left early, and instead met her as they made their way down to the dining room.

Wynne and Albert had long since departed for the range, and Mr. MacDiarmid and Laird were off somewhere, too, so only Mrs. MacDiarmid joined the two women at the table. Breakfast was accompanied by subtle, eloquent glances between the lovers, as their oblivious hostess chattered on about the upcoming commencement of school.

Her monologue was only interrupted by Mrs. Donnelly's entry into the room.

"Mrs. MacDiarmid."

The matriarch turned to her formidable housekeeper. "Yes, Mrs. Donnelly?"

"Word has arrived from town that Mr. and Mrs. Horace Mackey left Galbraith's Crossing rather hastily during the night."

"They did? Well, for heaven's sake. I thought surely it would be a week or two before they took their departure."

"I believe we all thought that, Madam, however it is being said..." Mrs. Donnelly hesitated, evidently reluctant to repeat gossip.

Mrs. MacDiarmid leaned forward eagerly. "Do tell, Mrs. Donnelly."

"I cannot say if this is the God's honest truth, Madam, but there is a rumour that Hugh MacDonald, having spent several hours last night in the bar at the Windsor Hotel, was seen carrying his old duck gun and walking in the direction of the Mackey residence."

Mrs. MacDiarmid nodded knowingly as Madelyn and Kicker exchanged puzzled glances. Their hostess explained. "Hugh MacDonald has been a farmer north of town for much of the last four years. He failed to prove his claim within the three year time limit, mostly because of his own shortcomings. As a result he was forced to give up his claim to new homesteaders and blames Horace Mackey for the downturn in his fortunes. He claimed that had he not been cheated on the grain rates, he would've proved up easily. Mr. MacDonald is well known hereabouts for having a deep fondness for rye whiskey, and an abysmally short temper."

"I suspect those failings came together last night to the detriment of the Mackeys, Madam, but in any case, their house now stands empty. Shall I take my staff in to begin preparations for Mrs. Bristow's move?"

Madelyn felt a carnal frisson ripple through her body at the thought that she and Kicker would soon be free to repeat the previous night's activities in their own home. A glance across the table indicated that, as evidenced by

Kicker's quickly suppressed smile and lowered head, the same thought had occurred to her.

Mrs. MacDiarmid sighed heavily. "As much as I regret relinquishing the company of our guests, I suppose you should, Mrs. Donnelly. We'll be in later to check on things." She turned to Madelyn, who immediately hid her glee behind a sombre expression. "My dear, Mr. Godwin said that your order would arrive on the afternoon train from Calgary. If it suits you, we'll go into town after lunch and inspect the shipment. I know you mentioned that you wouldn't have room for everything you originally ordered, but you know that you're more than welcome to store things here at the ranch."

"I appreciate that, Agnes, I truly do, but I think my cousin and I need to be practical about what to keep and what to send back. My husband would expect no less of me." Madelyn had learned that invoking the mythical Major Bristow put a swift end to any disagreement. "Now, if you'll excuse me, I have some letters to write before we go in to town."

At Mrs. MacDiarmid's affable wave of dismissal, Kicker rose and followed Madelyn out of the dining room and up the stairs. Upon reaching the landing, Kicker followed Madelyn into her bedroom. The door closed behind them and they regarded each other with sparkling eyes and heightened colour.

Kicker took a step towards Madelyn, who raised her hand and shook her head.

"I swear, dearest, if you so much as touch me, I'll not be responsible for what I do next."

Kicker chuckled, a blatantly carnal sound, and Madelyn quivered with desire. She took one involuntary step towards her, then another. Before she quite knew how it happened, Kicker had her pressed up against the door, kissing her with an ardour that threatened to renew their lovemaking where they stood.

Madelyn responded passionately, and it was only the sound of voices in the hallway that froze them in their pleasurable pursuits. They strove to suppress the sound of their raspy breathing as they listened to two young maids complaining about Mrs. Donnelly's orders for the day.

The servants stopped almost directly outside their door as they talked, and Madelyn and Kicker reluctantly drew apart. As they re-buttoned their clothes, Mrs. Donnelly called her staff from the base of the stairway.

"Here, you two, get a move on. We've plenty to do today and I'll not tolerate any lollygagging on your part."

The sound of their footsteps scampering down the staircase could be heard as they called, "We're comin', Missus."

Madelyn stifled a laugh, and by the twinkle in Kicker's eyes, she knew that the same thought had gone through her head. Determinedly fastening the last of the stays that Kicker had taken mere seconds to undo, Madelyn slipped around her.

With a rueful look in the mirror, Madelyn tried fruitlessly to pat her hair back into place. "You do realize, my darling, that thanks to your wandering hands, I now need to remake my entire toilette."

Kicker stepped behind Madelyn and wrapped her arms around the slender waist. "You did'na seem to min' my hands las' night, love."

Madelyn swayed in her embrace for a moment, then firmly removed the arms that encircled her. "No, dearest. Last night I was deeply grateful for these talented hands of yours, and I will be again...very soon."

"But not now?"

Madelyn turned to face her disappointed partner. "No, not right now. We took a chance last night. I'm delighted beyond words that you came to me, but we must not risk it again, dearest."

For a moment she thought Kicker was going to protest, but her companion simply nodded.

"You're right, Maddie. Tis soon enough we'll be in our own bed with naught to disturb our lovin'." Kicker made to leave, then turned back with a serious expression. "When you're goin' through your order this afternoon, don' sen' the Spencer or the huntin' knife back."

Madelyn regarded her with puzzlement. "But why? We'll not need those things living in town for the winter. I doubt very much that bears or cougars will stroll down the main street of Galbraith's Crossing."

Kicker began to speak, halted, and began again. "Tis important t'me, Maddie. Can that not be reason enough?"

"Of course it can, dearest. If you want those beastly things then you shall have them, and you'll hear no more about it from me."

Kicker received the assurance with a smile that took Madelyn aback with its underlying sadness. Before she could question her, Kicker departed and closed the door behind her.

By the time Madelyn and Mrs. MacDiarmid reached the former Mackey residence, it was redolent of lye soap. Mrs. Donnelly had directed her staff in scrubbing the tiny house from the crawlspace to the low-hanging ceiling of the sleeping loft. Nothing was overlooked: not the dense grime collected under the old wood stove, the abundance of ash in the parlour fireplace, or the profusion of cobwebs that had spun across every angle and protrusion.

Windows thick with two decades of filth were polished to a crystalline shine. The old mattress ticking had been hauled down the loft stairs and thrown out on a growing pile of garbage, along with frayed rag rugs, broken dishes, and tattered, stained curtains. Of the few pieces of furniture the Mackeys left behind, Mrs. Donnelly deemed only the kitchen table and iron bed frame suitable for retention.

Even Mrs. MacDiarmid reluctantly conceded that the house was clean and habitable, though she adamantly refused to acknowledge it had any other attributes.

Her housekeeper, reacting to Mrs. MacDiarmid's pronounced lack of enthusiasm, reassured her. "At least it's well insulated, Madam. By the time the men put a couple of coats of whitewash on it, Mrs. Bristow and her cousin will be as comfortable as any in the Territories."

Mrs. MacDiarmid offered a half-hearted objection. "There are not even two bedrooms, Madelyn, and not an inch of extra space for your cousin's mattress. Whatever will the Major think about his wife having to share her bed like a...a commoner?"

In her most soothing tone, Madelyn calmed her distressed benefactress. "My husband will be pleased that, until his arrival, I'll have the benefit of my cousin's warmth to fend off the worst of winter storms. Since we were children, she and I have often shared a bed, and we're accustomed to it."

"But when the Major returns..."

"Then, of course, my cousin shall find other lodgings, but in the meantime she'll be welcome company to ease the long winter evenings. Truly, Agnes, I am as certain as one can be that I'll be perfectly comfortable here for the winter."

The whistle of the westbound train as it approached Galbraith's Crossing was a welcome diversion, and Madelyn sighed in relief as Mrs. MacDiarmid ushered her down the boardwalk toward Godwin's General Store.

An hour later, Madelyn had sorted through the shipment sent from Eaton's. Despite Mrs. MacDiarmid's protestations, she returned many of the items that simply would not fit in the small house.

Madelyn kept a large tin tub that would hold water for washing themselves and their clothes, cookware, a pair of lamps and two chairs for the kitchen, a rocking chair and matching divan as well as a side table for the parlour, a commode, a large dresser and washstand for the bedroom, two blue and burgundy English art carpets, and enough lace curtains to cover the half dozen small windows. The sea moss and cotton mattress she had splurged on was delayed, but Mrs. MacDiarmid quickly offered the loan of a horse hair mattress from the ranch.

Madelyn also kept the horse tack she'd ordered as a gift for Kicker, as well as the Spencer shotgun and hunting knife, even though she did not understand Kicker's insistence on the weapons.

By the end of the afternoon, Madelyn had organized her new belongings and paid Mr. Godwin for a large supply of kitchen staples. With the contents of the chests they brought from England, Madelyn was certain that she and Kicker would be quite comfortable.

As she and Mrs. MacDiarmid climbed aboard their carriage, Madelyn was relieved that the results of the day's labours signalled their imminent departure from the ranch. Whether finest manor or meanest hovel, Madelyn wanted nothing more than to share four walls alone with the woman she loved, and the sooner, the better.

The big move began on Saturday afternoon, after Mrs. MacDiarmid had done a final inspection and could come up with no justifiable reasons to further delay Madelyn's departure from the ranch.

The task should have taken no more than a few hours, but turned into a marathon as Mrs. MacDiarmid insisted on rendering an opinion on everything. Madelyn grew increasingly frustrated as Agnes repeatedly changed her mind and issued contradictory dictates to her domestic staff every few minutes. Finally, with the remaining hours of light waning, she quietly appealed to Wynne, who had dropped by to see how things were going.

With a grin and a wink, Wynne coaxed her mother from the scene. Shortly after, Madelyn sent Mrs. Donnelly and her staff on their way with profuse thanks. It was only when she stood on the edge of the porch to wave goodbye that Madelyn heard a soft hiss from behind her.

Glancing to her left, Madelyn saw Kicker's head appear over the buffalo berry bush at the corner of the house.

"Are they gone for good, Maddie?"

Madelyn shot Kicker an exasperated look. "Yes. And exactly where did you disappear to? The last I saw you was more hours ago than I can count."

Kicker emerged from her hiding spot and mounted the single step to the porch with a sheepish grin. "I borrowed some tools from John an' I bin workin' out in the barn, makin' sure Rabbit and Galahad have a decent place to stay, too."

Madelyn planted her hands on her hips and glared at Kicker. "The horses looked perfectly happy grazing in the yard to me. I think it would've been a wiser use of your time to ensure our comfort first."

Kicker hung her head and mumbled an apology.

With a sigh, Madelyn forgave her. She knew how ill at ease Kicker was around Mrs. MacDiarmid, who made no bones about her disdain for the unconventional newcomer.

Madelyn was well aware that the matriarch of the Steeple Seven merely tolerated her partner. Though Kicker took pains to avoid Mrs. MacDiarmid, and was on her best behaviour when contact was unavoidable, there was no doubt that Mrs. MacDiarmid was discomfited by the odd cousin.

It had often made Madelyn wonder how Agnes dealt with the eccentricities of her own daughter, but for the moment, that thought was secondary. She and Kicker were finally alone together and standing on the porch of their new home.

Madelyn extended a hand. "Come see."

Madelyn woke first to a dull, grey light that barely illuminated their sleeping loft. The cool morning air coming through the open windows made her grateful for the thick, warm quilt. Madelyn's eyes, still half closed, focused on the woman next to her as she watched the steady rise and fall of her lover's chest.

After christening the loft with their lovemaking the previous night, Kicker had insisted that they don sleep wear, but several buttons of her nightshirt had come open. Madelyn stilled her impulse to slide a hand under the soft cotton and rediscover the delights of Kicker's body. She knew it had been a deeply stressful week for Kicker, and she wanted her partner to sleep for as long as possible.

Madelyn wrenched her gaze from the temptations of her bed mate and examined the room around them. The cleaning and whitewash had improved it immeasurably, but nothing could disguise its limited size. They had pushed the bed against one wall, and the peaked ceiling sloped to within two feet of their heads. In the absence of a closet, Kicker had hammered nails into one of the ceiling beams from which to hang clothes. Agnes had given them a short oak and brass screen that concealed the commode and wash stand in the corner opposite the stairs to the lower level, and the dresser took up the rest of the space.

The only spot that Madelyn could stand fully upright was in the centre of the room, and she ruefully predicted to Kicker that by the time they moved out to their property, she would have a dowager's hump.

Kicker took her hand, led her to their bed, and reminded her without words that having the privacy of their own room was more than ample compensation for its limited size.

Madelyn's unconscious smile at that memory wavered as her gaze moved to the shotgun that hung on the wall next to the bed. She argued vehemently against its placement and pressed to have the weapon banished to the kitchen, but Kicker refused to budge. The disagreement almost ruined their first night in their own home, until finally Madelyn accepted that Kicker was going to be implacable on this issue.

"I liked your smile better, Maddie."

The sleep raspy voice warmed Madelyn's heart as Kicker rolled toward her. Opening her arms, she felt her lover snuggle into her.

"What were you thinkin' on so hard?"

The words tickled Madelyn's neck, and she revelled in the sensation. Letting her fingers wander through Kicker's hair, she replied lightly, "Mmm, this and that, dearest. Nothing too terribly important."

That seemed to satisfy Kicker, as she wriggled closer and wedged one leg between Madelyn's.

A peaceful silence settled over them and Madelyn felt an unaccustomed serenity. Though this was not exactly what she had envisioned for them, at the moment she could not think of a single place she would rather be. Far too realistic to believe their current idyll would remain inviolate, she made herself a promise to remember this tranquility when difficult times loomed. "Will you join me for church this morning, dearest?"

"I tol' Seamus I'd help him set up their rooms so he can bring Pudge home once Esther says tis a'right. He's so busy learnin' on the job that he ain't e'en had time to breathe."

Unsurprised, Madelyn murmured acknowledgement and she caressed Kicker's back.

"Are you ready for school to start t'morrow?"

"I believe so. I spent quite some time this week writing up lesson plans and reviewing the materials from the Council of Public Instruction. Agnes told me that there had been some resentment from the bachelor homesteaders at having to pay a school tax of ten cents an acre, but she and a few of the others did a little genteel arm twisting. As a result, I'll be starting the school year with new textbooks for almost all the standards."

"That's wonderful, Maddie. Your students are so lucky to have you."

Madelyn smiled at the genuine supportiveness in her partner's voice. She wrapped her arms tightly around Kicker and nuzzled her hair. "It is wonderful, isn't it, dearest? Here we are, in our new country, in our own home, with jobs and friends, and things finally settling down for us."

"An' wakin' up nex' to each other." Kicker's hand slid lower and slipped under Madelyn's nightgown. "Tis the bes' part of all."

Madelyn gasped and rose to Kicker's touch. "God, yes."

As she exited the church, Madelyn shook hands warmly with the elderly minister. She would have enjoyed the chance to discuss his sermon, long winded though it had been, but the momentum of the crowd kept her moving in Wynne's wake. She soon found herself standing on the edge of a large crowd of women, half hidden behind a matron of substantial bulk.

Wynne bent her head to say something, just as Madelyn heard Kicker's name. Instantly alert, she strained to hear what was being said.

"I completely agree, Mrs. Lynley, and she certainly reflects poorly on her cousin, too. Why, it's disgraceful, I tell you. Nellie Cornwell told me that she saw Miss Stuart walking unescorted with that redheaded Irishman down by the river."

"She certainly has not the least sense of propriety. Have you seen the clothes she wears? No proper woman would ever wear such things. In heaven's name, what kind of an example is she setting for our daughters? Why, someone ought to tell her in no uncertain terms that we simply won't stand for that kind of behaviour around here."

Madelyn's mellow mood instantly vanished, but before she could vent her anger, Wynne took her arm and steered her away. Seething, she allowed herself to be manoeuvred away from the crowd to the shade of a nearby willow.

Wynne regarded her sympathetically, even as Madelyn glared and sought to identify which of the women had been the source of the nasty comments.

"Forget it, Madelyn. They're not worth it. Those old biddies just love to tattle like three year olds."

"It's not fair, Wynne. Kicker is one of the sweetest, most kind-hearted, most honourable women I've ever met, and they're unwilling to give her a chance. I'll bet not one of them has so much as spoken to her."

Wynne shook her head sadly. "Nor are they likely to, I'm afraid. But your cousin can handle herself. Unfortunately you're going to need the good will of those old hens when you begin teaching their precious darlings."

Madelyn forced herself to breathe deeply. Lost in her indignation, she did not realize that Agnes and several others approached them.

"There you are, Madelyn, dear. I wanted you to meet the mothers of a few more of your students."

Madelyn forced a smile to her face and turned to greet the newcomers, shaking hands politely. Conversation turned to the opening of school the next morning, and Madelyn did her best to answer all the questions put to her. It was only after Wynne drifted away to talk to a group of fellow ranchers and Agnes excused herself, that two of the mothers brought up an unexpected subject.

The woman Agnes had identified as Mrs. Mortimer Mason addressed Madelyn in a hushed voice. "So, what do you plan to do about the Indian girl?"

Madelyn blinked. "Pardon me?"

"The Blue Wolf child. What do you plan to do with her?"

"Do? Well, if she is to be in my class, I'll teach her as I do the others."

Mrs. Berg frowned. "I suppose you must, of course, but mind now, I don't want my Lillian sitting anywhere near her." She turned to Mrs. Mason. "You know, actually that child is not even really old enough to start school. I think we should speak to the District Superintendent right away."

Stunned, Madelyn took faint heart from the way the three other women, clearly uncomfortable with the turn of conversation, collectively drew back from Mrs. Mason and Mrs. Berg. Aware that she was probably about to make her first enemies, she opened her mouth to respond when a cold voice from behind cut her off.

"Do you have some sort of problem with my niece, Mrs. Berg?" Wynne insinuated herself into the circle of women and fixed the offender with an icy gaze.

Mrs. Berg shrank back, her eyes darting about for allies. "Oh, Mrs. Glenn. I didn't see you there."

"Clearly." Wynne advanced, her angry gaze taking in both Mrs. Berg and Mrs. Mason. "Did I hear you say you were going to attempt to keep my brother's daughter out of school?"

Mrs. Berg whined, "But really, Mrs. Glenn. She's only four years old..."

"Four and a half, and smart as a whip. She'll leave your Lillian in the dust—academically speaking, of course."

"Well, I never." Mrs. Berg drew herself up, then quickly deflated as Will and his wife, Ruth, flanked Wynne. Three sets of angry eyes regarded Mrs. Berg and Mrs. Mason, who quickly mumbled an apology and hastened away. The other three women, clearly discomfited by the confrontation, also departed.

Will spat in the dust. "Bloody bigots." Ruth laid a calming hand on his arm. "Well, damn it, Ruthie, you know they are."

"Of course they are," Wynne agreed, her eyes still blazing with anger. "But the real question is how we're going to protect little Marie from their bigotry."

"I assure you, I'll not tolerate any such nastiness in my classroom," Madelyn said.

Wynne nodded. "We know that you'll do your best, but the problem is going to be when the children are outside the classroom."

"Will she be my only native student?"

All three nodded, and Will explained. "John and Esther are the only Stoney or Métis living close enough to school their children in town. Not many would have the courage to put up with what they do."

"What about Marie's brothers and sisters? Are any old enough to join her?"

Wynne shook her head. "Not really. The next oldest, Lucas, is three. The only reason John and Esther are allowing Marie to go to school this year is that she spent most of last year squatting below the window or huddled in the cloak room, eavesdropping on the teacher's lessons. They decided it was better that she attend than freeze to death."

Ruth smiled. "You'll find her a pure pleasure to teach, Mrs. Bristow, that is, if you can get her to speak. I've never seen a child with such a thirst to learn." Then she sobered. "But be careful. Archie Mason and Lillian Berg will make Marie's life miserable if they get half a chance. Those two are natural born bullies, just like their mothers."

Madelyn nodded her understanding. "I don't wish to be presumptuous, but will your children stand up for Marie? It would help immensely if she is not made to feel that she's completely friendless."

The three started talking at once, then Wynne held up her hand to silence her brother and sister-in-law. Obediently, they fell quiet and allowed her to speak for the family, as always.

"We'll talk to all the children, Madelyn, and make them aware that they need to look out for their cousin. I think I'll speak to Laird and see if he and Billy will make it their mission to protect Marie."

Madelyn gave a sigh of relief. Throughout her years of teaching, she had found bullying one of the most intractable problems to deal with. Though she clamped down firmly on any manifestations in the classroom, she knew that most of the damage to vulnerable children was done away from her oversight.

With a shake of her head, Madelyn made a wry prediction. "It's going to be quite the year, isn't it?"

CHAPTER 17

KICKER FINISHED WITH A NEWLY repaired plough blade as John entered the shop carrying a cracked sleigh runner.

"Cybulski's ordered a replacement; you should be able to reuse the iron. Get started on this while I make a run up to the lumber camp to deliver the new boom chain."

Kicker nodded and set the plough blade aside. She took the sleigh runner to the handyman's bench on the opposite side of the room.

"Ranholm, or one of his boys, will be around shortly to pick up the plough blade. He paid in advance, so you just have to hand it over."

Kicker nodded again. In the months since she had begun work, they had developed a system. Many of the locals were leery about letting a woman handle their trade, so she worked in the shadows as much as possible. This allowed John to negotiate prices and deal with customers.

With harvesting completed, much of their business now was in the repairing of farm implements and preparation for the oncoming winter. There were also three sleighs behind the smithy that awaited their attention, and they'd received an order for four new barrels.

"I won't be back until tomorrow. However, that doesn't mean you are to work until midnight again." John looked sternly at Kicker. "You're burning up too much coal oil."

Kicker ducked her head to hide her grin. She was aware that her days were uncommon long at times. But she enjoyed knowing that her employer valued her and worked hard to earn his approval. Kicker knew that her taking over much of the iron work had freed John to focus on the equally lucrative woodwork his shop handled. Profits were rising steadily, and three weeks earlier, John had given Kicker a small raise.

Kicker was grateful for the increased wages, but it was John's words she held close to her heart. He told her that part of the upturn in the business was due to the growing population, but he also credited Kicker's skill and dedication for their ability to meet their customers' increased demands.

Kicker thrilled to the knowledge that despite having to stay out of sight, she made a real contribution to the smithy's reputation for excellence. Each day John's esteem warmed her against the increasing cold; each evening she lay with Madelyn in their bed, still enchanted by the reality of falling asleep next to the woman she loved.

The only hitch in their happiness was Madelyn's frequent absences during evenings and weekends. Though Kicker tried to understand and accept the demands of teaching, she couldn't help but wish for more than their precious nighttime hours together. It seemed to Kicker at times as if the entire world conspired to keep the lovers apart. But she had no wish to add to Madelyn's burden, and kept her qualms private.

It helped considerably that the angst of their early weeks in Galbraith's Crossing, and the guilt and sorrow over her friends' misfortune had eased with time. Even the fear of what could happen to Madelyn should Kicker's vigilance ever slip, faded as they settled comfortably into the joyfully mundane reality of their lives.

Rick Biggart had vanished. General consensus held that the town was better for his absence. By all appearances, Rupert Arbuster had been neutered by Kicker and Madelyn's powerful friends and allies. The women had a snug home, which, while not fancy, would ward off the worst of winter blasts while sheltering their love from prying eyes.

The worst thing they'd had to deal with since the initial turmoil was the visit by a school inspector with a Napoleonic complex. Mr. Harlbert Gilford, his physical stature smaller than Kicker's, rode into town on the tallest standard bred horse Kicker had ever seen. As if to belie his diminutive height, he wielded his considerable authority with tyrannical impunity. Gilford represented the territorial government and held the power of the purse over teachers, students, and school boards.

Immediately upon his arrival, the inspector had put Madelyn, her pupils, and the board of trustees through an inquisitorial afternoon. After several hours of rapid fire questions and individual interrogations, Mr. Gilford pronounced himself satisfied. Every citizen of the town heaved a sigh of relief. But that was well behind them now. Mr. Harlbert Gilford would not return until the crocuses appeared in spring.

"Blue Wolf."

John turned as his name was called from the street. "Ah, there's Ranholm now." He picked up the plough blade and went outside to make delivery.

When John returned, he admonished her again. "I mean it, Kicker. When the sun goes down, close up. Go home and have supper with Mrs. Bristow. I'm sure she misses seeing you."

After he left, Kicker paused in pulling the old nails that affixed the shaped iron to the cracked wood of the sled runner. Her eyes became distant as she considered John's parting words. *Misses me? Don' hardly seem so some days.*

Kicker sighed and returned to work as she mulled over Madelyn's absences like a broken tooth her tongue couldn't stay away from. She reviewed her partner's situation for the hundredth time and tried to convince herself it was understandable that she had fallen to the bottom of Madelyn's priorities. The summer's influx of immigrants into the district had added to the class load. The demands of teaching eight grades to thirty seven students were overwhelming. Three of Madelyn's students would be writing the all-important entrance exam for high school in the spring. Only one came from a family that could afford to send their son away to boarding school, but Madelyn spent many after-class hours tutoring all three boys.

Several students had little command of the English language. They, too, required extra help. In addition, the annual Christmas concert meant rehearsing children's dialogues, recitations, and songs, and coordinating parental help with costumes and sets.

The crucial preparations for the school inspector's visit had been all consuming for two months. Madelyn drilled her students obsessively in preparation, and conferred repeatedly with anxious trustees and parents.

Kicker could not remember the last time she had seen Madelyn for more than a rushed meal in the evening. Tonight Madelyn's obligation was the annual ratepayers meeting to elect a new member of the school board. Kicker glanced out at the angle of shadows on the street and guessed that it was just getting underway.

No point in goin' home.

Having worked herself into a mild depression, Kicker packed up for the day as she considered her options. She decided to check her most productive snare and see if there was anything to take over to the station house.

Since Esther released Pudge to Seamus' care, Kicker made it her business to share such small game as she could trap or shoot. John had taught her new techniques and the best trapping locations. Kicker had become a proficient provider for both her own and the Kelly households.

Kicker was such a frequent guest at the Kelly dinner table when Madelyn was busy, that Seamus simply added a plate without asking when she showed up at the station house door.

Seamus and Kicker dedicated themselves to recovering the routines of their lives before the fire. They were determined not to let Pudge slip further into the depression that overwhelmed him once he realized the severity of his injuries. Together they cajoled Pudge into some semblance of normality, with one exception. Music had been banished from the Kelly home.

Though the fusion of Pudge's right arm was far less serious than Esther first feared, Seamus and Kicker had been entirely unsuccessful in convincing Pudge to try playing again. And when Seamus saw that he pained rather than pleased his brother, he set his fiddle aside too.

Kicker missed the music, but mostly she missed the old Pudge—and hated the two bastards who had so violently changed her friend's life.

Wynne idly watched Will chat with Madelyn and several farmers at the front of the schoolhouse. Desks had been pushed aside and space cleared for the annual ratepayers meeting.

They'd dealt with most of the mundane business. Congratulations on the successful inspection by Mr. Harlbert Gilford were offered all around. Bob Whitney was designated to provide a wagonload of logs, split and stacked on the school woodpile for the winter. An update on the school well was given and detailed needed repairs. A lively argument over a small tax increase to effect the repairs ensued, before eventually being passed.

It was decided that the school roof would be adequate for another year, despite damage to some shingles that had been caused by June's hailstorms. Madelyn reported that preparations for the annual Christmas concert were going well.

The first half of the meeting wrapped up with a decision that a cat must be brought in. Field mice were finding the school an excellent sanctuary now that the weather had turned colder.

The election of a new board member was the only issue left to deal with. Before they tackled that, the ratepayers broke for coffee and cake.

"I didn't think you normally bothered with these things, Wynne."

Wynne turned her head to see her northern neighbour, Reed Nichols from the Bar N Ranch, smiling down at her. "Hi, Reed. You're right, I usually don't, but I had to come into town anyway, so I thought I'd sit in."

Reed took a seat beside Wynne and folded himself uncomfortably into a chair made for a ten-year-old. He jerked his chin at a man who sat alone in the back corner of the room. "And here I thought it might be because that polecat came."

Impressed by Reed's insight, Wynne glanced at Rupert Arbuster. As soon as she heard that Rupert planned to attend the ratepayers meeting, she sensed trouble. Her presence was directly related to Arbuster's, but thus far, he had given no indication of why he was present.

Reed tapped his cold pipe against his hand and looked caustically at Rupert. "We all know that where he goes, problems follow. And since he ain't got any children, why's he here?"

Wynne shrugged, even though that was exactly what she had asked herself. "Guess he's got as much right as anyone. The Arbusters are taxpayers, just as we are."

Reed's reply was cut off as Will hammered on the desk to get everyone's attention.

"Okay, if you'll all sit down, we'll finish up with the last business of the evening." There was a rustle of voices and an ebbing of the noise as people resumed their seats. "As most of you know, I've done my three years and it's time one of you lazy bunch took your turn." Will grinned at the catcalls and turned to the two men sitting next to him. "Mr. Samuel James will head up the new board; Mr. Dave Asher will be his second. We just need a third for a quorum, so, any takers?"

Will surveyed the dearth of volunteers with amusement. "Come on, you shirkers, volunteer or I'll have to nominate someone and have you vote him in. Henry, how about you?"

"Aw, Will, my oldest is barely into grade one. Give me a few more years and I'll do my part."

"Fair enough. Mr. Fairclough, what about you? Your son will be sitting the high school exam this spring, and—"

"I'll do it." Will's words were cut off as Rupert Arbuster rose to his feet. "I'll volunteer."

Wynne's eyes narrowed. Rupert had made his play, but she still didn't understand it. She wasn't alone. There was shock and consternation on the faces of most of her fellow ratepayers.

Will had to gavel the room to silence before he could speak.

"Well, now, Rupert, that's mighty big of you, but—"

"But what? My family pays its taxes. I'm eligible."

"That's true, but you don't have any children attending school."

Wynne rose to her feet. "I believe I'll add my name to the ballot, Will."

Rupert shot her a venomous glare. "Last time I checked, Wynne, there weren't no women on the board."

Wynne met his stare coldly. "Why don't we let our neighbours decide which is more important: having another man on the board, or having someone who actually has a child in the school and who really cares about the welfare of all the children."

A loud buzz of conversation broke out and Will again employed his gavel. When things quieted enough that he could be heard, he looked sternly at the crowd. "All right, folks, we have two fine volunteers. We only need one, so we're going to do the democratic thing and vote. Wynne, will you and Rupert step outside for a few minutes?"

Wynne nodded and headed for the door, followed by Arbuster. They let the heavy door close behind them and stood silently apart in the cool night air.

Brander had been curled in a ball under a nearby wagon. He immediately came to his mistress and stood between the two rivals, hackles raised as a growl rumbled low in his chest. Wynne reached down and ruffled his fur. She softly reassured the collie as she studiously ignored the palpable waves of hostility rolling off Rupert.

Finally Reed swung open the door and gestured them in. Wynne estimated it had barely been five minutes, yet it had felt like an hour with her unpleasant, though thankfully wordless company. Giving her canine companion one last soothing stroke, she pointed to the wagon.

"Go lie down, Brander. I'll be back shortly."

Rupert stalked stiffly ahead of her into the schoolhouse. As Wynne walked by Reed holding the door, he winked at her and smiled. More smiles greeted her when she entered the room.

Will brought the gavel down once and gave the crowd a satisfied grin. "By the power vested in me as outgoing chair, I declare Wynne Glenn the newest elected trustee." Turning to the two relieved looking trustees at his side, he handed the instrument of office to the nearest. "Okay, Sam, it's all yours. Good luck, and watch out for raccoons in the attic."

Sam rose to his feet. "I'd like you all to offer up a hand for Will MacDiarmid in appreciation of his fine service, and for going above and beyond to find our kids such a wonderful new teacher."

During the hearty applause and teasing hoots that followed, Wynne noticed Rupert slip out the door. Despite her contempt for the man, she shuddered at the look of frustrated malevolence on his face. Wynne still had no idea what his game was, but for now, at least, it seemed she and her neighbours had stymied him.

As Wynne joined the crowd gathered around her brother to shake his hand and slap him on the back, she inwardly cautioned herself against complacency. *Whatever he's up to, Rupe isn't one to give up easily. He bears watching... as always.*

Seamus pushed back from the table with a contented sigh. "Miss Kicker, you are truly a Renaissance woman. I believe these biscuits are worthy of the Queen's kitchen."

Pudge grunted his agreement as he sopped up the last of the gravy on his plate.

Kicker beamed at them. "Well, you can thank Cook Hannah for that. She taught me everythin' I know about cooking."

Seamus raised his glass. "Then let us toast the inestimable Cook Hannah. Long may she reign over her kitchen."

Kicker raised her glass too, but noted sadly that Pudge did not join in their playful toast. She glanced at Seamus and saw the melancholy way he regarded his brother, who was hunched over his plate.

Pudge's habitual pose kept the worst of his ruined face hidden; he wore his wide brimmed leather hat pulled low, even at the table. Besides Esther, Seamus and Kicker were the only ones allowed to see him undisguised, even briefly.

"Hey, you fellows up to a game of checkers, b'fore I go home?"

Seamus gave Kicker a grateful smile, which faded as Pudge shook his head.

"You two go ahead. I'm going out for a walk."

Kicker knew it would be a dark night if Pudge intended to go out. She wondered briefly how he would cope when summer brought longer hours, and hoped that by then he would be comfortable in the daylight.

"If you wait until I process the eight-thirty train, I'll come with you, Pudge."

"No, that's fine, Seamus. I like the quiet. I think better."

Seamus and Kicker watched as Pudge lifted their loaded shotgun down from the rack with his good left arm. He threw on a warm coat and silently departed through the side door.

"He takes a weapon but not a light, never a light."

Kicker looked at her friend. "Why?"

"He says he does not require light to see. I believe it is more that he cannot bear to be seen, even if it means falling in the river and drowning."

"You don' think—"

"That he would commit the mortal sin of suicide?" Seamus patted Kicker's hand comfortingly. "If I thought that, nothing in the world would keep me from his side, no matter how much he demurred. No, my brother is not self-destructive."

"But the gun?"

"He claims he is hunting."

"At night? Has he e'er brought anythin' home?"

Seamus gave her a measured look. "I do not think my brother hunts the deer in the forest."

Kicker stiffened in alarm. "He'll not go after Arbuster, will he? Seamus, we talked about this..."

"I know. I believe I made a grave error in judgement when I told Pudge who it was brought this calamity down upon us. I fear that the consequences of that lapse will return to haunt us one day, but appealing to my brother's good sense falls as short today as ever it did. He was always headstrong; now he is a veritable force of God."

"Bless'd Jesus. They'll hang him without a second thought if he kills Arbuster. They know what a weasel the man is, but they look after their own."

Seamus put a calming hand on Kicker's forearm. "Having come so close to losing his life, I do not believe Pudge would throw it away so carelessly. He will not assassinate Arbuster."

"But he says he hunts—"

"More, I believe, in the spiritual sense, Miss Kicker. He is seeking a reason for what happened, a sense of how to accept his circumstances. Perhaps even to learn, once again, how to plan for a future."

"With a gun?"

"I believe the weapon gives Pudge a sense of security. This time he feels himself prepared, whether beset by man or beast." Seamus gave a deep sigh. "But I fear his thirst for vengeance overwhelms him at times, and I have as yet been unable to temper his demons."

Kicker ducked her head. Despite assurances from both Seamus and Pudge that she bore no responsibility for the fire or Pudge's injuries, they had never fully dispelled her sense of guilt. Reminding herself not to distress Seamus, she shook off her remorse. "Should he e'en be out on his own so soon?"

"I did ask Miss Esther that very thing, but she informed me that as long as he does not exceed his limits..."

The two friends exchanged wry grins.

"An' Pudge is so good at knowin' his limits."

"Indeed. My brother... Some things, at least, have not changed. But leave Pudge's welfare to me. I will not fail him again."

Seamus stood and picked up their dishes. When Kicker made to help, he shook his head. "Go home, my dear. I'm sure Mrs. Bristow wonders where you are."

"I doubt it."

Seamus looked at her curiously but did not challenge her statement. Instead, he escorted her through the station's office to the front door. As they stepped out on the landing, Kicker saw that snow had begun to fall. She held out her hand and delightedly examined the flakes she captured.

Kicker looked at Seamus, who examined the dark sky with a similar air of wonder. "P'rhaps Pudge'll stay home when the snow gets deep."

"Perhaps."

But as Kicker strode away to her own home, she knew he didn't believe it. Nor did she.

When Kicker arrived home, Madelyn was not there. She lit one of their lanterns and busied herself lighting a fire in the stove that warmed both the kitchen and, to a much lesser degree, their bedroom. After setting a kettle of water to boil, Kicker sat down at the table to finish a letter to Adam.

Madelyn had left a letter she was writing to Lil in the stationery box, and Kicker carefully set it aside so she would not spill any ink on it. She smiled as she remembered what Madelyn had told her of its contents.

"I told Lil to have her soldier lad in South Africa post the letter we composed about mid-January. Sadly, I am afraid I shall be a heartbroken widow before spring."

They had chuckled together over the demise of Madelyn's fictional husband. But in truth, Kicker was nervous about Madelyn officially entering widowhood. It had not escaped her notice how the new schoolteacher attracted a great deal of male attention. Kicker knew that after two years of mourning, Madelyn would be considered fair game amongst the large pool of local bachelors.

Her only consolation lay in reminding herself that Madelyn was an excellent actress. If anyone could convince the townsfolk that she was emulating Queen Victoria in a permanent state of mourning for a beloved spouse, it would be her partner. But Kicker doubted that anyone dared pressure the Queen the way eager swains of Galbraith's Crossing would pressure Madelyn once she was officially available.

Kicker kept her fears to herself. Madelyn often exulted over the way their plans had worked out and Kicker did not wish to put a damper on her glee.

Adam's letter was almost completed when the sound of the door opening coincided with the sizzle of the kettle boiling. Kicker hastily lifted the kettle off the stove and turned to greet Madelyn. "You look tired, love."

Madelyn accepted Kicker's embrace before shrugging off her heavy coat. "It was a most long and wearisome day."

Kicker steered Madelyn into a chair. "I'm jus' making tea. Would you like some?"

"Please. And some biscuits with honey, if there are any left."

Kicker bustled about the kitchen fixing Madelyn a plate. "Did you get some supper? I lef' the last of the ham in the icebox and there's smoked beef in the root cellar—"

"I was not hungry, but thank you." Madelyn smiled at Kicker and accepted her tea and biscuits. "You're so good to me."

Kicker took her place across the small table and enjoyed the warmth of the cup between her hands. "How did the meetin' go t'night?"

Madelyn nibbled on her biscuit, a frown on her face. "It really was the oddest thing. I must be missing some of the local undercurrents. Apparently a gentleman who submitted his name for the board of trustees is not well liked or trusted in town. There seemed to be a great deal of consternation when he volunteered."

Kicker felt her breath catch. "Who was't?"

"One of the Arbuster family—Reuben, perhaps? No, that's not right... Rupert, that's it. Rupert Arbuster. Quite a handsome man if he did not scowl so much."

The tea curdled in Kicker's stomach. "Arbuster? He's the new trustee?"

"No, dearest. As I said, he seemed to arouse the ratepayers' enmity simply by volunteering, but it quickly became moot when Wynne too stepped forward."

Kicker stifled a sigh of relief. "So Wynne's the new trustee?"

"Yes. Apparently Mr. Arbuster doesn't have any children in school, which most seemed to regard as a mark against him. Actually I thought it was rather civic minded of him to volunteer despite not being a parent, but I'm pleased that Wynne will be on the board. They've never had a woman, but then Wynne is an exceptional figure, is she not?"

"Aye, that she is." *Bless you, Wynne Glenn.* In the fifteen months since Kicker had met Madelyn, she had become well acquainted with the power of a school board to make a teacher's life pleasant or sheer misery. Not only did they control hiring and firing, but they also allotted money for supplies and governed a teacher's standard of living and standing in the community.

Madelyn might be unaware of Rupert Arbuster's motives in seeking the trustee position, but Kicker would have staked Rabbit on a bet that he was up to no good. She was not sure exactly how, but she suspected that both of them had had a narrow escape that night.

"Did I tell you that I had to discipline that horrid Archie Mason again? I detest using the strap, but that boy simply won't respond to anything but physical punishment."

"What did he do this time?"

"Well, Clarence and George were helping me clean up at lunchtime. You remember me telling you about them, don't you, dearest?"

Kicker nodded absently. "Cousins. Family moved here from Brittany this summer to farm. French speakin'."

"Correct, though their English is really becoming quite good. I think playing with Laird and Billy has helped a lot. Those four are inseparable. Anyway, the boys were tidying up while I graded papers, and suddenly there was this terrible noise, like a clap of thunder. There was smoke coming off the top of the stove. Poor George was closest to the stove and he stumbled around holding his ears. I saw Archie peer in the window, laughing at the results of his latest prank. He'd been angered by the boys ganging up against him on behalf of little Marie Blue Wolf. He didn't even try to deny that he had sprinkled gunpowder on the stove to get back at them. Well, I marched him smartly into the classroom by the scruff of his miserable neck..."

Kicker made the appropriate responses as she listened to Madelyn's indignant recitation of Archie's most recent misdemeanours, but most of her thoughts revolved around the implications of Rupert Arbuster's latest tactic.

What does it mean? And what'll he do next?

The cabin door opened and Biggart glowered at the new arrival. "What the hell took you so damned long?"

"Quit whining. I'm here, ain't I?"

Biggart shot his patron a savage look. "Whining? I don't see you stuck out in the middle of nowhere, in a God-cursed trapper's cabin that's so bloody cold it's this side of useless at keepin' the wind out. I've never been so damned frozen in my life."

"At least you ain't dangling at the end of a rope." Arbuster tossed a canvas sack at Biggart's feet. "Besides, you only got yourself to blame. If you hadn't lost your damned gun..."

"It wasn't my idea to burn the cabin. I told you I could've grabbed the bitch anytime she was ridin' between the Steeple Seven and the Shadow Creek site. I could've made her regret the day she was ever born and had a little fun on the side, but you had to complicate things to hell and gone."

Arbuster ignored Biggart's pointed accusation. "And if you hadn't been so bloody vain about showing everybody in the territory what a fancy piece you carried..."

Biggart looked up from examining the contents of the sack with an acid expression. "Like you haven't bragged to everyone that crosses your path 'bout that plug ugly, hand tooled saddle you imported from Oregon. 'Sides, every man in this territory carries a gun—"

"Pearl handled? With your blasted initials—all four of them—engraved on the butt? You might as well have left a signed confession nailed to the burnt out ruins."

"They ain't found it." Biggart's voice was lethally soft.

"Yet."

Forcing himself to be patient, Biggart rose to his feet. "I told you—if no one's found it yet, it ain't gonna be found. There's no case against me, and if there's no case against me, then there's no case against you. There's not a reason in the world for me to rot out here any longer, and I don't plan to."

Arbuster gingerly took a seat on a wobbly chair by a table that was missing several boards. He wrapped his hand around the rum bottle sitting there and gave his right hand man a baleful glare. "Have you forgotten about the eyewitness?"

Biggart shrugged and leaned against the table. "So I'll take care of him—both of them. Who's gonna miss a couple of Irish anyway?"

After tipping the bottle to his lips and taking a long swallow, Arbuster shook his head with a sneer. "It would be a bit obvious, don't you think?"

Tired and cold, Biggart was uncharacteristically forthright. "So what? All you got to do is alibi me like you always do. Ain't nobody brought us down before. You gonna let a couple of Irish and that horse lovin' little freak, one up us?"

"No one's one uppin' me. Ever."

Biggart forced himself to adopt a conciliatory tone. "That's all I'm sayin', Rupe. We've played this cagey long enough. We just take care of this the way we always do, and everything's back to normal."

"I don't think that's going to work this time, Rick."

"Why not?"

An uneasy expression crossed Arbuster's face as he took another drink. "Because they got friends. Beats the hell out of me why, but the whole damned MacDiarmid bunch are in that freak's pocket. Well, not so much her pocket, but her cousin's. I'm not saying anybody would miss the freak, but we'd be stirring a hornet's nest if anything happened to the new schoolteacher. Old Lady MacDiarmid worships the ground the teach walks on, and God help us if we get caught doing anything to her."

Biggart held out his hand for the bottle and Arbuster passed it over. "I'm well aware of all that. I'm not sayin' we necessarily go after them openly. Accidents happen all the time, especially in the winter. We can be subtle when we have to. After all, it was my idea to get you on the school board, wasn't it? How did that go, anyway?"

"I didn't get elected; Wynne Goddamned Glenn did."

Jesus Christ! Shit for brains. Send a boy... Biggart raised the bottle and took a long drink.

"It wasn't like I wanted it anyway. I still don't know why the hell you convinced me to volunteer. Who the hell wants to be stuck with a bunch of snot nosed brats and their moronic parents, anyway?"

Biggart shot him a disgusted look and passed the bottle back. "How many times do I have to explain this? I told you—the freak's under her cousin's protection. We kill her, we upset the teacher. We upset the teacher, she goes cryin' to Old Lady MacDiarmid. Old Lady MacDiarmid gets upset, and the fat's in the fire, boy. She'll have half the territory huntin' for both our miserable hides, and you know she could do it, too."

"I know that, Goddamnit!" Arbuster rolled the bottle glumly between his gloved hands. "And that's all I'd need. But I still don't see how me being on the school board solves our problem."

"Christ, you just don't understand strategy at all, do you? If the teacher was single, I'd have told you to court her—"

"The hell, you say!"

"Ain't like she's hard on the eyes, Rupe. But my point is, you can't court her 'cause she's married, but you could've controlled her if you were on the board. You control her, and it gives us power over the cousin. A little tug here, a little twist there, we could'a made the bitch's life a livin' hell. Even you gotta understand that's a much more effective revenge than just burnin' a cabin they'll probably rebuild in the spring."

"Huh."

Biggart was relieved to see a glimmer of understanding cross his patron's face. Rupert was thicker than a plank, but he was the one with money and social status. As a boy, Biggart decided he would ride Arbuster's coattails as far as they would take him. Though at times he doubted the wisdom of his original decision, he knew he was stuck with it. It was the only game in town.

"Course, since you didn't get on the board, we're gonna to have to come up with somethin' else. I do not plan to rot away in the bush for much longer."

Arbuster looked at him in alarm. "Rick, we've got to be careful—"

"I know that." *Jesus, like I don't do the thinking for both of us.* "I'll stick it out here for another week or two to see if my gun shows up, but that's it."

"But, I put the word out with the boys a long time ago that I'd pay good money for the gun. Same time as I told everyone you went to Montana. No one's approached me yet."

"That's because it ain't our boys that's got it; it's one of the Steeple Seven bunch. I thought the reward offer would convince whoever had it to give it up, but I figure they've had the fear of God put in 'em by Donnelly. Whoever had it probably already tossed it so the wrath of the MacDiarmids doesn't come down on 'em, but I want you to stir the pot again. Double the reward offer and let the boys know that you'll pay the same amount to anyone who can broker a deal. Our guys will be on the Steeple Seven boys before the words are even out of your mouth."

"Pretty damned free with my money."

Biggart ignored his patron's grumbling. The dynamics of their relationship had been established when they were eight years old. Rick let Rupert think he ran the show because Arbuster supplied the capital and the protection of his name. *Ol' Rupe couldn't pull his dick outta his pants without me telling him how.*

"Of course if nothing happens then, it means the gun surely was ditched months ago. Either way, it means I'll be leavin' this damned ice cave for good."

"There might be a problem."

Biggart narrowed his eyes at Arbuster, who refused to meet his glare. *What's the hell's he done now?*

"The old man has been on my back lately. I'm not sure he'll let you back on the ranch."

Rage surged over Biggart. Through gritted teeth, he ground out, "And when exactly were you plannin' to tell me?"

"Hell, you know—"

"No, I don't know. I've been hiding out in this bloody hole for months, and now you're telling me it's for nothin'? I ain't gettin' my life back?"

"Look, it's not for certain, Rick. I figured I'd just give the old man time to calm down and sneak you back on the ranch. Everything would be back to normal again. Just don't do anything stupid in the meantime."

"Don't do anything stupid?" Biggart's voice was a silken lash over his craven patron. "Would that be somethin' as stupid as runnin' your mouth and your temper until you make a fool of yourself over a mustang mare, of all things? Something stupid like lettin' some little freak bitch get under your skin until you can't even think straight? Like makin' enemies of the most powerful family in the territory because of your blind stupid pride?"

"Hey, the MacDiarmids aren't—"

"Yes...they are. But you don't have to deal with the consequences, do you, Rupe? You've never had to deal with the consequences. Your mama always wiped your butt for you, didn't she? And if she couldn't, then your daddy just hired someone to clean up your shit. And now you're tellin' me that Daddy ain't gonna do that no more?"

Biggart could see his words tear at Arbuster like barbed wire, but for the first time, he didn't care. He had endured every miserable moment of the past few months hiding out in this godforsaken cabin for one reason—to resume his comfortable life on the Arbuster ranch at the right hand of the youngest Arbuster scion. Who conveniently forgot to tell him that it probably wasn't ever going to happen.

Biggart's hand balled into a fist but Arbuster jumped to his feet and held up both hands in a placating manner.

"Look, you just got to give me some more time, Rick. You know I'll make this right. I always do, right? Right?"

Arbuster obviously thought his grin engaging. Biggart thought it ghastly, but he reined in his temper and waited. "I'm listenin'."

"Look, worse comes to worst, not that I think it will," Rupert added hastily, "I'll pay to send you to Mexico myself. Set you up in fine style down there for as long as it takes. But you know I got my mama wrapped around my little finger, and I've got her working on the old man. You'll be back on the ranch by Christmas... New Year's tops."

Biggart's eyes snapped shut. He could sense Arbuster holding his breath. When he opened his eyes and gave a single sharp nod, Rupert released his breath in a long stream of condensation.

"Okay, okay then. We're square. I'll be back in a day or two with more supplies." Arbuster started to back away towards the door, keeping a sickly smile on his face.

"Bring more blankets...and rum."

"You got it. The finest blankets in the house and all the rum you can drink," Arbuster babbled as he fumbled for the door handle. "Nothing but the best, too; none of that rotgut they serve in the Windsor."

Biggart watched his cohort stumble out the door, briefly amused at Arbuster's haste. His amusement faded as he listened to the sound of a horse beating a rapid retreat.

Biggart opened the door. All that could be seen of his visitor was a dark blur disappearing into the forest, but the three quarter moon illuminated the horse tracks in the snow. His own mount, stabled in a lean-to at the rear of the ancient trapper's cabin, whinnied softly, but he ignored it.

He stood silently until the icy chill of the air forced him back to the relative warmth of his dilapidated hearth. As Biggart stood and stared into the weak flames, he made himself a promise.

Someone's gonna pay.

CHAPTER 18

MADELYN FINISHED REWRITING THE EQUATIONS on the board and stepped back to review them. She had learned that it was easier to work sequentially through the standards. Each hour she changed the mathematical questions just enough to challenge the next grade up. The brighter students worked ahead, often doing two or three grade levels in one day.

She stood for a moment with her back to her pupils and absorbed the sounds of her school. The squeak of chalk on slate was comforting, but it had taken Madelyn a while to become accustomed to the constant murmuring as younger students sought help from older children. However, she found that those who taught, also learned their own lessons most thoroughly, and she encouraged the process.

The consolidation of eight grades in one room and the speed required to guide everyone through an assortment of lessons had been one of Madelyn's most difficult adjustments. There was little time for more than rote learning and teaching the basics. Long gone were the days when she could spend several hours with bright young women examining William Blake's break with the Neo-Classicism of eighteenth century poets, or how Wordsworth and Coleridge ushered in the Romantic period. Now Madelyn was lucky if half her pupils didn't nod off to sleep two minutes after singing *God Save the Queen* to begin the school day.

The first time that had happened, she slammed her ruler down on the desk of the dozing miscreant and startled the boy so badly he fell to the floor. It was then that Madelyn learned her students were usually up for hours doing chores before the school bell rang. It was wrenching to accept that the majority of parents put priority on farm chores over schoolwork, but it was simply one more adjustment that Madelyn was forced to make. Subsequently, she exercised compassion, and allowed those who needed it to sleep for a brief period before rousing them.

Madelyn turned to face the pupils and sighed inwardly as she caught sight of Lillian Berg's ink spattered face. When Lillian's mother saw her precious angel, there would be hell to pay. No amount of explanation would convince the righteous Mrs. Berg that her daughter hadn't been deliberately targeted by class hooligans.

How in sweet heaven's name could I have known that Clarence's ink well would blow up at the worst possible moment?

Lillian's misfortune was an unfortunate confluence of several events: cold weather that froze the ink wells overnight, Clarence's unpredictable homemade ink, and Madelyn's attempt to warm and dry all the children by rotating their seats. Lillian had just moved to the seat nearest the stove when Clarence's thawing ink well blew its cork, spattering the girl's face, hands, and outer garments.

Madelyn calmed the shrieking victim and cleaned her clothes and face as much as possible. Sadly, Clarence's potent home brew of mountain ash bark, lamp black, and iron sulphate proved to have staying power. Despite the teacher's best efforts and the passage of several hours, Lillian still looked as if she recently emerged from a coal mine.

"All right, children, sixth grade equations are now on the board. Fifth grade, we'll be reviewing your spelling—"

The back door swung open and John Blue Wolf strode in through the cloak room. He stopped behind the last row of desks with his hat in hand. "I do apologize for intruding, Mrs. Bristow, but may I have a word?"

"Continue with what you were doing, children." Madelyn cast a stern eye over her curious students and made her way back to John. They stepped into the cloak room and lowered their voices. "What is it, Mr. Blue Wolf? Is Marie needed at home?"

"I will be taking her with me, Ma'am. There's a bad storm moving in from the northwest. You should dismiss the children immediately so they can get home."

Madelyn was surprised. The day had been grey and overcast, with the occasional flurry, but not particularly threatening. "A storm?"

"Yes, Ma'am, and it's going to be a fierce blow."

"I can certainly release the town boys and girls early, but Mr. Bolton is not due back to pick up the outlying children for another..." Madelyn glanced at the clock at the front of the room, "...two hours yet."

"I've got Kicker stoking the stove in the spare sled, and she's harnessed Rabbit. She'll stop in along her way and tell Bolton he doesn't have to make his run, that she'll do it. He'll be glad enough not to have to go out again today."

John's dark eyes were startlingly intense, and Madelyn shivered.

"There's really no time to spare, Mrs. Bristow. This one is coming in hard and fast and heavy. I expect it will shut down the whole town for a couple of days."

"Very well." Madelyn stepped briskly back into the classroom. "Students, attention, please. Mr. Blue Wolf tells me there's a very bad storm heading in our direction. Class is dismissed for today. Put your things away immediately and get your coats on. Those of you who live in town proceed directly home. Those of you who take the school sled gather at the front door. It will be here momentarily to pick you up."

The excited buzz of children washed over Madelyn as she turned back to John. "Thank you for the warning, Mr. Blue Wolf. I'm sure parents will feel much relieved to have their children safely at home."

John held out his hand as his daughter approached him. "You'd best get home, too, Mrs. Bristow. And check your guide lines and wood supply. Make sure you've got enough wood for at least three days. If the lines are loose, tighten them, or the wind will rip them right off and you won't find your barn or anything else until the storm ends."

Madelyn nodded nervously. Before the first snows, under John's direction, Kicker had secured ropes running from their house to the privy and to the barn, though they hadn't as yet had need of them. She had no doubt that the wood supply on the back porch was already topped up. Kicker hadn't let it get low since the cold weather had set in.

The thought of her partner raised a sudden concern. "Will Kicker be safe out in this?" Madelyn's heart sank when John didn't answer her immediately, but only stepped back to allow the swarm of children clear passage.

As children burst out the door, Madelyn could see the lowering clouds overhead. Ominously dark, they chilled her soul as she registered the thickly falling snow. "Perhaps I should keep the outlying children here for their own safety."

"Kicker has time to get them home, Mrs. Bristow; trust her. I do."

John buttoned Marie's coat and led her outside. Madelyn sought comfort in his assurance, but when Kicker pulled the sledge up in front of the school door, she could not help the fear that swelled up within. Despite her best intentions, she knew Kicker would see it in her eyes.

As a dozen children piled into the sled and huddled around the small stove in the centre, Kicker winked at her cheerfully. "Not to worry, Cousin. I'll be back b'fore you know it."

A gust of wind swirled snow around the sled as Kicker pulled away. The last Madelyn heard was Kicker ask, "A'right then, which of you lot gets off firs'?"

Madelyn saw Clarence and George wave their hands wildly as Kicker headed east out of town.

Laird and Billy, mounted on their own horses, stopped at the bottom of the stairs.

"Will you be all right, Missus? Shall I have Grandmother send help?"

Madelyn forced a smile to ease Laird's worried expression. "I'll be fine, Laird. You and Billy be on your way now, and with all good haste. Don't stop for any reason until you get home, is that understood?"

"Yes, Ma'am." Laird turned to Billy. "Race you home."

"Boys, wait..."

Before Madelyn could caution them to clear the main street first, they kicked their horses into a gallop. Mr. Godwin, who was crossing from the railroad station to his general store, jumped out of their way as they dashed past. She shook her head and made a mental note to have a word with them when school reconvened.

Madelyn went back inside and quickly gathered up her papers. Normal after class tidying chores would have to wait. She was going home.

The next hours were hellish. The wind howled and snow piled in deep drifts against the house. Madelyn paced the small parlour and constantly peered through the windows.

"Dear God, please, please, please, keep her safe. Bring her home to me, I beseech You."

In her more contemplative moments, Madelyn was quite certain that God would have nothing to do with a gleeful sinner such as herself. Tonight, however, her prayers were born of primal need. *Kicker has to be safe.*

The last of the winter's daylight faded, and Madelyn could no longer see the lights of the Blue Wolf home across the street. Though she stood no more than four feet from the blazing fireplace, she felt an icy chill settle into her heart and bones.

For one mad moment, Madelyn considered saddling Galahad to go in search of Kicker. Propelled by desperation, she ran through the kitchen and wrenched open the back door. The wind whipped the door out of her hand, and even the overhang of the small porch was no protection against the snow that pelted her.

Madelyn struggled to close the door against the gale that sought to tear it from its hinges. Finally she got it shut and sagged against it, panting from exertion and convinced that there was no way Kicker could find her way in such a storm. Wind-dashed tears clouded her vision, and for an instant she thought she saw Kicker sitting at their table, grinning at her. But when Madelyn drew her hand over her eyes, it was nothing—a trick of light. The tears began in earnest. She sank to the floor and sobbed.

"No, no, no, no, no... Why in the name of all that is holy did I bring you to this unforgiving land?"

A surge of irrational anger swept through Madelyn: at herself; at this harsh new country; at the children who needed a ride home; at the regular sledge driver snug at his own hearth; and at John Blue Wolf, who allowed Kicker to go out in the storm instead of driving the sled himself. As she beat her hands impotently against the floor, Madelyn even turned her wrath on Kicker for agreeing to her foolish plans.

There was a fleeting measure of comfort in allowing fury to supplant fear, but when she cried herself out, only fear remained. Madelyn dragged herself up off the floor and staggered back to the parlour. She huddled on the chaise lounge, her eyes fixed on the fire as her lips whispered the terror she couldn't keep at bay.

"What if Kicker dies..."

Many do in this blighted land.

Adelaide's bitter words echoed in her ears. Bleakly, Madelyn recalled more of her old friend's diatribe.

I'm sorry that I did not tell you true and advise you against leaving England. This is a fierce, harsh land. The summers burn the crops, and the winters sear your lungs. Every day is a struggle to live...to see your children live...while a vengeful God sits on His throne and laughs at your best efforts.

The house creaked under the assault of the unrelenting blizzard.

Go back, Maddie.

"I have to find her, Adelaide. I can't abide living without her."

Return to the gentle land of our birth. There is no escape for me, but the trap has not yet closed over you. You can go back.

"I cannot, Adelaide. It is too late..."

What will you do when your cousin dies, and you are left alone in your new home?

Madelyn moaned and shook as if afflicted with ague.

...spring before they find her frozen, lifeless body...

Blindly, Madelyn fumbled for the afghan that hung over the arm of the divan. She pulled it tightly around her body, as if to shield herself against her old friend's prophetic words.

Go back, Maddie. Go back...go back...go back...

"Go back...go back...go back..." Madelyn's fevered murmuring was cut short as something seemed to break the unrelenting blackness outside the front windows. She sprang to the window but was unable to see anything in the dark save for the snow beating against the glass.

Desperately grasping at hope, Madelyn ran to the back door. Though she was prepared this time, the wind still tore it from her grasp. But it didn't matter.

Kicker, hunched low over Rabbit's neck looked up at Madelyn's appearance in the doorway. She shouted at Madelyn, but her words were lost in the roar of the wind. Madelyn urgently beckoned her in, but Kicker shook her head and pointed toward the barn.

Relief and dismay co-mingled as Madelyn screamed at her, "Damn Rabbit! Just come inside!"

Again Kicker shook her head. She stabbed a gloved finger at Madelyn and pointed emphatically into the house. Madelyn watched in disbelief as Kicker reached down to grab the rope guide line which connected the house and the barn. Holding tight to the rope, Kicker and her horse moved beyond the dim reach of the kitchen glow and disappeared.

Emotionally numb, Madelyn retreated into the kitchen. Time seemed to stop altogether. Sounds faded. The howling of the wind, the drumming of icy pellets on the windows, the crackling as another log snapped in the parlour's fireplace—she heard none of these. Only the sound of her ragged breath penetrated as she waited for the one sound she needed to hear.

The door swung open and Kicker fought to pull it closed behind her. "Bless'd Jesus. Tis colder than Beelzebub's ba... um, sorry, Maddie." Kicker gave Madelyn a sheepish look and started to strip off her outerwear. She turned to hang her gear on the hooks next to the door as she scolded Madelyn. "What were you doin' outside? You could'a froze to death."

"I thought that you had." Even with Kicker safely back in their home, Madelyn could not move beyond the horror of the past few hours and she knew her voice trembled with barely suppressed emotion. Lingering dread battled her new-born anger when Kicker behaved as if nothing untoward had occurred that day.

"Aye, I'm sorry, love. The bloody sled o'erturned jus' as I dropped off wee Margaret Paxton. She's fine, but the sled will need some repair. I'll have to go get it after the storm dies down. An' it was fierce goin' from there to home. Times I thought sure Rabbit was lost, but I let her have her head and here we are."

Madelyn watched Kicker kneel to untie her boots. She could not make herself move; she could barely make herself whisper, "Why didn't you stay at the Paxtons'?"

Kicker looked up at her in surprise. "They did offer, but I knew you'd be worried."

"Better worried for a short while than devastated for the rest of my life."

The brittleness of Madelyn's voice reached Kicker. She regarded Madelyn thoughtfully and quickly finished with her boots. "Maddie, I did not mean to scare you. Had the sled not o'erturned, we'd ha' made better time, Rabbit and me. As twas, I had to wrestle it upright, gather up the stove that broke off, and store the harness in Paxton's barn b'fore I could leave."

"Why?"

"Why what, love? The sled was blockin' the Paxtons' gate and had to be moved. And I could not leave the harness untended. It b'longs to John an' would ha' been much the worse for wear had I left it lyin' in the snow an' ice 'neath the sled. Who knows how long b'fore this storm ends?"

Appalled that such considerations could have cost Kicker's life, Madelyn wanted to scream at her, to rail that none of it mattered compared to the terror she'd endured and the danger Kicker incurred. But she leashed her anger tightly, aware that Kicker was simply being Kicker—responsible, reliable, rational Kicker.

Subconsciously Madelyn knew that the delay at the Paxtons' was probably no more than fifteen or twenty minutes. But even such a short span, measured in the dread she had felt in Kicker's absence, was almost more than she could bear.

Then arms, cold from the storm but strong and steady in their embrace, closed around her as a dearly familiar voice sounded in her ear. "I'm so sorry. I ne'er meant to scare you so." Madelyn closed her eyes and a small whimper escaped her lips. "Shhhh, love, I'm here. I'll always be here. Everythin' is a'right now."

This time. Will it be so the next time, or the time after that...

Cold fingers brushed Madelyn's cheeks, and she realized she was crying. She wondered if she would ever stop, but the normalcy of Kicker's voice coaxed her away from her dark thoughts. "Do I smell somethin' good on the stove? A hot meal would sure serve to warm my cold bones about now."

With a faint chuckle that melted some of the chill in her heart, Madelyn pulled away from Kicker's grasp. "You know me. I'm not much of a cook at the best of times, but yes, dinner is ready. Do change into something dry first, though."

Kicker gave Madelyn a quick kiss and hastened for the steep, narrow staircase that would take her to their attic bedroom. As Madelyn watched Kicker go, a creeping lassitude made it impossible for her to move. Only the reassuringly familiar sounds of Kicker's footsteps overhead finally enabled her to shake off her numbness and move to the stove.

Much to her surprise, the stew appeared to be fine, and the liquid was not even close to being burned away. Puzzled, Madelyn stirred it. Had time played a trick on her? Surely it was many hours since she set it to simmer.

The sound of Kicker's footsteps bounding down the stairs ended her reverie, and Madelyn pushed the small mystery aside. She forced a measure of cheer into her voice and called over her shoulder, "Everything is ready. Have a seat."

She carried the pot to the table and set it on the trivet. Kicker inhaled deeply and grinned at her. Madelyn froze. It was the smile she pictured after her first futile attempt to go outside. *She's here. She's not out there—lost. She's sitting right in front of you and awaits her supper.*

Madelyn didn't trust her trembling hands to ladle out the stew so she pushed the pot in Kicker's direction. "Help yourself, dearest."

As Kicker enthusiastically filled her plate, Madelyn sank into the other chair. When it came time to serve herself, she took the smallest amount she could without arousing Kicker's concern. Even that proved almost impossible to swallow.

"No slight to your teachin', Maddie, but I think the chil'ren were glad of the unexpected holiday. They were chatterin' away in the back of the sled like a pack of squirrels. Mind, by the time I dropped the Anderson boys off, those lef' were hunkered down nex' to the stove jus' to keep warm. The las' half of the way was hard. Got bogged down by driftin' snow turnin' into Paxton's farm. That's how the sled flipped, though Rabbit worked hard to get it out."

Madelyn murmured an acknowledgement as she fought her rebellious stomach. Each small bite she forced down felt like a victory.

"But up 'til then, it was a pure treat. Twas like a winter wonderland, Maddie. The snow fallin' thick and hard, makin' everything so white and clean. Had it not bin for the bloody wind, it would've bin Heaven."

Madelyn shuddered at Kicker's enthusiasm for the weather that could so easily have taken her life. *How can she treat this as some adventure? How could she be so heedless of my fears? Did she give no thought at all to me being left here all alone?*

The anger that Madelyn had tamped down threatened to burst forth. Abruptly she stood, knocked over her chair, and startled Kicker.

"Maddie? Are you—"

"Fine. I'm fine. I'm just weary, fatigued from the day's travails. If you'll excuse me, I believe I shall retire early tonight." Madelyn could not bear the confusion and concern on Kicker's face a moment longer. She bolted for the stairs and ignored her soft query.

"Maddie?"

When Kicker came to bed several hours later, Madelyn feigned slumber. Kicker curled around Madelyn as was their custom, particularly now that the nights had grown so cold. And though part of Madelyn wanted to roll over into the warmth of Kicker's embrace, residual anger and resentment rendered her stiff and motionless until sleep, uneasy and haunted, finally claimed her.

"So, how'd you boys weather the storm out on the Steeple Seven, Milos?"

Milos accepted the glass that slid smoothly across the polished bar. "At last count, we lost about fifty head." He drained the glass and pushed it back for a refill. "Donnelly thinks it'll go higher, though. Some places we just couldn't push through the damned drifts to check."

"Wolves and cougars will be eating well, that's for sure."

Milos spat to one side at the mention of the ranchers' nemeses.

The door of the Windsor Hotel bar swung open and three Arbuster hands sauntered in.

Milos tensed. He was drinking alone, rare on a Saturday night. His usual cohorts, Whitford and Tyler, were absent—still out on the range rounding up strays.

"No trouble, Milos." The bartender gave his best customer a stern glance before moving down the bar. "Welcome, boys. Have the usual tonight?"

Milos sullenly hunched over his drink, idly eavesdropping on the Arbuster hands. Their talk was of the severity of the storm, the scarcity of women, and the weakness of the whiskey—when suddenly their words caught his attention.

"I swear. I heard young Rupe is offerin' twenty dollars for Rick-the-Stick's gun."

"Twenty? No word of a lie?" An incredulous whistle punctuated the second man's exclamation.

"Yep, twenty. Wisht to hell I knew where it was. That reward would buy me a mighty fine, mighty loooong time with them Calgary girls." He smirked at his friends and hitched his jeans.

His companions greeted the cowboy's cocky declaration with hoots of derision.

"Hell, Tommy, you'd hafta pay 'em twice that just for one night. 'Sides, they'd rob you and run you back to the ranch before you could even drop your drawers."

The rest of the cowboy's taunt was lost on Milos as he licked his suddenly dry lips. When the door swung open to admit another couple of men, lively music could be heard from down the street.

Milos jerked his head at the eastern wall of the hotel. "You know what's going on, Joe?"

The bartender nodded. "It's the annual Christmas pageant and box social down at the school. They're raising money to buy each of the kids an orange and some candies for Christmas. My youngest, Eugenia, has been so excited that she can barely sleep at night. I wish I could be there, but someone's gotta keep you boys from dying of thirst."

Milos mustered a weak grin and tossed back his drink. He shook his head when Joe began to tip the bottle again. "No, that's enough." He ignored the look of surprise on the bartender's face and dropped some coins on the bar. "I think I'll check out the excitement."

Milos headed for the door and made a point to avoid eye contact with any of the Arbuster hands. Milos had his own reasons for shunning their company and it had nothing to do with the traditional rivalry between the Steeple Seven hands and the Arbuster boys. Their words hadn't surprised him. He had heard rumours for the past ten days that Rupert Arbuster had increased the reward for the missing gun.

Milos tilted his sheep-lined collar up and stepped out into the cold. He stopped on the boardwalk and looked around. He hadn't really intended to follow through with going down the street to the school; it had just been an excuse to allay Joe's shock at his early departure.

Milos sighed deeply and exhaled a long stream of condensation into the still night air. *When the hell did it all get so complicated? Goddamnit!*

Unwilling to return to the Steeple Seven and face the amiable jibes of his fellows, Milos wandered toward the music. His early departure from the Windsor meant some of his pay was still in his pocket, and he had a hazy inclination to join the box social. Maybe he would even buy a lady's box lunch, if he wasn't too late.

By the time Milos reached the school, it was clear that the merriment had been underway for quite some time. The yard was filled with wagons and tethered horses. He heard spirited fiddle music and even frosted windows couldn't conceal the shadows of dancers stepping lively to a square dancing call.

Milos hesitated as a long submerged instinct nudged him. He unexpectedly craved the company of the settled and staid townsfolk who looked down on ranch hands like him. Then the momentary impulse was subsumed by the more urgent call of his bladder.

With a quick glance around to ensure there were no ladies present, Milos walked toward the far side of the school. As he turned the corner, he stumbled over a still figure, crouched below a window and leaning against the wall. The contact knocked the silent listener's hat off and made him drop the rifle that had rested between his knees.

"Shit! Sorry. I didn't know you was here. I was just gonna—"

The man scrambled for his hat, but a shaft of light from the window fell across his face.

"Jesus Christ!" Milos shuddered at the damage. "Pudge? Is that you? Bloody hell, man!"

Pudge jammed his hat down on his head and darted away, his back turned to Milos.

Openmouthed, Milos watched his one-time friend lope away, the rifle tucked under his arm. The last time he had seen Pudge was the night of the fire. Even then he had only had a glimpse of the unconscious man. Whitford had helped Seamus Kelly lift his brother into a wagon, while Milos fought the fire and Tyler rode for help.

Milos knew Pudge had been severely burned, but in his mind's eye, Pudge was still the cheerful Irishman with an endless supply of songs, stories, and jokes.

Most appreciated by Milos, though, had been Pudge's generosity with his home brew during his brief stay at the Steeple Seven. After the Kelly brothers were injured, he, Whitford, and Tyler had taken over running the small still Pudge had secreted in the woods. They gave a ritual toast to the Irishman with each new batch of the potent spirits.

What shook Milos the deepest was not the melted side of his former bunkmate's face or the missing ear, but the tears that ran unchecked down the unblemished half. Milos felt like he had been kicked in the balls by the MacDiarmid's prize bull. "Oh fuck! Fuck, fuck, fuck, fuck, fuck..."

Falling to his knees, Milos retched up every drop of the Windsor's best rye whiskey.

On days like these, Kicker really appreciated her job. Out on the street, the weather might freeze a rabbit in mid-jump, but inside the shop, it was toasty warm. Except when the door swung wide open and admitted some of the Arctic air.

Kicker looked up to admonish the newcomer for letting the cold in, only to smile when she recognized her customer. "Wynne. Haven't seen you in a month of Sundays. What can I do for you?"

Wynne sauntered over to Kicker's bench. "Actually, I have some news you may be interested in."

Just then John came in from the backyard carrying a half-finished barrel. He set his load down and nodded at the new arrival. "Wynne."

"John. I was just telling Kicker that I have some news that concerns her."

John raised an eyebrow and Kicker cocked her head inquisitively. She could see the gleam in Wynne's eyes. Whatever the news was, it was obviously very pleasing to her.

"You remember Del Milos, Kicker?"

Kicker shook her head uncertainly. John spoke up.

"You would probably be more familiar with him as part of the trio of Milos, Whitney, and Tyler."

Kicker's confusion cleared. "Oh, aye. They work for you, and they're...uh..."

"Fond of their drink. There's no disputing that, for sure. But they're decent men and good workers. Will and I figure as long as they don't let their moonshining get out of hand, they've got a job at the Steeple Seven."

Kicker looked at John. Judging by his smile, he knew what Wynne was about to say. When she focused back on Wynne, the look on her face reminded Kicker of an illustration she had seen of Alice's Cheshire Cat.

"So, he finally confessed, did he?"

"Yes, John, he did. Brought it to Donnelly Sunday morning, bright and early. Put his X on a statement attesting to where and when he found it, too. Swears that if it comes to trial, he'll be right there to testify."

John chuckled. "You might want to dry him out for a week beforehand, if it comes to that."

"Hah. He'd need drying out for more like a month before he could take the stand."

Kicker frowned at the dialogue going on over her head. "Excuse me, what are you talkin' about?"

Wynne shot her an apologetic look. "Aw, I'm sorry, Kicker. I'm just so pleased that Fortune finally smiled on us. Milos turned in Rick Biggart's gun yesterday. He swears he found it the night of the fire, right next to where Mr. Seamus Kelly and his unknown assailant had been rolling around in the dirt fighting. Says he just tucked it in his belt because he was so busy, and didn't even look at it until long after the fire was out. He apologized good and proper for not coming forward sooner. Says he forgot all about it until he overheard some of the Arbuster boys talking in the Windsor on Saturday night. I figure he had it hidden somewhere and got nervous about being found with it, but whatever the reason, I'm just glad he finally coughed it up."

"Biggart's gun? So that's evidence, right? He can be charged now?"

"Charged, yes. But remember, Kicker, we have no idea where he is, so it may all be moot."

"But if he's charged, an' if he's caught someday, then maybe we can get Rupert Arbuster, too."

John and Wynne exchanged glances and Wynne cautioned Kicker, "We don't know what Biggart will say if he's caught. Even if he implicates Rupert, there's nothing but his word against Arbuster's."

"An' who'd take that?" Kicker fought the bitterness that welled up inside her. She reminded herself that it was good news they could punish Biggart for his monstrous crime—if they could find him.

"Kicker." John quietly caught Kicker's eye. "Remember what I told you. Biggart is the brain that drives the beast. Without the brain, the beast will founder."

"Maybe. But he won' be punished. Damn the bastard!" Though Kicker wanted to dash down the street to tell Seamus and Pudge the good news, she was also galled by the thought that Rupert had wreaked havoc with impunity.

"Undoubtedly the Hereafter will render that verdict. But at least you needn't worry that either of them will come after you again. We'll spread the word far and wide about the warrant for Biggart's arrest. If he's not already gone south, you can bet he'll be halfway to California as soon as he hears his gun has shown up."

At Wynne's assurances, Kicker involuntarily glanced at the corner of the shop farthest from the door. An old cougar hide hung in that corner, and though it was impossible to see from a distance, the hide was riddled with knife holes. She and John had used the hide for their daily knife practice ever since it became too cold to go outside. It amused Kicker that John seemed to take particular delight every time a sharp blade pinned the hide to the wall. They even threw in tandem, trying to see how close they could come to each other's knives without knocking them aside.

Though it was a relief to know the threat had been lifted, Kicker wasn't going to stop carrying her boot knife or keeping a loaded shotgun over their bed. She might never need either, but she preferred to err on the side of caution.

"Esther will have lunch ready shortly, Wynne. Would you care to join us?"

"Love to, John. Just want to finish up with Kicker, and I'm ready to go."

"I'll go on ahead and let Esther know to set another place."

As John left, Kicker looked at Wynne curiously. "Finish up?"

Wynne nodded. "I am the bearer of an invitation from my mother for you and Madelyn to join us for the holiday festivities. She instructed me to tell you both that she's not taking no for an answer, and that your room awaits."

Kicker shifted uncomfortably and Wynne chuckled. "Don't let my esteemed parent intimidate you. Besides, if nothing else, you can enjoy the holiday without lifting a finger. Mother is practically dancing on air at the thought of you returning to the ranch for a few days."

"At the thought of Maddie returnin' to the ranch, you mean."

"Conceded, my friend, but the rest of us are looking forward to seeing you, too. You and Madelyn will have to share a room, as Albert's fiancée, Sarah, has Madelyn's old room. But I imagine you won't mind."

Kicker glanced at Wynne sharply, but couldn't read anything significant in her good natured expression.

"Mother and Sarah are busy planning the wedding. I know Mother is looking forward to getting Madelyn's input. She thought maybe your cousin would have some ideas garnered from her own wedding."

Is she trying to warn me? Kicker made a mental note to tell Madelyn to be ready with details of her "marriage" to the fictional Major. She mumbled an acknowledgement.

"Mother said that you are to ride home with them from church two Sundays from now, and stay until New Year's Day. After all, it's not every year that we see in a new century. Mother's got quite the celebration planned."

Having delivered her message, Wynne gave Kicker a tip of her Stetson. "Well, I've got some of Esther's wonderful cooking waiting for me. If there are any objections to

Mother's plans, have Madelyn send a note home with Laird. Otherwise, we'll see you in a couple of weeks."

Kicker was left to brood over the invitation. Though she had expected the command appearance from the MacDiarmid matriarch, a small part of her had still hoped that she and Madelyn could celebrate alone together.

Madelyn had been curiously reserved since the night of the blizzard, and the strain of staying at the Steeple Seven was not going to help resolve matters between them.

At leas' we'll be sleepin' in the same bed.

It was not much comfort.

CHAPTER 19

KICKER HAD SAT PERFECTLY STILL for an extremely long hour in the luxury of the MacDiarmid sitting room. The book on her lap lay unchanged, still open to its first page. Kicker's every muscle ached from tension. She wanted nothing more than to jump to her feet and start running...anywhere. She wondered if this was how a rabbit felt when it emerged from cover.

Daft fool. You're fine. This won' las' forever. Stay calm.

The self-admonition was just another version of the inner refrain that Kicker had used since she and Madelyn arrived at the Steeple Seven four days earlier. Kicker was having a great deal of difficulty with their current stay. She knew why, but knowing didn't ease her discomfort.

Kicker's gaze was fixed on three women having afternoon tea. They were gathered around the small, lace covered table by the window.

Madelyn turned her head and caught Kicker's eye. "Are you sure you wouldn't care for some tea, Kicker? It's delicious, and Mrs. Donnelly has quite outdone herself with these scones."

Not trusting herself to speak, Kicker shook her head and offered a weak smile.

"So, dear Maddie, you were telling us about the mother of one of your students appearing at your door to upbraid you? My goodness, she sounds like a perfect termagant. I swear I could not abide such company for even one moment. You have far greater forbearance than I could summon up in a lifetime of trying."

Madelyn laughed and picked up her story about Mrs. Berg as Kicker focused on Madelyn's companions. She had not been surprised by Mrs. MacDiarmid's dismissive attitude; she had no illusions about where she stood with the matriarch of the Steeple Seven. It was the third woman, the one so sweetly beseeching Madelyn to continue, who was the cause of Kicker's present consternation.

Sarah Binnington, Albert's fiancée, arrived from England in late fall. She had been chaperoned by an elderly governess who soon passed away from the rigours of their arduous travels. Mrs. MacDiarmid had assumed the role of Sarah's guardian until the young Englishwoman and Albert were married. The nuptials were set for the spring, once the couple's new house was completed. It would stand next to the homes of Albert's brothers.

The new addition to the MacDiarmid clan had translucent skin, pale blue eyes, and a cascade of thick, golden hair. Sarah's excellent taste in clothing was apparent in the lavish fashions that perfectly flattered her slender figure. Albert was clearly besotted with her. Even Mrs. MacDiarmid appeared to be enchanted by the exquisitely mannered newcomer.

Sarah coolly dismissed Kicker immediately upon their arrival. Conversely, the newcomer promptly set her sights on charming Madelyn. The young Englishwoman constantly sought Madelyn's counsel, and hung on her every word.

Accustomed to being slighted by her social superiors, Kicker at first ignored Sarah's blandishments toward Madelyn. But much to Kicker's surprise, within a day Madelyn had succumbed to Sarah's spell.

Kicker saw her flattered lover fall willingly into the role of the worldly confidant. Mrs. MacDiarmid, Sarah, and Madelyn quickly became inseparable. Countless hours, even on Christmas Day, had been consumed with wedding plans and gossip.

With a growing sense of unease, Kicker watched as Madelyn's new best friend laughed coquettishly and flirtatiously touched Madelyn's arm at every opportunity. Kicker felt hopelessly outmatched. She lacked any feminine wiles to compete with the vivacious Sarah. What made the situation worse was Madelyn's attitude when Kicker finally summoned the nerve to broach her misgivings. Madelyn airily dismissed Kicker's concerns and assured her that there wasn't the slightest cause for worry.

When Kicker doggedly pursued the matter, Madelyn became irritated. She insisted that Sarah was simply seeking friends in the strange new world in which she found herself. Madelyn asserted that it would be cruel to reject Sarah's friendly overtures and accused Kicker of unjustified jealousy.

Kicker watched Sarah playfully offer Madelyn a taste of her cake. *Tis not unjustified, Maddie. I may not know what Sarah is calculatin' to do, but I can smell a fox when she's in the henhouse.*

Blessedly, Kicker's bleak thoughts were interrupted.

Wynne beckoned to her from the doorway. "Kicker, I'm taking Laird and Billy out tobogganing. Care to saddle up Rabbit and join us for a few hours?"

Better than sittin' here watchin' Maddie be ensorcelled. "Aye, that soun's like a fine idea."

"Go put on something warm and we'll meet you out at the barn."

Wynne disappeared down the hall and Kicker rose to go. "Maddie, I—"

"I heard." Madelyn waved without looking. "Have fun, and do try to stay warm."

Kicker left the room and half ran up the stairs, barely able to breathe for the lump in her throat. Only when she was finally mounted on Rabbit did the thickness in her chest ease. The cheerful chatter from Laird and Billy, who were on a toboggan being towed behind Ballantrae, was a welcome distraction.

The brilliance of the bright sun on the fresh snow was almost blinding. When the first snows came, John taught Kicker the trick of smearing ash under her eyes to cut the glare. However, she had not paused in her headlong flight from the house so, pulling her hat lower, Kicker shaded her eyes as best she could.

"Let out the rope, Mama. We're getting snow in our faces."

Wynne played out the rope she had looped over her saddle horn. Kicker looked back at the boys as the toboggan drifted further from the horses' heels. She grinned as she saw Brander leap on and off the wooden conveyance, and bark when the boys threw snow at him.

"I think Brander is havin' as much fun as Laird and Billy."

"He usually does," Wynne agreed. "That far enough?"

"Give it a coupl'a more feet."

Wynne did so, then snugged off the rope on the saddle horn. At a particularly loud whoop of laughter from the boys, she chuckled. "If you think they're having fun now, wait until we get to the hill. They'll be rousing the bears from hibernation with all their noise."

Kicker nodded at the gun strapped to Wynne's thigh and the rifle in its saddle boot. "That why you always carry those...in case of bears?"

"Not to mention wolves, coyotes, and cougars. There are a lot of predators out here, and they don't all walk on four legs."

A chill swept through Kicker. "You mean Biggart? You think he'll come after us?"

Wynne shook her head. "No, he's not a fool. I really think he's long gone by now. It was more a general observation. When my father realized I was happiest at his side out on the range, he made damned sure I knew how to defend myself. He told me there would be a lot of men who resented my intrusion into their world, and that some of them would try very hard to put me in what they considered my place."

"Did they? Try, I mean?"

"Some did. Rarely a second time, though." Wynne shot Kicker a wry smile. "No doubt you're familiar with what I'm talking about."

"I am. But I bin lucky, too."

"I suspect you've probably made much of your luck. You work hard and you deal honourably with people. That tends to overcome a lot of resistance. Well, that plus time and familiarity."

"Worked for you, too?"

"Aye," Wynne drawled in a teasing imitation as she winked at Kicker.

Kicker laughed and felt the burden on her heart lighten. She may have been excluded from Madelyn's new friendship, but she was not without friends of her own.

"Kicker, that gorgeous set of candlesticks you gave your cousin for Christmas?"

"Aye?"

"Could I commission a similar set from you? Your work is absolutely brilliant, and I think it would make an excellent wedding gift for Albert and Sarah."

Though Kicker couldn't suppress an involuntary grimace at Sarah's name, she also felt a glow of pleasure at Wynne's request. She had worked hard through the autumn, using scraps of iron to make a set of intricate candlesticks for Madelyn. It was very much trial and error as she had always focused on the utilitarian aspects of her trade. But when she wrapped them, she was confident her gift would equal anything under the MacDiarmid tree.

Kicker had been disappointed when Madelyn's response was less than she'd anticipated. While she knew Madelyn could not be too effusive in front of their hosts, she'd hoped for more than the polite expression of gratitude she received. Maddie seemed more taken by the gown Sarah gave her—part of the extensive trousseau the bride-to-be brought with her from England.

Now Wynne's words were balm to Kicker's wounded ego. "You really liked them?"

"Very much. I've never seen finer craftsmanship. You and John might want to consider making candlesticks as a sideline. I have a contact in Calgary who would be thrilled to take them on consignment."

Kicker gave the matter some thought. She got a satisfaction from creating the candlesticks that shoeing horses had never provided, but she'd assumed it was simply because she was making something for Madelyn.

"I'd be proud to make a set for you, Wynne."

"For Albert and Sarah."

Kicker wondered at the faintly questioning note in Wynne's words. "Aye, for your brother and his bride."

Wynne sighed, glanced back to check on the boys, then looked at Kicker. "Please don't allow Sarah to trouble you. I've seen her sort before. She needs to seduce every man or woman who comes within her orbit. Albert hovers about her like a love addled pup, so she is bored with him. Madelyn is an alluring challenge. Sarah will soon enough tire of the game and move on to someone else."

"Seduce?"

"Oh, I don't mean in the carnal sense of the word. Women like Sarah live entirely for the sensual hunt. They are a mile wide and an inch deep when it comes to...well, to actual consummation. I suspect my brother will find his wedding night far less...satisfying than he hopes for. Trust me. Your cousin's marriage is in no danger, but she may find her feelings deeply bruised by the time Sarah is done with her. Like a siren, Albert's fiancée loves to beguile the unwary until they find themselves stranded on the rocks of her indifference."

Much to her amazement, Kicker found herself aching to confide in Wynne. She reminded herself that Wynne was not Lil. Madelyn would never forgive Kicker if careless words precipitated the loss of the MacDiarmid patronage. But she was desperate. "It's not just Sarah."

"No?"

"Maddie...my cousin's been diff'rent since the big blizzard."

"How so?"

"She's bin distant, like she's cross with me."

"Why? What happened during the storm?"

Kicker shrugged unhappily. "I don' know. I was drivin' the chil'ren home, an' I was late gettin' back because the sled tipped out at Paxton's farm. I know Maddie was scared. I know she thought sure I was dead out in the snow. What I don' know is why she's angry at me."

Laird's voice cut in from behind them. "We're almost there, Mama. Can we go fast now?"

Wynne looked at Kicker apologetically. "I usually give Ballantrae his head for this last little bit. It gives the boys a thrill."

Knowing how the boys felt, Kicker gave an understanding nod. "Go ahead. Rabbit could use the exercise."

They kicked their horses to a faster pace, to delighted shrieks from the boys and boisterous barking from Brander. A few minutes later they arrived at the base of a hill and pulled up.

Steep and long, but devoid of trees across the wide centre, the hill offered speedy runs with an acre of flat ground at the base for the riders to coast to a stop. The only potential obstacle was a small creek to the northern edge, but it was solidly frozen over.

Toboggan tracks were just visible through the light snowfall of the previous night. Large tree stumps had been hauled there for seating. They ringed the blackened remains of a campfire, evidence that this was a popular gathering site for children of the Steeple Seven.

Kicker followed Wynne's lead and slid off Rabbit. Laird and Billy ran up, pulling the toboggan behind them as Wynne reeled in the loose rope and laid the coil over her saddle horn.

"Go ahead, but stay on this side of the hill," Wynne instructed as her son and his best friend darted off. She knotted Ballantrae's reins around his neck, untied a saddlebag, and slapped his haunches. He ambled off in search of accessible grazing, followed closely by Rabbit.

"Come on, let's get the fire going. By the time the boys are tired, they'll need to warm up."

An axe was buried in one stump, and a stack of cut wood neatly piled next to the makeshift firepit was covered with canvas. Within moments they had extracted enough dry wood to get a fire blazing. Kicker and Wynne settled on two of the stumps and watched the boys and Brander. Wynne dug into the saddlebag and came out with a flask. She twisted the top off and offered it to Kicker.

"What is it?"

"Mrs. Donnelly's special eggnog. Guaranteed to keep you warm on the coldest winter day."

Kicker took a sip. The initial sweet smoothness surprised her, as did the burst of warmth that flooded her belly.

"You like it?"

"Aye, tis tasty stuff." Kicker held out the flask, but Wynne shook her head with a grin.

"Keep it. I've got another." The rancher pulled a second flask from the bag and took a long draught. "So, Kicker, I've been thinking about what you said—about you and your cousin being at odds since the blizzard."

"Aye?"

"I sincerely doubt that it has anything to do with you."

Kicker flashed Wynne a sceptical glance.

"No, really. Look, I've never been to England, but over the years my parents have told us what it's like. Judging by what they've said, it doesn't seem like you often have blizzards like we just had, right?"

"We have storms."

"Right, but I doubt they engender the same sense of helplessness, of overwhelming isolation, of loneliness and fear that being blocked in by six feet of snow does. Kicker, I've seen hardened men, natives of this land, driven mad in the depths of winter, even when they were in no immediate danger and had plenty of supplies."

"But I was only gone for a few hours. An' she was in town, not stuck alone somewhere out in the bush. John and Esther were right across the street; Seamus and Pudge jus' down at the station. Hell, she knows ever'one in town, an' they'd all gladly take her in if need be."

Wynne shook her head at Kicker's protests. "If she'd tried to reach anyone in that blizzard, she'd have been lost within ten feet of leaving her front door. But that's not my point. She didn't know where you were, the person she cares most about and on whom she depends. She had no idea if you were alive or dead, and she had no way to help you in any event. She was utterly powerless. All she could do was wait out the worst storm of her life, and pray."

Confused, Kicker dug her toe in and kicked snow at the fire. It sizzled and hissed as she thought about what Wynne said. Finally, she raised troubled eyes to her friend. "I din't understan'. When Rabbit and I were out in the storm, it was excitin'. I was colder than I'd e'er bin b'fore in my life, but it was like..." Kicker paused, at a loss to put the exhilaration of that ride into words.

"Like you were one with the land; your soul so filled with joy and your body so rooted that nothing could ever beat you down."

Kicker stared at Wynne in awe. *She understands.* "Aye. Twas a powerful feelin', worshipful, almos'."

"Your cousin doesn't feel the same way about this country."

"No. She don', but I thought she liked it well enough till the blizzard."

"I suspect until that night, she convinced herself that it wasn't all that different from what she'd left behind."

"You would ne'er say that if you saw the mansion she grew up in an' the schools where she taught."

Wynne laughed and drank deeply of the potent eggnog. "I was thinking more of the social and cultural aspects. Our schools, our government, our laws, even our entertainments are often a throwback to those you find in England. Hell, the hottest topic at the Rancher's Association meeting a few weeks back was starting a polo club this spring. I suspect when Madelyn hears her students singing *God Save the Queen*, it doesn't take much to imagine she's teaching in some remote corner of England. It's only when she stops to realize that she can't return to the bosom of London society with a short train ride that it really sinks in how far she is from home."

Kicker pursed her lips doubtfully. "From the way she talks about her classes, I don' think she's foolin' herself about where she is. She's never taught in such diff'cult conditions."

"I guess my point is that some immigrants, like you, take to the West as if they were born here. But for others, the beauty and freedom and space just aren't enough to outweigh the inherent hardships. Eventually those turn tail and run for the comfort and safety of home."

Kicker felt like Rabbit had kicked her in the stomach. "You think Maddie will give up and go back to England?"

"I'm not saying that. But I've noticed that it's often the highborn who fold first. They're used to an ease of life and rigid social structure that we don't have here. To be honest, my friend, and with no offence intended, in England it's doubtful that you and I would be sitting and talking as we are right now. I think it's a marvellous thing that we can do so, but many, particularly those just off the boat, would not agree. And that's just one small example of how the Old and New Worlds differ."

"It was Maddie's idea to come. She won' give up so easy."

Wynne raised an eyebrow as she raised her flask. "I thought it was her husband's idea."

Kicker was saved from having to answer as Laird and Billy came barrelling down the hill and overturned in a tangle of sled, boys, and dog. While Wynne hurried over to check that all limbs were intact, Kicker chastised herself for the slip. When Wynne returned, Kicker steered the conversation to less sensitive matters.

It wasn't until they were towing a tired and contented trio home on the toboggan that Wynne raised the topic again. "I really don't think you need to worry. Whether or not your cousin is finding it difficult to make the adjustment, the essential thing is that she moved out here for love. And love is more powerful than any blizzard, any twister, or fire. If she stays, it won't be because of my mother's scintillating conversation or Sarah's ingratiating charms, or even the satisfaction of teaching a bunch of students like those two." Wynne jerked her thumb back at the toboggan. "It will be because the only possible place she can envision is being beside the one she loves."

"An' if she leaves?"

Wynne gazed at Kicker calmly. "Then it will be because love wasn't enough. But we won't know until...well, until the Major arrives, will we? So in the meantime, don't give yourself conniptions."

They were as quiet as the tired boys for the rest of the trip. Conversation was desultory as they sent Laird and Billy up to the house and unsaddled the horses. Lost in thought, Kicker barely noticed Mrs. Donnelly's arrival in a buggy driven by one of the hands until Wynne spoke up.

"Back from town, Mrs. Donnelly? I didn't think anything would be open on Boxing Day."

"It's not, but Mr. Godwin has been holding the ranch mail for me since before Christmas. I thought I'd just pop by and pick it up after I had a nice visit with Mrs. Thatcher."

Wynne looked inquisitively at Mrs. Donnelly's large handbag. "Anything for me?"

"Not today, I'm afraid." Mrs. Donnelly looked at Kicker with a smile. "I took the liberty of picking up your mail too, though, and your cousin got two letters. Would you like to give them to her?"

"Thank you, Mrs. Donnelly, but I've got to change into somethin' dry."

"Right then, I'll just give them to her myself." Mrs. Donnelly bustled away while Wynne and Kicker walked at a slower pace back to the house.

"I expect the boys will be asleep before dinner time tonight." Kicker nodded at Wynne's idle comment, but said nothing. "Are you back to work tomorrow?"

"Aye. John said to be there at the usual time. I've not decided whether to go home t'night, or ride in early t'morrow."

"Will you come back out to the ranch after work? You'd be more than welcome."

"I don' think I will, no. It makes no sense to ride back and forth to the ranch when the house is jus' across the street."

"But your cousin will be staying until the New Year, won't she? Mother would be terribly disappointed if Madelyn left before the celebrations."

As would Sarah, no doubt. "That's up to Maddie. I believe she does plan to enjoy your hospitality for a few more days."

As Kicker grasped the front door's handle, Wynne laid a hand on her arm.

"Kicker, please know you are every bit as welcome as your cousin under the MacDiarmid roof."

Keeping her doubts to herself, Kicker acknowledged Wynne's words with noncommittal thanks.

They entered the house just as Madelyn's voice cried out.

Kicker instantly ran towards the parlour, Wynne close on her heels. They found Madelyn standing, staring at a sheaf of papers in her hand. Sarah and Mrs. MacDiarmid were gathered around her, clucking worriedly.

"Bad news from home, dear Maddie?"

Kicker wanted nothing more than to wipe the sickly sweet expression from Sarah's face with her fists, and break the arm that was wrapped firmly around her lover's waist. She took half a step, but felt Wynne's hand knot in the back of her coat and pull her to a stop.

Madelyn looked up and met Kicker's eyes. "It's... Father. He's dead."

Madelyn pleaded a headache and excused herself from her sympathetic audience to join Kicker in going up to their room. As quickly as the door closed, Kicker turned and opened her arms. Madelyn walked into her embrace and sagged against her.

Unsure whether her reaction should be relief or sadness, Kicker held Madelyn quietly. Finally she offered muted words of consolation. "I'm sorry about the bad news, Maddie. I know you were not on the bes' of terms, but he was your da, after all."

Maddie just shook her head, clutched Kicker tighter and mumbled words into her shoulder.

Puzzled, Kicker tried to decipher what she heard. "Did you say 'Lil', Maddie?"

Madelyn pulled back and looked at Kicker with tear filled eyes. "Yes. Mother wrote that Lil is very ill, and may not live until spring."

"So your da is a'right, then?"

"No. He is dead. The servants found him in bed one morning. The doctor said he most likely had a massive stroke sometime in the night. But I shall never grieve his death. As far as I'm concerned, I hope Father is now reaping the eternal damnation he so richly deserves for all the evil he sowed in his lifetime. But Lil...my dear, sweet Lil—Mother put news of her ill health in a postscript, as if it were no more than an afterthought, but all I can think of is that she is alone, with none to care for her."

Saddened, Kicker thought of the woman whom she'd known for such a short time. The fact that Madelyn loved her would have been enough in itself to incline Kicker favourably towards the seamstress, but Lil won Kicker over with her warmth, generosity, and insight. She grieved for the elderly woman, too.

Madelyn clutched Kicker's arm fiercely. "We could go back, Kicker. With Father no longer a threat, we could return to London and I could take care of Lil."

Kicker did not like the fevered glitter in Madelyn's eyes. "Maddie..." Gently disengaging Madelyn's grip, she guided her across the room to the chairs that abutted the window. "Let's talk."

"Don't you see? The confluence of Father's death and Lil's illness—it's the hand of Fate. We must be meant to return immediately. We must be."

Bless'd Jesus. An' I thought Sarah was my biggest problem. Cautiously, Kicker tried to reason with her. "We knew when we lef' England that we would probably ne'er see Lil again, is that not so?"

Madelyn's rigid posture displayed a stubborn intransigence, and Kicker sighed inwardly. "Though tis sooner than we feared, we a'ready made our final farewells to Lil. She knew that to be so. Surely she would not ask us to rush back on her b'half."

"She shouldn't have to ask for help, Kicker. She was a second mother to me, often much more so even than Mother. I owe her everything."

"And what do you owe us, Maddie? We're buildin' a life here, a good life. What do you owe us?"

Kicker gave her a few moments to mull that over and then pulled out her trump card. "Do you remember, what you said to me on the train to Liverpool?"

Madelyn sullenly shook her head and refused to meet Kicker's gaze.

"You tol' me we were not leavin' for fear of your da. You spoke of dreamin' a life as you chose to live it. Do you remember that, love?"

"I suppose... I may have said that."

"But mos'ly, you spoke of freedom, Maddie. To be free of old b'liefs and rules. To be free to live the adventures you only e'er read about. To be free to choose our own destiny. We're not explorin' the wilds of Africa, love, an' tis not perfect here, but there is freedom in this New World, jus' as you said there would be. Would you turn your back now, with our dreams in reach? Lil would not choose that for you. You know tis true."

Madelyn's head dropped and her shoulders slumped. "Damn you." The words were weary rather than angered.

Casting around for a diversion, Kicker noticed two envelopes in Madelyn's hand. "Who's t'other letter from, love?"

Without glancing at the letters, Madelyn extended them to Kicker. "I didn't look after reading Mother's."

Kicker looked at the return address on the unopened letter and blinked in surprise. "Tis from Lil."

Instantly Madelyn snatched the envelope from Kicker's hand and tore it open. Before reading it, she looked at Kicker defiantly. "If Lil writes to ask me to return to England, I'm going, no matter what."

Damnation! Kicker held her breath while Madelyn scanned the page, then wordlessly held it out to her. Kicker practically sagged in relief as she read Lil's letter. *Aye, you knew your girl, Lil. Bless you.*

My dearest Madelyn,

I suspect that by now you have heard from your mother about my health issues. I was feeling poorly the day she dropped by. Though I begged her not to mention my troubles to you, I think it likely that, being kind-hearted, she did so nonetheless. I write now to urge you against precipitous action. In truth, my dear girl, I am fine. I merely had a touch of influenza, which has been making its annual rounds with particular fervour this year. I am now fully recovered, and I look forward to many more years of our correspondence.

I receive your letters with great joy and anticipation, and spend hours picturing your new life there. It sounds as if you and your cousin are faring well, and this pleases me deeply. I am so proud of you, Madelyn. If I have not told you that often enough, then please forgive this old woman. You carry my dreams with you, and always will. Of all the children I raised and cherished, you will do those dreams the greatest of honour.

You also carry my love with you, dear Maddie. I trust you know that, and will always hold me close to your heart. You are as dear to me as any daughter could be. If you will permit me the liberty of speaking to you as your own mother might, may I ruminate upon a matter of some import? From your earliest years, I tried to instil in you a balance of duty and independence. There were times I feared you erred in favour of the latter course. But now, with the virtue of age, I see with increased clarity that your independence was never a flaw of your character, but its defining attribute.

Maddie, you have chosen a difficult path, and for this I most humbly salute you. You have the courage that I lacked. Though I was not unhappy with my life—how could I be when it brought me both you and dear Vivian—I would not willingly choose the same again. My admiration for you and your cousin abounds, and I confess myself deeply envious of your adventure. Had I two score less years, I would join you and see for myself the wonders you so vividly relay to me.

As I conclude in the waning of this day, I beseech you to cling tightly to your dreams, Maddie. Though many would argue, I know with all my heart that dreams such as yours find favour in God's eyes. Hew rigidly to truth, fidelity, and loyalty, but most fervently, to love, for it will lift you up and bear you through the most difficult of times.

I remain as always,

Your devoted servant,

Lillian

Kicker closed her eyes momentarily in relief, then glanced at Madelyn. She stared absently out the window and rubbed Lil's gold wedding band on her hand.

"Maddie?"

Madelyn turned to her with a sad smile. "I'm fine, dearest. Forgive my momentary lapse. I did not mean to distress you."

"Tis a'right, Maddie. Twill all be a'right. You'll see."

"I know." With visible effort Madelyn drew herself erect. "I suppose we'd better pack for our return to town."

Kicker's eyebrows lifted in surprise. "I thought you were stayin' here for the rest of the week, love. Mrs. MacDiarmid and Sarah will be sore disappointed if you leave early."

"So be it. I want to see in the new century with the woman I adore."

"I could come back here on New Year's Eve—"

"Ah, but I wish to wake early on the first morning of 1900 and make love to the glorious creature next to me, without thought to who might hear her cries of pleasure... or mine."

"That may be the bes' idea I e'er heard."

"Yes?"

"Aye."

And for a brief while, the time for talk was over.

An hour later, pleading an inability to celebrate due to the strictures of mourning, Madelyn was able to extricate herself from the clutches of Mrs. MacDiarmid and Sarah. She and Kicker were on the road to town before night fell.

Kicker had never been happier to open the door of the nondescript little house. Though Madelyn was quiet during the ride, she too seemed pleased to be home again. While Kicker hastened to build up fires in the kitchen stove and parlour fireplace, Madelyn took their bags upstairs.

When the chill finally receded, they made a simple supper out of the bounty Mrs. MacDiarmid insisted on sending home with them. A short while later, they retired for the evening. Both were eager to pick up where propriety dictated they leave off in their bedroom at the Steeple Seven.

Later, with Madelyn sleeping soundly in her arms, Kicker tried to summon the resolve to follow her own ironclad rule. Since the day they moved in, no matter how long or how late they made love, she always insisted they rise and don sleeping garments before their final descent into sleep. But on this night, the bliss of their naked bodies entwined and the joy of renewed physical and emotional harmony made it impossible to break away from Madelyn, even for a few moments.

Jus' for t'night. Jus' one night...

It was Kicker's last conscious thought before she fell into a deep, restorative sleep.

The next morning, Kicker slipped quietly out of bed, not wishing to rouse Madelyn. But her lover rolled over to watch her dress and smiled sleepily in the near dark.

"Shhh, go back to sleep, love. Tis early. You needn't rise yet. I'll build up the fire b'fore I leave."

"And I'll have the fire stoked when you come home." Madelyn deliberately tugged the heavy bedding below her breasts.

Kicker's eyes widened and she dropped to her knees next to the bed. "How can you be so cruel when you know I have to go to work?"

"Cruel, dearest?" Maddie raised her arms above her head and arched into a long stretch. "Whatever do you mean?"

With a groan, Kicker thrust her hand under the covers and lowered her head to the irresistible temptations Madelyn's action exposed. Within moments Madelyn was writhing and clawing at Kicker's back, and when she arched again, it was with an abandoned cry of exhilaration.

Kicker gentled her lover back under the covers with a smug smile. Lowering her head for a kiss, she was surprised when Madelyn tugged on the waistband of her pants.

"Get these off."

"I've not the time, Maddie. I mus' get to work."

"Get them off now. Trust me, this won't take long."

Aye, that's the truth.

Kicker quickly shucked her pants, but left her shirt hanging unbuttoned as she straddled her lover.

The first touch of Madelyn's mouth left her holding helplessly to their iron headboard. Slender arms embraced Kicker's naked thighs as her lover's tongue worked its magic.

"Bless'd Jesus, woman. What are you doin' t'me?"

Madelyn didn't pause to respond. True to her initial assertion, it didn't take long before Kicker cried out her pleasure.

Kicker collapsed and stared blindly at the ceiling. "Sweet mother of...how d'you expect me to work all day after that?"

A warm hand slid up the center of Kicker's exposed body, caressing and exploring. Kicker seized the tantalizing fingers and held them tightly. "Oh no—no more, Maddie. I'll not be able to lift so much as a poker if you do that to me again."

Soft laughter met her feeble protests. A few minutes later Kicker summoned enough energy to roll off the bed and don her trousers again.

"Will you be home for lunch, dearest?"

Kicker glanced at the bed where Madelyn had huddled back under the bedding. "I'd thought to go see Seamus and Pudge, but if you're plannin' to serve lunch as you did breakfast..."

Madelyn reached from beneath the bedding and stroked Kicker's thigh. "That could be arranged."

Kicker stepped back with a grin that matched Madelyn's and shook her head in mock remonstrance. "Insatiable wench."

"Better have something to eat before you go, dearest. You'll need your strength...for later."

With those self-satisfied words, Madelyn rolled over and snuggled down in the pillows. Kicker watched her for a few moments as relief and love battled for ascendancy. She had her lover back for the first time since the blizzard. "I'll see you in a few hours, Maddie."

Madelyn murmured something unintelligible in response to Kicker's whispered words. Unable to keep the smile off her face, Kicker took the narrow stairs three at a time, landing on the kitchen floor with a soft thump.

The smile stayed in place through a hurried breakfast and as she made a quick trip to the barn to check on Rabbit and Galahad. It was only when she rounded the corner to find the barn door ajar that her grin vanished.

Even in the dim light, Kicker could see the bloody streaks that limned chaotic markings in the snow. She snarled and ran toward the door. She wrenched it open and saw Rabbit and Galahad standing calmly in their stalls.

Instantly understanding what had happened, Kicker knelt to look more closely at the snow. "Bless'd Jesus! The trap worked."

She rose to her feet and saw drag marks and a blood trail leading away from the barn. During the night, someone had crawled away with a heavy iron trap clamped on his leg.

And Kicker had no doubts about the identity of the night prowler.

CHAPTER 20

KICKER GLANCED FROM THE TELLTALE marks in the snow up to their small bedroom window. She bit her lip as she tried to decide what to do. Her first instinct was to brush away the evidence of the intrusion in case Madelyn decided to take Galahad for a ride today.

Kicker's second, stronger instinct was to seek advice and validation of her suspicions from her employer, mentor, and protector, the man who had proved his staunch friendship day after working day.

Tis possible I'm wrong. But as Kicker jogged across the street and around to John and Esther's back door, she was convinced she wasn't. Biggart had finally made his move. The thought of what could have happened the previous night terrified Kicker. At the same time she found a perverse relief in the near certainty that her enemy had failed in whatever he had planned to do.

Takin' a chunk outta his leg might not slow him down for long, but damned if the bastard won' think twice about comin' after me an' mine the nex' time.

Kicker took some comfort from her defiant thoughts as she rapped softly at the Blue Wolfs' kitchen door.

John was eating breakfast and looked up in surprise as Esther admitted their early visitor.

Kicker bobbed her head apologetically to Esther. "I'm sorry to disturb you, Ma'am."

Esther nodded calmly, accustomed to visitors with emergencies at all hours.

John rose to his feet. "Is there a problem?"

"Not at the shop; I've not e'en been there yet. But there may be a big problem with..."

Kicker trailed off, unsure how much Esther knew. She didn't want to alarm the woman unnecessarily. Fortunately, she didn't have to say another word. John grabbed his coat and hat, and followed her.

Kicker explained the situation as they crossed the street. "...an' I set it jus' like you showed me. He mus' not ha' known it was there til it snapped shut."

John said nothing as he followed the trail from the barn to the back of the school. Kicker restrained her impatience as she watched him examine the telltale marks. His face was unreadable. When at last John stood, his voice was grave and his eyes worried.

"I believe you are correct, Kicker." John pointed out the numerous tracks and droppings within a tight circle. The trampled snow told the story of a horse that had been tied in one spot for a long time, and the man who had alternately crouched and paced in the same area. "Your intruder lurked here for quite some time. I expect he was waiting for everything to quiet down. Were you and Mrs. Bristow up late last night?"

Kicker blushed as she remembered why their bedroom candle had burned until almost midnight. "Aye. Twas a late night."

"Esther was awake with the baby about one a.m., and our lantern was lit for almost an hour, too. I could still hear noise from the Windsor after that. Who knows how long he waited until he felt it was safe to make his move?"

"So you do think twas him, then?"

"Without witnesses we can't be certain, but the odds are good. Why would anyone but Biggart wait so patiently, for so long? Rupert certainly wouldn't. Judging by the colour and viscosity of the blood, it couldn't have been more than three hours ago."

Kicker nodded grimly. "I don' e'en know how he could'a remounted with that trap on his leg."

"Biggart is an unusually dogged man. If necessary, he would cut off his own leg to escape. If you hadn't blunted the teeth of the trap, we might now be looking at his corpse. The threat to you would be over, and the town would be better for his death."

John's tone was even, but Kicker felt the mild rebuke. When she first came up with the idea of some way to protect the horses the previous fall, John found her an old bear trap with offset jaws and nearly a foot spread. But it was Kicker's initiative to blunt the teeth. Then, as now, her imagination pictured what a fully engaged bear trap would do to a man's leg. She could not do it, even to Biggart.

Kicker admired John deeply, but she was aware that he put people in three camps—friends, enemies, or irrelevant. John had no compunction about doing whatever it took to protect those he counted friends and family. For Kicker, some things were not black and white. While she had no doubt she could kill in direct protection of her loved ones, Kicker had no experience with being in the eye of a feud.

Kicker hated the village schoolteacher of her youth from whose whip she frequently ran. She loathed Merrick Grindleshire for his arrogant courtship of Madelyn and his casual assumption that the teacher would be his. She feared Timothy Bristow in an abstract way for the danger he posed to her relationship with Madelyn. But until she became a target for Rupert Arbuster and Rick Biggart, Kicker never imagined the lengths to which an adversary might go.

So, unable to contemplate injuring any human being so severely, Kicker disregarded John's advice and filed the tips of teeth to blunt their murderous power. At the same time, though, she sabotaged the trip mechanism. It would be nearly impossible for someone to open the trap by themselves once it was sprung. Given her preparations, Kicker was incredulous that Biggart managed to get away.

"When I set the trap, I thought certain I anchored it soun'ly. Twas sure I'd hear him and catch him in the act. It must'a hurt like livin' death when it closed on him."

John nodded. "He's either abnormally resistant to pain, or you were sleeping unusually soundly."

As she and John retraced the drag marks splotched with blood to the back of the barn, Kicker chastised herself for the lapse in security. *Damn fool. E'en had you heard him, he'd ha' bin long gone by the time you donned your clothes and got out to the barn with the gun.*

Setting aside her self-remonstrations for the moment, Kicker pointed at the small, frozen pool of blood outside the barn door. "Could you follow his trail, John?"

"Not for long. Looks to me like he headed directly for the road. No way to pick his tracks out from everyone else's except by the blood trail, and it'll be churned up by now."

In the interval since Kicker fetched John, the townspeople had awakened. Horses and wagons were already moving on the street, and identifying one set of prints would be impossible.

"Biggart's no fool. He's kept out of sight for months now. You know he's got a secure hiding spot. He'll go to ground until he's fit to move about again."

Kicker knew John was undoubtedly right, but his calm assessment was chilling in its implications.

"He's a patient man. And now he'll be a very angry man. Biggart has always done Rupert's bidding and kept his own counsel, but this will make it personal for him." John lowered his gaze from the horizon to Kicker, and she was shocked at the concern in his eyes.

"Maybe he'll bleed to death." Kicker knew her words lacked conviction.

"Maybe. I'm going to go finish my breakfast, but we'll discuss our options at work today."

As John strode away, Kicker grabbed a shovel from the barn. She worked quickly to obscure the tracks and blood even as she sought solutions. *Depen's how bad he's hurt. We have at leas' a few weeks, or even months til he heals. Or he may be crippled up so bad he'll ne'er be a threat again. Best stay ready for the wors', though.*

By the time the snow was unreadable, Kicker had come to one conclusion: the teeth of the trap would never be blunted again. This was war, and the consequences if she failed to protect her own were too terrible to consider.

Kicker's imagination conjured up an image of a hamstrung Rabbit, or their barn or house in flames. As horrendous as those things would be, Kicker knew she would survive those disasters. She could even picture her own death with a certain degree of equanimity.

The one thing that almost brought her to her knees was the anguish of imagining harm to Madelyn. Turning to face their bedroom window, Kicker made a silent vow. *From now on, tis naught that I'll stay my hand from to protect you, my love.*

One trembling fist clutched an almost empty bottle. The other raised an axe, blunt side down. With a desperate inhalation of air and liquor, the axe swept downward and smashed against the implacable metal.

It held.

Enraged, the man swung again and again. He barely noticed when a poorly aimed swing caused the axe to ricochet off the trap and glance off his imprisoned leg.

Finally, a lucky blow sprang the trap, and a guttural scream of torment and triumph echoed through the old cabin.

Outside, a nervous gelding, with bleeding scrapes and welts on its flanks, flinched and reared. The unearthly sounds that came from the interior terrified the animal. He reared again and again, desperate to get away from the rage and the blood.

The animal's efforts did not loose him. The mad, pre-dawn sprint through the forest ended with the rider falling from the horse's back, but the wounded man tied his mount securely before he dragged himself into the cabin.

Finally there was silence.

Kicker knocked at the station house door, and swung it open.

Seamus was at his desk, sending a Morse signal. She hung up her heavy coat as she admired how rapidly his finger tapped the key. When Seamus finished transcribing the train order, he leaned back and smiled. "Well, Miss Kicker, I had no idea I would have the pleasure of your company today."

"There's not much goin' on right now. John said tis always like this at Christmas. He sent me home early."

"I was about to make some tea. Will you join me?"

Kicker followed him into the small kitchen and took her usual seat at the table. "Where's Pudge?"

"Out."

Shocked at the uncharacteristic behaviour, Kicker stared at her friend's back as he pumped water into the kettle. "Out? But...tis still daylight."

Seamus turned to face her. He leaned against the counter as if too weary to stand unsupported. "He ventured out on Christmas Day, and has gone out every day since. He's been using a pair of the snowshoes you gave us."

"But that's won'erful, Seamus."

"Is it?"

Kicker shot her friend a puzzled look. "Is it not?"

"Perhaps." Seamus said no more until he set the table and took a seat opposite her. "I thought I would be pleased when he finally felt secure enough to go outside in the daylight, Kicker. I thought it would be a start to him reclaiming his life. I could understand if he ever raged against the unfairness of what happened...if he cried for the dreams lost, or showed any emotion at all... But I have never seen any man so utterly focused, so preternaturally calm. I don't understand what drives him so. He barely returns here to sleep, and I cannot remember when we last shared a meal. I fear for his health and sanity."

Saddened, Kicker reached across the table and touched her friend's hand. "I'm so sorry, Seamus. I thought he was doing better. Mr. Godwin tol' me Pudge is supplyin' him with fresh game to sell."

A glimmer of a smile lightened Seamus' expression. "He has been, yes. And it is a good sign. At least there is a benefit to his incessant roving. I would never have considered my brother a hunter, but as his skills improve, he seems to have built a thriving little business. When things seem the bleakest and I've not seen him for days, I take comfort from that. I believe it builds his confidence, not to mention his purse. Having to abandon our homestead claim meant we could never be the potato kings he dreamt us, but we will be able to live a decent life."

"Then p'rhaps the wors' is behin' him."

"You could be right. But I will feel much better when he sleeps and eats and speaks as normal men do."

"An' plays music."

Seamus' expression grew doleful again. "That may be too much to ask for, though I would give anything to see him pick up his flute again."

"Is there naught we can do to help him settle, to draw him back into an e'ryday world?"

"I am certainly open to suggestions. I have tried everything I could think of to convince him that his life did not end with the fire, to encourage him to dream anew of a bright future. Before we left Ireland, every dawn saw him with a new scheme to win a girl's heart or pad his purse. Now, Pudge does not appear to plan beyond the next excursion into the forest." Seamus gave Kicker a wry smile. "God help me, I've even continued to pray on my brother's behalf, though I suspect my entreaties were ill received in Heaven, absent from His host as I have been this past year."

Kicker was surprised at Seamus' confession. Her friend rarely spoke of religion or his break with the Church. She fumbled for comforting words but could find none.

"Do not fret. Though I am bereft of my faith in many things, I hold tight to faith in my brother. It may take time, but Pudge will defeat his demons. One morning he will wake up and wonder why he has absented himself from the world he once enjoyed. This near recluse is not who he truly is. My brother could never be a genuine misanthrope. The fire may have ruined his face, but nothing can ever ruin his soul. We need only have patience and compassion, and he will again be the Pudge we love."

Kicker wondered if that would truly be enough, but for her friend's sake summoned up some optimism. "Aye, then. That we can do."

"We can, and we will." Seamus forced a smile and rose. "I hear the kettle summoning us to tea. May I offer you some shortbread? Grandmother Kelly gave me the recipe, and I swear an angel must have whispered it in her ear."

Whilst Seamus completed the preparations, Kicker mulled over her dilemma. She had planned to tell her friend of the morning's events and seek his counsel, but she did not wish to add to his troubles.

The issue was taken out of her hands when Seamus filled their cups. "And what distresses you this fine day? Is it the death of your uncle?"

My uncle? Oh. "How did you..."

"My telegraph wires are outmatched by Mrs. Thatcher when it comes to disseminating information. I encountered the good mistress at the general store earlier today, and she was eager to tell me the latest news from the Steeple Seven."

Kicker shook her head in amusement. "Villages are the same..."

"...on either side of the ocean. Yes, I agree. So, is it the passing of Mrs. Bristow's father that puts those worry lines in your forehead? Are condolences in order?"

"No, not at all. Maddie's sire was an evil man, and his passing is of no loss to the world. Even Madelyn will tell you her father mus' now sit at Satan's right han'."

One of Seamus' eyebrows shot up. "Truly, then?"

"Aye. I doubt any in his family will mourn him at length."

"Then if it is not his death, what perturbs you so?"

Kicker bit her lip as she stared into her tea.

"I hope that you know you may confide anything to me."

Kicker was startled by the depth of sincerity in Seamus' voice. She looked up to find him regarding her affectionately.

"Though I am no priest, I will treat your confidences as if they were uttered in the confessional."

"Aye. I know that. I only wisht not to add to your burdens, but p'rhaps tis best you know." Kicker took a deep breath and told of the trap she had set and of the quarry she had so briefly snared.

Seamus was silent after her recitation. Kicker wondered if she would see a resurgence of the icy wrath he had displayed on first learning the identity of the arsonist who had so severely injured his brother. To have been so close to catching Pudge's assailant and to have lost him would be nearly as hard for Seamus as it was for her. To Kicker's relief, he remained calm.

"And John believes it was Biggart?"

"Aye. By the brightness of the blood, John judged the time the trap was sprung to be long after midnight. An' whoe'er it was, stood an' watched from behin' the schoolhouse 'til he was certain to be unseen. Who but that bastard would have such patience?"

"I do not dispute Mr. Blue Wolf's assessment of the matter. Did he suggest a course of action?"

Kicker shook her head. "We talked it o'er t'day. He said the only surefire way to fin' Biggart's lair would be to follow Rupert Arbuster e'ry day from sun up to sun up. We've none of us time for that."

"Hmmm. Have you told your cousin of what transpired this morning?"

Kicker froze. That was the question that had torn at her all morning. It had been with reluctant steps that she had entered their home at noon. Much to Kicker's relief, Madelyn was doing laundry, her partner's least favourite chore. Dishevelled and soaked as she bent over the scrub board, Maddie was ill inclined to pursue the carnal promise she made Kicker that morning.

Kicker wisely kept her own counsel on the broken promise and instead offered assistance with the detested task. Madelyn testily informed her that no help was required, but that Kicker would have to make her own lunch.

Kicker grabbed some nearly frozen jerky and biscuits from the cellar, and retreated to the welcoming warmth of the forge. There she thawed out her meal, relieved that she hadn't had to feign a desire for intimacy when she had so much on her mind.

Now, however, Seamus was waiting for an answer. Kicker could tell he was not going to allow her to slip the question.

"No. I did not."

"Why?"

"I did not wish to worry her."

"And?"

"An'?"

Seamus fixed a mildly accusatory gaze on Kicker. "And what is it you are concealing, my friend?"

Kicker ran her hands through her hair. Though she averted her gaze, she knew Seamus regarded her steadily, awaiting her answer. "I don' wan' to give her any reason to think ill of this place, of the people here."

Seamus frowned at Kicker's muttered words and bent closer. "Pardon me?"

"I don' wan' her to think ill of Galbraith's Crossin' an' insist on returnin' to England."

"I see." Seamus straightened up and leaned back in his chair as he stared at Kicker. "Do you think this a possibility?"

"She's bin...unhappy of late. Knowin' that a madman has beset us...beset me..." Kicker could not finish the thought, but Seamus nodded slowly.

"I understand your dilemma."

They sipped their tea quietly and Kicker took a bite of Grandmother Kelly's shortbread. Though part of her mind registered its thick, sweet flavour, it might as well have been dust in her mouth.

"If Miss Madelyn made such a decision, what would you do?"

Kicker raised bleak, fearful eyes to Seamus. "I have no idea."

"Please don't insist we put our clothes on, dearest. Tonight of all nights, I want to lie this way with you until morning."

Madelyn felt Kicker go still beneath her, and wondered again at her lover's strange insistence that they always redress after lovemaking. She had initially assumed it was for warmth during the long winter nights. But as Madelyn had often pointed out, with both the kitchen stove and parlour fireplace well stoked and a pile of thick blankets and quilts over them, they were in no danger of freezing.

Playing her trump card, Madelyn pushed off her lover's body just enough to create a delightful friction as she let her breasts slide over Kicker's.

With a half groan, Kicker wrapped her arms around Madelyn and pulled her down. "You don' fight fair, Maddie."

Content that she had won, Madelyn chuckled and snuggled back into place. She loved the feel of Kicker's warm, naked body against her own. "I can't think of a better way to celebrate the coming of a new century, can you?"

A hand softly stroked her rumpled hair. "No, my love, but then I can think of no better way to celebrate the comin' of any day than to make love to you."

Madelyn did not try to suppress her delighted smile as she hugged Kicker even closer. "Do you suppose it's officially the twentieth century yet?"

"I didn't hear the clock strike, though given what you were jus' doin' to me, I may well ha' missed it."

Just as Madelyn opened her mouth to suggest a reprise their clock gonged and coincided with the sound of gunfire and exuberant shouts from the Windsor Hotel. The celebratory cacophony went on for several minutes as the women listened. When the last of the noise faded, Madelyn raised her head and looked down at Kicker by the light of their single candle.

"Happy New Year, dearest."

"Happy new century, Maddie."

Madelyn allowed herself a long moment to savour the love reflected in Kicker's eyes before she lowered her face for a kiss.

Like Kicker, the kiss was slow but ardent, powerful, and gentle all at the same time. While Madelyn's body revelled in the sensations, part of her mind marvelled at how far they had travelled since the day she and Kicker first met at the train station.

Such an unlikely union, yet never did I believe I would find one so perfect for me...

Then Kicker urged her up, and as Madelyn rose to her knees all thought fell away. Her sole focus on the tantalizing movements of Kicker's hand between her legs, Madelyn groaned at the sensations of being separated, stroked, and penetrated. Her eyes fluttered shut and her body flexed in the candlelight.

"Bless'd Jesus. You are so beautiful, Maddie."

The hissed whisper recalled Madelyn fleetingly from the edge, but then she opened her eyes and saw the smouldering intensity of Kicker's gaze as her lover's insistent fingers controlled her. In that instant Madelyn lost control.

With a cry Madelyn fell forward and strained against Kicker's hand to prolong her pleasure. Finally, she slumped over the wiry body and buried her face against Kicker's neck. Maddie could feel the wild pumping of her lover's heart, and knew hers beat the same.

Eventually Madelyn felt the chill of the room and pulled the covers up over them as she eased to one side. Languidly she posed an unspoken question by teasing Kicker's nipples, but a weary chuckle told her that Kicker was just as sated. Anticipating the swift arrival of sleep, Madelyn wrapped an arm and leg around Kicker. She was drifting contentedly towards sleep when Kicker's voice roused her.

"You said somethin' earlier about changin' the date for your late, lamented husban's passin'?"

"When I wrote Lil yesterday, I told her not to send the notice of passing until late spring. It's bad enough that I have to don mourning for Father. I certainly regret blurting out the news of his passing. I think I can get away with two months of half mourning for him, but of course once my putative husband dies, I'll have to don full mourning for at least two years. I'm not looking forward to such a lengthy period of unrelenting black, I can assure you."

"You look as beautiful in black as e'ry other colour."

"Thank you, dearest, but it can become dreary very quickly. My mother came from a large family, and when I was a child, she and Grandmother were forever in black, mourning one relative or another. Thank heavens traditions have eased with the years. Form does not seem quite as rigid here, though of course I'll have to adhere to the local customs."

"At leas' the men will keep their distance for that span."

"I suppose, and that is a benefit, but every now and then my soul simply cries out for colour." Madelyn felt an unexpected sadness overwhelm her. "There is so little colour around us in these winter months."

Kicker's arms tightened around her and Madelyn clung to her lover. *Whatever would I do without you, beloved?*

Resolutely, Madelyn pushed back the depression that had hovered just below the surface ever since the first snow flew. "Sarah has asked me to be her bridesmaid, and while I may have to wear muted colours, I do not intend to be in black for the wedding."

At the mention of Sarah's name, Madelyn felt Kicker's body stiffen. She sighed inwardly and wearily rallied herself to defend her new friend yet again, but Kicker said nothing. Trying to divert Kicker from groundless fears, Madelyn continued as if nothing were amiss. "Did you know that their wedding will be the first event to be held in the new opera house?"

That sparked a reaction from Kicker. "Tis a lark that they give it such a fancy name. Tis jus' a parish hall."

"Actually, it's to be more elaborate than that, dearest. I believe there will be an upper balcony surrounding the stage and seating area. According to Agnes, Will is working to have Galbraith's Crossing added to the itinerary of the travelling opera and play companies that pass through Calgary. And certainly magic lantern shows will come our way. It really will be a centre for entertainment as well as a community meeting place."

"Will it be built in time, d'you think? The groun's so frozen they won' e'en be able to start until late March."

"If Agnes MacDiarmid has anything to say in the matter, it'll be finished. She's quite insistent that Sarah and Albert are to be married by Easter, or as soon thereafter as possible."

"Mmmm."

Madelyn found Kicker's noncommittal murmur exasperating. She did not understand the instant dislike her lover had taken to Sarah. "Aren't you looking forward to the wedding, dearest? Agnes told me that Mr. Kelly has been invited to play with the band." Kicker was quiet so long that Madelyn wondered if she had drifted off. She nudged her. "I know you enjoy listening to him."

"I loved to listen to both of them. Twould barely seem fittin' to hear Seamus 'thout Pudge. Besides, it matters not. I won' be invited."

Madelyn rose on her elbow and stared down at Kicker. "Of course, you will. In fact, I thought that your rose coloured gown would be just the thing for you to wear."

"Maddie," Kicker's voice was gentle, but insistent, "Mrs. MacDiarmid and Sarah will not want me there, rose coloured gown or no. I matter no more to them than the meanest cowhand. You have to know that."

"But you mean everything to me. And if they'll not have you, then they shall not have me."

Kicker caressed Madelyn's face and brushed away the angry tears that had surfaced. "Shhhh, love. Tis of little import if you go without me."

"It matters to me."

Kicker pulled Madelyn down and held her close. One hand rubbed her back soothingly, but Madelyn's ire was unabated. While she knew that Kicker spoke the truth, the unfairness galled her.

If only they'd give her a chance. If only they really knew her... knew what a truly kind and loving and honourable woman she is. Wynne and Will know how wonderful Kicker is. Even Mr. MacDiarmid is fond of her. Why are Sarah and Agnes so blind?

Madelyn became conscious of Kicker humming below her breath. She concentrated and tried to identify the tune. It was a sweet, sad air; one she felt she had heard before, but could not place. "What song is that, dearest?"

"Tis Seamus'. He calls it *Kicker's Journey*. Says it remin's him of our meetin' on board ship."

"It is...haunting."

"Aye, but wait til you hear him play it. P'rhaps he will do so at the weddin'. My poor noise does it no justice."

Some of her irritation dispelled, Madelyn chuckled. "Granted, you may never be asked to perform in the new opera house, but your voice is the sweetest sound in the world to me."

Madelyn knew she had surprised Kicker by the catch in her breathing.

May it be enough to know how much I love you, dearest. And damn those who refuse to see your worth; I always shall!

The resumption of school after the Christmas holiday was nearly as exhausting as the last day before the holidays. The children still coasted on the euphoria of the season and seemed unable to settle into their routine.

Lillian Berg had begun the day with a crying fit because her best friend, Beatrice Blatty, failed to compliment her new dress.

Archie Mason and Thaddeus Whitney got into a fistfight at noon, though neither would confess to the cause. Madelyn regretted having to use the strap on their first day back, but was well aware that she had to keep a tight grip on Archie in particular or the young bully would seize control of her classroom.

And two of her favourite students, the Portier boys, were absent, but as they were rarely any trouble, she was sure there had been a good reason.

By mid-afternoon Madelyn yielded to implacable reality and split her students into two groups for a rousing game of Geography. The blue team was up twelve points to nine in identifying small countries on the big globe when the clock finally, mercifully, sounded the end of the school day.

As the children rushed to tidy up and depart, Madelyn consoled herself that they had all made it through the difficult first day back relatively unscathed.

The last of the children had left the schoolhouse when Wynne entered.

Madelyn looked up from her desk in surprise. "Wynne. How lovely to see you. Are you looking for Laird? I believe he and Billy already left."

Wynne shook her head as she approached the front of the classroom, hat in hand. Madelyn noted her friend's sombre expression and felt the first stirrings of unease. Instantly her thoughts flew to Kicker, though she was certain that had there been an accident at the forge, John would have notified her immediately.

"Madelyn, the Portier cousins, Clarence and George..."

Madelyn sighed with relief. "I know they were absent today, but I'm sure they were not truant without cause. I really think the school board can overlook this once. They are such good children, a pure delight to have in class. Their Grand-père Portier was coming for Christmas, and I'm certain they simply could not drag themselves away for class. They were so excited about his arrival. They'll be back tomorrow, wait and see..." Madelyn trailed off as she realized that Wynne was shaking her head. "Wynne? What is it?"

"I'm so sorry, Madelyn. I wish I were not the one to have to tell you this, but... Sam James is out at the Portier farm and Dave Asher is sending to Calgary for the District Health Inspector, so it falls to me."

"Oh, dear God! Are the boys—"

An image of laughing faces flashed into her mind. With their shy eyes, innocent smiles, and thick, wavy black hair, Clarence and George reminded her of what Kicker might have been like as a seven-year-old.

"Their grandfather did come for Christmas. Unfortunately he was ill when he arrived, and he infected both his sons' families, and God knows how many others on his journey. No one knew what was happening until Reed Nichols went by there this morning. He noticed an unusual lump in the snow out on the road just past their gate. It was young George."

Madelyn gasped and tears sprang to her eyes. "Oh no, no, no!"

"They think he might've been trying to go for help. When Reed reached the house, he found it full of the dead and dying."

"Clarence?"

"Alive, but barely so. Reed got the hell out of there and rode for town. Practically drove his horse into the ground to get help. Esther headed right out to see what she could do."

Madelyn half rose to her feet. "I must go see Clarence."

Wynne shook her head emphatically. "Absolutely not, Maddie. We've declared the Portier place a pest house; it is under quarantine. Will organized a crew to get the dead cleared out quickly. Asher's supposed to be bringing back as much bichloride of mercury as possible from Calgary. Mr. Kelly wired the authorities to have it standing by for transport. John and Kicker are building airtight, tin lined caskets as fast as they can. I sent some of the handier of my men over to help them."

Madelyn could barely speak for the lump in her throat. "What killed them? Does Clarence have any chance at all?"

"Hell, I can't believe he's still alive. He and one of his baby sisters are the only ones to survive so far, out of what...a dozen or more of them in the two families? And most of them so damned young, too. As for what killed them, I suspect it was probably diphtheria or maybe scarlet fever. All I know is that Mr. Kelly said he noticed the grandfather seemed feverish and had trouble breathing when he got off the train. At the time, Kelly attributed it to the gentleman's age and the cold weather. Now he's upset with himself for not doing something, but he's not a doctor; there's no way he could've known." Wynne shot Madelyn a look of compassion as she put her hat back on. "I'm afraid I have to get going. It's going to be a hellish couple of days and there's a lot to do." She spun on her heel, then turned back with a gentle question. "Maddie, I know this is quite a shock. Are you going to be all right?"

Though grief and despair threatened to overwhelm her, Madelyn nodded silently, even as Roddy's face, forever fifteen, flashed into her memory.

"Look...word will spread around town quickly, no doubt, but you might want to give some thought as to how to talk to your students tomorrow."

Ashen, Madelyn bowed her head.

"Maddie, these kids...well, they know what loss is. This won't be the first time any of them has encountered a death. It's a rare family that hasn't lost at least one member to the Fourth Horseman."

Madelyn raised anguished eyes to Wynne. "Your family, too?"

"Yes. Laird's big sister died when she was only a month old," Wynne swallowed hard against the rush of emotions, "and my brother Wally lost two sons before they were five. They lie near each other in the church yard. Sadly, each winter sees more children join them."

Madelyn saw tears fill Wynne's eyes and rose to her feet. She circled her desk and they shared a hug; a brief, mutual acknowledgement of sorrows and losses, old and new.

After Wynne left, Madelyn slowly gathered up her things. *It's been a harsh winter. Two souls, both taken too soon. Yet while I knew him such a short time, I will grieve for George as I will never mourn Father. The innocent and the evil—lives cut short and who can say why? Let the angels sort them out, I suppose.*

On her walk to the coat closet, she paused beside George's desk. The child had carved his name and the year into the corner. As Madelyn traced the crude etching, grief filled her heart and overwhelmed her.

"Did you even get to see the twentieth century, little boy?"

Her agonized whisper echoed in the empty room. Desperate to get away, Madelyn ran for the door. Outside, she forced herself to slow to a decorous pace, but tears blinded her as she stumbled to their home.

Madelyn's need for Kicker engulfed her, but even as she called her lover's name, she knew the house was empty. There were no arms to hold her, no soft voice to whisper reassurances, no gentle caresses to wipe away her tears.

Kicker was building coffins.

CHAPTER 21

THE SOUND OF MEN AT work—sawing, hammering, and barking orders—assaulted Kicker's ears. She watched in frustration from the shelter of a leafless aspen on a hill above the building site.

Having acquired substantial construction experience that spring while working with John Blue Wolf, Kicker longed to be among the community of workers raising the walls of Galbraith's Crossing's opera house.

After the Christmas tragedy that killed the rest of their family, Esther nursed the orphaned Portier children—Clarence and his baby sister, Ghislaine. By the time Clarence recovered, he and his sister were so attached to their nurse that John and Esther offered to adopt the children.

There were grumblings among some of the townsfolk about the propriety of white children being adopted by the half Stoney man and his Métis wife. However, Wynne and Will put the weight of the MacDiarmid name behind the adoption.

The additions to the Blue Wolf family meant cramped quarters, so Kicker and John spent six weeks building an extension to his house. They added two more bedrooms, enlarged the kitchen, and built a small clinic for Esther.

Sure that her skills were equal to those of the townsmen, Kicker chafed at the awareness she should be shunned from such a publicly unseemly role. *Tis only half tolerated I am in the shadows of the forge.*

Her sad gaze drifted from the two walls already erected and braced, to the far edge of the clearing, where women were setting out lunch for the workers and keeping children from getting underfoot.

As always, Kicker's eyes fastened immediately on Madelyn. Her lover, now clad in conservative blue rather than funereal black, was in charge of organizing the serving table as dishes arrived. Despite the bedlam, the women appeared to enjoy their first outdoor socializing of the year. Laughter erupted frequently, and every arrival was greeted enthusiastically as each cook proudly unveiled her culinary contribution.

Not welcome there, either.

Kicker searched Madelyn's face, hungering for comfort and reassurance. Madelyn's smiles disappeared with George Portier's death, and were seldom seen in these bittersweet days of spring's return. Though she had been drawn into the revelry at Agnes' insistence, Maddie's expression displayed no joy in the day's activities.

With a sigh, Kicker stood and brushed the dirt and dead leaves from her trousers. For a moment she lingered and watched the clutch of men grouped around Will. They were arguing over a set of blueprints laid out on a plank that rested on sawhorses.

Kicker particularly eyed the two men who flanked Will. His brothers, Wally and Bruce, had returned from the Yukon the previous month. The prodigal sons, with nothing to show for their long absence except empty pockets and the tallest of tales, were greeted boisterously. The ensuing party thrown by the MacDiarmids, as much to defy the cold, dark days of February as to welcome the men home, was already a part of local legend.

Even Kicker and John joined in the merriment, though both returned to town long before the bacchanalia wound to a close. Kicker did not see Madelyn until the celebration finally ended two days later, but she had not begrudged her partner the fun.

"Bin a hard spring all way 'round, eh, Maddie?"

Kicker's soft words went unheard. She allowed herself a moment more to watch Madelyn, then departed for the place she was always welcome.

The front door of the station house was open, admitting sunshine, fresh air, and tepid warmth. Kicker could hear Seamus whistling within. She smiled. Even her often melancholy friend had responded to the unusually early advent of spring.

"Permission to come aboard, Cap'n?"

Seamus beckoned her inside with a smile. "You are most welcome, Miss Kicker. I warn you, though, the Canadian Pacific Railway is keeping me very busy today."

Kicker ducked around the heavily laden clothesline and into the station house. "Has bin a lot of trains through the las' coupla days."

"Apparently the Crowsnest Coal Company has powerful connections back East. They complained they were producing coal faster than the CPR could haul it away. Ever since, additional tonnage has been rerouted from east and west down to the Pass at an unprecedented rate." Seamus stopped talking as his telegraph key began to chatter.

Kicker slid onto a tall wooden stool that Seamus had installed in his office just for her. She rocked idly back and forth on the uneven legs until her friend finished transcribing the train orders.

Seamus sat back and swivelled his chair to face her. "So, what brings you here on such a fine Saturday? If I could conjure a way to get my telegraph outdoors, I would certainly be out there, myself."

Suddenly weary of her own thoughts, Kicker shrugged.

Seamus eyed her closely. "Kicker? Is there a problem?"

Instead of answering directly, Kicker told him of the excellent progress being made on the opera house. "...an' I expect all they'll have left by day's end is the interior work."

"So then, it will be ready for the grand matrimonial celebration in two weeks."

Kicker gave a half-hearted grin. Though they had missed Agnes MacDiarmid's Easter deadline, Mrs. MacDiarmid's determination to see her youngest married as quickly as possible was no secret. "If the Missus has anythin' to say about it. She's been on 'em like a rabid badger e'er since they started. But I saw Albert finally take her aside an' she ain't bin back to bother the men since."

Seamus chuckled. "She is quite the determined lady, is Mrs. Agnes MacDiarmid. I would not willingly stand in her way when she has her mind set on something."

"Well, she's surefire set on seein' Albert marry sooner rather than later."

"I rather imagine Albert is keen on that himself."

Kicker thought back to the welcome home party, the last time she had seen Albert and his fiancée together. Albert had seemed far more interested in his brothers' return than in his fiancée. This had the curious effect of causing Sarah to cling to him like a Scottish thistle.

Sceptical, Kicker shook her head. "Maybe."

"You seem doubtful, my friend. Perhaps there is a reason for Mrs. MacDiarmid's haste? Has young Albert's ardour dimmed since he lured Miss Binnington to this side of the Atlantic?"

"It won' matter. They'll be married anyway."

And the sooner the better, as far as Kicker was concerned. Albert's fascination with Sarah may have waned, but Sarah's infatuation with Madelyn continued unabated. When Sarah wasn't clinging to Albert, she fawned all over Madelyn. It turned Kicker's stomach, and when John sought her out, she leapt at the chance to leave the party early and return to town.

"As Mrs. MacDiarmid decrees, so shall it be done?"

"Aye. Tis about the size of it. So, Seamus, on more pleasant topics, how goes your music these days? I know you could ne'er replace Pudge, but..."

"True. My brother's inimitable joie de vivre and talent were nonpareil, but I have found an unexpected degree of harmony with Geoff Mansell, Andrew Payne, and Matt Galloway. I find myself quite looking forward to our practice sessions."

"So your band will be playin' at the weddin' then?"

"So it seems. And you? Will you also be attending the nuptials?"

Kicker beat her heel against the stool leg. "S'pose so. I was included in the invite, and Maddie insists I go."

"It could be fun."

"It could be hell."

They shared a rueful chuckle. Kicker knew that they were both picturing the same thing—Mrs. MacDiarmid ruling over the festivities with a sharp tongue, short temper, and an iron fist not even marginally clothed in a velvet glove.

"At leas' the music will be good."

"Thank you, Kicker. I will ensure that we play all your favourites."

"Includin' *Kicker's Journey*?"

"Of course, though you will understand if I do not name it so to the gathering."

Again the friends shared a look of understanding. They were aware that many of the townsfolk thought their unusual relationship verged on indecent. Madelyn had been quietly advised to either rein in her odd cousin's dalliance with the unmarried Irishman, or see that the two courted properly, preferably in the presence of a chaperone.

Despite the annoyance of being grist for the gossip mill, Kicker derived comfort from the erroneous assumptions. If the good women of the town assumed Kicker was engaged in scandalous activities with Seamus Kelly, it protected Madelyn's reputation from any speculations.

Dolts. If they only knew. Kicker felt the familiar tingle in her body. The distance that had grown between the lovers that spring always stopped at the foot of their bed. Sometimes Kicker thought it was only their frequent, passionate lovemaking that kept her from plunging into despair. Sadly, it did not have the same effect for Madelyn, who had grown progressively more withdrawn since New Year's.

"I am surprised that you're not working at your cabin today. I've barely seen you since the weather turned halfway pleasant."

Kicker blinked at the sudden change of subject. "I should be." She did not know how to explain that the satisfaction from the solitary work of clearing the site of the burned cabin had paled since work on the opera house began.

Seamus leaned forward and patted her arm comfortingly. "A day off here and there is not a bad thing. Besides, once the colliers have enough rolling stock to carry their coal, I may have time to lend you a hand."

Kicker tried to muster a grateful smile, but knew she had failed by the concern in Seamus' eyes.

"Tell me."

To Kicker's shock and embarrassment, tears filled her eyes at Seamus' tender tone. Unable to censor herself, she blurted out the truth. "I don' know what to do."

"About what? What troubles you so?"

"Maddie. I try—Bless'd Jesus, how I try. But nothin' I do lif's her spirits."

Seamus nodded thoughtfully. "Your cousin has been unusually reserved, but I thought perhaps with time and the passage of winter, her customary sanguinity would return."

Kicker shook her head, mortified at her inability to stop the tears from spilling over. "It has not. I thought... I thought if I got workin' right away to rebuild the cabin, it might help cheer her, might get her lookin' to the day we could move into a new home, but she won' e'en talk about it. Tis like she cares for naught anymore."

"Given that you have been out there every day since before the last of the snow melted, none could fault either your work ethic or enthusiasm." Seamus shot a keen look at his disconsolate guest and drew a clean handkerchief from his pocket. Kicker accepted it and mopped her wet eyes. "Do you know what lies behind your cousin's melancholy?"

That question had consumed Kicker for weeks. She was certain that Madelyn's love for her had not wavered. If anything, it had deepened to the point where Madelyn appeared to find her only comfort in Kicker's arms. There had been times of late when the profundity of Madelyn's naked need unnerved Kicker. But she could not tell Seamus that. "I think tis partly...when we were leavin' London, Maddie's young nephew, Peter, was worried that she would die far from her family. I think George Portier's passin' maybe got Maddie ponderin' how far from home she is. I remind her o'er an' o'er that we're fam'ly an' we've made a home here, but it don' seem to help any."

Seamus leaned back in his chair, a meditative look on his face.

With little appetite for conversation, Kicker allowed him the uninterrupted contemplation of his own thoughts for long moments until an old thought recurred.

"There is somethin' else..."

"And what would that be?"

"B'fore we lef' London, an old frien' of Maddie's tol' me—she warned me that Maddie might have secon' thoughts, that she might waver and come to regret our gran' adventure." *An' I promised Lil I would care for her in any case. I'm doin' a bloody good job of that, ain't I? In bed, I can get her to plead, to deman', e'en cry out in ecstasy. But put us back in clothes, an' I can ne'er e'en coax a simple smile from her.*

"You think she is a poor fit here, in Galbraith's Crossing?"

Kicker shook her head. "That's the curious thing, i'nnit? She ain't the misfit; I am. Tis her who's loved and appreciated by all. Me, many would ha' run out of town by now except for Maddie. But still I like this place fine. Tis not a day goes by I'm not glad we came."

"I think you underestimate the esteem you yourself are held in by quite a number of people, Kicker. But be that as it may, I do understand your point." Seamus hesitated and bit his lip.

"What's on your mind, Seamus?"

He took a deep breath and met her gaze squarely. "You know that I would never say anything to hurt you..."

"Aye, I do know that. You're a staunch frien'. So speak your min' openly."

Seamus rolled his chair across the wooden floor until his knees almost touched her. "I have never related this to anyone, not even Pudge. It still shames me to a great degree, though I know it should not. Kicker, I am intimately familiar with what it is to be a misfit, to know how it feels when the world defines you in a manner that begins to cage and crush your soul."

Kicker momentarily lost her own concerns in the pain in her friend's eyes. She reached for his hand and he gave it to her. "Sem'nary?"

"Yes. You have to understand, my whole life was shaped by the assumption that I would be a priest, the first in my family. My mother's hopes, my father's status, the pride and envy of my brothers, sisters, grandparents, cousins, uncles and aunts—all rode on my shoulders as I entered my last year of studies."

Seamus paused to take a deep breath and Kicker gently squeezed his hand. "What happened?"

Seamus gave a short, bitter laugh. "I asked questions."

"About what?"

"Everything. Theology, biology, anthropology—unanswerable, irreverent, blasphemous questions. Questions that brought the Brothers' wrath—and their scourges—crashing down upon my shoulders. But still I could not let their cant go unchallenged, could not stop asking questions, even though I knew that each time I opened my mouth, I endangered all the hopes and dreams of my family. Finally I was ordered to leave. Their parting words were that I should be grateful I was not excommunicated."

Kicker knew confusion must be apparent on her face, as Seamus gave a small smile and shrugged.

"The nature of the questions does not matter, Kicker. My point as it relates to your cousin is that Miss Madelyn may be finding herself similarly stifled, with no way to relieve the pressure and tedium. The immigrant, the teacher, the wife away from her loving husband—all these things shape how people regard and treat her. Perhaps her spirit cries out to return to the comfortable and the familiar. This life is not for everyone. Perhaps Miss Madelyn's soul withers as she feels trapped with no way out. Is that possible, my friend? If so, how may you help your beloved cousin?"

Kicker was saved from answering by the clacking of the telegraph. Seamus spun back to his desk and grabbed his pencil as his finger swiftly tapped out a response.

However, the chatter of the machine could not save Kicker from her thoughts. Though Seamus' personal revelation was new, nothing else he had said about Madelyn was. Kicker had spent countless hours mulling over her lover's growing despondency and ways to remedy it.

Thus far, much to Kicker's frustration, Madelyn refused to even acknowledge her sadness, lightly deflecting attempts to engage in a heart to heart. If Kicker persisted, Madelyn sidestepped or seduced her to shortcut any dialogue. As obvious as Madelyn's tactics were, Kicker was unable to counter them successfully.

The sound of the telegraph ceased, and Kicker watched Seamus slowly turn to face her. The look on his face was sombre.

"Tis bad news for someone, then?" Kicker knew that was the only part of the job that Seamus hated.

"For Miss Madelyn."

Kicker's eyes widened. She sprang off the stool and seized the telegram from Seamus' hand. Her eyes scanned his writing, and the signature of the sender at the bottom—Charles Whittaker. "Bless'd Jesus."

"I am so sorry, Kicker. Were these unfortunate people friends of yours?"

"Of Maddie's. Bloody hell. Adelaide, her daughters an' their newborn ... all dead? Poor Charles."

Her heart ached for the hard working Manitoban, now widowed and left to raise his two sons alone. While Madelyn renewed her friendship with Adelaide, Kicker spent most of her time on the Whittaker farm helping Charles. After their initial reservations, Charles, Charlie Jr. and Benjamin all accepted her. Kicker had grown fond of the taciturn farmer and his quiet sons. "There was no more, no tellin' of how they died?"

Seamus shook his head. "No, I'm sorry. That's all there was. I can send a query back, if you wish."

"No. I'll not bother the poor man. P'rhaps twas fire or illness took them."

"That could well be. I heard that Manitoba endured a much harsher winter than we did this year."

Kicker felt pole-axed as she folded the telegram and stuffed it in her pocket.

"You will ensure that Miss Madelyn gets that?"

Kicker nodded absently. "Aye."

There was relief in Seamus' voice. "Good. I most gratefully leave it in your capable hands. Please extend my condolences to Miss Madelyn on the loss of her friends."

"I will. I'd bes' go, then."

Seamus murmured sympathetically and walked her to the door. He gave her shoulder an affectionate squeeze as she left, but Kicker barely felt it.

What do I do? What if tis the last straw? It could break Maddie's will, sen' her packin' on the nex' train east.

Kicker was nauseated with fear. She walked toward the river, which though clear of ice, had barely begun to swell with spring runoff. Following the bank, Kicker walked west along the Bow, feeling the telegram in her pocket as if it bore the weight of a boulder.

She debated furiously with herself, presenting one side of the argument, then taking the other as she tried to thrash out her next step. By the time she turned and began the trek back to town, Kicker had come to a conclusion.

She would withhold the telegram for now. It would serve no purpose to add to Madelyn's emotional turmoil by telling her of the deaths.

Maddie ain't e'en heard from Adelaide in months. An' she ne'er speaks of her no more. Sure an' certain she could not get there in time for their funeral anyway...

Kicker reviewed and analyzed her justifications over and over as the town came into view. But no amount of reason or logic or persuasion would settle the roiling in her stomach.

The hall still smelled of freshly cut timber, but Kicker was impressed by Galbraith's Crossing's newly finished opera house. Neither the scarlet and gold paint, nor the heavy velvet draperies arrived in time, much to Mrs. MacDiarmid's dismay, but a couple of coats of whitewash concealed the raw lumber.

Kicker wasn't bothered by the absence of gilt and glamour. She surveyed the stage where the band was warming up and the dance floor surrounded by small, linen covered tables, where the locals in their best dress mingled and chatted. Her gaze drifted up to the balcony where the children had been sent to eat and play under watchful eyes, and she decided that the opera house was a worthy addition to the town.

Even the sight of the finely clad bride and groom brought a smile to Kicker's face. She had not anticipated the feeling of relief that swept over her when Miss Sarah Binnington formally and definitively tied her future to Mr. Albert MacDiarmid in St. Mark's Anglican Church.

Aye, I hope he gets you pregnant t'night. Then maybe you'll be too busy to bother with my Maddie. Kicker knew she should feel remorse for her uncharitable thoughts, but she missed her lover deeply. As wedding preparations swept to a crescendo, Madelyn spent the past four days out at the ranch.

Madelyn caught sight of Kicker, where she stood just inside the doorway, and left the bride's side to make her way across the floor. Kicker was startled to see the look of anticipation in her eyes as she approached.

Maybe she missed me too...

Then Madelyn was in front of her and Kicker shivered as warm breath caressed her ear.

"You look absolutely beautiful in that gown, dearest. Would that we were home right now so I could watch you remove it—very, very slowly."

Kicker could only nod, her mouth suddenly too dry to respond to her lover's whisper. Madelyn chuckled and, laying her hand lightly on Kicker's arm, pointed toward a table on the edge of the dance floor. Just down from the bride and groom's table, Wynne, Will, and his wife, Ruth were already seated there. "That's our table for the festivities, dearest. Why don't you join our friends, and I'll be with you as soon as possible."

Suddenly Sarah could be heard calling Madelyn's name as the bridal party assembled near the food tables. With her back to the bride, Madelyn rolled her eyes. "Good Lord, I swear that woman could not lift her own fork without assistance. I'm so sorry, Kicker. I promise to make this up to you later."

The annoyance in Madelyn's voice was as satisfying as the ardent look she shot Kicker before departing.

Kicker crossed the floor to join Wynne and Will with a grin wider than she had sported for many months. Even the persistent, niggling guilt of the hidden telegram was temporarily pushed aside. As Will stood up at her approach and Wynne gave her a welcoming smile, Kicker revelled in a long absent sense of contentment.

The wedding was well attended, with all of the MacDiarmids' fellow landowners and most of the townsfolk present. Even the entire Arbuster family had made an appearance. Kicker could not help scowling when she saw Rupert, but she was in far too good a mood to allow his presence to ruin her evening. It wasn't until they had gotten their food from the lavish buffet that Kicker noticed some absentees. "Wynne, will John and Esther be comin'?"

"Unfortunately, no. Albert hand delivered their invitation, and tried to persuade them to join us, but John said they couldn't leave the children. Albert told him to bring the children along, but Esther said that Clarence wasn't up to festivities yet. Knowing John, though, I suspect he was worried that his and Esther's presence might cause problems with certain people, and he didn't want anything to spoil Albert's big day." Wynne shot a pointed look at Rupert and his cronies, who had been slipping out the side door at regular intervals, growing more boisterous with each return.

"Tis not fair."

Wynne sighed. "No, it is not." Whatever she was about to add was lost as the band began to play a lively air. Those not partaking of the meal swarmed onto the dance floor.

Kicker caught Seamus' eye and was rewarded with a wink. She was delighted to see the smile on her friend's face as he and his three bandmates entertained the crowd. *P'rhaps someday Pudge'll be up there too.*

The next several hours passed swiftly with music and merriment. The children, protesting all the way, were eventually taken from the hall while the adults continued to celebrate. More of the men slipped outside and returned with suspiciously glazed eyes, wide grins, and pungent breath. Madelyn returned to their table as soon as possible and, as they passed the evening together, Kicker could not remember the last time she had had as much fun.

Will asked Kicker to dance, and to her own surprise, she accepted. Though Kicker had not danced since she was a child, she was nimble enough to follow Will's lead without embarrassing herself. That seemed to break the ice, and other invitations to dance were soon extended.

Kicker was dancing with Mr. Godwin, close to where Madelyn danced with the groom, when the music ended abruptly. Dancers stumbled and came to a stop. Kicker and Madelyn ended up next to one another and looked around curiously. People began to draw back, clearing a path as everyone stared at the apparition that had just entered.

Rick Biggart stood inside the front door, leaning heavily on a makeshift cane. He brandished a Winchester repeating rifle as he stared at the merrymakers. Those nearest him wrinkled their noses as the stench from his body sullied the air.

Biggart was gaunt to the point of emaciation; long, greasy hair dangled rope-like over his shoulders, and a matted beard covered his face. His eyes, dark and wild, were sunk deeply in his face and he gave a vulpine sneer as he lurched forward a couple of steps. Then Biggart cast his cane aside and drew his revolver.

There were shrieks from the unarmed assembly, and a woman screamed. Kicker held her breath and unconsciously reached for Madelyn's hand as the intruder looked over the crowd.

"See here..." Albert began, stepping away from Madelyn's side.

Biggart swung his rifle until it was pointing at the groom's chest, and Albert wisely fell silent. Biggart spotted Kicker and his eyes widened with malevolent glee. The rifle moved again, targeting her.

Kicker spared one desperate thought for the boot sheath and the deadly blade she had practiced with for so many hours. Left behind when she donned her wedding finery, the weapon was back in their little house—a house that, judging by the hatred and triumph in Biggart's eyes, she would never see again.

Then to Kicker's amazement, Rupert Arbuster stepped forward, all slurred arrogance and addled bombast. "Rick, what in God's name are you doing? This is neither the time nor place. I really must insist that you leave immediately."

The rifle moved again. This time it centred on Rupert, who swayed, blinked, and took an involuntary step back.

"You must insist? Who the hell are you to insist on anything, Rupe?"

Arbuster's voice was shaky as he responded, "I'm...your friend, Rick. You know that. We can settle this peaceably, but I really think you should—"

"Friend?" Biggart spat loudly, and the woman nearest him crumpled into the arms of her escort. The gunman ignored her, his gaze riveted on Arbuster. "Friend? What kind of friend abandons someone to die, crippled up and starving?"

"I never—"

Ignoring Rupert's feeble protest, Biggart roared his bitter rebuttal. "Week after week, I waited for you to show, waited for the supplies you promised. I couldn't get out and hunt; I couldn't fish. I had to kill my goddamned horse just to survive!"

"I thought you'd left long ago. I gave you the money to go. I couldn't—"

"No, you never could do anything, could you, Rupey? Year after year, if you needed something done, you'd send me. Steal a horse—send me. Break a man's leg—send me. Burn a house down—send me. Hell, about the only thing you had the balls to do was your own raping."

A collective gasp went up and all eyes turned to Rupert, who cringed from Biggart's words as if they were blows. Those standing near the disgraced rancher pulled away and left Arbuster isolated.

"Since we were knee high to a grasshopper, I did your thinking and I did your nasty work, and what did it get me?" Biggart rested his rifle down the length of his stained and torn pant leg, staring down at it for a moment before bringing the weapon to bear again. "You're a halfwit, Rupe, and I'm a no wit for ever listening to you."

As Biggart's thumb moved to the hammer of his revolver, Arbuster grabbed Mrs. Nichols, who was standing nearest him, and pulled her over to shield him. She cried out, and her protest was echoed resoundingly from guests throughout the hall.

Biggart sneered and cackled, "About what I'd expect from you, Rupey-boy. Your whole life, you've hid behind your mama's skirts and your daddy's name." He spat in Arbuster's direction and contemptuously turned away from him. Again the rifle targeted Kicker.

She dropped Madelyn's hand and stepped away. She allowed herself one quick look at her lover, aching at the confusion and fear in Madelyn's eyes, then Kicker faced her nemesis.

Biggart staggered a step closer to Kicker, his gun unwavering, his face contorted. "Dress a freak up in a pretty gown, she's still a freak. I been dreaming of this, girl. Every night, for so long I can't even remember. I'm going to blow you into so many pieces that Satan will need a basket and a broom to sweep you up."

Kicker heard Madelyn's shocked gasp. She wished she had time to explain, to apologize to her for the secret between them, but she knew she didn't.

"No!" Madelyn stepped forward, holding out her hand. "Wait! You do not know what you are doing!"

"I know exactly what I'm doing." In one fluid movement, Biggart thrust his pistol back in its holster, cocked the rifle and drew a bead on Kicker's chest, too close to miss.

Madelyn screamed and jumped in front of her.

The gun barked twice and Kicker felt wetness spatter her face. Horrified, she grabbed for Madelyn and spun her around. Blood soaked the front of Maddie's lavender gown.

Kicker searched frantically for the wound as she prepared to ease her to the floor.

But Madelyn did not slump. She did not fall or cry out in pain. She simply stood and stared in shock at the blood soaking her bodice.

Over the screams of women and shouts of men, Kicker heard a thud from beyond Madelyn. Instantly she pushed Madelyn into Albert's arms and stepped forward, prepared to draw Biggart's focus.

To Kicker's shock, Biggart sprawled motionless on the floor, a pool of blood spreading beneath him.

Pudge stood just inside the door. He eyed the corpse as a smile slowly grew on his ruined face. Coolly, he tipped his hat well back on his head with his smoking double-barrelled shotgun, then, with a nod to the frozen crowd Pudge turned and sauntered out of the hall.

"...so after the trap sprung, John and I thought sure Biggart was gone—killed or crippled too bad to come after us again. Din't see any sign of him til t'night when he..."

Kicker trailed off. There was no reason to review what had happened that evening.

Kicker leaned back in exhaustion and tried to evaluate the effect her lengthy story had on Madelyn. Though it was well after midnight, the two women still sat in their parlour as Kicker tried to explain how she became Rick Biggart's fixation.

Madelyn refused to meet Kicker's eyes. She stared instead into the flames which consumed her dress and destroyed the carmine evidence of that night's bloodshed. "And you never once thought to tell me?"

Kicker flinched at Madelyn's quietly wounded tone. "I thought of it many times, but I was tryin' to pr'tect you."

"Did it never occur to you that if I had known about all this, perhaps I could have protected both of us?"

That thought had not crossed Kicker's mind. She had been obsessed with the overwhelming need to safeguard Madelyn, to the exclusion of all else.

When there was no response, Madelyn raised her head. "He was going to kill you. You would've been dead, and I would've had no idea why the woman I love past the point of sanity was so savagely taken from me."

"But he din't kill me, Maddie. An' he's dead. He's no more threat to me...to us."

Madelyn rose to her feet and gazed down at Kicker distantly. "That's not really the point, is it?"

Kicker watched helplessly as Madelyn walked away. She heard the soft echo of footsteps as Madelyn climbed the stairs to their bedroom. At a loss, Kicker sat and stared into the fireplace as the flames incinerated the last of the blood-soaked gown.

"Oh, hello, Mrs. Bristow. How are you doing?"

Madelyn knew that the sympathy in Mr. Godwin's voice shouldn't grate on her, but she had tired of overly solicitous behaviour in the ten days since the shooting. Everyone in town appeared certain she must have been traumatized by her near brush with death, and treated her with kid gloves.

"I'm fine, Mr. Godwin, thank you. Do you have any mail for me today?"

"Yes, Ma'am, I do. There's a couple from London, something pretty official looking here from South Africa, and a letter for your cousin, too, if you'd like to take that."

"Thank you, yes."

Madelyn accepted the thin packet of mail the storekeeper handed her and noted without enthusiasm that the long awaited letter from South Africa had arrived. But before she could scan through the rest of the envelopes, a voice sounded behind her.

"Good day, Mrs. Bristow. Lovely weather we're having, is it not?"

Madelyn turned and gave Seamus a tired smile. "Yes, it is, Mr. Kelly. And how are you doing?"

"Well, thank you."

"And your brother? I hear he has taken employment in the coal mines of the Crowsnest Pass?"

As Seamus' face dropped, Madelyn instantly regretted her words. Since the night of the wedding, locals had alternated between reviling Rupert, who wisely decided that it was time to take an immediate and indefinite vacation in England, and hailing Pudge as a hero.

Townsfolk spoke in hushed and admiring tones of Pudge's long and dogged search for Biggart; of how he had hunted the villain for months, braving the cold and the midnight hours, and learning the terrain as he went. People who'd previously averted their eyes if they happened upon him, now went out of their way to salute him.

But with his self-appointed mission complete, and uneasy with the unwanted attention, Pudge Kelly decided it was time to move on. Gossip was that his brother attempted to go with him, but Pudge refused to allow Seamus to leave the life he'd already built for himself.

"I'm sorry, Mr. Kelly. I did not mean to..."

Seamus gave Madelyn a thin smile. "Quite all right, Mrs. Bristow." He tipped his hat politely, and stepped around her to accept the letter Mr. Godwin extended to him.

Madelyn had almost reached the door when she heard her name called again.

"Oh, Mrs. Bristow, please pardon my deplorable manners. I have been meaning to extend my condolences on the unfortunate loss of your friends."

Madelyn turned to face Seamus, puzzlement clear on her face. "Loss of my friends, Mr. Kelly?"

"Oh...my mistake. Please, do accept my apologies again. I...well, I am obviously in error."

Madelyn advanced on the flustered man. "That would be entirely unlike you, Mr. Kelly. Please enlighten me: to whom and what were you referring?"

Seamus' eyes swivelled to the door and Madelyn thought he looked like nothing so much as a rabbit caught in a trap. "Mr. Kelly?" She knew her tone was exactly the same as the one she used on Archie Mason when he was at his most obnoxious. "I am very, very weary of secrets, Mr. Kelly."

"I...uh... a telegram arrived for you over a fortnight ago, telling of the sad passing of a Mrs. Whittaker and three of her children. Miss Kicker said they were friends of yours."

Madelyn gasped. Grief warred with anger as she forced her next question past a huge lump in her throat. "So you gave the telegram to Kicker to deliver to me?"

"Yes, Ma'am, but perhaps in all the furor of the wedding and Mr. Biggart's demise, she forgot to pass it along. I am sure she intended to."

Seamus' voice was faintly pleading but Madelyn was not fooled. "Over a fortnight ago, you said? That was well before the wedding."

Without giving him another chance to suggest an alternative, Madelyn turned and strode out of the store.

Tears burned at Madelyn's eyes, and she hastened toward home. *Adelaide—my poor, dear, Adelaide. I was not a very good friend to you, was I? And Kicker, in the name of all that is holy, what were you thinking? How could you keep such news from me? Am I an infant that you thought to shield me in such a manner?*

By the time Madelyn slammed the kitchen door shut behind her, her wrath had escalated to biblical proportions and it overwhelmed her sorrow. She stormed up the stairs, intent on finding the telegram. She tore open drawers, threw items haphazardly about in a blind rage, and searched the pockets of Kicker's clothes.

Madelyn's chest heaved with exertion and emotion by the time she finally paused and tried to think the matter through logically. *Where would Kicker put something such that I would never accidentally encounter it?*

Instantly it came to her, and Madelyn grabbed the box of shells she had tossed aside in her search. She opened it and saw a neatly creased piece of paper tucked along the edge. Her hands trembled as she unfolded it and read Charles' stark and limited account of the death of Adelaide and their daughters.

Madelyn sank down on the bed amidst the chaos she had created. Head bowed, she allowed herself to cry at length.

Kicker found Madelyn there an hour later when she arrived home from work.

Standing in shock at the top of the stairs, Kicker stared around their bedroom. "Bless'd Jesus! What happened here?"

Wordlessly, Madelyn held out the telegram. Kicker paled and walked over to kneel at her side.

"I can explain..."

"No need. I think I understand everything quite clearly now."

Madelyn knew her voice was hollow, and that she was scaring Kicker. Her partner tentatively laid a hand on her knee. Madelyn stared at that hand, at once small, but strong; callused, but gentle. It was a hand that could mould iron to Kicker' will, or draw exquisite pleasure from Madelyn's body.

"Maddie, I'm sorry, so sorry."

"I know."

"I...I don' know what to say. I jus'...I jus' din't want you to hurt anymore."

Madelyn tried to summon a smile. She was too exhausted to talk any further. With an effort she stood up and began to unbutton her dress. When Madelyn glanced at Kicker, she could see confusion in her eyes. She shook her head.

"I'm very tired, Kicker. I just need to sleep. We can talk about this later."

Kicker sat back on her heels and watched Madelyn disrobe. It was usually a preliminary to their lovemaking that Madelyn enjoyed very much, but tonight it was simply a perfunctory action, devoid of any sensuality.

Madelyn donned a nightgown, got into bed, turned away from Kicker, and closed her eyes. She heard Kicker quietly gather up strewn clothes and slide drawers shut, but she did not move. Emotionally drained, Madelyn was certain she would fall asleep immediately, but long after Kicker descended to the lower level, her thoughts still tumbled and taunted her.

When Kicker came up to bed hours later, Madelyn feigned sleep. Though she ached for her lover's embrace, Kicker stayed stiffly on her side of the bed. Finally, silent tears soaking her pillow and very conscious that Kicker's breathing signalled her wakefulness, an enervated Madelyn fell asleep.

Wynne gently ushered the black-clad Madelyn to a chair. "I was so sorry to hear about your husband's passing. My whole family extends our deepest condolences."

"Thank you, Wynne. I received the notes. I am grateful for everyone's consideration."

"Please don't think you need to rush back to the classroom. Ruth has been filling in just fine, though Will had to let young Mr. Mason know who's in charge."

"Yes, Archie can be a handful; that's true. I will not miss him one bit."

Wynne straightened in her chair and eyed Madelyn closely. "Miss him?"

"Yes." Madelyn drew an envelope from her bag and laid it on Wynne's desk. "Major Bristow's passing has given me cause to re-evaluate our move to Canada. I believe it is the right decision for me to return to England. I will not leave you, the Board, or the children without tutelage, however. I'm submitting my resignation for the end of the school year and will book passage home for Kicker and myself in early July."

Wynne's face fell. "I'm awfully sorry to hear that. You've been a wonderful teacher, and besides that, a real asset to the town. You'll be impossible to replace, as will Kicker. You're both special people."

"I appreciate you saying so. I'm not sure what we would have done without your guidance and friendship this past year. I'm deeply grateful to all of you."

"I can see there is no talking you out of leaving, but Lord, Mother is going to be devastated." Wynne shook her head. "Guess Will and I can flip a coin to see who has to tell her."

"I'll tell her. I believe I saw her in the gardens when I arrived, and I'll speak with her before I leave. I'm sure she will understand. There has been so much loss this year..."

Madelyn's voice trailed off and she saw the sympathy in Wynne's eyes. She gathered herself and forced a smile. "I've already written my mother to advise her of our return. I know my family will be delighted to welcome us back."

"Their gain is definitely our loss. I trust you and Kicker will allow us to throw you a farewell party before you depart?"

"We would be honoured. Thank you."

As Wynne provided an escort out of her office, Madelyn was surprised that she did not feel better. When she finally made the decision after long, sleepless nights since the wedding, she was certain that she would feel a forgotten lightness of spirit.

Maybe once I tell Kicker.

"Dearest, would you come sit with me for a moment? I need to tell you something."

Madelyn could tell that Kicker did not know whether to be relieved or apprehensive. Kicker had walked on eggshells for the last three days. Though there had been no ill words exchanged, they also had not touched, either in passing or in bed.

Madelyn gave Kicker a reassuring smile and held out her hand. Kicker took it and trailed Madelyn into the parlour. They settled on the divan, still holding hands.

"I've come to a decision." Madelyn felt Kicker stiffen, and squeezed her hands soothingly. "I think you will agree that things have not worked out here quite as we thought they would."

"Tis not been all bad."

"No, dearest, it has not, but I believe it's past time for us to face reality and accept that we made a mistake—that I made a mistake, for which I accept full blame. I rushed into the move without giving due consideration to what awaited us. Father's death facilitates remedying my poorly made decision. Poor Adelaide was right. This is a harsh and unforgiving land, and it's time for us to quit it."

Kicker abruptly pulled away. "Bloody hell! What have you done?"

Puzzled at Kicker's reaction, Madelyn shook her head. "Only tendered my resignation. We will take the train in early July and be back in England by month's end."

"I see. An' once back in England...what then?"

"What then?"

"Aye. You decided we were comin'; you decided we're leavin'; surely you mus' have decided where we will live an' where we will work. No doubt you have decided how of'en we'll make love once back there, too."

Madelyn recoiled from the anger in Kicker's voice, then her own temper blazed. "What is the matter with you? Surely you can see this is for the best? This journey has been one disaster after another. Why in God's name would we persist in it a moment longer than we must?"

Kicker gave a short, bitter laugh and leapt to her feet. "An' to think I bin' feelin' guilty about that damned telegram."

Madelyn rose to her feet, hands on her hips. "As well you should. You had no right to keep such information from me. Just as you had no right to keep all knowledge of what took place between you and Mr. Biggart and Mr. Arbuster hidden from me."

"An' what right do you have to decide my life for me?"

Shocked, Madelyn stared at her usually amenable lover. She could not remember ever seeing Kicker so angry, let alone had that anger directed at her. "But I...surely you can see that I can no longer stay here? This is a vile and violent land, scarce fit for gentlemen let alone gentlewomen. It's not simply the beastly nature of some uncivilized inhabitants, but the land itself is a constant threat. Every season is a battle, Kicker. We fight against soul-sapping snow and cold in winter, the deluges of spring, the fires of summer—there's never any peace. I yearn for the green and gentle ways of our homeland, and I will not abide here a moment longer than I must. I find it incomprehensible that you would dispute the need for us to leave when I absolutely cannot stay. Did you not tell me, that first night at Grindleshire's when you came to my bedroom that you would come with me always?"

"Aye, I did." Kicker would not meet Madelyn's eyes. "An' you said you would have to be tied in chains to re-board a ship."

Madelyn shuddered. "I did say that, dearest, but with your help I'm sure I can manage. And knowing that England lies at the end of our journey will make all that misery bearable."

Kicker turned and strode away.

"Where are you going?"

"Takin' Rabbit out for a ride."

This was not going at all as Madelyn had expected. "Kicker, surely you understand. I cannot live here, but I cannot live without you. I love you. You must come with me, dearest. You must."

As she reached the back door, Kicker paused and turned. "No, Maddie. I will not."

Kicker grabbed her coat and disappeared through the door, as Madelyn, dumbfounded, stared after her.

CHAPTER 22

THE BLACK PRAIRIE SKY STRETCHED overhead for as far as Kicker could see. She let herself get lost in counting stars. She hoped it would distract her from the unremitting pain that had wracked her since she bolted from the house hours earlier.

Kicker reached twenty-nine before she gave up. She shivered and sat up to feed the small fire. Though the mid-May days were warm, the nights were still cold, and the tiny flames did little to ease Kicker's chilled body and soul.

"Am I daft, Rabbit? Should I have stayed e'en when she was bein' so irrational? Maybe I could ha' talked those bloody fool notions outta her head."

Rabbit snorted from the far side of the fire where she grazed.

"She's givin' up, Rabbit. Why? She don' believe in our future anymore? She don' believe in us? Maybe she don' believe in me."

Kicker laid back and rested her head on Rabbit's saddle. She stared up at the sky that had enchanted her from the moment she arrived on the prairies.

"Maybe she don' love me anymore." But even as she murmured the words, Kicker knew they were not true.

True, Madelyn had been coolly distant and formal with her for the past few days. Kicker did not blame her for that. She knew she had handled her feud with Arbuster and Biggart badly. And she could not herself believe that she had kept Charles' telegram hidden. From the moment she had tucked the telegram in her pocket and not gone directly to Madelyn with it, Kicker was keenly aware that fear had overridden good sense. But with each passing day, it grew more impossible to own up and make good her error. She procrastinated herself into deeper trouble.

Kicker understood the source of Madelyn's desire to leave, but the irony was galling. Both of them had based decisions on fear when they should have talked things out together and allowed logic and sound judgment to rule.

It was clear that Madelyn construed the recent string of troubling events not only as an indictment of their life in Canada, but as a breach of trust. Rather than give up, however, Kicker longed to put those things behind them and move forward.

With bone deep certainty, Kicker knew that they had a unique chance to build a rewarding life together in Galbraith's Crossing unlike any they could have in England, but she despaired of being able to get that across to Madelyn.

Madelyn was the one skilled with words. All Kicker had was the passion of her convictions, and she was not sure that would be enough to sway Madelyn.

Kicker was far too practical to brood for long, and she felt her resolve grow and solidify. She knew whatever her verbal inadequacies, she had to try; she had to fight with every weapon she had to keep Madelyn with her. Whatever had been said or done, all that really mattered was how they felt about each other and how they dealt with their problems from this point on.

Her mind returned again to Lil's cautionary words, and her own promise. If it was within her power, Kicker would not let Madelyn make the mistake of leaving Galbraith's Crossing.

As to her own mistakes, Kicker vowed that, given another chance, she would never again withhold anything from Madelyn, not even in a well-meaning attempt to protect her. If she expected Madelyn to treat her as an equal in the new life they were building, she knew she had to respect her enough to do the same. And though she was still very angry about Madelyn's arbitrary decision, Kicker had no doubts about the depth of her all-consuming love.

Madelyn's fervent words rang in Kicker's head. *I cannot live here, but I cannot live without you. I love you. You must come with me, dearest. You must.*

No, love was not the problem, nor was lovemaking. Kicker knew that whatever happened, it would only be a matter of time before Madelyn reached for her again. Their need for each other outweighed every other element of their lives.

"Maybe tha's it, Rabbit. E'ry time I try to talk serious to her, she slips a han' into my pants an' I forget my own name." Kicker glanced at Rabbit with a smile. "Prob'ly a good thing I came out here then, eh? If I stayed, she'd give me one of those looks an' I'd agree to anythin' so long's she'd touch me."

Kicker folded her hands behind her head with a sigh. In truth, she knew she held equal sway over Madelyn. However, with their views about life in Canada so diametrically at odds, it left them stalemated.

Reluctantly Kicker considered what Madelyn asked. *Would it be so bad to return to England? I could see Adam again.* Kicker's lips curved in an affectionate smile, but as she pictured her big brother, another's face supplanted the image. *Twould be farewell to Seamus, then, an' jus' when Pudge lef' him, too.*

Kicker grimly dismissed these factors. As much as she adored both Seamus and Adam, neither of those brotherly relationships came close to what she felt for Madelyn. Ultimately, the only thing that mattered was her partner.

It would be so easy to give in, as easy to bend to Madelyn's will as she bent her body to Madelyn's touch. And it would be so wrong.

As Kicker had done on the aimless ride eastward from Galbraith's Crossing, as she had done while she unsaddled Rabbit and made her small camp next to a prairie slough, as she had done through the long, cold hours staring up at a brilliant night sky, Kicker pondered her stand.

She loved Madelyn; Madelyn loved her. In an ideal world, they would never be parted. Nothing would ever put asunder their God sent union of body and soul. In an ideal world, Madelyn would join Kicker in embracing their new life—a life that sometimes offered rewards too ephemeral to grasp and challenges too overwhelming to see beyond, but always a freedom they would never replicate in England.

But it was not an ideal world. So the only question that remained was making the best decision for them...

For me. Kicker examined that thought. *What if I cannot convince Madelyn to stay? She seems hard set on sailin' back. Do I stay? Or will I fore'er go where e'er she goes, with nary a question asked nor protest raised?*

She thought of the small business she had been building since Wynne requested a pair of ornate candlesticks similar to those she had given Madelyn for Christmas. True to her word, Wynne put Kicker in touch with her contact in Calgary. Several shops now carried not only Kicker's candlesticks, but other of her small, ornamental ironwork creations. John was tolerant of Kicker's sideline as long as she completed their projects first, and she insisted on paying him a portion of her profits for the use of his equipment.

But Kicker dreamed of someday setting up her own shop and expanding her business beyond Calgary and Galbraith's Crossing. She knew that as a stable hand at Grindleshire's, she would never have conceived such a dream, but in this new land, anything seemed possible.

More importantly, Kicker could not visualize any circumstances in England that would allow her and Madelyn to live together as equals. She knew how lowly many of the townspeople regarded the schoolteacher's odd cousin, and that it took sustained chicanery to create their situation. But ultimately all that mattered to Kicker was sharing a home with the woman she loved.

She doubted that any amount of skilled deception could create similar conditions in their former home. She would never ask Madelyn to descend to her lower social standing, but Kicker's great fear was living out a charade as some sort of lady's maid, simply to be close to Madelyn.

"Plain truth of it, Rabbit, I jus' don' want to go back, but am I bein' selfish? In England, Maddie's got a home an' family, an' a life any would envy. Would it be better to jus' let her go? If she sees all else here as worse than England, is my love enough for her?" Kicker chewed that over, then shook her head firmly. "We have friends here, good friends—friends that will grow close as family with the years. An' I know she loves teachin' those chil'ren, no matter what. But mos'ly, tis what I see in her eyes when she hol's me, Rabbit—that's what I fight for. Tis worth fightin' for, I swear. An' if she'll jus' give it a little more time, I know she'll see that too. She can no more live without me than I can live without her."

Kicker rolled to her feet and brushed at her clothes as Rabbit came to her side. She slid an arm around the mare's neck and laid her face against Rabbit's muzzle. "Our life is meant t'be here, girl. I know that with all my heart. I jus' have to convince her."

With a quick glance at the sky which had lightened almost imperceptibly in the east, Kicker began to break camp. It was time to go home. It was time to talk some sense into Madelyn.

Madelyn stared morosely at the whitewashed ceiling. The dawn light that seeped into the tiny bedroom did not signal the end to a restful night's sleep. Rather, it emphasized her exhaustion from endless hours of worry alternated with defiant anger, spiced by confusion and exasperation.

She rolled onto her side and savagely punched her pillow for the umpteenth time. "Damn you, Kicker!"

Unlike the horrible night when she imagined Kicker lost in a snowstorm, Madelyn was not worried about her safety. The weather was good. Kicker was warmly dressed, mounted on Rabbit, and had repeatedly proven her competence and ability in this often hostile land to care for herself.

And me. Madelyn angrily dismissed the uninvited thought. *This is about Kicker refusing to listen to good sense and reason, nothing else.*

But her gaze rested on Kicker's pillow, and Madelyn's fatigue tricked her into seeing Kicker's face as it appeared when she woke to each new day. Dark eyes alight with love turned toward her and the shadow of hands reaching to pull her close felt so vivid that Madelyn groaned with desire.

Aggravated as much by her own need as with Kicker, Madelyn pushed herself onto her back and stared again at the ceiling so close above her head. When she tilted her head back, she could see the place where she had once cracked her head against a beam in the course of enthusiastic lovemaking. An unwilling smile curved her lips as she remembered how Kicker had distracted her from the pain in her head. But the blatant carnality of the memory only stirred Madelyn's emotional turmoil.

"Damn you, Kicker."

The words were soft this time. She did not want to fight. She did not want to argue. She wanted to feel Kicker wrapped around her, one sturdy arm nestled below her breasts in her lover's favourite sleeping position.

How many mornings had Madelyn waited for Kicker to awaken? She always knew the moment Kicker reached consciousness by the way the buttons of her nightgown suddenly came undone as a searching hand slipped beneath the heavy cotton.

Madelyn's favourite mornings were when Kicker's intentions swiftly became clear; when she would return the pressure of her lover's body and invite the soft caresses that sent her hunger soaring.

Madelyn's body stiffened uncontrollably under the memory of Kicker's hands: exposing, touching, thrilling her beyond measure.

"Damn you, Kicker."

The soft, half-hearted moan echoed in the quiet room.

Momentarily Madelyn toyed with her nightgown, tempted to pull it out of the way and relieve the ache herself, but the thought held no allure and she abandoned it.

She allowed her listless gaze to drift about the room. She dwelled first on Kicker's work shirt and trousers hung on nails that jutted from the outside beam, then on a stray sock half-hidden under the corner of their dresser.

She focused on the torn curtain that hung at their window. It was a casualty of a night when they had not even made it to their bed, despite it being only a foot away. Madelyn closed her eyes and remembered how she clutched frantically at the fabric as Kicker worked magic on her naked body. They had not noticed the tear until the next morning. Madelyn had sewn it up, but their eyes had only to meet over the rough repairs for them to break out in mutual laughter.

And usually a quick return to bed. Angered by her unruly thoughts, Madelyn grabbed Kicker's pillow and pulled it over her face to muffle a brief, frustrated scream. It didn't help. The pillow's redolence was all Kicker, and Madelyn, eyes closed, curled it into her chest.

She lay like that for a long time, no longer trying to control the paths her memory took. Kicker's word echoed in her mind... *Bloody hell! What have you done?*

"Only what I thought best for both of us, dearest." Madelyn wearily considered her response to her phantom accuser. Had she genuinely taken Kicker's wellbeing into account when she'd decided they should leave? Or had she taken an impulsive leap, as she reluctantly admitted she was wont to do?

Surely you mus' have decided where we will live an' where we will work.

"Well, we will go to Mother's first, dearest, and decide from there..."

Am I to be a scullery maid again, then?

Madelyn blinked in astonishment. *Kicker never said that.* But her mind flooded with images of Mrs. Edward Stuart as she washed dishes in the kitchen, served deferentially at the Bristow family table, and ducked her head obediently when Madelyn imperiously summoned her for hasty, secretive, impromptu lovemaking.

But it wasn't like that. Her father's lecherous face flashed in Madelyn's mind. After Timothy Bristow's death, Kicker finally told her of what the man had been up to in the servants' quarters. She had been sickened then, and was sickened now. *I'm not him. I love her. I would never take advantage of her. We were merely playing roles to protect our relationship. Kicker is my beloved, not any manner of servant.*

Revolted by the involuntary comparison of herself to her predatory father, Madelyn sat upright and rested her head on her knees as she rocked back and forth.

"If I hadn't made all those decisions, we wouldn't even be together. You'd still be working in the stables at Grindleshire's Academy."

"Where I was happy."

It took a moment for Madelyn to realize that her mind had not projected that response to her self-justification. She looked up to see Kicker. She leaned against the wall at the top of the stairs and regarded Madelyn solemnly.

"Are you saying that you regret me taking you away from Grindleshire's? Are you sorry we ever met?" Madelyn held her breath until Kicker slowly shook her head.

"No, Maddie, I'm not sayin' any such thing. I was content then, and I'm mos'ly content now. Tis naught I've regretted from the moment I met you. I would do it all again t'be in this place, in this time, with you."

"But this place is no good for us."

"You're wrong."

Madelyn knew by the intractable look in Kicker's eyes that there would be no reasoning with her at the moment. *Later, when we are well rested and our tempers are not so short, she will be more reasonable.* "You look utterly exhausted, dearest. Come to bed."

For a second, Madelyn thought Kicker would refuse, but her shoulders slumped and she nodded. "Aye. I could sleep."

"Thank heavens it's Sunday so you need not go to work."

Kicker grunted as she shucked her shirt and unbuttoned her pants. Madelyn watched her, unable to deny the hunger that swept over her. Naked, Kicker reached for the nightshirt slung over a chair.

"Please, leave that off, dearest."

Kicker turned to face the bed, her eyes unreadable as she studied Madelyn.

"Please... I know you're tired. I just want to hold you."

Wordlessly, Kicker dropped the nightshirt back onto the chair and crossed to the bed. "Am I t'be the only one nude?"

Madelyn hastily shed her nightgown and tossed it to the floor as she opened her arms to Kicker. When the familiar warmth of her lover's body snuggled against her own, it took all of Madelyn's willpower not to initiate lovemaking. She desperately craved the reassurance their union always brought her.

When Kicker fell asleep almost immediately, Madelyn was equally relieved and chagrined, though neither feeling did much to lessen the temptation.

Finally, emotionally drained, Madelyn too fell asleep. Hours later the tolling of the church bells woke them from the longest night of their lives. The ensuing lovemaking was silent and desperate. When it was over, they rolled away from each other, and the tears neither could stop were just as silent...and just as desperate.

Kicker stopped and wiped her sleeve across her brow. Though summer was officially still one week away, it was hot work felling trees to rebuild the cabin in the woods.

Across the clearing Seamus trimmed and shaped the logs they'd cut that morning. He looked up, met her gaze, and set down his axe.

"I believe it's past time for a break, my friend."

Kicker shook her head. "You go on, Seamus. I'm not tired."

"As my sainted Grandmother Kelly would say, that is a load of pig slop. Now put down that axe and come with me."

Startled, Kicker paused with her axe in the air.

Seamus gave her a stern look, and for an instant she had no trouble picturing him as a priest. She gave him a reluctant grin and lowered the axe. "Oh, a'right then. I guess a break won' kill me."

Kicker followed Seamus down the slope to the edge of the creek. As they dunked their heads to cool off, Kicker felt the absence of the third member of their little construction crew as keenly as she knew Seamus did. For her, their rest breaks always resurrected bittersweet memories of playing in Shadow Creek the previous summer. "What news from Pudge?"

Seamus towelled his face with his sleeve and tapped a well worn letter tucked in his breast pocket. "I received this one last week. As ever, my brother asked me to convey his affectionate regards to you."

Kicker sat back on the log that had become their de facto bench. "He's doin' well, then?"

Seamus smiled as he took a seat next to her. "He is doing exactly as Pudge always has—getting by, getting along, and getting in trouble. He tells a story of one of the miners who invited several of his bachelor friends, including Pudge to dinner. Just as the guests walked up the steps for dinner, there was a tremendous explosion."

"Bless'd Jesus! Is Pudge a'right?"

"He is, though as usual he keeps his guardian angel working around the clock. Their host, as is the custom with miners, kept his dynamite dry in the oven, it being useless if it gets wet. However, having been down at the local hotel for the afternoon, he forgot he had not removed the dynamite prior to lighting his stove. Fortunately none were hurt, though the chicken dinner was deemed beyond consumption."

Kicker gave a relieved laugh. "So aside from dinner blowin' up on him, things are well?"

"I think so, though I am not sure Pudge would tell me if that were not the case. He informs me that he has just been hired for the night shift at Turtle Mountain, and will be moving to the town of Frank within the week. My brother seems to have an affinity for working nights and sleeping days."

Kicker did not have to ask why. Though Pudge's aversion to showing his face had lessened in the aftermath of Biggart's death, it had not been eradicated. She suspected that even finding acceptance and camaraderie with men who worked deep in the earth would never put him fully at ease when the end of shift brought a return to day's light.

"Apparently my brother's only regret about relocating is leaving his current lodging. There, along with his room and board, he may have his choice of a morning shot of hard liquor with hot water, or a cold glass of beer on his return from the mines. He tells me that we have stumbled upon a very enlightened society."

The friends chuckled together and Seamus turned to face Kicker. She braced herself, aware of what was coming.

"Enough of my brother and his antics. How are things with you and your cousin?"

"Could be better."

"Elucidate."

Kicker shrugged and picked at a loose thread on her trousers.

Seamus' voice was gentle but insistent. "The time grows short, my friend."

"D'you think I don' know that!" Kicker instantly regretted the harshness in her voice. Seamus did not deserve to bear the brunt of her frustration.

"Then I take it you've had no success in convincing Mrs. Bristow of the error of her decision?"

Bitterly, Kicker shook her head. "Night after night, week after week, we both say the same words o'er and o'er. I hear them in my sleep. But she will not budge, and I cannot."

"Then perhaps..."

"P'rhaps, what?"

"I take no joy in saying this, Kicker. I have come to value our friendship more highly than I can possibly tell you, but—"

Kicker stared at Seamus incredulously. "You're goin' to tell me to jus' give in? When I know with all my heart she is makin' the wrong decision?"

"You are a deeply principled woman. I would never dispute that, nor entreat you to contravene your heartfelt convictions. But I want you to think, to consider how you will feel if Miss Madelyn climbs aboard that eastbound train without you."

Kicker shook her head stubbornly. "She won' do it. I jus' need to hol' firm, an' when it comes right down to it, she won' get on that train. There's naught for us back in England."

"Kicker..." Seamus shot her a troubled look, "the date of her farewell party is set. The search for next year's teacher has begun. It does not appear likely that Mrs. Bristow will reverse her decision."

"You don' know her like I do." *You don' know how she clings to me in the night, how she reaches for me at the end of every argument and holds me like she'll ne'er let me go. When it comes to it, she won' leave me—she cannot leave me.*

The friends sat quietly, both intently watching the creek as though it held the secrets of the universe. Kicker was the first to break the silence.

"D'you e'er regret not becomin' the Potato Kings of the West? I mean aside from Pudge's tribulation, of course."

Seamus shook his head. "It was more my brother's dream than mine. I quite enjoy the work in which I am now engaged. Euan Farrell—he is the gentleman that assumed our renounced homestead—tells me that the potatoes Pudge and I planted are keeping his family well provided this summer. That pleases me."

"Mmmm." Kicker felt Seamus fidget and unconsciously braced herself.

"Kicker...sometimes, like our potato farming, dreams do not take shape as we first envisioned them. That does not mean—"

Kicker cut Seamus off before he could go further. However willingly he surrendered his dream, she refused to surrender hers. "C'mon. Let's get back to work. Maddie will be much happier once she's got her own home."

As she climbed the bank, Kicker felt Seamus' worried gaze on her. But as had become her pattern in the past month, she furiously fended off even a hint of doubt with the refrain that had become her constant mental companion. *Maddie loves me. I know she does. She would ne'er leave me. Ne'er.*

Their voices were low. No matter how ferociously they fought, they never raised their voices. They were far too aware of how rapidly gossip spread in a small town.

The arguments came more frequently now. The departure date swiftly approached and each grew increasingly frantic to prevail upon the other.

"How can you condemn me to cross the ocean without you? You know I will suffer the agonies of the damned."

Kicker glared back across the table. Their dinner, as so frequently happened, grew cold between them. "Then tis simple—don' go."

"I must, you know I must."

"I know nothin' of the kin'."

Madelyn shook her head helplessly. She had never seen Kicker so entrenched in a position. She had never before been unable to reason her into at least admitting there were two sides to an issue. She decided to use the final ammunition she had held in reserve, and prayed it would be enough.

"I received a letter from Charles last week." Madelyn saw Kicker flinch and stifled the instant urge to comfort her. "I wrote him to express my condolences and apologize for the delay in sending them. I explained that you were unaware of the contents of his telegram and had accidentally mislaid it. He accepted both the condolences and apologies, and expanded on the tragedy."

Though Kicker did not meet her eyes, Madelyn knew that she hung on every word.

"Kicker..." Madelyn drew a deep breath to overcome the sick sensation that overwhelmed her every time she contemplated Charles' letter. "Adelaide and their daughters did not die by illness or accident."

Kicker raised her head, confusion plain in her expression. "What happened, then?"

"It was several weeks after their baby daughter, Miriam, was born. Charles and the two boys had gone out to the barn to start the day's chores. Amelia and Joanie were helping their mother in the house. Charles said he wasn't gone from the house more than an hour when he went back in for something before he and the boys were to go to the fields. He found Adelaide first—hanging from a beam in the kitchen. He ran through the house, and found Amelia and

Joanie tucked in their beds, dead. The baby girl, too, dead in her crib. He thinks they were probably all smothered. A note from Adelaide said she could not condemn her daughters to her wretched life, so she'd taken them with her to a better place."

"Bless'd Jesus! She killed them? Her own children?"

Madelyn shuddered at the shock and disbelief in Kicker's voice. It reflected her exact emotions each time she considered the despair that Adelaide must have felt to do such a horrifying deed.

"Adelaide was so much stronger than I, Kicker. I'd looked up to her since I was a child. I tried to emulate her and always set my standards by hers. When she became a Suffragette, I could hardly wait until I was old enough to join the movement, too. If this land, to which she came with such dreams and hopes, made her do such a terrible thing, if it broke her—and it did—it will break me, too. I just cannot chance that, dearest. Can you not understand that?"

Kicker was silent and Madelyn's heart leapt with hope. *Maybe now she will understand. Maybe now she will agree it is best for us to leave this place forever.*

When Kicker slowly shook her head, Madelyn's hope crumbled.

"You are not Adelaide, Maddie. Whate'er you saw in her back in England, the woman I met in Manitoba was nothin' like you. She had not your courage, nor wisdom, nor fortitude."

Madelyn pleaded openly. "But do you not understand, Kicker? I've none of those things without you. You make me better than I am. If you don't return with me, I will once more be the woman who allowed her father to separate her from the one she loved. Who did not have the courage to steal away—to abandon the life of luxury he gave her, to find the woman she loved no matter how long or what sacrifices it took. Without you, I am a lesser woman, a weaker woman. Without you—" Madelyn broke off despondently. *Why even try? I know that look on her face. She is obduracy incarnate. She will not be moved, no matter what I say.*

As was the pattern of their fights, Kicker swiftly went on the offence. "How would you e'en explain my presence to your ma? I'm supposed to be with my husban', homesteadin'."

Madelyn knew that Kicker deliberately attacked the weakest part of her plan. "I've told you and told you, you may abide with Lil until we make further plans. She has already agreed to take you in."

Kicker gave a dismissive snort. "An' am I to be her apprentice, to trade the forge for a sewin' needle? Would you cage me like that when I have lived like this?" She cast her arm in a wide circle and Madelyn knew she was not just indicating their home.

Madelyn was sure that was the crux of it—Kicker's unwillingness to give up the freedom she found in this new land. She deeply resented being put second in her lover's priorities, and she allowed anger to leak into her voice. "You know very well that it's to be a temporary placement only, until we can make long term plans. Neither Lil nor I expect you to be her apprentice. I'll pay Lil for your room and board, and you can help out around the place in whatever manner you both deem fit."

Kicker leaned back in her chair, her eyes flashing. "I see. An' whene'er you get an urge, you'll jus' come by and order me to drop my pants, is that it? I'm to be your concubine, then."

Again her father flashed through her mind, and Madelyn blanched. She bolted up, knocked over the kitchen chair, slammed her hands down on the table, and hissed at her lover, "Damn you! You know bloody well that's not what I mean! I'm only trying to make things work out, but as always you refuse to compromise."

Kicker rose to her feet. "I refuse to compr'mise?"

"Yes! It's as if you deliberately go out of your way to make our lives harder!" Madelyn knew she'd lost control and should hold her tongue, but frustration boiled over and she was helpless in its grip. "Even so simple a thing as putting on a dress and attending church once a week, or observing social proprieties so that the whole blessed town would stop gossiping about you and Mr. Kelly. If only I didn't have to defend you at every turn. Life would be so much simpler if you would just—"

Dark eyes went cold. "Jus' what, Madelyn?"

Madelyn's wrath deflated and she shook her head hopelessly.

"Be a lady? Be like you? I ne'er lied to you about who I am. Not once. I'm a sow's ear. Bin so since I were born. Those that care for me...accept me thus. I thought you did too."

"I did... I do."

"I don' think so. You can go anywhere. You can be anyone you choose to be; you'll always fit in. There are few places I fit, includin' the place I were born. Grindleshire's was one, but tis not a part of your plans, nor could it be with the way we lef'. Then, with God's blessin', I foun' another place where I don' have t'feel like a freak from sun up to sun down. I don' think that wheel will e'er spin my way again, Maddie."

The sadness in Kicker's voice almost broke Madelyn's heart. She tried to speak, but Kicker raised a hand to forestall her.

"Let me finish. I know you love me, but I question that you've e'er accepted me as a true equal. Tis understandable. You're so far above me that were we any other two, you'd ne'er e'en give me a second glance. But I won' accept that any more, Maddie. I'll not be your lesser e'er again. If I do as you wan' me to, if I follow you onto that train, twould not be true t'me, or our love."

"What are you saying?"

"What I've said all along, but you were not listenin'. You mus' make a choice now: commit to me as a full an' equal partner in our love and the life we're buildin' here, or walk away from me for good." There was no anger in Kicker's voice, only quiet, unyielding determination.

Tears rolled unchecked down Madelyn's face. She felt as if her legs would not hold her another instant. She groped to right the fallen chair, collapsed into it, and buried her face in her hands.

"I cannot, Kicker..." *I cannot walk away from you. I cannot stay...*

There was a long silence, then Madelyn heard Kicker turn and mount the stairs to their bedroom. She felt ill. Leaving the table, she stumbled into the parlour and lay down on the divan. Within moments, a blinding headache had her curled into a fetal position, her fists pressed against her temples. She did not hear Kicker descend the stairs until a voice sounded from the kitchen.

Madelyn forced herself to look up and saw that Kicker carried a bulging burlap sack in one hand and the shotgun in the other. There was a look of ineffable sadness on her expressive face.

"You once tol' me that no matter what I decided, you'd still love me. Now I'm tellin' you the same. I love you. I always will."

Alarmed, Madelyn sat up, only to have the pain in her head intensify. Barely able to focus, she managed a question. "Where are you going?"

"I will not stay and watch you leave. Be well, Maddie... always." Kicker turned and walked out the door, closing it softly behind her.

Madelyn stared at the door, willing Kicker to return, to admit that she could not live without her and that no matter what, they had to stay together.

But the door remained closed.

In deference to Madelyn's recent widowing, the farewell party was muted. But as nearly the whole community wanted to attend, the gathering was too large to be held at the school and had been moved to the opera house.

Everyone was aware of the terribly long hours that Madelyn had worked in the final weeks of the school year, so those present accepted her pallor and sunken eyes as a sign of her fatigue and state of mourning. All were deeply sympathetic as they paid their respects.

Many brought small gifts. Her students presented her with an embroidered linen bag of buffalo bean, Old Man's Whiskers, columbine and prairie crocus seeds. They asked her to plant the seeds at her new home to remember the wildflowers the children often presented to her at school.

Agnes MacDiarmid, her eyes conspicuously reddened, hovered about Madelyn, as did her pregnant daughter-in-law, Sarah. Seamus and his band mates played quietly in the background as a grand feast was set out on long tables.

Everyone complimented Madelyn on how well her students had scored in the all-important year end entrance exams for high school. Even Archie Mason, much to everyone's shock—including his own—achieved a respectable passing mark out of grade eight, though, like most of his fellows, he was bound for his father's farm, not higher education.

John and Esther Blue Wolf, their children hanging shyly on their legs, came to extend their best wishes for a safe journey. After giving Clarence and Marie warm hugs, Madelyn looked up eagerly at John. "Mr. Blue Wolf, may I have a moment of your time?"

John nodded and stepped forward, ducking his head to listen.

"I wondered...that is, I've not seen my cousin for the past week or so." Madelyn knew John was aware of her frequent visits to the forge in a fruitless effort to find Kicker. "I know you said she'd gone up to the lumber camps to deliver some things, but I thought she might be back by now. Would you by any chance be aware of where she is?"

"Not really, Mrs. Bristow. When Kicker got back from the camps yesterday, she asked to have a few days off. She's certainly earned them, given the hours she's worked, so I granted her request. I expect her back to work in two days' time."

The day after my train leaves. Madelyn sighed and offered a wan smile. "Would you tell her...no, never mind."

"Perhaps she will return in time to see you off, Mrs. Bristow."

"Perhaps." *No, she won't. She knows I made my choice, and she's turned away from me. God help me—what have I done?*

She was barely saved from an emotional collapse by the sudden appearance of Laird and Billy. They giggled and egged each other on. She fought back tears as she smiled at them. "What are my favourite rapscallions up to?"

The boys suddenly turned shy, until Wynne rolled her eyes and gave her son a nudge. "Laird, I believe you have something for Mrs. Bristow?"

Laird cleared his throat and brought a thin, flat package out from behind his back. "We wanted you to remember us." He glanced up at his mother for support and she gave him an encouraging smile. He handed the package to Madelyn, who busied herself with unwrapping it.

When the wrapping fell away, Madelyn found herself looking at a photograph of all her students in front of the schoolhouse. At the bottom was written in large black letters, "To the best teacher ever! Don't forget us!"

Tears spilled from her eyes as Madelyn traced the faces of the children who had become so dear to her.

Laird looked up at his mother in a panic. Wynne ruffled his hair. "It means she likes it, Laird."

Madelyn pulled Laird and Billy into her arms. "I could never forget any of you."

The boys wavered between triumph and unease as they hugged Madelyn tightly then broke away.

Wynne laughed as she watched them scamper over to the food table. "You should see what I have to go through just to get a goodnight kiss." She turned back to Madelyn and a look of concern crossed her face. "Are you all right, Maddie?"

When Madelyn was unable to answer, Wynne took her arm and waved other well-wishers back. "Let's let Mrs. Bristow get some air, shall we?"

A short, sharp whistle and Brander led the way as Wynne steered Madelyn to the side door and guided her outside. She shot her mother a warning look when it appeared that Mrs. MacDiarmid was going to follow them.

"Come on, Maddie. We'll go over here and let you settle yourself a bit. I don't doubt everything has been more than overwhelming these past few days."

Wynne placed a firm hand on Madelyn's elbow as they crossed the grass to a bench that had been set under some trees. The young couple who sat there took one look at Wynne's stern face and hastily departed, mumbling their apologies.

Madelyn gave a weak laugh. "You'd have made a good teacher. One glance and you put the fear of God in them."

"Actually, that was Elliot Costain and Reid Nichol's daughter. Since I pay Costain's wages, and my good friend Reid isn't thrilled by a cowhand courting his eldest, Elliot wasn't about to stick around. At any rate, have a seat here and rest a bit."

The women sat, Brander curled comfortably at their feet. Madelyn, aware of the concerned looks Wynne directed her way, tried a diversionary tactic. "How on earth did you ever get all the children together for that picture without me knowing?"

"Mother's idea, believe it or not. Remember that weekend she and Sarah took you into Calgary for some shopping?"

"Of course. Oh, for heaven's sake, we even passed the photographer getting off the train at the station. I practically tripped over his equipment."

Wynne gave a satisfied chuckle. "Mother arranged everything. The photographer stayed a day, and made a fair bit of money working around Galbraith's Crossing. A lot of people like the idea of being immortalized. Even Mother made sure she got her money's worth. She had pictures taken of the whole family before she gave the photographer his wages and traveling money."

Madelyn was moved by Agnes' thoughtfulness. *I'm really going to miss her.* Her eyes filled with tears as she acknowledged what she had known all along. *I'm going to miss all of them so much, even Archie.* But it was the thought of the one she would miss more than she could ever bear that caused the tears to spill over.

Wynne took a folded handkerchief from her handbag. "Here. There are lots more where that one came from. I had a hunch they might be needed tonight. Now, tell me what has you looking like you lost your best friend. Or perhaps I'm being indelicate. Certainly the loss of your husband is more than sufficient reason for you to exhibit such woe."

Madelyn shook her head and dabbed at her eyes daintily. "No, that's not it. The Major and I...well, we spent more time apart than we did together since we married. I often felt as if I barely knew him."

Wynne gave a sympathetic murmur. "So, not your husband... Your cousin, then? I noticed Kicker's absence from the party. I take it things are not harmonious between you?"

It was the warmth and concern in Wynne's voice that broke the fragile hold on propriety that Madelyn had maintained since the night Kicker left. Sobs shook her body as she wept freely into Wynne's handkerchief.

Brander sat up in alarm and Wynne reassured him, motioning him back to the ground.

An arm encircled Madelyn's shoulders and Wynne quietly offered support without demanding any answers.

When Madelyn finally tried to speak, Wynne hushed her gently. "Let's go for a walk, shall we? It will be a bit more private further down the road."

Madelyn leaned on Wynne's arm and followed her friend's lead, the border collie close at their heels. She paid little attention to their direction and was surprised when they stopped on the porch of her own home.

Wynne gestured to one of the two chairs and, despite her dress, took a seat on the railing. Her kind eyes regarded Madelyn with determination. "So tell me, Madelyn Bristow, what has you looking like your world is ending?"

"Kicker isn't coming with me."

"I know. John told me."

"Matters between us are...difficult. She's angry with me for returning to England. She feels that I've made a poor decision and will come to regret it."

Wynne narrowed her eyes shrewdly. "Strikes me that you already regret it. I've seen lots of would-be homesteaders leave here. Some of them are embarrassed about their failure; some of them are defiant; most can hardly wait to get out of here. But I've never seen any of them looking like it was Judgment Day and they'd ended up on the wrong side of the scale."

"It is the right decision for me. I know I'll be much better off back in England." Madelyn knew her words were unconvincing by the scepticism on Wynne's face.

"And you think Kicker would be too?"

"No." Madelyn's eyes widened in shock at her response. As if a dam finally broke, the words came straight from her heart. "Kicker is absolutely right that her home is here; this is exactly where she belongs. Taking her back to England with its societal constraints would be like putting Rabbit to work pulling a London cab. It would be the height of cruelty. It would kill their beautiful spirits. Neither belongs in the city."

"I agree. So?"

"So, what's right for her is not right for me. I have a life there. My family and friends await my return. My uncle wrote to tell me that after a suitable interval, he will ask for my mother's hand in marriage. He was always more of a parent to me than my father. My dear old nanny is getting on, and I want to be there for her as she was always there for me." Madelyn rose to her feet and leaned against the railing next to Wynne. "Please don't take this the wrong way, but London is home. Here is—"

"Not home."

"Not home."

"I understand, Maddie. Surely Kicker will come to understand too, in time."

My sweet, stubborn woman. No, she will never understand why I relinquished our love. "I know she respects you immensely, and holds both you and Will in the highest regard. Will you be there for her, Wynne?"

Wynne nodded solemnly. "Kicker has friends here. We'll stand by her. Don't you worry about that."

"There is one more thing." Wynne raised a quizzical eyebrow. "The property out by Shadow Creek. I know that by ending my contract prematurely, I abrogated any claim to that land. However, I have some money of my own, and I'd like to buy the land outright from you."

"And deed it to Kicker?"

"Yes. I also want her to have Galahad, and all our household goods. Can that be arranged before I leave?"

"Have you told her?"

Madelyn gave a bitter laugh. "When? I've not been able to find her for the last week, and no one seems to know where she is. Your brother said she is to return to work the day after I leave Galbraith's Crossing, and knowing Kicker, she will hold to that. Would you please deliver the deed to her when she returns?"

Wynne took Madelyn's hand and squeezed it lightly. "I promise."

Madelyn could not help comparing the crowd on the station platform that had come to see her off, with their welcoming committee a year ago of one small boy. She assumed her brief walk to the train station would be solitary as Seamus had collected her trunk earlier that morning. But when she emerged from her house a short while before, a crowd, headed by the MacDiarmid clan, had already gathered to escort her. As they made their way down the street, more and more people joined in the impromptu parade, jostling to get close to her and bid a personal farewell. Madelyn tried to convey her appreciation to each well-wisher, even as her eyes frantically scrutinized every shadow for the only person she really needed to see—the one person who never appeared.

Now, even as she felt hemmed in and trapped by friends and supporters, Madelyn took some small comfort from the evidence that she would be missed. But it did little to stem the grief that threatened to overwhelm her at every turn. *I will get used to it, to her absence. It's only been a week. Time will help. Dear God, it has to. I cannot possibly endure this agony much longer.*

She spotted Seamus Kelly standing by the station door. Madelyn made her apologies and pushed her way through the crowd to his side. Just as she reached him, the departure whistle sounded. Madelyn hastily took a letter out of her handbag. "Please, Mr. Kelly, will you give this to her?"

Seamus accepted it with a solemn nod.

Madelyn worried that he would be angry with her for hurting his friend, but she saw only sorrow in his eyes. "Would you tell her that I will write? Would you tell her—no, would you beg her from me, to write back? Please, Mr. Kelly..."

The whistle sounded again and helpful hands tugged Madelyn away. As she was rushed to her carriage, she twisted to see Seamus, her eyes pleading with him.

He nodded, and waved the letter in a farewell salute.

Before she could say anything further, Madelyn was smothered with hugs from Agnes and bundled aboard the train. She took a window seat with a view of those on the platform. She desperately scanned the crowd, but though she knew them all, nowhere was the face she yearned to see.

Madelyn took her final leave and forced herself to wave as they began to pull away from the station. Within moments the engine picked up steam as the train moved out onto the open prairie.

She stared blindly out the window at the familiar landscape, a sense of unreality filling her. *This cannot be happening.* Her gaze shifted from the slowly passing scenery to the seat across from her.

Madelyn could hear the older couple in the seats behind her, but their words did not penetrate as she stared helplessly at the emptiness of her compartment. *No, no, no...* Then a woman's raised voice pierced her consciousness.

"Good heavens, Roland! Is that a Native chasing the train? You don't suppose he plans to attack us, do you?"

Madelyn blinked and ignored the husband's reassurances as her eyes searched for the source of the woman's fears. *Kicker!*

Kicker and Rabbit raced parallel to the train tracks, close enough that Madelyn could see her lover's eyes searching the carriage windows. Instantly she stood and wrenched open the small upper window. But as she thrust her arm out to wave, the train began to curve around a copse of trees and Kicker fell out of sight. Madelyn made a dash for the back of the carriage, but as she reached the door to the exterior platform, the conductor entered.

He held up his hands. "Whoa, Miss. You don't want to go out there. It's far too dangerous. Let me help you back to your seat, and if there's anything you need, anything at all, I'll be glad to fetch it for you."

I need her!

The conductor took Madelyn's arm firmly and escorted her back to her seat. As she collapsed onto the padded bench, her eyes searched the horizon. There was no sign of Kicker and Rabbit. They had been left far behind by the iron horse on its eastward passage.

Did she change her mind? Dear God, was Kicker trying to come with me after all? Should I get off at the next station and go back, just in case?

As much as every part of her wanted to believe that, wanted to return instantly to fetch Kicker back, Madelyn knew she had not changed her mind.

Kicker had found her place in the world, and neither the depth of Madelyn's love nor her longing to be with the woman was going to change that simple fact.

Madelyn's black mourning clothes had never felt more appropriate.

CHAPTER 23

KICKER TOOK NO NOTICE OF the rider who approached her campfire until a cold nose touched her face. Momentarily startled out of her misery, Kicker fended off Brander's exuberant greeting as Wynne reined Ballantrae to a halt. Inwardly, Kicker groaned. Company was the last thing she wanted. It was also the last thing she'd expected at her isolated campsite.

Wynne swung down from her horse, crossed to the fire, and wordlessly squatted next to Kicker.

"How'd you fin' me?" Kicker did not care if her question was abrupt. She did not care why Wynne had come looking for her. She could not find it within herself to care about anything at all.

Wynne met Kicker's scowl with a level gaze. "Mr. Kelly gave me a general idea of where you might be; Brander did the rest."

Kicker could barely summon up the emotional energy to be annoyed with Seamus, but Wynne read it in her expression anyway.

"Don't be angry at Mr. Kelly. He strongly suggested that I leave you be; he told me that you would be back in town in your own time and on your own terms."

"Said I'd be at work t'morrow, an' I will be."

"I know. John didn't send me."

"Then why're you here?"

"To give you this." Wynne drew a long envelope out of her vest. When Kicker made no attempt to take it, she tossed it in Kicker's lap. "You might as well read it. I'm not leaving until you do."

With that motivation, Kicker opened the envelope and disinterestedly scanned the words on the enclosed papers by the light of the campfire. Slowly it sank in what she was reading, and she started again from the beginning.

The papers Wynne had handed her did not make sense. Nothing made sense anymore. Finally, after the third reading, Kicker raised bleak eyes to her friend, who responded with a half-smile.

"Madelyn wanted to ensure you were taken care of, Kicker. She bought the land out by Shadow Creek and deeded it to you. It's yours now. She also gave written instructions that everything left in the house goes to you, including Galahad."

If Kicker had been able to feel anything, she would have felt shock. But nothing penetrated the numbness that had settled around her when she had finally accepted that Madelyn was leaving her.

Wynne laid a hand on Kicker's shoulder and shook her softly. "Do you understand? It's yours, all yours."

Kicker managed to rouse herself enough to respond. "I... thank you, Wynne."

"I merely had our lawyer draw up the papers; this is Madelyn's gift to you. She needed to know you would be all right without her."

Kicker felt the bile rise in her throat. *A'right without her? How could that e'en be poss'ble?*

The tears that had flowed freely as Madelyn's train rolled beyond Rabbit's ability to pace it, returned. Crumpling the papers, Kicker buried her face in her hands and sobbed.

From one side, Brander whined and nudged at her knee; from the other, strong arms closed around her and held her tight. Kicker sagged against Wynne, unable in her utter desolation to reject the comfort of her friend's embrace.

"Shhh, shhh, it'll be all right, Kicker. I know how hard this is, I understand, but it will be all right some day."

Kicker shook her head, unable to speak through her tears but certain her world would never be completely all right ever again. Wynne held her tightly and rubbed her back in wordless comfort. When finally the tears subsided, Wynne released her, took a seat on the ground next to Kicker, and handed over a handkerchief. "Between you and your cousin, I seem to be going through a lot of these lately."

Kicker wiped her eyes and blew her nose. She stared morosely into the fire, but warmed to the solid strength of the friend beside her. Gratitude seeped through the cracks of her misery, and, turning to face Wynne, she allowed herself a once unthinkable question. "D'you understan' truly?"

A deep sadness etched on her face, Wynne nodded. "Yes, Kicker, I do. And I envy you."

"Why?"

Wynne's voice was so quiet that Kicker had to strain to hear her. "For having the courage I lacked."

Kicker was not really surprised. "D'you wan' to tell me?"

"What's to tell? I was very young when I fell desperately, passionately... inappropriately in love. Fearful of the consequences, I ran from that love." Wynne laughed bitterly. "I promptly landed in the arms of the most unsuitable mate possible, but as a mate, he had the virtue of being a man, so I married him."

"Laird's da?"

"Yes. So it wasn't a complete loss. But still, I envy you so."

Kicker understood that. Even to abate her current agony, she would not surrender a moment of the past year's joy. *If I ne'er again have but the mem'ry of that joy to warm me at night, I count myself the mos' fortunate of women.*

For a long time the women sat together silently, shoulders braced against each other, each lost in thought as they stared at the fire.

Eventually, Kicker cleared her throat. "I'll not go back to that house."

"I didn't think you would. You once spoke of making the barn at Shadow Creek into a temporary home. I took the liberty of having some of my men clear out the old Mackey house and transport your goods to your property. You can use whatever you need to make the barn liveable while you build the cabin; store the rest in the shed and root cellar. I had Galahad moved out there, too."

Kicker had given little thought to her living arrangements. Her spare camp would have sufficed until the weather worsened, and she assumed she would find something else at that time. She appreciated Madelyn's thoughtfulness and Wynne's initiative in taking those concerns out of her hands. "Would you take Galahad back to the Steeple Seven?"

Wynne turned to Kicker in surprise. "Why?"

"Tis not fair. Rabbit will be in town with me all day whilst I work. Galahad would be alone too much." *Alone too much. Twould make two of us…no point in that.*

Wynne considered for a moment and then shook her head. "Galahad is accustomed to being around Rabbit. I think you should keep him, at least for now. If it becomes too much to care for him this winter, I'll take him back then, all right?"

Too drained to argue, Kicker shrugged her acquiescence. She tilted her head and looked up at the darkening sky. "We should have ridden more. Twas what brought us t'gether in the firs' place. She craved the freedom ridin' gave us. We always meant to, but Maddie was so busy with school. Maybe had we done so, she'd have fallen in love with the country the way I did. Maybe then she ne'er would have left."

"Kicker, if Maddie's love for you wasn't enough to hold her here, no force on this earth could have."

"An' twas not enough." The simple truth of it closed Kicker's throat with grief. She leaned against Wynne, who put her arm around Kicker's shoulders. By the time they spoke again, the moon could be seen above the tree line.

"I'd best get back to the ranch."

"Aye." Kicker rested her head on Wynne's shoulder for a comforting moment, then stood and shook off the numbness from sitting too long in one position. "Thank you for comin' out here."

Wynne rose to her feet, Brander instantly by her side. "You're welcome. Remember you are not alone, Kicker. You have friends." She held out her hand and Kicker grasped it firmly. "I need to caution you, though—you must be careful what you allow others to see. They will expect you to be sad at your cousin's departure; they will not understand that you are shattered."

Kicker saw the sympathy in Wynne's eyes.

"I know it will be hard. God knows I do, but when it gets too much to bear, send for me. I've walked this road, and may be of some help if you'll let me."

"I'll be a'right, though tis grateful I am for your sympathy and understandin'. You're a good frien'."

Unexpectedly, Wynne pulled Kicker into an embrace. "She made a mistake, Kicker. She knew that when she bought you that land, and she knew that when she climbed aboard that train. Don't give up hope." Wynne released Kicker, wheeled about and strode over to Ballantrae.

Kicker watched Wynne ride away. *Don' give up hope? Far too late for that.*

Kicker knew Seamus would give her time to indulge her desolation. She also knew the instant that time was over, to his way of thinking, he would seek her out, even though she consciously avoided him.

She was consciously avoiding everyone. Until Kicker was sure she could maintain a calm demeanour, she did not want to handle any inquiries about her cousin's departure.

Seven days had passed since Madelyn boarded the eastbound train. Kicker only made it through each day by keeping awareness of Madelyn's absence rigidly at bay. She arrived at work before dawn and left long after John had called it a day, unless he insisted she do otherwise. When she departed, she rode Rabbit east out of town, then doubled back to skirt the northern edge as she returned to Shadow Creek to avoid any townsfolk.

Days were relatively successful. Backbreaking work, either at the forge or on her cabin, made it easy to stay focused on the task at hand and not let her mind wander. Nights were hellish, so Kicker kept them as short as possible. She worked late into the evening by lantern and torch light, until she could fall asleep from sheer exhaustion.

Fortunately Wynne and Will had gone down to Montana on a buying trip, so Kicker had not had to evade her friends' well intentioned sympathy. Her only interactions these days were with John Blue Wolf, but even with her employer, conversations had dwindled to solely essential communication.

When Seamus finally cantered up to the Shadow Creek cabin, Kicker reluctantly set down her tools. She knew she had pushed his patience as far as she could.

"Kicker."

"Seamus."

Seamus dismounted and Kicker hid a reluctant smile. Her friend was not a natural horseman, and no matter how much he rode, always appeared as awkward as a chicken riding a goat. *It can be done, but there ain't nothin' pretty about it.* "You can put that ol' nag in with Rabbit and Galahad, if you want."

Seamus nodded, and led his ancient gelding to the corral next to the barn.

Without waiting, Kicker headed for the creek. She suspected this was going to be a lengthy talk and knew they would be more comfortable in the shade.

Kicker did not have long to wait before Seamus took his place beside her on the old log. Wordlessly she handed him the tin dipper and he drank his fill of creek water.

"This certainly is a welcome respite from the heat."

"Aye. Tis a hot one, t'day."

"I find the flies far more bothersome than the heat, though. And the mosquitoes were surely dispatched from the Underworld itself."

Kicker shrugged. She had spent so much time at the Shadow Creek site that summer that she had become inured to the omnipresent pests.

"Were you aware that your old house sold?"

"Aye. John said as much. No concern of mine. Twas the town's to do with as it pleased."

"To a dentist, is what I hear. The gentleman apparently plans to convert the parlour to his shop and continue to utilize the bedroom and kitchen as his living quarters."

The thought of a stranger sleeping in the tiny attic bedroom where she had shared such happiness with Madelyn pained Kicker far more than she had anticipated. She drew in a deep breath and struggled to calm herself.

Seamus quietly gave Kicker time to regain her equanimity as they both gazed out over the creek. When her breathing returned to normal, he spoke again.

"I cannot allow you to become a hermit, my friend. I understand the instinct to hide—truly, I do—but I will not make the same mistake again."

"Again?"

"I thought I was doing the right thing by indulging Pudge's reticence, by allowing his near pathological fear of people seeing his injuries to set the course of our days. I assumed, particularly given the ebullience that was his birthright, he simply needed time. I was wrong. I refuse to lose you, too."

Kicker twisted to look at Seamus. He did not meet her eyes but she could see the determination etched on his face.

"You're not... I'm not los', only grievin' a little."

"A lot, if you would permit me to say, and that is your right. But I plan to come out here every chance I get to help you build, and I would appreciate you stopping in for supper when you finish work. I am used to cooking for two, and you—" Seamus finally turned to look at Kicker. He frowned at what he saw. "...apparently have forgotten how to cook for one."

Kicker guiltily lowered her eyes. She had punched a couple of new holes in her belt to pull it in tighter. She knew she was foregoing meals, but her appetite fled the day Madelyn announced her decision to leave Galbraith's Crossing. Though she suspected hunger of any kind had vanished permanently, she knew Seamus had a good point. "A'right. I'll stop in now an' again."

"Every evening. I will not insist you stay. I will not even insist you converse with me, but if you do not make an appearance, I will march supper over to you at the forge."

Kicker snorted, amused in spite of herself. "Won' that give the good people of Galbraith more to talk about."

Seamus didn't chuckle, as he normally did when they spoke of the misperceptions of their fellow townsfolk.

"Seamus?"

It was his turn to draw in a deep breath. "Kicker, I...well, I know the way of things, and if you want...that is, I know you do not want, but if it is necessary...if you find yourself in a difficult situation...not that I want to make things any more difficult, but..."

As the most articulate man Kicker knew stumbled over his words, she stared at him in amazement. "Seamus?"

Seamus grabbed for the discarded dipper and scooped out more creek water, drinking half and pouring the rest in his hand to dash over his face.

Struck by her friend's obvious distress, Kicker gentled her tone. "Jus' spit it out, Seamus. What's on your mind?"

"I apologize for sounding like a pure dolt. I have given this matter much thought, and only wish to offer a solution to a problem that may or may not arise."

That sounds more like him. Kicker nodded encouragingly. "An' that is?"

"Please understand that I do not wish to take advantage of either your unfortunate situation nor our friendship, which I cherish greatly."

"I know." And though Kicker still did not know what Seamus was talking about, she did know with absolute certainty that her honourable friend had only her best interests at heart.

"Kicker, life can be terribly difficult for a woman in your circumstances."

My circumstances? Kicker's eyes widened as she suddenly understood the direction of Seamus' thoughts. "You mean a woman alone...without a man?"

"Or another woman...as a companion." Seamus half turned on the log and his long legs dragged against the moss. His expression, flustered mere moments ago, was now serious. "I have little to offer anyone in this life. But what I can offer you, should you ever need it, is the protection of my name."

"You're talkin' about marriage?" Kicker wondered if she sounded as dumbfounded as she felt.

"I am, but not in the traditional sense. I would neither ask nor expect...well, this is difficult, but...consummation." Seamus' pale face turned bright red, however he doggedly pushed on. "None need know that, of course, but you could pass the nights in Pudge's room. To the world at large, we would be as husband and wife. We certainly get along well. Next to my brother, you are my dearest friend. I would consider myself a fortunate man indeed to spend the remainder of my years as your putative husband, and I swear on all I hold holy that I would never ask for more than simply your companionship."

Stunned speechless, Kicker stared at Seamus.

"I know this has come as a shock. I certainly do not require an answer at this time. In fact, I do not require an answer at any time. I only wanted you to know that if it ever becomes onerous or dangerous to continue life as a single woman, I would be honoured to stand by your side as your spouse. You need only come and tell me, if ever I can help."

Bless'd Jesus! I ne'er saw that comin'!

Seamus turned back, his gaze again across the creek as he fell silent.

Kicker saw the beads of sweat on her friend's face and knew how hard it had been for him to speak. Affection swelled her heart and she nudged him gently. "I cannot begin to tell you how grateful I am. You are a staunch frien', an' tis bless'd I am to have you. But what if some day a lady comes along that you truly wish to marry, to have a family with? Twould not be fair to you to be tied to me. Are you sure you would wan' to do this?"

He nodded. "I've not told you the whole story about my leaving—" Seamus broke off abruptly and Kicker saw his prominent Adam's apple bob convulsively. "I am sure, Kicker. There will be no other woman—no children, no family."

For the second time, understanding washed over Kicker, and she ached for her friend. *He un'nerstan's lonely.* "I thank you. I don' think it'll e'er come to that, but if it does, you may well see me standin' on your doorstep." Kicker saw Seamus' shoulders slump in relief, and with a half-smile, she joined him in staring out across the creek.

Kicker could not imagine a time or circumstance desperate enough that she would give up her independence to become Seamus' wife, even in name only. But it warmed her heart that he had made an offer so obviously counter to his own nature, all in an effort to protect her.

Birds had resumed singing and squirrels were again chattering by the time Kicker spoke again. "I knew the depth of her distress, but I ne'er thought she'd leave, you know?"

"I know."

"Twas arrogant of me to think she'd stay jus' for me, I s'pose."

"No, not arrogant, my friend. It is human nature to pit absolute hope against all evidence to the contrary. You did nothing wrong."

"I mus' have. She lef' me."

Seamus had no answer for that.

"I don' know how what we had between us was not enough. Is such a love so common that she could abandon it easily?"

"There was...there is nothing commonplace about your love for Miss Madelyn, Kicker. I truly believe that she will feel its absence forever."

"Pretty words, but they mean naught in the long run. She'll be aboard that ship to England soon, if not a'ready."

Seamus heaved a deep sigh but said nothing.

"I know we could've worked it out, had she stayed. I know it, Seamus. With all my heart, I know it."

"I've no wish to cause you pain, but given what I understand of your feelings, do you now regret not boarding that train with her?"

"E'ry hour of e'ry day." Kicker shot Seamus a rueful look. "An' I still think I made the right decision. Twas right to try to anchor Maddie here. Twas right to oppose goin' backwards. Our future was here, not back in England. I believe that now; I'll believe that always."

"I am so very, very sorry."

"Aye, as am I."

Seamus drew an envelope from his pocket.

"You heard from Pudge?"

Seamus shook his head and extended the envelope to Kicker. "No, this isn't from Pudge. This is from Miss Madelyn. She gave it to me the day she left. I would have brought it directly, but I thought you might need some time, first. Miss Madelyn said to tell you that she will write from England, and begs that you will write in return."

So there are to be letters, are there? Does she think twill make up for her absence from my arms, from our bed? Tis cold comfort indeed, Maddie love. Kicker accepted the letter and turned it over in her hands as she stared at the familiar writing on the envelope. Reading it would be like rubbing salt in a wound, but she was struck by the knowledge that it held Madelyn's last words to her.

A hand patted her shoulder and Seamus rose to his feet. "I will leave you with that. I must be getting back. Shall I see you at supper tomorrow?"

Kicker nodded absently. "Aye. I'll stop by after work."

It was long after Kicker heard Seamus ride away that she finally broke the wax seal, opened the envelope, and extracted the single sheet of paper within.

My dearest Kicker,

I am in a state of utter disbelief. My train departs in less than two hours, and only now am I coming to accept that you will not board with me. I cling to the diminishing hope that you will have a last moment volte-face. How can our impending separation not sear you as agonizingly as it does me?

And yet, my beloved Kicker, even as I write these words, I know how selfish I am. I know that you belong here, in this place, in this world. Still, the pain that I feel overwhelms every other consideration. I do not care what it costs either of us; I only want us to be together. Nothing else matters.

I love you—beyond all measure, dearest. Had I found you these past days, I would have flung myself at your feet and begged you to come with me. I believe you knew that, and with the wisdom that has always surpassed mine, you would not allow such abasement. For it would have done no good, is that not so, dearest? On this matter, you are as staunch and unyielding as those damnable mountains.

All the words in the world would not have changed your mind. In the bitterly lonely days and nights to come, I will endeavour to respect that, to respect you and your choice. If I am never again to touch you, never again to know the joy of your kisses and the warmth of your body, then I shall try with all my heart to remember to be grateful for the time we have had.

Please forgive me for all the occasions I wounded you, and for this irreparable rending of the heart. May you find solace in knowing that I did myself as grievous an injury. It is a pain that shall never end, even should I live to the age of our good Queen. Perhaps some day you will forgive me for not being strong enough to live for love alone.

Your final words to me were that you would always love me. Let my final words to you be the same. I will always, always love you, my dearest Kicker.

Forever your,
Maddie

Renewed anguish doubled Kicker over, and tears dropped to the ground between her feet. *How could we have given this up? What fools we are.*

Kicker ran her sleeve over her face. As July moved into August, the heat had grown oppressive, even at twilight, so she chose to work in the shaded interior of her cabin.

With Seamus' help, Kicker had the walls of the cabin up, the doors and windows roughed in, and most of the roof on. Though she felt no sense of urgency and was willing to spend the winter in the barn, Kicker was satisfied with the progress they'd made.

As she hammered another plank into place on the floor, Kicker considered her next step. She needed to finish the roof and chink the spaces in the wall between the logs. Though there was still plenty of summer left, she did not want to wait until the leaves began to turn and the cold winds to blow.

Suddenly Kicker felt another's presence. Expecting Seamus, who had promised to come out after his last westbound train went through, she turned to the door.

Madelyn stood there.

They stared at each other for a long moment, then Kicker dropped her hammer, rose to her feet, and jammed her shaking hands into her pockets. She fought tears of grief and joy with every bit of will she had, but kept her voice calm. "I bin waitin' for you to come back. Thought I might have our home finished firs', though."

Madelyn's eyes welled up. "I am a fool, Kicker."

"Aye." Kicker's dry answer drew a shaky laugh from Madelyn.

"How could you possibly be so certain I'd return?"

"I will not lie. For the firs' while after you left, I was certain I'd ne'er see you again. I'd promised Lil that I'd anchor you, no matter what. I swore to her I'd be strong enough to hol' us t'gether if...when you allowed your fear to push me away, but it was desperate hard, Maddie." Kicker paused, her tenuous control savagely undercut by the memory of too many unbearable nights alone. She swallowed and went on, her voice trembling. "Sometimes, though...when it was too much to endure... I'd tell myself you had to come home. If I was in such agony, then you mus' be, too. You had the means to end our pain. I had to b'lieve some day you would choose to do so. I had to b'lieve..."

Madelyn gave Kicker a bittersweet smile. "Your faith in me was hardly warranted, dearest. When I left here, I intended never to return. I spent weeks in Montreal at L'Auberge de St. Christophe, passing up every outbound ship until Monsieur and Madame Gagnon must have thought me quite mad."

"Because you were afraid of sailin'?"

Madelyn shook her head. "No, dearest. Because the only thing that I was afraid of—the only thing that sickened me to my very soul every single hour of my absence—was the torment of thinking I would never see you again."

Kicker took a step toward Madelyn, who held up a hand.

"Let me get through this. If you touch me, I shall instantly forget everything but my desire to hold you. Since the moment I got on that train, I've done nothing but reflect upon my words and actions of this past year, and before anything else occurs between us, I need to tell you of my conclusions."

"But, Maddie..." Kicker inched forward, then stopped as Madelyn took a step back. Resigned, though barely able to restrain the need to touch Madelyn, Kicker signaled her acquiescence.

"I truly have been a fool, but I would have you understand why."

Kicker suspected she understood more than Madelyn knew, but she simply nodded encouragement.

"You scared me."

I ne'er expected that. Kicker's eyes widened in shock.

Madelyn shook her head. "No, dearest, I don't mean in the physical sense. I know you would never harm me in any way." Madelyn glanced around the cabin and avoided Kicker's eyes. "May we walk a bit?"

"Aye."

Madelyn stepped outside and Kicker joined her, careful to keep a space between them. They strolled slowly, without talking. As they passed the corral, Madelyn stopped. Galahad trotted over and whickered as Madelyn stroked his nose.

The women did not touch each other until they reached the edge of the bank by the creek. Kicker planned to dig in wooden steps eventually, but re-building the cabin had taken precedence. She hesitantly offered Madelyn her arm to descend the slippery embankment, and rejoiced when it was accepted. As she tucked Madelyn's arm inside her own, Kicker could not help an involuntary shiver. Madelyn's warmth and nearness were balm to her senses.

When they got down the embankment, Kicker offered Madelyn a seat on the log, but it was declined. In the cool shade, Madelyn unpinned her hat and loosed her long, thick hair.

It took all of Kicker's resolve not to plunge her hands into that glorious mass and pull her in for a fierce, proprietary kiss.

"Where did I leave off, dearest?"

Kicker dragged her eyes from the coppery cascade and met Madelyn's gaze. "I scared you."

"That was misleading. I scared myself." Madelyn drew a deep breath. "I have a confession to make. Do you remember when we took the train away from Grindleshire's?"

"Aye. The conductor would have thrown me off for gettin' in your carriage."

Madelyn chuckled and Kicker closed her eyes at the sound that had been too long absent. "I believe he might have tried, but I sincerely doubt he'd have prevailed."

"Because you protected me."

"Did I?"

"Aye. You did then, and e'er since."

"And that, dearest, is the crux of the matter."

Madelyn turned to face her and tucked her hands into Kicker's welcoming grasp. Her expression begged Kicker to understand.

Lost in the exquisite sensation of once again holding hands, Kicker strove to focus on Madelyn's words.

"From the moment you told me you would accompany me on this wild journey, I felt that I was responsible for you. I promised your brother I would take care of you always. I took that vow very seriously. I was convinced that as I had taken you away from all that you knew, it was up to me to protect and guide you every step of the way. I was equally convinced that eventually I would fail miserably at my self appointed task."

"I were no chil', Maddie."

"I know that, beloved woman. I know that so well. I'm well aware that you protected me every bit as much as I shielded you. But my point is that even when I thought I was taking responsibility for you, inwardly I quailed at and fought against the idea. When it came to affairs of the heart, I'd only ever been responsible for myself."

"Charity?"

"No, Kicker. Charity took the lead in all our intercourse, until the moment Father seized upon her and threw her out of my life."

"An' t'others? I know twere others, Maddie."

"Yes, dearest, there were. Though perhaps not as many as you may have imagined." Madelyn grimaced at Kicker's involuntary expression of disbelief. "Truly, beloved, I was never as given to flights of fancy as my comportment may have suggested. After the disaster with Charity, I never again allowed my heart to be engaged. I gave only fair words and a willing body to the women I courted thereafter."

Kicker wanted to believe that. From the moment she had learned of Madelyn's inclination towards women, she had tried very hard not to speculate about her former lovers. "An' when you met me? Was that the way it began for us?"

"No. It was as different as night from day. None, not even Charity, affected me as you did from the moment you came for me at the station. I'd never met one as utterly honest and artless, and it is to my eternal shame that I mistook your lack of guile for lack of competence in dealing with the new and unknown. I was convinced it was up to me to shield you from the world, while uncertain that I would be able to do so."

"I needed you thus in London."

"But not here, Kicker. Never here. You fit this world like the missing piece of a puzzle, and I resented that. You didn't need me—"

"Not true." Kicker clutched Madelyn's hands fiercely to her chest. "Twas ne'er a moment that I did not need you."

"Perhaps that is factual in an emotional sense, but in the much wider sense of things, you really did not need me. Ironically, I was absolutely correct when I told you at the Canada High Commission that your practical knowledge would be of far greater use in this land than my poetry and pence ever could be. Look how well you've done in my absence."

"Done well?" Kicker stared at Madelyn in consternation. "Are you daft? I barely make it from one day to the nex'."

"But you do make it, don't you? You continue to work, to build, to see your friends. You continue to live."

"Tis not a life, love. Without you, twas only a half life at bes'." Kicker frowned at Madelyn. "An' how d'you know how I've been, anyway?"

"Mr. Kelly gave me a ride out here. We talked about you the whole time."

Kicker wondered briefly whether that conversation had included Seamus' proposal, but suspected it had not. She and Seamus had never mentioned it again themselves.

Madelyn drew Kicker's hands to her lips and bowed her head for a long moment.

Desire surged through Kicker and heated memories of her lover's touch overwhelmed her. She struggled against the urge to throw propriety to the winds and return to the fevered couplings of their early months together. It would be so easy to rip Madelyn's clothes apart and take what she knew Maddie was just as eager to give. *God gi' me strength. I need you so.*

When Madelyn looked up, Kicker saw her eyes were bright with unshed tears. Instantly her desire melted into a need to comfort. She ached to take Madelyn in her arms and kiss those tears away. But Kicker knew they had to resolve matters between them first, before they allowed themselves the reunion they craved. Too much had been left unsaid already.

Though Kicker was certain they could, with joy and abandonment, pick up physically where they left off, she wanted more. She wanted—she needed the confidence that nothing would ever again separate them. To gain that surety, Kicker knew they could no longer ignore the issues that had divided them.

"What I'm trying very hard to make clear, dearest, is how much in error I was and what it did to me when I came to that realization. I was so utterly convinced that I needed to protect you, but day after day, the reality of our lives here made it clear you needed no such protection. It left me feeling completely adrift, unsure of my moorings or what to do next. What could you want or need from me, if I could not provide you this essential part of our partnership?"

Kicker nodded slowly. It was becoming clear to her. "An' you thought by goin' back—"

"That our roles, as I perceived them, could be restored, and I would avoid losing you."

"Tis daft, Maddie."

"It was damnably foolish, was what it was. But I never reasoned it out in those terms, not until I got to Montreal. Until then, I'd only a bone deep sense that I needed to get you back to England or you would be lost to me. I didn't really understand why. And failing in that understanding, I thoughtlessly left behind my whole reason for leaving... and living."

Kicker's heart leapt at the candour and sincerity of Madelyn's words. "An' when you come to that understandin'?"

"I knew my decision for the ludicrous thing it was. Oh, Kicker, I can apologize until the end of our days together, but I can never convey how truly sorry I am. You are fully an equal in this union of our love. All I can do is plead for forgiveness, not only for being so mistaken, but for leaving you when it was the cruellest thing I could do to either of us."

With a touch more delicate than most would think her capable of, Kicker caressed Madelyn's face. "Tis forgiven."

Tears rolled down Madelyn's cheeks. "As easily as that, dearest?"

"Aye. I know how much courage it took for you to come back. I know the mistakes I made, and how hard on you this life has been—"

Madelyn laid her fingers across Kicker's lips and shook her head. "I purposely disregarded all the wonderful parts of our life over this past year thus allowing myself to focus solely on the travails. It was only when I lost the many pleasures of my life here, that I admitted their existence."

"All life is hard, Maddie. Were we in London or Galbraith's Crossing, twill ne'er be easy for such as us."

"I know that, dearest. Believe me, I do."

"Twill be times still that life hurts us, that we hurt each other."

"I know that, too. But I also know that the only thing that matters is going through life with you forever at my side. We'll deal with all the rest as it arises."

"Aye, we will." Kicker gently brushed away Madelyn's tears. "It won' be easy, love. We'll have to live in the barn for a bit."

"I would live in the hollow of a tree if it meant being with you."

"Wynne's ma will have a fit."

"Let her. I'll never again allow anyone or anything to separate us for even a day."

Kicker was not sure if her heart could contain her explosion of joy. She wanted nothing more than to lead Madelyn to the barn, and the bed that had been empty for far too long, but she tried to remain practical for just a few moments longer.

"I hear they hired a new teacher, love. She's boardin' at Mrs. Thatcher's."

Madelyn shrugged, the wide smile on her face evidence that she truly was prepared to overcome all obstacles. "You know what Will said, dearest. They have a terrible time holding on to single teachers around here. I need merely bide my time until the first box social and undoubtedly the new teacher will be swept off by an eligible bachelor. I'll be patiently waiting in the wings. I have the funds to carry us for a few years—"

"I earn a decent wage, Maddie. We will carry each other."

"Exactly so, dearest. I'll undoubtedly falter in my new determination from time to time, but bear with me. I swear I will never again let you down."

"I know, love. I understan'."

"No matter how long it takes, I fully expect the Widow Bristow to teach at Galbraith Crossing's school and live with her cousin at Shadow Creek, until you and I are in our dotage."

Kicker gently drew Madelyn closer and wrapped her arms around her. *Heaven can be no sweeter than this.* "I'll build us a porch to rock on."

Madelyn pressed her body firmly against Kicker's. "As long as you have a bed for us to share, little else matters."

Kicker's breath shortened and she saw the answering desire in Madelyn's eyes, but before she could claim her, Madelyn grew serious.

"May we go back to the way it was then, dearest?"

"No." Kicker felt Madelyn's instant distress, but this time she had to make her point. "We cannot go back, Maddie, but we can go for'ard."

Relief and exultation filled the eyes Kicker had dreamed of every night since Madelyn boarded the eastbound train. "Truly? You will have me back then, body and soul?"

"Aye. With all my heart, b'loved."

Madelyn's kisses were at once delicate and demanding, ardent and giving. Her hands moved over Kicker's body with an urgency rarely matched in their time together. The sounds that spilled from her throat were an unabashed vow of intimacy renewed and devotion reborn.

Kicker could not remember an occasion—even the first time they made love—that she had felt greater elation. Madelyn was safely back in her arms, and together they would face inner demons and external obstacles. Whatever the world thought of their socially mismatched relationship, in this place, they were perfectly paired. Lovers, friends, partners—at once both teacher and student—their roles were for them to define and explore.

She and Madelyn would build a new life, taking the best from the old. They would not forget the heartbreak or the misunderstandings, or the misery each had caused the other. They had learned too much from the pain to discard such memories. But ever triumphing over those remembrances would be the joys they embraced—commitment, belief in each other, and faith that their love would sustain them to the end of their days.

Madelyn fell to her knees and pulled Kicker's shirt open. Kicker groaned as she felt Madelyn's mouth close on her breast. If they did not move soon, she knew it would only be moments before they were naked on the mossy ground at their feet. Struggling for breath, Kicker stilled Maddie's hands as they reached for her belt.

"Not here, Maddie love. Come with me."

Barely able to separate for even an instant, they climbed the bank hand in hand, and left the creek behind. When they reached the barn door, Kicker stopped and drew Madelyn into her arms. "Thank you for coming back, Maddie. Twas ne'er home when you were away, but twill be home fore'er now. I love you. I'll always love you."

Tears spilled down Madelyn's cheeks, but Kicker wasn't worried. Elation shone from Madelyn's eyes as she cradled Kicker's face in quivering hands.

"Dearest woman, my home is wherever you are...from now until forever, I swear."

Kicker pushed the door open. "Then welcome home, love."

They entered together and closed the rest of the world outside their door. The journey that had begun for the women one hot summer afternoon at an English train station had taken them far from the land of their birth. But the journey they began now would take them even further. From the gentle lands of rural England to the harsh winters of western Canada, from school to forge, from mansion to barn, they journeyed now as one, sharing love, courage, and commitment that was both destiny and destination.

ABOUT LOIS CLOARECHART

Born and raised in British Columbia, Canada, Lois Cloarec Hart grew up as an avid reader but didn't begin writing until much later in life. Several years after joining the Canadian Armed Forces, she received a degree in Honours History from Royal Military College and on graduation switched occupations from air traffic control to military intelligence. Having married a CAF fighter pilot while in college, Lois went on to spend another five years as an Intelligence Officer before leaving the military to care for her husband, who was ill with chronic progressive Multiple Sclerosis and passed away in 2001. She began writing while caring for her husband in his final years and had her first book, *Coming Home*, published in 2001. It was through that initial publishing process that Lois met the woman she would marry in April 2007. She now commutes annually between her northern home in Calgary and her wife's southern home in Atlanta.

Lois is the author of four novels, *Coming Home*, *Broken Faith*, *Kicker's Journey*, *Walking the Labyrinth*, and a collection of short stories, Assorted Flavours. Her novel Kicker's Journey won the 2010 Independent Publisher Book Award bronze medal, 2010 Golden Crown Literary Awards, 2010 Rainbow Romance Writer's Award for Excellence, and 2009 Lesbian Fiction Readers Choice Award for historical fiction. *Broken Faith* (revised second edition) will be published in print and e-formats in winter 2013 and *Coming Home* (revised third edition) in spring 2014.

Visit her website: www.loiscloarechart.com
E-mail her at eljae1@shaw.ca

OTHER BOOKS FROM YLVA PUBLISHING

http://www.ylva-publishing.com

WALKING THE LABYRINTH

Lois Cloarec Hart

ISBN: 978-3-95533-052-1

267 pages

Is there life after loss? Lee Glenn, co-owner of a private security company, didn't think so. Crushed by grief after the death of her wife, she uncharacteristically retreats from life.

But love doesn't give up easily. After her friends and family stage a dramatic intervention, Lee rejoins the world of the living, resolved to regain some sense of normalcy but only half-believing that it's possible. Her old friend and business partner convinces her to take on what appears on the surface to be a minor personal protection detail.

The assignment takes her far from home, from the darkness of her loss to the dawning of a life reborn. Along the way, Lee encounters people unlike any she's ever met before: Wrong-Way Wally, a small-town oracle shunned by the locals for his off-putting speech and mannerisms; and Wally's best friend, Gaëlle, a woman who not only translates the oracle's uncanny predictions, but who also appears to have a deep personal connection to life beyond life. Lee is shocked to find herself fascinated by Gaëlle, despite dismissing the woman's exotic beliefs as "hooey."

But opening yourself to love also means opening yourself to the possibility of pain. Will Lee have the courage to follow that path, a path that once led to the greatest agony she'd ever experienced? Or will she run back to the cold comfort of a safer solitary life?

CHARITY

(REVISED EDITION)

Paulette Callen
ISBN: 978-3-95533-075-0
362 pages

The friendship between Lena Kaiser, a sodbuster's daughter, and Gustie Roemer, an educated Easterner, is unlikely in any other circumstance but post-frontier Charity, South Dakota. Gustie is considered an outsider, and Lena is too proud to share her problems (which include a hard-drinking husband) with anyone else.

On the nearby Sioux reservation, Gustie also finds love and family with two Dakotah women: Dorcas Many Roads, an old medicine woman, and her adopted granddaughter, Jordis, who bears the scars of the white man's education.

When Lena's husband is arrested for murdering his father and the secrets of Gustie's past follow her to Charity, Lena, Gustie, and Jordis stand together. As buried horrors are unearthed and present tragedies unfold, they discover the strength and beauty of love and friendship that blossom like wild flowers in the tough prairie soil.

BACKWARDS TO OREGON

(REVISED EDITION)

Jae

ISBN: 978-3-95533-026-2

521 pages

"Luke" Hamilton has always been sure that she'd never marry. She accepted that she would spend her life alone when she chose to live her life disguised as a man.

After working in a brothel for three years, Nora Macauley has lost all illusions about love. She no longer hopes for a man who will sweep her off her feet and take her away to begin a new, respectable life.

But now they find themselves married and on the way to Oregon in a covered wagon, with two thousand miles ahead of them.

COMING FROM YLVA PUBLISHING IN WINTER 2013 AND SPRING 2014

http://www.ylva-publishing.com

FERVENT CHARITY

Paulette Callen

Fervent Charity continues the story of the friendship of five women who have nothing in common but the ground they walk on and the vicissitudes of post-frontier prairie life.

Lena, a young mother living on the edge of heartbreak. Her sister-in-law, Mary, more beautiful than loved. Alvinia, midwife to the county and mother of ten. Gustie and Jordis, trying to make a home together but finding their place on either the reservation or in Charity precarious.

The women come together in the face of natural hardships—childbirth, disastrous weather, and disease—and the unnatural malevolence of people who mean them harm. In the end, they find themselves bound by a secret none of them could have predicted.

HIDDEN TRUTHS

(REVISED EDITION)

Jae

"Luke" Hamilton has been living as a husband and father for the past seventeen years. No one but her wife, Nora, knows she is not the man she appears to be. They have raised their daughters to become honest and hard-working young women, but even with their loving foundation, Amy and Nattie are hiding their own secrets.

Just as Luke sets out on a dangerous trip to Fort Boise, a newcomer arrives on the ranch—Rika Aaldenberg, who traveled to Oregon as a mail-order bride, hiding that she's not the woman in the letters.

When hidden truths are revealed, will their lives and their family fall apart or will love keep them together?

Kicker's Journey

ISBN: 978-3-95533-060-6

Also available as e-book.

Published by Ylva Publishing, legal entity of Ylva Verlag, e.Kfr.

Ylva Verlag, e.Kfr.
Owner: Astrid Ohletz
Am Kirschgarten 2
65830 Kriftel
Germany

http://www.ylva-publishing.com

First Edition: 2009 by P.D. Publishing
Revised Second Edition: October 2013

Credits:
Edited by Judy Underwood
Cover Design by Streetlight Graphics

Made in the USA
Coppell, TX
08 December 2023